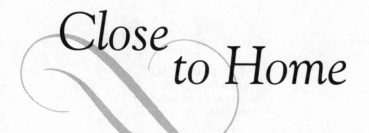

Close to Home

Barbara Hall

Simon & Schuster

SIMON & SCHUSTER
Rockefeller Center
1230 Avenue of the Americas
New York, NY 10020

This book is a work of fiction. Names, characters, places, and incidents either are products of the author's imagination or are used fictitiously. Any resemblance to actual events or locales or persons, living or dead, is entirely coincidental.

SIMON & SCHUSTER and colophon are registered trademarks of Simon & Schuster Inc.

Designed by Deirdre C. Amthor

Manufactured in the United States of America

1   3   5   7   9   10   8   6   4   2

Library of Congress Cataloging-in-Publication Data
Hall, Barbara.
Close to home / Barbara Hall.
p.   cm.
I. Title.
PS3558.A3585C58   1997
813'.54—dc21   96-54872   CIP
ISBN 0-684-80981-8

Acknowledgments

FIRST I'D LIKE to thank Lyla Oliver and Yossi Sharon for all but adopting me during this process, and for never sending me to bed without dinner. I appreciate you and I love you. This book was guided by two extraordinary forces: my editor, Chuck Adams, and my agent, Cynthia Manson. I know how lucky I am. Thanks to my sister Karen for a lifetime of encouragement, and for making me laugh even when it's not funny. And thanks to Dave Marsh, for being around, and for being Dave Marsh.

Thanks to Arion Berger, Tom Carson, David Chase, Robin Green, and Marti Noxon (winner of the captive audience award). Thanks to Jim Rice who added another dimension to the story. And I'd like to thank my daughter Faith who is, in the words of Bruce Springsteen, "a walking, talking reason to live."

FOR BOB

Prologue

THE FIRST TIME Lydia ever saw her husband, she made fun of him.

The place was Myrtle Beach, South Carolina. She was reclining on a towel, her elbows digging into the warm sand, her face turned like a flower toward the sunlight. Her friend Camille lay in a similar pose beside her. They were twenty-eight. They were beautiful. The world was theirs to ridicule.

Lydia watched the middle-aged women lumbering past, stuffed into violently floral swimsuits, their pink thighs rubbing together, hair pulled back or held in place by mastic sprays. Some were accompanied by husbands, their spreading bellies and bald knees separated by baggy plaid trunks. The men always glanced at Lydia and Camille, then looked quickly to the ground, kicking at seashells.

"Shoot me now," Camille said, watching them.

"That won't ever happen to us," Lydia reassured her. It had become Lydia's role over the years to reassure Camille. It was a pointless exercise, as Camille's self-esteem was perfectly intact. But this was the game they had played since high school. Camille criticized herself, pointing out some phantom imperfection, and Lydia told her how silly she was and extolled her virtues. Lately she was starting to grow tired of this routine. She felt they were too old for it, but it was too late to change. They were stuck.

Many of the things in Lydia's life felt stuck. It was as if her story had already been written, and all that remained to be played out was the slow, unsurprising resolution, the moral. She wasn't quite sure what the moral was, but she supposed that would be the point of the next fifty years.

Lydia knew it was ridiculous to feel old at twenty-eight, but she did, and in an effort to fight off that feeling, she mouthed reassurances. She didn't know how to tell Camille that the fat women with the distracted husbands filled her with a cold terror. She could see herself in them, bloated and resigned. She could see Ham, the man she intended to marry in less than three months, glancing at beautiful girls on the beach, then looking away, ashamed of his desire.

"I mean, for one thing," Lydia said, "we can afford liposuction."

"You can afford it, with Ham's money. Me, I'll probably marry some amateur musician or a government lawyer or something."

"No, come on," Lydia said, her reassurance now taking on a half-hearted tone. "You'll marry anybody you want to."

Camille sighed and stared at the Atlantic Ocean as if she were in the market to buy and it wasn't quite big enough. That very look was the thing that made Lydia certain Camille would get what she wanted.

Even sitting there on the beach, Lydia saw the way a man's eyes would flit over her and land hard on Camille, sensing her desire to be pleased. Camille ignored them, of course. She was so accustomed to attention that it bounced off her, as if she hadn't the ability to absorb any more.

Lydia watched her friend, envying her unique talents, one of which was a capacity for sitting in direct sunlight without sweating. She seemed impervious to the elements. The wind left her hair alone and even the insects kept their distance.

"Oh, look," Camille said, sitting up suddenly, shielding her eyes from the sun. "What have we here?"

She also possessed an ability to spot men from great distances. This, Lydia suspected, was the secret to her indifference. By the time a man noticed her, she had already thoroughly reviewed and rejected him.

"Look where?" Lydia asked, squinting.

Camille nodded at two figures moving along the shoreline. Lydia could barely make them out.

"Not bad," Camille said, watching their approach with intense concentration. "Still warm." And, finally, as they got closer, "Never mind. Chromosome damage. Bad gene pool."

"What makes you think so?" Lydia laughed, though she felt uneasy about it. Camille had always been hard on people, and her strict standards made Lydia feel that her own ability to judge character was radically inferior. The fact that Lydia recognized a more generous instinct in herself seemed a weakness. It gave her the sense that she was missing the point.

"One's got a fake leg," Camille said, still scrutinizing them as they approached.

Now they were in focus, and Lydia could see that one of the men walked with a slight limp. His left leg ended at the knee where a piece of flesh-toned plastic took over. She was ashamed of how unappetizing she found it, yet she stared as the two men staked out a spot in the sand. She was fascinated and repelled, as he detached his prosthetic and set it carefully aside like a radio or a thermos, an everyday piece of beach equipment.

"He could have lost it in an accident," she suggested.

"Worse. Farm labor." Seeing Lydia's skeptical frown, Camille said, "So how many rich people do you know with prosthetics?"

"He could have lost it in a skydiving accident. Or racing in Monte Carlo."

"You optimist," Camille said. She lit a cigarette, letting her eyes comb the sand again.

Camille was looking for an affair. Not for herself but for Lydia. She was thoroughly convinced that Lydia needed to commit some radical deed before she went down the aisle with Hamilton Crider. "You're marrying your high school sweetheart, for God's sake," Camille was constantly saying. "You're morally obligated to do something bad."

Actually, in high school, Lydia and Ham had only been flirtatious and cruel to each other. Their love, in those days, was like any young love: afraid of itself, resentful of its obligations, looking for an escape route. It was much later, after she had graduated from college and dropped out of law school, that she and Ham reunited with the degree of maturity needed to pursue anything resembling a relationship. Now she felt comfortable with him. She felt it was something that was meant to happen. She didn't even mind the disappointing sex. That seemed to be a part of the bargain.

"The thing you always have to remember," Camille had told her when she first got engaged, "is that you're doing this to make your parents happy. Marrying Ham is your way of apologizing."

"For what?"

"Dropping out of law school."

"That's ridiculous. I've loved Ham forever." She made the statement without emotion. She declared it on a daily basis, like a catechism.

There was much to admire in Ham. He was smart but not arrogant, Harvard educated but humble about it. He rarely told anecdotes, but when he did they were witty and succinct. He had money but disguised it well. He was an investment banker, but he never talked about work. He read. He cried at old movies and he loved going to restaurants and throwing dinner parties. He liked dogs. He wanted children. The list went on and on.

So why did certain aspects of his personality nag at Lydia like food caught between her teeth? The way he called people by their first names, immediately after meeting them. The way he had to qualify every moment together, constantly rating their experiences, as if their lives together were some sort of Zagat guide.

Most troubling, however, was his sense of social responsibility. He worried about the underprivileged, but he seemed to ride his compassion like some noble carriage. She always felt that lurking somewhere in his empathy was a degree of superiority. All those "poor" people were consigned to an existence he knew he'd never have to endure. His pity had a generic quality that troubled her.

Once she had made the mistake of voicing some of these concerns to Camille. She really had only wanted to sound out her theories, but Camille had taken it a little more seriously.

"Honey, you are looking for demons. Leave that poor man alone and go have yourself an affair. Get it out of your system."

Lydia was not particularly interested in having an affair—the thought of all that subterfuge exhausted her. But she did recognize a need to get away. There was so much to escape, she didn't know where to begin. She wanted to escape the scrutiny of her parents, who were always present, even though they lived in Springfield, Virginia, and she was safely ensconced inside an Upper Northwest townhouse with three other law school dropouts. She wanted to escape D.C. altogether, with its pathetic attempts at grandiosity (did the Kennedy Center really fool anybody?), and its pandering to tourists with gentrified little pockets of hipness, such as Adams Morgan, an area whose idea of being multicultural meant putting an Ethiopian restaurant next to a tapas bar. One ethnic restaurant after another, all full of white Georgetown students.

Lydia hated the traffic and the distant sound of gunshots from the other side of the Hill and the gray-suited lawyers bumping up against each other in the metro. She hated the self-conscious secondhand-book stores with the snarly attendants, professional students with unfinished novels in their backpacks, and the chatter of activists on the street—save this animal, that Slavic country, the other endangered root vegetable. She hated the legislative assistants spouting off their narrow political philosophy in crowded Irish bars. She disliked knowing that these uninspired, pimply youth would be the leaders of tomorrow. She hated the busking at Dupont Circle, the middle-class kids with dreadlocks moaning about conditions in countries they'd never even glimpsed. D.C. was the land of safe rebellion. Sitting right there under the Supreme Court, everyone with an opinion felt free to air it with a tune, a shout, or a flyer.

Lydia longed for stillness, quiet streets, a little taste of apathy. People who still thought that the rain was clean and Democracy worked and God was coming. She thought constantly of a place where people might actually have an interest in living rather than exhibiting their lives.

There were few people she could air such complaints to. Ham, for all his calculated compassion, had a low threshold of boredom when it came to her soul-searching. Her parents would be appalled at the mention of her dissatisfaction. Her parents didn't just live in Fairfax County. They were the Hunts of Fairfax County. Every other library, museum, or hospital ward was named after one of Lydia's relatives. The notion of ever leaving the place had never occurred to any generation of Hunts. Therefore, the fact that it was occurring to Lydia was something she needed to keep to herself. Her parents were still convinced that Lydia would eventually go back to finish off her law degree at UVA and abandon her current studies toward teacher certification at Georgetown. Her mother referred to Lydia's sudden desire to teach as her "little fit." Secretly she worried that her mother might be right about that. But getting married was no fit. It was an act of stone-cold sanity. It felt inescapable and final, like the right thing to do.

The one-legged man and his friend spread their towels a few feet from Lydia and Camille, a location too close to the water. The tide was coming in, and in no time they would be scrambling for higher ground. They didn't seem to care.

Lydia stared at the men as they settled down. No one else was looking at them, but she found it hard to stop. She couldn't tear her gaze away. She wanted to defend them.

"Yeah, okay," Lydia admitted. "That one lost his leg to farm equipment. The other one's body makes up for it, though."

"That's the spirit, lusting after farmhands. It's very D. H. Lawrence. But let's not take this thing too far, Lydia," Camille said.

The one with the fake leg looked like a carnival worker. Thin and reedy, his ribs pushing against the skin as if they were trying to escape. His hair was an ash blond, his skin so white it looked bleached, taking on the pale blue tint of his veins. He had a wispy mustache and smoked constantly, staring at each woman as she walked past. He stared at them all—thin, fat, young, and old. He seemed to find some merit in all of them.

His friend, Lydia thought, was different. His friend was dark. Not just his hair, not just his skin but his whole persona. The darkness ran deep; it connected to his soul. He seemed dominated by a sense of detachment, oblivious to his immediate surroundings. He did not look at the women. He stared at the horizon, as if picturing something beyond it, like heaven or Europe.

It was Camille who spoke to them first.

"You're in my sun," she said.

The dark one turned to look at her. Lydia stared at him. His face is a cloud of doom and worry, she thought. She had never seen anyone whose concern seemed so intense, whose ruminations seemed in complete control of him. He looked young, barely into his thirties. What could this man already be burdened with? she wondered.

"Your buddy," Camille said, pointing her cigarette at the carnival worker. "He's casting a shadow on my shins."

The reedy friend looked over his shoulder and grinned, revealing gapped teeth turned sepia from nicotine. "I reckon somebody'll have to move the sun, then."

"Kyle, slide over an inch," the dark one suggested.

"Shit, no. Women have took over enough of the world. They can't have my patch of sand."

Camille gave Lydia an eye roll of the told-you-so variety. Lydia smiled and wondered why her heart felt suddenly fat, incapable of getting enough blood to her brain.

"What's your name, sweetheart?" Camille asked.

"Danny," the dark one answered. "What's yours?"

Camille only smiled and said, "Y'all staying here?"

She affected a thick accent and jerked her head toward the Myrtle Beach Hilton behind them. She assumed that they must have wandered up the beach from the cheaper hotels on the strand.

Lydia felt embarrassed now. Even though she was just as critical as Camille and enjoyed a nice, confidential laugh at someone else's expense, she didn't enjoy humiliating people. And she especially did not enjoy humiliating this man. His worried eyes were starting to get to her, and the way he stared curiously at Camille, his head slightly cocked, as if he could not fathom her motives.

"As a matter of fact, we are," Danny said.

"Oh? Well, let me commend you. The grounds are absolutely lovely," Camille said.

Lydia shot to her feet, brushing sand off her legs. She felt hot with embarrassment, though Danny did not seem annoyed.

Lydia said, "I've had enough sun."

"See what you've done? You've run my friend away," Camille said.

"And what would it take to get you to go with her?" Danny asked. It happened so quickly, so smoothly. Camille was caught off guard. She opened her mouth and finally succumbed to a cackling laugh.

Lydia gathered up her towel and Danny watched her with unapologetic curiosity. The wind whipped up, blowing sand from her towel in his direction. He rubbed his eyes, then looked at her again. She returned his stare but didn't speak. Under his scrutiny, she found she had nothing to say.

The next day Camille was stricken with a serious case of sun poisoning. Her body swelled until she resembled a large pink cushion. She lay in a dark room with cold washcloths on her face, trying to preserve what was left of her complexion.

"Sun damage," she moaned. "I can feel the wrinkles spreading like fire across my forehead. I am going to look like Ronald Reagan when I leave here."

"Oh, stop it," Lydia said irritably. She had been cooped up in the room with Camille too long. She had lost the desire to reassure her.

"You'll have to carry on without me. Go, find the groundskeeper. Tell him it's your last chance for happiness or something."

"Who?"

"The guy on the beach."

"He's not a groundskeeper," Lydia said, embarrassed by her desire to defend him. "I'm not going to see him again, Camille. I just want to go home."

But they didn't go home. They stayed, and she did see Danny again. First in the lobby of the hotel, then later in the bar, then by the pool where he complimented her bathing suit and bought her a drink with a parasol in it.

His one-legged companion, Kyle, who turned out not to be a carnival worker but a former appliance salesman living on disability, had mercifully found a new set of friends, some generous drinkers on a printers' convention. This left Lydia and Danny alone most of the day, discussing in casual detail their backgrounds and plans for the future. No messy analysis of families or neurosis or frustrated ambitions. Just talk. Unemotional history. Danny was from Virginia, too. He had acquired an economics degree from James Madison University and was working at a commercial contracting firm, only months away from taking the reins from the founder. He lived in a small town in the southwestern part of the state, famous for nothing but the fact that it sat on one of the largest natural deposits of uranium ore in the country.

"About once every five years some company tries to buy off the land and mine it, but the environmentalists get on their high horse and some actors get involved and it goes away. Sissy Spacek came to town one year. You'd think she was a Kennedy. Everybody in town came to the rally, and half of them had no idea what uranium was."

Lydia laughed, trying to picture a small town set aflutter by the arrival of an actress. In D.C., any day of the week, you could bump into the people who were manipulating the legislation of the most powerful country in the world. She didn't tell him that, though. She was afraid it would sound belittling.

They disclosed their likes and dislikes, and not surprisingly, there wasn't a great deal of overlap. It wasn't just that he didn't like theater; it was that he'd never seen any. And it wasn't a matter of not caring for Turgenev; he didn't know who he was. Lydia's stomach did a flip and she almost sneered, but when she tried to explain who Turgenev was she found she couldn't, beyond the fact that he was a Russian writer. She'd read him, she was sure, but for the life of her she couldn't remember what he believed or why he was significant.

Danny had an interest in economics, the stock market, anything to do with numbers. Lydia admitted she couldn't balance her checkbook. He tried to explain his passion for architecture, not the aesthetics but the numbers—the angles, the space, the logic. The thought of it all gave her a headache, but the way his eyes lit up when he discussed it caused her heart to race, and she forgot to eat. At night she lay awake listening to the ocean and reconstructing his face.

Over the next few days they talked incessantly, analyzing their interests, celebrating their differences. Each considered the other unusual and enigmatic, hard to pin down. They were tolerant of each other and kind; there was no criticism, no confessions. Later she would look back and wonder if they had spared each other the details of their demons out of politeness or fear of alienation. No one wanted to discuss troubles when love was parked at the door with the engine running.

Words like love and desire flitted into Lydia's head like a short circuit, the way foreign voices sometimes broke through a telephone line. What could it mean? She loved Ham. She had to. She knew everything about him. But maybe this was the point. Maybe this was the reason the fat women walked ahead of their husbands on the beach. There was nothing to learn, so they moved ahead, looking for mystery.

Was it possible, Lydia wondered, staring at Danny's inscrutable profile, to marry mystery? Was it possible, or even desirable, to commit to that? She didn't know the first thing about Danny, and he gave her the feeling that she never would.

The night before Lydia left, they drove to a local seafood place called the Rice Plantation, which no visitor to the area was supposed to miss. The restaurant was a restored Victorian house, and the patrons waited on a long porch, sitting on rocking chairs or porch swings or leaning against the railing while they waited for their names to be called. It took forty-five minutes to be seated, but neither of them mentioned the wait. They talked rapidly about anything they might have forgotten to cover.

Once inside, they were seated at a table in a massive room with hardwood floors and ceiling fans and Victorian memorabilia nailed to the walls. Their waitresses wore starched white aprons and lace bonnets. They were served huge platters of fried seafood and french fries and hush puppies. They sipped iced tea from mason jars, and the cold liquid made the grease congeal and stick to their gums. None of it mattered.

Lydia sat across from Danny, staring at him as if she'd just discovered something of vital importance to the human condition. He stared at her the same way.

His face was sharp, severe, full of angles. When he smiled, his eyes brightened, but only a degree.

"You should come to Fawley," he said.

She laughed. The name itself sounded so improbable. She tried to picture herself writing down her address, Lydia Hunt, followed by a two-digit number on some street named after a tree or a president—Fawley, Virginia.

"What's in Fawley, besides uranium?" she asked.

"I am."

"Yes, but what else? What would I do there?"

"We have schools. You could teach."

"What else?"

"On the weekends we could drive to Greensboro."

"What's in Greensboro?"

"Factory outlets."

She laughed. "And this is how you choose to live."

Danny smiled. "It's hard to describe the virtues of a small town. You have to live it. After a while you don't know where the place stops and you begin. It knows your history, it owns you."

"You're not being very persuasive," she said, smiling. "Maybe you should come to D.C."

"Why? Even you don't like it there."

She shrugged. "At least it doesn't own me."

"Then why are you still there?"

The coffee came. They sipped it in silence.

Finally Lydia said, "What about that person you hang around with?"

"Kyle?"

She nodded. "He's a good friend of yours?"

"No. He's my cousin."

She waited for him to elaborate, but he didn't.

"How did he lose his leg?" she asked.

"Car wreck. He nearly died."

Danny seemed to clam up at the mention of Kyle. Lydia considered this slightly odd, but she tried to remind herself that most people weren't as interested in character analysis as she and Camille. There were those who just let things be.

The check came. He refused her efforts to split it. The waitress took his credit card away and they sat staring at each other over their half-eaten plates of food. In their faces there was a kind of desperation, the heightened attention usually given to war or natural disasters. What happens next? How do we get out of this one?

Looking at him now, Lydia remembered his story of humble origins and modest ambitions, and she realized that Danny was, as her mother would put it, "not her kind." He was so different that it felt as if they weren't even part of the same species. Yet she felt connected to him. She felt relieved in his presence, as if all the stringent standards she'd imposed on people her whole life, and which had been imposed on her, were completely meaningless. He had little in the way of advantages or breeding. What he had instead was an unapologetic gaze, a straight back, a quiet confidence that surrounded him like a nimbus. He had nothing to protect and nowhere to fall. He moved forward, aware that there was no greater plan following him, making him doubt his decisions.

Oh God, she thought, I want some of that. I want to possess that, whatever it is.

He caught her look and said, "What?"

"I'm about to get married," she said abruptly.

"I know," he said.

"You do?"

"Well, that ring."

She blushed and twisted the diamond around on her hand. She had somehow forgotten about it, a monstrous, two-carat thing in a Tiffany setting. It felt like an aberration, like Kyle's false leg.

"It's quite a ring," he said.

"But you're with me anyway," she said.

"I'm with you anyway."

"Why?"

"Because," he said, pausing to clear his throat. "I've got a better idea. I think you should marry me."

She laughed nervously. "Well, all right. You talked me into it."

He didn't smile. It scared her. The ring on her hand felt enormous, and her finger was itching underneath it.

He stared at her, unblinking. She massaged her temples, fighting back a dull roar in her head. When she looked up again, he was smiling at her. She wasn't sure she'd seen him smile this way before—a long, sustained expression, as if he knew something she didn't. He had thin lips, but from where she was sitting, she could tell they were soft. As if they'd never been chapped. As if they'd kissed no one but his mother.

Her heart raced, and she had a sudden image of what it might be like to make love to him. She could picture him putting on a rubber, kneeling on the bed, his head bowed in concentration. And she could see herself lying on the bed, one hand on her breast, waiting. It felt like a real memory, but she had never been there before.

"Are you okay?" Danny asked. "Your face is flushed."

"Yes. Fine."

He cleared his throat, then he reached across the table and picked up a box of matches. He took out a single match and laid it on the table next to the box.

He said, "How do you get all the rabbits in the world in this room, just by using these two things?"

Lydia smiled. "I don't know. How?"

He picked up the match and stuck it in the side of the box like an antenna, creating a tiny version of a walkie-talkie. He put it next to his mouth and said, "Calling all rabbits. Calling all rabbits."

Lydia laughed, deep down. It felt good, like an answer. Like a reason.

Six months later, they were married.

Part One

1

THE HOUSE WHERE Danny Crane grew up, and where his parents and brother Rex still lived, did not have a number. The road it was situated on did not have a name. The rough asphalt that twisted through farmland was simply called Route 48. The Crane home was a modest L-shaped brick house with a carport and a screened-in back porch. It looked lonely and alienated from its surroundings. There was a mailbox jutting out like an elbow in the front yard. There was neatly trimmed boxwood on all sides, and an ornate letter "C" on the metal screen door. Other than that, the house had nothing to say for itself.

None of this struck Danny as particularly strange, but to Lydia, even after three years of marriage, the whole concept was exotic and mildly disturbing. Danny had grown up in one of those sad, detached places she remembered passing on long road trips with her parents. She'd watch those isolated houses shoot past and she'd wonder who could be content to live in them. Where were their neighbors? What had they done to deserve being stuck out in the wilderness? And if they were there by choice, what had driven them to that kind of seclusion?

Every Sunday she and Danny made the trip from town out to his parents' house for lunch, and every Sunday she entertained these thoughts as they drove down the winding country roads. She wasn't sure if she was disapproving; perhaps she was just fascinated. Perhaps she was even charmed. All she knew was that as they pulled up in front of the house, greeted in the yard by his father's hunting dogs, she had the sensation she was being sent on some sort of field trip. In the presence of his family she felt like an anthropologist, her mission to observe the behavior of an obscure, aboriginal culture.

There was never any question of skipping the Sunday lunch. It was written in stone. Once she had suggested to Danny that they spend a quiet Sunday to themselves and he looked at her as if she'd suggested they try drugs or yoga.

"Well, we could," he'd said, scratching his chin in contemplation. "I'm not sure how that would go over."

"Let's try it and see."

So they had, one Sunday two years ago. She had cooked a chicken and they'd eaten it together in the stiff silence of their kitchen. Danny had kept giving her tense smiles and complimenting the food beyond its merit, and when the exercise was over he'd excused himself and gone to the phone to call his parents.

The rest of the day was lost. Danny hadn't been able to concentrate on any of his usual activities—gardening, watching football, paying the bills. He'd paced the house, looking out the window, checking his watch to see if it was time for bed.

Lydia had thought about confronting him, suggesting that his connection to his parents was a little too strong. She was his family now, after all. But then she remembered that Danny didn't really pay an excessive amount of attention to them; during the week, he hardly mentioned them. It was just this Sunday thing. It was a tradition. And as Lydia came to learn, Danny had trouble extricating himself from traditions. There weren't many, but the ones he honored were as inviolable as any law of God or nature.

You wanted something different, Lydia reminded herself as the truck bounced over the rutted asphalt. Well, this is different. Sometimes, indeed almost every time, she tried to picture her own family, who usually ate out on Sundays, brunching at the Ritz Carlton or the Four Seasons, then wandering through the Dumbarton gardens to examine the foliage. Her parents did not speak to her anymore. They had disowned her after her marriage. She and Danny had made a fruitless pilgrimage to her home to announce their engagement. Her parents had treated Danny with cool respect, but Lydia had endured the journey, fully aware of what was smoldering beneath their inescapable politeness. The way they avoided her eyes told her that it was over. This trip was not an introduction; it was a farewell.

They had not attended her wedding, naturally, and the only communication they kept up was a coldly engraved Christmas card each year. She knew this was one of the reasons she was so hard on Danny's family. They had to take the place of her own now. And that was no easy task.

"What are you thinking about?" Danny asked, not every time, but on this particular Sunday, early in March, as the first signs of spring were struggling to arrive.

"The dogwoods," she said, gazing out the window. "Wondering when they'll bloom."

"When they're ready," he said, and squeezed her shoulder.

This Sunday, as always, lunch was an overdone affair. Sally, Danny's mother, cooked enough for an army, then looked wounded by the amount of food left over.

"I can't believe what y'all didn't eat," she said, pinching her lip. "Look at what I've got to put away."

"Surprise, surprise," Danny's brother, Rex, said. "The fifth battalion didn't show up."

Rex was a sickly, waifish man. His hair was racing to desert him and his skin was the color and consistency of tapioca pudding. But he always dressed well and scrutinized the appearance of everyone around him. Rex seemed misplaced, for many reasons. One, of course, was that he was almost twenty-nine and still lived at home. Another was that he possessed a kind of sophistication out of keeping with his surroundings. His vocabulary was extensive. His mannerisms were slightly effete and superior, as if he had spent years studying abroad and felt he had no place to practice all the skills he had acquired. The truth was, Rex had never left home at all, scarcely ever ventured further than the public library, where he worked four days a week.

Danny's parents were more consistent. His mother was an attractive woman with too many years of cooking around her middle, but other than that, not much to betray her lack of exposure to the world. She was simple yet composed. Her dark hair was just turning gray and was always neatly styled. She wore just enough makeup and very little jewelry. She had a warm smile and melancholy brown eyes that had been passed on to both of her children. Both of them had been imprinted with her physical characteristics. Neither of them even remotely resembled Nelson, her husband. He was of grade A Scotch-Irish stock, complete with bone white skin, broken blood vessels around his nose, thin, sandy blond hair, and fierce blue-green eyes, roughly the same color, Lydia imagined, as the North Sea. Sometimes Lydia wondered if Nelson felt slightly betrayed by the fact that his children looked nothing like him. But it was hard to imagine Nelson feeling agitated about anything. Danny claimed his father had had a ferocious temper at one time, but it was gone now, like an old skin he had shed.

Danny could do no wrong in his father's eyes. Only Rex could get to him. This was visible only to those curious enough to look, and Lydia was always looking.

"Oh, damn," Nelson said quietly, swiping at a gravy stain on his shirt. "Brand-new shirt."

"Daddy, don't fret. That shirt just might see in the millennium," Rex said. "That fabric would survive a nuclear war."

"What? It's a J. C. Penney shirt."

"Oh well, far be it from me to insult the Patron Saint of Wash 'n' Wear."

"Rex, you didn't eat any of your squash," Sally interceded, sensing trouble.

"I don't like yellow vegetables, Mother. This you know. Particularly when they are cooked beyond their original molecular structure. Daniel isn't exactly devouring his portion," Rex observed, suddenly turning his attention to his brother. "What's troubling you? Things slow in the land of concrete?"

"Business is fine," Danny said defensively, spearing his squash, which hung limply on the fork.

"We can't eat a lot," Lydia said, "because we have to go to church tonight. For the potluck dinner."

"Oh, you don't have to go to that," Sally said. "They have too many functions, if you ask me. Just another excuse for that John Evans to run his mouth."

Lydia smiled, relieved by her mother-in-law's critical streak. Buried beneath Sally's compliant nature there was a seed of something dark and suspicious. Sometimes Lydia thought that if she could get Sally drunk, the two of them would finally connect. Lydia liked her mother-in-law, but it was no secret to her that Sally distrusted her. No woman would have been good enough for Danny, but certainly no woman with her credentials. Danny, in Sally's mind, needed a good, salt-of-the-earth gal who'd live to please him and let her own needs go untouched. Instead, here was Lydia, with all her breeding and her career and her ideas. What on earth did Danny need with that, when he had plenty of ideas of his own?

Then, too, Lydia was sure Sally could detect her own detachment, the way she held herself just outside the immediate experience, observing and analyzing. Sally had once confided to Danny that she felt Lydia was like somebody from the IRS, constantly looking for a mistake. Danny had thought that was enormously funny; to his credit, Danny enjoyed his wife's tendency to scrutinize everything. He wanted Lydia to like his family, but he did not mind the fact that she did not accept them at face value.

Out of nowhere, Nelson said, "Pike never did like squash himself."

The table went silent. They all stared at their plates, as if they were required to meditate at the mention of his name.

Uncle Pike, Nelson's brother, was the family's acknowledged saint. He'd been dead some twenty years, but it was as if it had happened yesterday. This was one of the first things Lydia had learned after she'd married Danny—that Pike's death presided over the family like an ominous but sacred cloud.

Pike was Kyle's father. He had also fathered four girls, three of whom still lived with their mother, Rita, in a farmhouse down the road. The women had hardly ventured out of the house since Pike's demise. No one was sure why. More frustrating, at least to Lydia, was that no one even asked why. Like so many things about this family, Pike's death was shrouded in mystery. Lydia had heard the story a number of times but still could not make sense of it.

It went something like this: when Kyle was a teenager, he'd been shot in the foot in his own front yard. He told his father that a black man, driving past, had shot him for no particular reason. In a violent rage, Pike jumped in his truck and went chasing this loosely described culprit. As the odds would have it, since half of the county was black, Pike had found a black man and confronted him. The black man, in a panic, had shot Pike dead. And nothing since had been the same.

This was a long time ago, long before Kyle had lost the same leg in a car accident. Bizarre accidents seemed to visit this family as regularly as the Avon lady. Lydia could make no sense of it, but she had decided that it wasn't really her business to work out the details. Still, she wondered. Every day she wondered how a family could accept these occurrences, never asking why. She had never really understood the concept of stoicism until she married into the Cranes. Maybe she could learn something from them, the freedom of not knowing.

After a respectable silence, Rex said, "Well, there you go. I take after Uncle Pike, and he was perfect."

"You're damn right he was," Nelson said, his eyes flaring, revealing something of the temper Danny always talked about. "He was as perfect as anybody could be."

"People always get perfect after they die," Sally said quietly.

"What the hell does that mean?" Nelson demanded.

"Nothing. He was a good man."

Lydia wasn't sure if Sally truly respected Pike as much as she was required to. Maybe he had bothered her, the way that Kyle bothered Lydia, although thankfully, she rarely saw him. She had gotten a bad feeling about Kyle that first day she had laid eyes on him at Myrtle Beach. It wasn't just the missing leg. Something else was missing in Kyle, something that made him dangerous, even from a distance. Just knowing he was there, and that she was related to him, made Lydia feel uneasy. The fact that Danny seemed tenaciously protective of him made her uneasier still.

Sally slid her chair back and started collecting dishes. Lunch was over. Pike's name had ended it, like a benediction.

Lydia helped Sally wash the dishes and listened to her talk about what she'd read in *Redbook* or seen on *Montel Williams*. Lydia did little talking herself, except to say that teaching was fine, Danny's work was fine, and she was looking forward to summer. From the den Lydia could hear the TV inevitably tuned to the featured sport of the day. Upstairs, from Rex's room, the music from *Phantom of the Opera* drifted down. Sally lifted her eyes to the ceiling and gave her head the slightest shake. Lydia caught her eye and smiled.

"How are your parents, dear?" Sally asked her.

Lydia shrugged, concentrating on the plate she was drying. "I suppose they're fine."

"It's so sad. They still haven't forgiven you?"

Lydia shook her head, then said, "I don't think it's a matter of forgiveness. They're just waiting it out."

"Surely they don't think you're going to come back, after all this time."

"My parents never give up."

"Well, I think it's ridiculous. Disowning a child. Life is short, don't they know that?"

"I don't think that's how they look at things."

"Well, I still don't know what it is about Danny they don't like. Maybe they just don't understand him."

Lydia just smiled and reached for another plate. It was pointless trying to explain the way her parents worked. The way Camille worked, all of her friends from her former life. They were not interested in changing. As far as they were all concerned, they were at the top of the ladder. And to understand anyone else, they would be forced to look down.

"I mean, around here he's considered a star," Sally said. "Maybe in northern Virginia that doesn't mean anything. Maybe you have enough stars up there."

The star quality Sally was referring to had to do with Danny's brief excursion into minor-league baseball. Just after college he'd been drafted by a farm team somewhere in North Carolina. He'd done pretty well there until an injury cut his career short. The whole episode, like Pike's death, was shrouded in folklore. Danny didn't like to discuss it, so Lydia had a hard time getting any perspective on it. She wasn't sure if Danny had been on his way to greatness or simply holding his own among the also-rans. What she did understand was that he was the only thing resembling a celebrity that Fawley had to offer.

"I'm sure if my parents got to know Danny, they'd feel differently," Lydia offered, though her mother-in-law seemed less than comforted. Why should her son have to prove himself to anyone? Lydia didn't know how to answer that. The question ran too deep and took her places she did not want to revisit.

Danny and Lydia left the Crane home with an armful of leftovers, sealed in Tupperware. They wouldn't eat them, she knew. The containers would take up space in the refrigerator until a gray, fuzzy mold grew on the top, and as Lydia pushed the contents down the garbage disposal she'd think of Sally, as if she were destroying a part of her mother-in-law's soul. Sometimes she imagined that Sally, wherever she was, would jump as the disposal blades went into action, as if she could feel her maternal instincts being devoured.

"So how bad was that?" Danny asked as they drove away. He always asked that, and Lydia always smiled and put her hand on his knee.

The Milton Memorial United Methodist Church quarterly potluck dinner was full to overflowing. For the first time that anyone could remember, there weren't enough chairs. The minister's wife, Dee Evans, brought down some red and blue plastic Fisher Price chairs from the nursery and sat on one herself, balancing her Chinet plate full of baked spaghetti, egg rolls, and carrot salad on her lap. Her husband, the Reverend John Evans, smiled at the sight, though it was obvious he felt such a show of sportsmanship was a little overdone. Long ago John had stopped trying to control his wife's behavior and instead prayed for the fortitude to understand and appreciate her whimsical nature.

There were a couple of reasons for the above-average attendance. One was the weather. It was only the first week in March, and the temperatures had soared into the eighties. The promise of spring made people more trusting. It made them want to congregate and converse. It made them forget.

Spring arrived in Virginia like a charming but conniving adolescent, full of promises it couldn't keep. Only the most naive would fall for it. Only the most trusting would pack away their sweaters, turn off their furnaces, take down the storm windows. Even the intelligence of the flora was tested. The dogwoods, too sophisticated to be fooled by a sudden rise in the thermometer, would keep their buds clenched tight. But the buttercups, the idiots of the plant kingdom, would jump out at the first sign of warm weather, turning their foolish yellow faces toward a capricious sun. Their unquestioning nature would eventually be their undoing. They were the first to succumb to a late frost.

Lydia was not fooled. She did more than question the good weather; she detested it. She hated to say goodbye to her flannel nightgowns and cups of hot cocoa and fires popping in the fireplace. She loved putting her bare feet to a cold floor in the morning. She loved the metallic smell of frosted glass as she pressed her nose to the window. Something about the iced lawn and the low, gray sky made her feel comfortable. Spring was demanding. It wanted her to come outside and appreciate it. Lydia had never wanted to do what she was told; she wasn't going to be bullied by a warm breeze and a robin or two. As a result of her skepticism, she was the only one in the crowded room wearing a black turtleneck sweater. She was a dark cloud in a sea of pastels and bright floral prints.

The weather went a long way toward waking up the congregation, but the most important reason for tonight's high attendance was the title of the devotional to be served up after dinner—PLEASING GOD IN THE COMMUNITY. It was a vague enough thesis, but the inhabitants of Fawley were sensitive to its meaning—how to stop the Quality-Mart from opening.

For over a year now, the town had lived with the threat of the discount department store opening on the Greensboro Road, just seven miles outside the city limits. The Fawley town council, in conjunction with the churches, the Jaycees, the Lions Club, the Masons, and pockets of concerned citizens, had done its best to destroy the plans. The small town (population 1,800 counting the farmers in the surrounding county) saw little good in the coming of a discount store, covering two city blocks, offering a full gamut of decadent items—guns and gym shoes, Japanese cameras and televisions, costume jewelry and cosmetics, school supplies and sports equipment, and designer clothes with slight irregularities. The store was being imposed on them by the machinery of some northern conglomerate, developers who had no respect for the town's needs. It was a plan concocted by business school graduates who could only appreciate profits and had no sense of the serenity their project might be threatening.

Fawley was an old town, a post–Civil War pocket of Victorian houses, turn-of-the-century churches, horse ranches, and farms. The half-a-mile stretch of stores had served its community well for over a century. The merchants and the townspeople relied on those small businesses. The well-being of the town depended on the fact that the outside world rarely encroached on its boundaries. No one ever came to Fawley in search of bargains. No one came to Fawley in search of anything but gas and fast food, interrupting their travels along the highway toward some more desirable place. The employment that Quality-Mart might bring to the town did not outweigh the other, undesirable elements that would surely follow in its wake. Northerners would come. Gangs would come. The businesses in town would suffer. People would be laid off. Crime was waiting like a dog at the door, ready to race through the slightest opening.

These were, more or less, the words of John Evans as he approached the pulpit every Sunday. And they were the words perpetuated on the lips of the congregation and beyond, every day of the week. No good would come of this. No good at all.

John was preparing to make yet another speech of this nature. He stood at the front of the fellowship hall, setting up a slide show with some help from the laymen in the church. Dee watched him indifferently, more interested in her starchy dinner than anything her husband might have to say. Dee regarded her husband's status as one of the four Protestant preachers in town as a quirk of personality rather than a calling. She tolerated it, as if it were a phase, and any day now he'd find a real job.

Lydia sat among the congregation members, taking small bites of the broccoli and wild rice casserole prepared by Inez Milton. Being related to the original founders of the church, Inez felt obligated to prepare special meals. Inez seemed to have no identity outside the church. Sometimes Lydia had difficulty recognizing her in town. Inez was rich, and everyone knew it, but she lived as if she didn't have a penny to her name. She was the first person to appear at the sidewalk sales, sifting through the clothing as if she couldn't afford a new winter coat. When church fund-raising came around, however, Inez happily ripped off a five-thousand-dollar check with no more thought than if she were buying Girl Scout cookies.

Lydia was still full from the meal at her in-laws', but she feared her lack of appetite would be noted by others. She glanced around the room, trying to determine if her Rice Krispies squares were being consumed. She saw at least six people either biting into them or keeping them perched on the edge of their plates. She'd already learned a big lesson about the potluck dinner after the last round, when she'd brought some beautiful espresso brownies purchased at a bakery in Greensboro. Only two had been missing from the plate—one taken by herself, the other by her husband. Later she was informed by Dee that store-bought goods were a no-no, bordering on sin.

"You must cook," Dee told her the next day. "You must turn on the oven, even if what comes out is inedible."

This proved to be good advice, and she watched the cheap, sticky squares disappear.

There was so much to be learned about a small town, Lydia thought. She'd been here three years and every day another secret was revealed. All her education—boarding schools in New England, the College of William and Mary, two years of the University of Virginia Law School—really could not help her at all where the unwritten rules of Fawley were concerned.

The slide show finally in place, John took his spot in the middle of the fellowship hall, turning to his congregation with the serious expression of one who had seen the end of the world and was now obliged to spread the news.

"Quality-Mart is coming," he said solemnly. "There's nothing we can do to stop it."

Lydia cleared her throat in an effort to stifle a laugh. Danny reached out to touch her hand, hoping to quiet her.

"Now, this is nothing new to us. Five years ago they were going to dig up our farms and expose us all to uranium. This time they're going to put some monstrosity out on the Greensboro Road. We fought them and kept them out of the city limits, but we could not send them away completely; we've only kept them at bay. Why is everybody so hell-bent on destroying this town, you ask? Well, people, it's simple. They don't understand a community that cares more about their families and their neighbors than their wallets. People who'd rather watch a clean sunset than buy a new automobile. They don't want to know about people whose first priority is serving God in the community."

"Clever how he slipped the theme in there," Lydia whispered to her husband.

"You could say we've lost to Quality-Mart," John went on. "Or you could deny that it has anything to do with us. You'd be in good company if you wanted to deny it. Peter denied knowing Christ. *Three times!*"

John held up three fingers, gazing around the room with a half-smile.

"Three times," he repeated with the exact same inflection. Lydia was starting to recognize certain tricks of his ministry. Repeating things, that was key. Finding moments in the Bible where admirable men had fucked up. Smiling in that ironic, superior way. Pausing before the delivery of a particularly good line. It was like watching a well-timed comedy routine.

"Three times Peter said, 'Hey, I never heard of this guy.' And then the cock crowed. And what happened?"

No one answered. Inez Milton bit into a Rice Krispies square.

"Nothing, folks," said John. "Peter went on to be one of Christ's most loyal servants. Why? Because he admitted his betrayal to Christ. Then there's Judas who took it a step further. He denied his own *denial* of Christ. Denial happens everywhere, in bad guys, like Judas, and in good guys like Peter. We're doing it now. We're denying the evil of Quality-Mart. We have convinced ourselves it won't ruin our lives. And maybe it won't. But we must all stand as guards, ready to recognize its evil potential. Let's be like Peter, folks. Let's admit our denial and try to make it right. Let's admit that Quality-Mart is not for us. We can't stop it from coming. But we can stop it from succeeding."

The slide show followed, consisting of the architectural plans for Quality-Mart—basically an enormous warehouse surrounded by an enormous parking lot. These images were followed by picturesque shots of Fawley, the string of small stores along Main Street—the pharmacy, Oliver's Grocery, Leggett's, the bank, the Dollar Store, Whitney's antiques, Nathan's Hardware. Most shots included one or more of the proprietors standing in front of them, gesturing toward the signs, wearing solicitous smiles.

This is all too good to be true, Lydia thought. The blueprint of her life appeared before her—months and years of patronizing these shops, sending her children to the local schools and occasionally to Oliver's for a quart of milk, buying them shoes at Leggett's, medicine at the pharmacy, inflatable backyard pools at Nathan's Hardware. The thought that these plans might be threatened made her equally hostile toward the sinister Quality-Mart, even though in her more lucid moments she knew the panic was overstated.

"I'd like to encourage you all to keep faith," John said at the end of the visual display. "We've lost the battle but not the war. Here's my wife to tell you about how you can participate in the boycott."

Dee rose, somewhat reluctantly. She was a former hippie and still had trouble disguising that look. Not a hippie, exactly, Lydia reminded herself, since the movement had not really made its way to this remote location, except in the form of a fashion statement. But Dee was one of those girls who always wore fatigue jackets over tight T-shirts and hiphugger jeans. Her hair, in those days, had been unwashed and uncombed. She spent her lunch hour smoking behind the cafeteria, talking about motorcycles with the boys, calling the teachers "dickwad" and "fuckface."

These days Dee just looked like a tired, disheveled housewife. She wore men's shirts, untucked, with jeans and battered Keds. The only association one might make between her and her husband was the thin silver cross that hung in the hollow of her throat.

"Okay, if anybody's interested," she said, brushing her dark curls away from her face, "there's going to be a boycott. I'm head of the boycott, and you can just call me or put your name in the collection plate if you're interested in participating."

John trained his eyes on her, a stern but patient expression.

"Oh yeah, and there's going to be a peaceful protest in town on open-ing day, which is just a week away. So you can call me about that or sign up in Sunday school."

Dee sat back down, but not before making eye contact with Lydia and rolling her eyes. Lydia covered her smile with her fist.

"Any questions?" John asked, taking center stage again.

John was a handsome man in his late thirties, of medium build with a shock of dark hair, big brown eyes, and strong features. His skin looked scrubbed, pink, healthy as a baby's. He always wore khakis and buttoned-down oxford cloth shirts. It was hard to look at him and know the things that Lydia knew, mostly from her conversa-tions with Dee.

"Do you have any idea," Dee had confessed to her once, "how excit-ing it is to have sex with a man of the cloth?"

"No, I don't," Lydia said. It made her uncomfortable to talk about sex with anyone other than Camille. It always made her feel like those ridicu-lous women on sitcoms or talk shows, whose willingness to say the word orgasm was supposed to be an indication of how far women had pro-gressed. Maybe it was a throwback to her mother, the outdated gentility of her upbringing, but Lydia thought sex should be a private issue.

Still, she was interested and hoped Dee would elaborate. She al-ways did.

"Honey, it defies description," Dee had admitted, sitting at the kitchen table, folding the twins' footed pajamas. She and John were parents to two adorable and completely unruly three-year-old boys, Matthew and Mark. ("Saints in the making," Dee often laughed.)

"All that Bible thumping all week," Dee explained, "all that do-gooding, visiting hospitals, talking to teenagers about abstinence. He comes home, bursting at the seams. All I have to do is tug at his ear and he's dropping trou. I sit in church while he's preaching, and I think if only the congregation could know what he was doing a half an hour be-fore he got into the pulpit."

Lydia liked Dee. She reminded her of a bucolic version of Camille. She had the same sharp tongue and observant eye. Her candor sometimes bordered on cruelty. But it only bordered; Camille's frankness often went the distance and beyond.

Lydia spent most of her afternoons with Dee, drinking beer out of coffee mugs (in case John came in unexpectedly), talking about sex, the men they should have slept with, the drugs they missed taking now that they'd both sworn off.

"Couldn't you go for a joint right now?" Dee would ask, getting up to stir the Brunswick stew on the stove, pausing to yell at the twins for fighting over the TV remote control.

"I never really did that," Lydia said. She did not add that marijuana was beneath her social circle. They never fooled with anything so cheap. Her high school friends used cocaine, her college friends flirted with heroin, and everyone took Xanax like vitamins. But mostly, they drank.

"Boy, I did," Dee said. "Sometimes I dream about my bong. I kept it tucked under the mattress for years. I didn't know how to get rid of it. You can't exactly give it to Goodwill. Finally I smashed it and buried it at the bottom of the garbage can. I was so depressed I drank an entire bottle of red wine."

Lydia laughed, as she always did, starting to feel giddy from the beer. "How in the world did you end up married to a preacher?"

"I'm telling you, it's the best sex I've ever had. And I love him, of course. I love that he's so rigid. I love breaking him out of that mold. And he loves it, too.

"The real question is," Dee asked her more than once, "how did you end up married to Danny Crane?"

Lydia felt stumped for an answer. It frightened her that she couldn't come up with some great, poetic reason that she had dumped her fiancé and abandoned her former life to be with Danny. She felt, in some irrational way, that people should just understand it. They should be able to look at the two of them and realize it was meant to be. Danny had offered her everything she never believed she could have. A remarkable escape from her family of high achievers, from the predictability of marrying someone with an MBA and settling down in Georgetown. Danny had saved her from being one of those fat women on the beach. Would Dee ever understand that? Would anyone?

Then there was the joke about the rabbits. Sometimes it was hard for her to admit how much that had played a part, the fact that he'd told a simple, unsophisticated joke which surprised her and made her smile.

And then, without question, there was sex. She had known it, from the moment she stared at his thin lips across the table at the Rice Plantation.

There was the image of him putting on the rubber, which had actually transpired very close to the way she had pictured it. It made her feel as if she had had a premonition.

Sex was never playful with Danny. When he entered her they both were slightly relieved, as if something important had been accomplished, something they both doubted was possible. They never talked during sex. Once, in the early days, she had whispered that she loved him and he immediately lost his erection. She had learned her lesson; it was an encounter to be played out without emotion. And when it was over they could say whatever they wanted. But the act itself was to be observed and carried out in serious silence.

It was not a problem. In fact, Lydia got excited just thinking about it. But she did not tell Dee. She did not want to reveal that secret. It was almost as if she did not want anyone to know that she and Danny made love. She had a strange feeling that if she gave up this information, she would be surrendering the part of her marriage that made it work.

"Danny's a great husband," Lydia answered simply, whenever the question came up.

"Of course he is. For years he was regarded as the only man in Fawley worth marrying. But he never seemed interested. Then suddenly there was you. It's safe to say you broke some hearts when you arrived on the scene."

Lydia knew she should feel proud, but such statements made her slightly uncomfortable. It was hard for her to face the fact that almost every person in Fawley had known Danny longer, and therefore better, than she did.

"But not *your* heart, right?" Lydia had asked her.

"Honey, you don't have to worry. Danny and I tried real hard to feel some enthusiasm for each other. Our parents were swooning at the thought of us getting together. But it was no use. It's real hard to roll around in the backseat with somebody when just a decade ago you were playing in the sandbox together wearing nothing but hand-me-down underpants."

Dee had a great talent for distilling all of Danny's mysterious past to such unremarkable moments.

"Well, that concludes our discussion," John said.

Lydia came back into the present, surprised to discover the program was over, and that she was smiling pointlessly at her feet. She noticed

Danny looking at her, slightly worried. Danny was always slightly worried, of course. Her original assessment of him had remained intact. The man always had something mildly disturbing on his mind, and these days she wondered if she were contributing to that. He never said so, but he sometimes stared at her with a look of nameless concern.

"Any questions," John asked, or rather stated, indicating that he truly did not expect any.

A hand shot up. It belonged to Celia Burnette, known as Sissy among the congregation. Sissy's husband, Brian, had been unemployed for the last year, partly because of his premature arthritis, mainly because of his drinking.

"I know that Quality-Mart is a bad idea and all that. But they are hiring now, and I was wondering if applying for a job was a violation of the boycott."

John stared levelly at her. "Most definitely."

"But it's not like I'll be buying anything there. It's just, Brian's been laid off. And I was just wondering . . ."

John was distracted by Martha Dawson, who had suddenly started moving through the crowd like a union organizer, passing out flyers to the people.

"Excuse me, Martha, may I ask . . . ?"

"Letters," she answered back quickly. "Letters I've composed to our congressmen. All you have to do is sign them and mail them back."

"Well, I'm not sure Congress is the way to go here."

"What do you suggest, Reverend? Should we just pray until that monolith disappears?"

Lydia sat forward in her seat, hoping to see something interesting. Martha Dawson, the prim, stridently opinionated high school typing teacher, almost never showed her face at regular church services or events. But when a controversy arose, she would be the first to arrive on the scene. Martha liked nothing better than wrestling demons—as long as they weren't her own.

"Please, Martha, the church has not sanctioned this . . ."

"Sanctioned, my foot. We have to do something."

"I'm sorry, if I could just see the letter . . ."

But John was fighting a losing battle. Martha had distributed them all and was collecting her belongings. The crowd had started to disperse and move toward the door, eager to revisit the spring weather.

Danny and Lydia stayed long enough to help stack the folding chairs.

"John's going to be St. Jerome the martyr tonight," Dee grumbled. "Nothing he hates worse than not getting the last word at a church event."

"I think he did a good job," Lydia said.

"Look, I hate to do it but I have to ask. Are you available to picket on opening day?"

"I think you know me better than that," Lydia answered.

"Danny?"

Danny smiled. "You're cute when you're irrational, Dee."

"Give me a friggin' break," she said, grinning, and moved off to find another victim.

Lydia smiled and waved to Alicia Clay from across the room. She was another colleague, the gym teacher at the high school. Alicia enjoyed being the only black member of Milton Memorial. Given her nature, she would not for a moment entertain the notion of going to the all-black Baptist church.

"Y'all want some collard greens to take home?" she asked, approaching them with a tin-foil-covered dish. "Nobody touched them."

"Alicia, you are evil," Lydia said.

"What? I'm trying to share my culture with the congregation."

"When was the last time you fixed collard greens for yourself?"

Alicia smiled and wrinkled her nose. "Personally I think they smell like the stuff that comes back up your garbage disposal."

"Well, I was raised on them," Danny said, taking the dish from her.

"Did you get a whiff of Martha Dawson?" Alicia asked. "Her breath and a match could blow up Quality-Mart, and that would be the end of that."

"Maybe it was cough syrup," Danny said.

"Your husband is so cute," Alicia said, once Danny had stepped away to help collect the trash. "I don't know how you manage to leave him in the mornings."

Lydia smiled gratefully. She still loved getting compliments about Danny. Every favorable remark made her believe she'd made the right choice.

"I don't leave him. He leaves me. He goes to work at six o'clock," Lydia said.

"Oh my God. My whole life I've been looking for a man who gets up earlier than I do. Does he have a friend?"

"No," Lydia said. It was true. He didn't. He only had Kyle.

"Well, keep me in mind if he gets one."

At last they went out into the cool spring night. The thermometer was already starting to dip, but people walked bravely to their cars, shivering in their shirtsleeves, refusing to relinquish their belief.

Danny and Lydia walked hand in hand to the brand-new pickup truck. The sight of it made Lydia smile, but she could see Danny wrinkling his brow, and she knew he was wondering, again, if they could afford it. He'd had to talk himself into buying it right after Christmas. The contracting firm where he worked had had a stellar year, but Danny was always reluctant to trust good fortune. He kept waiting for the recession that seemed to lurk around every corner. It was curious, Lydia thought, the way Danny always acted as if his career were on the verge of ending, rather than moving forward. He was only thirty-four, and he was preparing for the lean years.

"I can't believe we own this thing," he said as they approached it.

Lydia smiled tightly. It was stressful to her, his cautious attitude. She had been raised to look ahead, to think bigger. Danny's scope of anticipation, she realized, was limited. Visibility was no more than a few feet at a time.

They drove through the dark streets of Fawley. It was only nine o'-clock, but it felt like midnight. The sidewalks were empty but for a few young men collecting like bugs next to the streetlights. The storefronts did not look real at night. With their crudely painted signs and handwritten posters in the windows advertising sales, Fawley's merchant section looked like a kindergarten version of a town. Let's play store. Lydia liked that quality, of course. It was unobtrusive and humble. The merchants behaved as if advertising or updating their image was a sign of vanity. No, worse: immorality. The stores of Fawley did not shout or twist anyone's arms. Come here if you like, they seemed to say. If not, go to Quality-Mart. The equivalent of hell.

"How come no one ever says anything to you about Quality-Mart?" Lydia asked.

"What would they say?"

"That you helped build it."

Danny frowned. "The company contracted it. I didn't lay any bricks. I didn't even hire the subs."

"But still."

"I'm not to blame. It's not like I run the company."

"No, it's not like you do."

If Danny heard the edge in her voice, he ignored it. When he first met her, he had claimed to be months away from taking over the company from the retiring founder, Howard J. Mecklin. Three years later, Howard was still retiring, and his son, Ben, was being groomed to take the reins. Danny was supposed to be Ben's partner, as Ben had no real experience in the contracting business. But so far, there had been no changes. Danny was still a sales manager, meeting with clients, writing bids, negotiating with subcontractors. He even spent time on the building sites, overseeing the work. Lydia wasn't sure why he hadn't been promoted. The idea had been advanced that Danny would be the person to prepare Howard J. Mecklin & Co. for the future, for the global economy. The reality was that Danny was a glorified construction worker, a foreman in a tie.

The situation, however, did not seem to bother Danny, so Lydia tried hard not to let it bother her.

He turned the truck into the driveway of their modest two-bedroom home on Roosevelt Hill. The front-porch light was on, illuminating the wicker rocking chair and antique milk can, both presents from his parents. Danny's parents always gave them old things. Their wedding present was an antique washbasin and pitcher. Lydia felt as if his parents were preparing them for old age. In fact, turning into the driveway this late, Lydia felt as if she were already old. Their house looked as if it belonged to someone's grandparents. If I live here now, she wondered, where will I live when I'm eighty?

It was an unremarkable house, one of several post–World War II homes that had cropped up almost overnight to accommodate the returning veterans. The floor plan was a masterpiece of utilitarian thinking. Each room was a perfect square, each with a closet of identical proportions. Bathroom separating two bedrooms. Kitchen in the back with a screened-in porch. Living room in front with a fireplace. No frills, no unnecessary attention to detail, no impractical (forget ornamental) placement of windows. It was comfortable and pragmatic, free of any clutter that might get in the way of the business of living.

One day she and Danny would live in one of those fabulous Victorian houses on Main Street, just north of town. Their beautiful antebellum features had been untampered with over the years. The Doric columns, the wrought-iron balconies, the turrets, and the wraparound porches were all still as they might have been in the 1860s. No one had torn anything down or built anything on or painted them inappropriate colors. It showed a remarkable consistency of taste, an understanding of aesthetics that Lydia didn't always believe the inhabitants of Fawley possessed. They did not have much perspective on where the town was headed, but they did understand the importance of its past.

Buying one of those homes was not so far in the future, Lydia thought as she shed her clothes and slipped into bed. Danny had gotten a nice raise last year, and once he made vice president, she was certain they could afford it. Once he made vice president, a lot of her problems would be solved. She wasn't sure why she believed that, or even what problems she was referring to. It just felt like they were moving toward that goal; then everything could happen the way it was supposed to.

Lydia thumbed through *People* as she waited for Danny to bathe. Tomorrow was Monday, but she didn't have to teach, as it was still spring break. She felt the same sort of recklessness she felt as a child whenever school was not in session. Part of what she loved about teaching was being on the same schedule as the kids. She was just as excited on a Friday as her students, just as undisciplined during her breaks, just as given to counting off days on the calendar and dreaming of June.

Danny slipped into bed next to her, smelling of Irish Spring. She hooked her arm around his still damp chest.

"What do you make of John?" she asked him.

"What do you mean?"

"Dee says he's great in bed."

"What people do in their bedroom is their own business."

"They do things with Magic Shell. You know, that chocolate stuff that dries hard on ice cream?"

Danny gave in to a smile. "Why am I not surprised that Dee's become your best friend?"

"Three years you've been harping on me to socialize. Now you're disapproving?"

"Men don't harp. They persist."

"You like Dee. She was your girlfriend," Lydia reminded him.

"I took her to the senior prom. We were so drunk we passed out in the car and woke up in time for the final dance."

"And what was John doing?"

Danny shrugged. "Dealing dope, probably. He was making over

twenty grand a year growing pot in his backyard and selling it over in Greensboro. They never caught him, though. He got nailed for shoplifting, of all things. Went away for a while, came back a preacher."

"Why do you think he did that? Turned to God, I mean?"

"It figures. John was always looking to be a celebrity. When you're young, the way you do that is by being the wildest and most outrageous. Then one day you realize that as you get older those characteristics will only make you pathetic. So instead of being the worst person in town you decide to be the best. This is John's way of getting people to listen to him. He's always been a man of action, and now his actions are acceptable and beyond reproach."

She loved to hear Danny talk this way. His insights always seemed so far-reaching. Not in a general sense. He wasn't going to win any Nobel Prizes. Semantics confused him and his hold on language was shaky. But sometimes his ruminations were so pure, and so incongruous with the way he lived his life. The fact that he analyzed people in this way made her feel excited and glad to be alive. It was like hearing truth distilled to common sense. Just plain thinking.

"I don't think Dee believes any of it," Lydia said.

"Dee talks a big game. But at the end of the day, she wants security. She wants something predictable."

"Do you believe any of it?" Lydia asked.

"You know I'm not religious. Going to church in Fawley is more a social obligation. It keeps my parents happy."

"No, I'm talking about Quality-Mart."

"Oh, that," he said, stifling a yawn. "You have to understand, this town treats any kind of change like Armageddon. It was the same thing when the bypass was built. The town was going to die. It was going to be the end of civilization as we knew it. Of course, Quality-Mart isn't going to affect us at all. But I guess we should be grateful that people care so much."

"It scares me, though. All that uninformed passion. Like the Third Reich."

"Well, that's *you* overreacting."

Lydia thought about arguing. Lydia loved to argue, but at the moment she felt too tired and too content to pursue it. So she moved on. "Do you think Rex is gay?"

"Oh, Lydia. Don't start."

"Danny, he's almost twenty-nine and still lives with your parents. He does four days a week in the library and builds models."

"That doesn't mean he's gay. Why can't he just be odd?" he asked.

"He *is* odd. But he might be gay, too. I mean, how else do you explain him?"

"I *don't* explain him. That's your ambition."

He began to kiss her neck. A chill shot through her and she shuddered. He kept kissing her and she started to feel weak.

"Tell me about Pike again. Tell me what happened."

"Later," he said.

Now he was kissing the nape of her neck, and that was always her undoing.

"Thank you for bringing me here," she said as his callused hand traveled over her breasts. "Every day is a miracle. Where do you think I'd be now, if you hadn't come along? I'd be an alcoholic with a face-lift. Slap me if I ever forget that."

He moved on top of her, putting his mouth to hers less out of passion than a desire to shut her up. Danny had never been comfortable with gratitude.

2

THE PHONE RANG in the middle of the night. Lydia swam out of the darkness, trying to identify the sound. In the split second between dreams and consciousness, she ran through the possibilities—a fire alarm, a school bell, the microwave. Her brain didn't want to identify it as the phone, because no call at this hour could be good news.

Danny was up and out of bed, bumping into things, swearing. Lydia sat up in bed, her heart racing, as if every bit of horror she had ever encountered had come to her in just this way. Ancient deaths, one after another, lining up to remind her of her past. But she had never received terrible news at night. Her grandfather had died in the middle of the afternoon. Her mother's car accident happened one lazy Saturday morning. Her favorite cat was mauled on a bright, cold Christmas Day.

Still, she sat there clutching the sheet, watching Danny pick up the phone, feeling that those few seconds between knowing and not knowing represented her last chance for peace. This is it, the moment between contentment and everything else. The moment that changes everything. Years later she would tell her children, "Then came the phone call."

But it was only Kyle. It was always Kyle.

Danny mumbled into the receiver, scratching his bare chest. He tucked his hand into the waist of his boxer shorts and nodded as he listened. Lydia felt her heart sink, and she tried to tell herself it wasn't disappointment. It was relief, which sometimes, this late, felt like the same thing.

Danny hung up the phone and rubbed his hand over his unshaven chin, making a whispering sound.

"He's in the hospital," he said.

"Is he okay?"

"I guess. I have to go down there and see."

"What is it?"

"Car accident," Danny said. "What else?" He stared at his fingers, flexing them. He did this a lot lately, Lydia noticed.

"But, I mean, what is it?"

"How the hell should I know?" he asked, fumbling in the darkness for his jeans. "It was my mother calling. She doesn't deal in facts."

Lydia nodded. She could hear Sally now, her dark, worried voice, tense with drama, as if she were almost enjoying it: "It's Kyle again. You'd better come." And then she probably hung up, in an effort to heighten the effect of the moment.

Like the rest of the women in his family, Sally did not handle tragedy well. She unraveled. These were not the strong Southern belles who had hidden the money and fought the Yankees off their farms and plowed the fields with the bare white hands. These were the women left unmentioned by the history books. The ones who hid in closets and cried until the men came home.

Lydia got up and put her robe on. Every time, she felt the need to respond. She felt guilty about staying in bed, turning over and going back to her dreams, which was what she was always tempted to do. One day, if she and Danny stayed together long enough and Kyle didn't kill himself, that was what she would do. But not yet.

Lydia still had trouble understanding the loyalty Danny felt toward his cousin. She had two or three first cousins she'd never met. For her, the word was synonymous with those family members who were too distant to be concerned about. But not yet.

She sometimes wondered how she might feel about Kyle if she could not remember those early days, the first time she saw him limping along on the sands of Myrtle Beach. Perhaps she would have given him the benefit of the doubt if she did not have Camille's voice still ringing in her ears: "Never mind, chromosome damage." That remark had stuck with Lydia an unreasonably long time. It was as if Camille had accurately diagnosed the damage, a bad chemical in the brain, some vital genetic information gone wrong. Lydia had to remind herself that in the final analysis, there was nothing mysterious about Kyle. He was just what Southerners called "no good."

"Want me to come?" she asked, because she always did and because she knew she wouldn't have to.

"No, no. Of course not. Why don't you just go back to sleep?"

"I can't sleep when you're not here."

"Better learn."

"Why? Do you intend to be your cousin's keeper for the rest of your life?"

Danny zipped up his jeans and made a halfhearted attempt to tuck in his T-shirt.

"It's not exactly my choice."

"Whose is it, then?"

"Do you want to argue, on top of everything else?"

"Of course I want to argue," she said, following him to the door. "Kyle is thirty-four years old, Danny. This isn't a phase anymore. It's his life. You can't save him from his life. At some point, you'll have to leave him to the mercy of it."

"Not tonight," Danny said, sounding like an exhausted housewife. "Not tonight, okay?"

"Okay," Lydia agreed. She was already looking forward to the cup of hot chocolate and the late movie—two treats she only enjoyed when Kyle got himself in trouble.

Danny didn't kiss her before going out the door. She felt confused and irritable as she stood at the window, watching the pickup truck spinning gravel into the lawn she had just mowed that afternoon.

The late movie was a vampire thing, a delicious, low-budget production that usually comforted her like macaroni and cheese. But tonight she just couldn't concentrate on it. She was busy thinking of her marriage, her own deal with the devil, and whether or not it had paid off.

"Do not do this," Camille had pleaded when Lydia showed her her small, plain diamond—such a stark contrast to the monstrosity Ham had given her. "Find some other way to have a breakdown, Lydia, for God's sake."

"You'll never understand what this feels like," Lydia had said, bristling, defensive. Her head was full of white-hot conviction. She was as right about this as anything in her life, and the certainty of that made her hard and unapproachable.

"Thank God I'll never have to understand," Camille had responded. "He's a construction worker, Lydia. I'm sure the sex is great, but we're talking about your life. Marry Ham and cheat with this guy. Kind of long distance for an affair, but it can be worked out, can't it?"

"I feel sorry for you," Lydia had shot back.

"Oh, please. Keep your pity for yourself. You'll need it."

Lydia did not think of her marriage in terms of rebellion. It couldn't have been, for she entered into it seeking everyone's approval. She wanted Camille to understand. She wanted her parents to approve. She had spent hours trying to convince them that Danny was much more than they thought, and that this life was what she had always been looking for. She pleaded for her happiness like a lawyer. She stated its case with passion and self-righteousness. She rebutted and cross-examined and summarized. But in the end, she lost her case. She went into her marriage alone, leaving a trail of bitter and broken hearts.

"Young girl, don't come crying to me," was the last thing she'd heard her mother say.

"Mother, I wouldn't ask you for water if my lungs were on fire."

Only love could have caused Lydia to say such things to her mother. Only young love and seasoned hate could be so certain.

Most of the time Lydia now felt vindicated about her choice. Her marriage to Danny had lasted three years and was still strong. (Camille's misguided marriage to Christian French, a local millionaire, heir to his father's scrap-metal fortune, had already faltered.) She and Danny were poor by her family's standards, but she truly did not feel it. She had clothes and food and neighbors. Beyond that, wanting things felt like some irrational desire, the denial of which made her feel pure.

Sometimes, though, particularly on the evenings when Danny went off to rescue Kyle, she felt the doubt creeping up like a low-grade fever.

Kyle was the first real adjustment she'd had to make when she moved to Fawley. They had only been married a week when the phone call came in the deep of the night. She'd actually accompanied Danny to the hospital that time, thinking this was a rarity, a special occasion that required her presence and support. She had entered into the equation with wide-eyed concern, chewing her nails in the waiting room and rubbing her husband's back whenever he sat down long enough to be comforted. She knew that Danny and Kyle were close. She did not, at that time, recognize the degree of that closeness. She was no better at understanding it now, but at least she was prepared for it. Danny felt obligated, and such obligations were foreign to her. She tried to appreciate his loyalty. Because loyalty was a good thing, wasn't it, regardless of how misplaced it seemed?

She and Kyle had never connected, despite Danny's attempts toward that goal. She'd had him to dinner a couple of times and he did nothing to make her revise her first impression of him. He drank too much, became belligerent, made fun of her. "That how rich girls wear their hair? It's in style to look like a dyke? Is this what rich folks call food? What was this meat before it went to college?" Danny made an attempt toward damage control, but by the end of the evening Kyle had become overtly hostile, even to Danny, whom he claimed to love.

"So what's next for Dan the Man," Kyle had slurred on that occasion. "Got the wife, got the house, got the shirt and tie job. What about golf? What about a boat? Hey, what about a baby? Or do rich girls have babies? Maybe they order them from New York or somewhere. Hey, here's the ticket. A mistress. Some skinny little schoolgirl who'll—"

Danny had shoved Kyle at that point, mainly, Lydia thought, to prevent him from saying anything that Danny would be forced to acknowledge as the end of their relationship. As usual, Danny was saving Kyle from himself.

Lydia sipped her hot chocolate and looked at her watch. Danny had been gone two hours. This could be the big one he was always predicting, the act of whimsy that finally did Kyle in. If so, it would be the first person close to her, other than grandparents, who had died. This, she thought, was another class issue. Death seemed to tiptoe around her social circle. Danny, by contrast, had a whole catalogue of relatives who died young, many of them violently, like his Uncle Pike. Kyle would be next, whether it was tonight or a decade from now. And his death would be gory, stupid, and sordid.

Lydia sometimes surprised herself at how much she disliked Kyle. Staring at the vampire on television, with his bone white skin, hollow jaws, protruding teeth, she realized that somewhere inside of her, she thought Kyle was evil. Supernatural, almost. Certainly beyond redemption.

These thoughts spooked her. It hit her, as it sometimes did, that she knew nothing about her husband and his family. Nothing but what they told her. Those strange tales of saintly relatives and violent deaths. The details that, in tiny increments, kept changing. Something left out here and added there. Perhaps she was making too much out of it. It was late, and the hour made her feel crazy.

Still, she had a sudden urge to look for answers. She went into the bedroom and started opening drawers. This was something she used to do as a child whenever her parents weren't home. She was drawn to the mystery of their bedroom, searching for clues to the people they really were, parts of themselves they did not reveal to her. Once when she was thirteen she had found a love letter her father had written to her mother before they were married. It started, "My Darling Margo, Why can't I seem to forget your eyes?" She didn't read any more. It made her feel embarrassed and slightly sick, the fact that her strong, reticent father was capable of such sentimentality. It made him seem foolish and unreliable.

She felt the same sort of fear as she looked through Danny's things. Her heart was pounding and her palms were starting to sweat. It seemed so dirty, what she was doing. What did she expect to find? Nothing, of course, but it disturbed her that she wanted to do this. It proved that she did think Danny was capable of deceiving her.

His sock drawer revealed nothing. Just socks, all neatly folded together, arranged by color. His underwear drawer was equally unimpressive. Boxers on one side, briefs on the other. Lydia smiled as she touched them. Danny always insisted on doing the laundry. He was better at it than she was. He placed a higher value on order and symmetry.

She turned to the nightstand next to his side of the bed. She rarely opened it, and she was surprised to see that it was slightly messy. A hodgepodge of things—loose change, sunglasses, condoms, a pocket dictionary, a small black Bible, a deck of cards, loose photographs.

The photos interested her. She picked one up—it was the two of them on their honeymoon on Hilton Head Island. She was tanned, holding a drink, sitting on his lap. She was smiling too much. Danny was not smiling at all. He was looking at something off to the side. Lydia could not remember the moment or who took the picture. But she could see a vague sense of panic in her eyes. Danny, on the other hand, seemed calm, unperturbed.

She found another photo, this one of Danny and Kyle together as children. It was black and white. They could not have been more than twelve. Danny was holding a baseball glove and Kyle was raising a BB rifle in the air, above his head like a soldier about to charge. There was rage in his face. Danny's expression, as always, was inscrutable.

Looking at it, she realized Kyle had both his legs in this photo. Of course he did. The accident happened much later, in his twenties. It felt odd to know that Kyle had once been physically complete. His missing limb seemed so much a part of who he was.

Squinting, Lydia could make out another form in the picture. Deep in the background a young girl lurked. One of Kyle's sisters. It looked like Joyce, the oldest. She was watching the boys from a distance, frowning at them. Lydia wondered who had taken the photograph, if that had something to do with Joyce's expression. Or maybe Joyce had learned to hate Kyle already. Maybe it started that long ago.

Lydia picked up the Bible and opened it. The smell wafted up, that Bible smell. Odd how no other book smelled that way. She thumbed through the thin paper until she found something—a newspaper clipping. She unfolded it carefully and read the headline: LOCAL MAN FATALLY SHOT IN MYSTERIOUS DISPUTE. And there was Pike, bald and smiling, his eyes a kinder version of Kyle's. She'd seen Pike before in family albums, but somehow this picture was more haunting. She couldn't stop staring at it.

She heard the sound of tires on gravel. Headlights washed over the window, and she jumped. She put the Bible back in the drawer and was about to close it when she saw a small bottle of pills. Taking them out she quickly read the label: Ativan. One tablet as needed for sleeplessness. Since when? she wondered. Danny never had trouble sleeping. But maybe this was why.

She had very little time to wonder about it. She dropped them in the drawer and slammed the drawer shut. She rolled over and lay on the bed, waiting for Danny to come in.

"The TV was on," he said. "What are you doing in here?"

"I got bored. What happened?"

"It was nothing," he said. "Kyle ran the car into a guardrail and bruised his forehead. But we had to wait for a bunch of doctors to come. First, to test him for drugs. Then to test his sanity."

"Well?"

"He'd had some beers. Maybe a joint. No coke, thank God."

"What about his sanity?"

Danny leaned against the door as if he longed to dart back out. Finally he said, "They said he had some delusions which could be attributed to the drugs. But that he had a very real fear of abandonment, and could I think of where that came from?"

"Could you?"

"Yes, of course I could. I said his father died when he was young and he never got over it. Then Aunt Rita started screaming about Uncle Pike being the highest saint in heaven, and the doctor looked like the job was just too big for him. So he gave Kyle a shot and went home."

"Did you try to explain about your family?" Lydia asked.

"Aunt Rita was there. The doctor could see for himself what the problems were."

"Kyle needs help."

"That's why I was there."

"Professional help."

Danny sighed and looked out the window at the flat, gray dawn approaching.

"You believe in professionals," he said. "We don't. Professionals are people who come in and give names to problems which have been plaguing families for decades. They define it, they don't cure it."

"Well, who's going to cure Kyle?"

"He's going to cure himself one day."

"By wrapping himself around a tree?"

Danny tightened his jaw and looked out the window again. A bare black branch scraped against the pane, making a sound like a cat's hoarse cry.

"Let me ask you something, Danny. What has Kyle ever done for you?"

"He's my cousin," Danny answered flatly.

"That's not an answer."

"I've tried to explain this before," he said with dull impatience. "I promised Uncle Pike that I would look out for Kyle."

"But you weren't there when he died."

"Before," he said in a weary tone. "Years before. It's like he knew he wasn't going to be around."

"I don't think it was fair of him. What the hell was he doing talking to a child about things like that? Didn't he know what kind of burden he was placing on you?"

His dark eyes fell on her, hard and disapproving, full of self-righteous anger. When he looked at her like that she felt horrified, as if he, too, were seeing her as an outsider.

"Family matters to people around here," he said simply.

"Oh yes. Up North we eat our young."

"Lydia, you don't speak to your parents."

"I sacrificed them for you!"

"I never asked you to."

"But why would I have anything to do with them, Danny? They hate you. They told me I was making the biggest mistake of my life. You know what my mother called it? 'A spoiled little girl's fascination with farm trash.' So you want me to speak to them? Let's call them right now." She grabbed the phone and thrust it at him. "Here, you dial."

He stared at her for a long moment, his eyes blinking languidly. He looked at his hands, flexing his fingers.

"I'm going to bed," he said.

But he walked away from her, toward the guest room.

3

WHEN LYDIA CAME into Oliver's Market on Monday morning, Joyce Crane felt her knees go weak. She froze at the cash register, a can of creamed corn in her hand. She wanted to disappear. Lydia looked in her direction and waved; Joyce smiled tensely and nodded. She dragged the corn across the scanner.

"Joyce, you charged me for that already," the customer, Mrs. Parrish, complained.

"Sorry."

Maybe she could take her break now and hide in her office until Lydia was gone.

Don't do this, she told herself, trying to breathe normally. She's just a person, just a normal person, and she likes you. You can talk to Lydia, you want to talk to Lydia, and anyway, there is no other choice.

"That's Danny's wife, isn't it?" Mrs. Parrish asked as Joyce bagged her groceries. She was scrutinizing Joyce's every move.

"Yes, ma'am."

"An interesting girl, isn't she? Watch the bread, please. Last time it was crushed."

Interesting. To call Lydia interesting was to call the core of the sun rather warm. It seemed like a minor miracle that Lydia was a part of her family. How could any of them ever have imagined a person like that taking up a limb of the family tree? Sometimes Joyce thought about what it would look like, years in the future, when someone dissected their genealogy. Years of subdued, unquestioning, uneducated women, interrupted by this unlikely figure. Where had she come from?

From Danny, of course. He was the only one who ever brought anything good to the family. The college graduate, the baseball player, the one who'd monopolized all the gene pool had to offer in the area of looks and intelligence and grace. Danny promised to restore the family's good name. It had had one once, so Joyce was told, before her father's death. Before Kyle. As hard as Kyle tried to destroy the Cranes, Danny struggled to save them. Lydia was a prime example of that. She was the new blood that they all needed.

This did not mean that Joyce was comfortable with Lydia. Far from it. Whenever she saw her, she felt overcome with fear. She had an overwhelming impulse to hide something. And that thing, she eventually came to understand, was her brother Kyle. She was scared he would drive Lydia away. Joyce wanted to take her aside and say, "Everybody knows what Kyle is. Don't let him ruin us. Give us a chance." Or something to that effect, but the conversation never happened, even though Joyce never stopped rehearsing it in her head.

Lydia was the only person that Joyce wanted to talk to in any sort of meaningful way. Joyce actually had fantasies about going out for a drink with Lydia and, after a couple of beers, telling her all the things she'd never told anyone.

Suddenly a voice echoed through the store, like the voice of God: "Joyce to the produce department."

Joyce's heart was racing as she walked the short distance to the so-called produce department, which amounted only to a small refrigerated counter and some vegetable bins at the back of the store. She had forgotten it was produce day. A farmer was waiting, with his face pinched in a frown and his body already set in a defensive posture. The farmer was Clive Lewis, one of their trouble clients. He was lazy and angry, a dangerous combination, always trying to unload inferior produce and responding to Joyce's low bids as if he'd been mortally wounded.

"How are you, Mr. Lewis?" Joyce said.

"Don't start with me, Joyce," he said, plopping down a basket of shriveled carrots, and another equally unimpressive basket of sweet potatoes.

Clive, like many of the farmers, had trouble accepting Joyce's position. She had recently been promoted to assistant manager, and along with the slight increase in pay and the freedom to move beyond the checkout counter came the responsibility of overseeing the delivery of goods. It had never occurred to her when she first started working at the cash register that one day she would be forced into a position of negotiation. The most difficult encounters she'd ever had in those days were the customers complaining, usually in a good-natured way, about the high costs or the shortage of items. Occasionally she'd have to tell someone that food stamps could not be used for alcohol or pet food. But no matter how disgruntled they became, she could always shrug and say, "I'm just the cashier. I don't make the rules."

She still wasn't making the rules—Mr. Oliver set the standards—but she was in the dubious position of defending those standards as if they were her own. If a certain crop of tomatoes was disappointing, it was her job to refuse them or underbid them. If cucumbers were small or ears of corn were shriveled, Joyce had to be critical, to explain that they could not accept what they wouldn't be able to sell. Farmers were always difficult; they regarded their crops as extensions of themselves, as children, who were perfect in their eyes and beyond reproach.

Once when Joyce had rejected several bushels of peaches, she'd actually reduced a farmer to tears.

"Okay, then," he'd said, wiping his nose with a worn handkerchief, "you tell my children why they won't be getting anything for Christmas."

Joyce knew it was theater, manipulation, but it was all very convincing. She actually believed that she was denying some seven-year-old the latest Barbie or a pair of Nike gym shoes. The only way she could stand her ground was by convincing herself that she was protecting her customers. Somehow it had become her job to provide the town with the best choice of produce.

She didn't really care about quality produce. All she cared about was protecting her job. Her job, which allowed her an income, gave her the freedom to move out of her mother's house and set her apart from her sisters, who still lived at home and cowered at the thought of confronting the world. Her job, which afforded her a tiny apartment on Elm Street, was the thing that constantly reminded her she was different. She was not doomed. Let them all hide in that house. She would not live in fear.

She did, in fact, live in fear, but she did not give in to it. Every morning when she woke up, the thought of the day ahead was almost overwhelming. The idea of taking a shower or making toast or choosing a pair of shoes seemed like a challenge; the idea of going out there, conversing with people, making decisions, or even answering the phone seemed insurmountable. She always set her alarm early to allow for the half hour of dread. It took her that long to calm herself, lying in bed and staring at the ceiling, repeating to herself like a chant, "There's no other choice."

Every day, she wanted to bolt her doors and pull the covers over her head and disappear. But she knew if she ever gave in to that temptation, she would be just like the others, and that was a fate she could not accept. She was not like her sisters. She was different.

But then, Joyce had always been different. Her reflection in the mirror always confirmed it. She did not look like other girls. (Women, she tried to remind herself. For though she was approaching thirty-nine, she had trouble thinking of herself as a woman.) Her face, which in the best light could only be described as plain, was actually grotesque. A portion of her right cheek looked as if it had been bitten. It was sunken in, cavernous, the result of a childhood accident. A venetian blind had sheared it away, and a plastic surgeon's attempt to repair it had gone horribly wrong. A keloid had developed, inches of unwanted tissue growing up over the wound, overdoing its attempt to replace what was missing. The cheek dipped in, then bulged out, in layers of overdeveloped skin, forming railroad tracks of pink scar tissue. Her face looked like something a kid would spend hours trying to concoct on Halloween. It had earned her many colorful nicknames at an early age—Frankenstein, Scarface, Vampira. The names had eventually worn themselves out, and now she'd reached another level, which was equally disturbing. She was so much a fixture in the town that the children of those who'd once made fun of her no longer noticed her. They'd been trained by their parents to accept and ignore her deformity. She felt like Hubble, the drunk street artist, or Lucinda Greely, the local retarded girl (body of a forty-year-old, mind of a sixth-grader), a part of the town's folklore that children had learned to accept. She was local color. She was the scarred woman at the grocery store.

Their silent acceptance was worse. Their silence felt like pity, and pity was something she detested.

The farmers never pitied her. This was why she greeted each produce day with a mixture of fear and excitement. The strong words she'd have to use sent her shivering. But the excitement came from the fact that the

farmers couldn't give a damn about her face. They didn't want to be attracted to her; they only wanted to sell to her.

"Just don't start with me," Clive repeated. "I've got a lot on my mind
and I don't want to argue with you."

"Then don't argue with me," she said, running her fingers through the
carrots, locating one of average size and holding it up to the light. The
skin was reasonably healthy, but the texture was soft and malleable.

"You won't find any better, with the winter we've had," he claimed.

"Hmm," Joyce replied, locating a carrot no thicker than a cigar and
balancing it on her palm.

"There's a runt in every litter," Clive said, issuing a smoker's cough
into his fist.

"I'll tell you what I think," Joyce said. "I think it's an early crop. These
carrots—those potatoes, too—belong in the ground. You harvested them
too soon."

He had no response to this, but his face grew red as he heard her offer.

"Highway robbery," he said. "I'll take my business over to Quality-
Mart."

She shook her head. "They don't sell fresh produce."

"Then I'll sell 'em to Birds Eye. No way I'm giving away my hard
work. This is my lifeline we're talking about."

"Ours, too, Mr. Lewis. And I can't buy what I can't sell."

"Fine, then go without."

"Whatever you say."

"I want to see Oliver."

"I believe you know where his office is."

Joyce was not impressed by such a threat. She knew, as well as Clive
did, that Mr. Oliver hated to be bothered with such matters, and the im-
position would cause him to reject not only this shipment but anything
Clive brought in that year. Mr. Oliver was very bloody-minded that way.

"It's criminal, that's what it is," Clive said.

"I agree. You got impatient, harvested too early. You were trying to
manipulate the market. My advice to you is leave the rest of your crop
in the ground and take a chance on the going rate."

Mr. Lewis stood tall, jutting out his chin in a gesture of defiance.
"What you know about farming wouldn't fill a thimble," he said.

"Well, I don't need to know about farming. I just need to know buying and selling. And I can't sell this crop."

They compromised. He cut his price and she bought both baskets, enduring his insults as he went out the door.

"You'll be lucky to see me again," he grumbled, and she just smiled and nodded.

It was going to be nice to show Mr. Oliver that they had acquired an early shipment of fresh carrots and sweet potatoes at a cut rate. The sweet potatoes were a particular triumph, as they were reasonably healthy. But the inferior carrots had brought down the farmer's confidence and caused him to act too quickly.

Jeffrey the bag boy was sitting on the counter, scowling, when Joyce returned.

She gave him a look. He jumped down, but he never lost his scowl. He had hated her ever since she'd caught him stealing from the store. Little things like candy and magazines, but it was enough to get him fired. Mr. Oliver didn't tolerate any sort of dishonesty. Joyce felt she'd done Jeffrey a favor by giving him a second chance, but he hadn't interpreted it that way. He blamed her, somehow, for his own misdeeds.

"I don't need this shit," he'd said when she confronted him. "Nobody calls me a thief. My father is an influential man."

Jeff's father was an influential gas station manager who'd been investigated on embezzlement charges himself. Joyce had ignored whatever veiled threat he was making and told him if he'd pay for the items, she'd let it go. He had grudgingly written her a check, from his father's bank account, and she'd never mentioned anything to Mr. Oliver.

Today he looked at her as if he wanted to spit on her.

"Good afternoon, Jeffrey," she said.

"Yeah, right," was his reply, as he stared at her scar. People did that often; it was as if they hated her for inflicting her ugliness on them.

Lydia came to the front then, a basket hooked over her arm with a few cans rattling around in it. She smiled and suddenly Jeffrey's expression brightened.

"Delivery?" he asked.

She laughed. "I don't think so. I've got four cans and some peas and some noodles."

Jeffrey looked disappointed.

"Jeffrey, we have a whole case of coffee that needs unpacking," Joyce said.

Jeffrey gave her another look of pure contempt and moved off.

Joyce pretended not to see it and turned back to Lydia. "Why are you doing the shopping?" she asked.

She hated the way it sounded, even though she'd rehearsed it. Danny usually did the grocery shopping on Fridays, when he also did his mother's. He shopped at the Food Lion out on 29. It was rare to see either one of them in Oliver's.

Lydia said, "It's spring break and I don't know what to do with myself. I had the urge to make a tuna casserole and I knew you'd have fresh peas."

Joyce smiled. She felt proud about the peas. Lydia had that talent. She made people feel good about small things. Unless it was someone she didn't like. Then she could give them hell. Like the time she told Mr. Oliver, "It's shameful the way you wax your cucumbers and apples. Do you think that fools anybody? It takes hours to get that crud off." On another occasion she'd challenged his refusal to buy an ad in the high school yearbook: "My students come in here every day after school for junk food. When it's their turn to sell something, you turn on them."

Lydia saw through people. She evaluated them. Joyce was no exception; she felt herself being sized up whenever Lydia stared at her, but she was relieved that the assessment always seemed to be an honest one. Lydia still looked at the right side of Joyce's face, not critically, but as if the sight of it always made her want to know exactly what happened. After years of dull stares, repulsion without interest, the curiosity in her eyes was a comfort. Once, in the early days of their acquaintance, Lydia had come right out and asked.

"It was a childhood accident," Joyce had replied, hoping to end it at that, yet oddly relieved when Lydia would not let it go.

"Danny said it was something about venetian blinds? How did that happen?"

"They fell on me. I was too young to remember."

"They just fell? Just dropped down?"

"You'd have to ask my mother," Joyce had said.

Lydia had rolled her eyes and said, "I've never had any success in getting an answer out of your mother. The longest conversation we ever had lasted about two minutes."

"That's a minute longer than most people get," Joyce had replied, and she'd been thrilled at the way Lydia had laughed.

Remembering that, Joyce felt brave. She smiled at Lydia and asked, "Is it a good tuna casserole recipe?"

"Is there such a thing? I don't know, it's easy. I'm lousy at this stuff. Martha Stewart has nothing to fear from me."

"Well, at least you've got a better haircut," Joyce said, surprised and thrilled at her retort. Occasionally lines like that came out of her, like a gift from heaven.

Lydia laughed a deep, genuine laugh and ran her fingers through her thick blond hair. "Really? I think I look like Joan of Arc. But I can't stand messing with hair, you know? Life is short, so hair should be, too."

Joyce felt her courage building, whisking the products across the scanner in an easy, consistent motion which, she thought, made her look coordinated if not brilliant.

"So what do you think of Quality-Mart?" Lydia asked. "Is it going to hurt your business?"

The question threw a wrench into her rhythm and the scanner refused to acknowledge the noodles. She tried three times and drew an obnoxious, atonal bleep. She fumbled to punch in the numbers on the UPC code.

Joyce didn't like to think about Quality-Mart. Mr. Oliver had already warned that if business went down by even a third, he'd have to think about selling out. He couldn't compete with Food Lion and Quality-Mart too. He was getting on and early retirement was not the worst thing that could happen to him. But unemployment was something Joyce could not even fathom. Having to pick up and start over. In Fawley, there was no place to start.

She delivered the company line: "If people want to buy an inferior product, there's nothing we can do. Here you get locally grown produce, fresh meat. You can't get that there. There you don't know what you're getting."

"Hey," Lydia said, "you're preaching to the converted."

"There's a special deal on the generic tuna," Joyce said, holding up a can of Starkist.

"I want the dolphin-safe stuff," Lydia said.

Joyce nodded and rang it up.

"I thought I'd see you at the church potluck," Lydia went on. "We had a big meeting about Quality-Mart."

"Oh well. It's here now. There's nothing we can do."

"Not true. They're organizing a boycott, and a peaceful protest."

Joyce stared at Lydia and wondered how such a woman could be interested in these issues. She was clearly so much of another place, with that hair, her bangs falling over her eyebrows, the rest disappearing behind her ears. And then the clothes, odd things thrown together that somehow always looked great. Loose sweaters with a shirttail hanging beneath them. Short skirts with ribbed tights and thick hiking boots. Floral dresses that touched her ankles, with a denim jacket. And those earrings. Lydia always had something dangling from her ears—bold hearts, strings of crosses, or hoops the size of Oreo cookies. Today she wore a pair of jeans, a black blazer over a white T-shirt and black Converse sneakers. In her ears were vertical strings of silver circles, like Christmas tree ornaments. She wore no makeup except a ruddy brown lipstick.

"How's Danny?" Joyce asked.

"Oh, the same. Making deals, doing paper work. Sometimes he goes off to hammer nails or pour concrete. He tries to hide that from me, but I know. He's got this weird love of construction. It seems to make him happy. We had lunch with his family yesterday, as usual."

"Oh? How are they?"

"The same. Sally trying to please everybody and Nelson being oblivious and Rex . . . just being Rex."

Joyce giggled.

"I mean, honestly," Lydia went on. "Will that man ever come out of the closet?"

"Oh God!" Joyce said, now laughing in earnest. "Don't ever say that to Sally. Or my mother, for that matter."

"But don't you think it's about time?"

Joyce could not speak now from laughing. It felt good, like a release, but at the same time she felt ashamed of herself for acknowledging such a stark admission of an unspoken truth. As far as her family was concerned, Rex wasn't gay until someone said he was. And, naturally, Lydia was just the person to say it.

But then, Lydia was from Washington, D.C., a city Joyce had never seen, even though it was only four hours away, up Highway 29. The thought of it, with all those monuments and buildings full of lawmakers, cabs and a subway and two airports, malls and five-star restaurants, sent her shivering with anxiety. For Joyce it was scary enough living in an apartment building, full of people she only knew to nod to. One such neighbor had been robbed once. This was all she wanted to experience of crime, and D.C. was overflowing with gangs and drugs. How people coped with such knowledge and went on about their business was beyond her. Even in Fawley, Joyce felt constantly at risk. She kept an old hunting rifle under her bed just in case, even though it was unloaded and she wasn't all that certain how to use it. It just made her feel better.

Lydia was the bravest person Joyce had ever met. Nothing seemed to scare her. Her ideas were brave, too. She hated guns, for example, and thought they should be outlawed, though she didn't go around saying that very much in Fawley.

"Do you have any coupons?" Joyce asked before she hit the total button.

"No. I'm terrible about that. I cut them out and then I lose them."

"I'll give you a discount anyway," Joyce said, her heart pounding. It was wrong, and she'd have to cover for it when she did the books. But she felt the need to do Lydia a favor.

She told her the total and watched as Lydia wrote a check in bold, reckless handwriting, swirling letters and putting long, emphatic crosses through her t's. She ripped the check out, tearing a corner.

"We should get together," Lydia said. "Why don't we have lunch sometime?"

"I don't know," Joyce replied without thinking. "I'm so busy right now."

"Maybe on a Saturday."

"That's our busiest day."

"Well, during the week."

"Don't you have school?"

"Spring break. I don't go back until next Monday."

"Oh. Okay." She felt trapped. Though she had fantasized about such an outing with Lydia, the reality of it paralyzed her. She'd have to think about what to wear. She'd have to plan the conversation beforehand. The dread descended on her, the notion that she was not up to the task. What could she possibly say that would hold Lydia's interest?

"You know what we could do?" Lydia said. "We could go to the opening of Quality-Mart."

Joyce stared at her. "That's not a good idea, is it?" she asked nervously.

"Well, we don't have to buy anything. Just going there isn't a violation, is it? The first rule of war is to know the enemy."

"What if someone saw us?"

"Of course someone will see us. Because no matter how much everyone in town claims to hate it, they'll all be there for the opening. They'll be drawn to it like an accident. Believe me, there'll be so many familiar faces it'll feel like a family reunion."

"But aren't you on the boycott committee?" Joyce countered.

"I was. It started out just to be a research committee, a fact-finding mission. When it turned into a boycott, I quit. I don't do boycotts. Feels too much like fascism to me. Boycotting today, book burning tomorrow."

Lydia was full of such arguments. It came from too much thinking, Joyce's mother often said. All that education, letting in ideas. Joyce's mother would definitely not be at Quality-Mart on opening day. But Kyle might. It was the kind of thing Kyle would do. In fact, Kyle would be first in line to buy something.

"I don't know," Joyce said.

"It's just an idea. If it makes you nervous, forget it."

Joyce smiled. Lydia should have understood that it made her nervous—everything made her nervous. Every conceivable activity made her want to chew her nails and lock the door and turn on the television set. Every prospect of facing the world made her want to retreat from it.

She realized, in a wave of despair, that she and Lydia would never have that drink together, and she would never reveal her secrets, whatever they were, or ask Lydia to reveal her own. No matter how hard she struggled, she would be forever separated from those things she most desired. She had gotten out of her mother's house, but she had not traveled very far at all. She had simply built her prison in a new location, and had devoted all her time and energy to trapping herself in a different set of circumstances. Here she was, surrounded by bananas and lettuce, instant coffee, Hamburger Helper, and Pledge. This was what she called a job. Arguing with farmers was the most spectacular confrontation she would ever have. She suddenly felt overcome by a sense of missed opportunity. She had been denied a normal life by the random circumstances of her childhood. It was not fair, and yet no one would ever have to pay.

"Are you all right?" Lydia asked. "You've turned pale."

"I'm fine," Joyce said. "Paper or plastic?"

4

A FACULTY MEETING was held on Thursday before school was set
to resume on Monday. Nothing was ever really accomplished in such
meetings. It was more an effort to remind the teachers that even though
they'd been allowed a respite from the daily grind of public education,
they must now start to take the profession seriously again.

Lydia was two minutes late and the meeting had already started.
Everyone was present and the principal, Nigel Hayes, had already begun
complaining about the low standardized test scores and how he'd received a letter from Congressman Kloony as to how the district was
bringing down the national average.

Lydia slipped into a chair beside Rick Gunther, the history teacher and
assistant varsity football coach. Rick always sat slumped in the last row,
one leg extending into the aisle, a posture that suggested an unwilling-
ness to commit and a desire to vacate the room as soon as possible. He
stiffened when Lydia sat beside him, uncomfortable at the thought of
someone noticing or impeding his quick escape.

Still, he gave her a grudging smile. Rick's rules for being friendly
were simple—to attractive women, he was cordial. To everyone else, he
was openly hostile.

"What have I missed?" Lydia whispered to him.

"New carpet for the faculty lounge."

"Really? I've grown so attached to the coffee-stained pea green shag."

This forced Rick to smile, but he shifted his weight on his other hip, slightly away from her.

"Now," Nigel spoke, tucking his chin and looking over the top of his glasses, "that stated, we move on to an equally serious matter concerning the content of the classrooms, curriculumwise."

In both manner and physical appearance, Nigel Hayes resembled Ed Sullivan. Lydia had trouble taking him seriously, as she always felt he was about to announce a musical act. But Nigel was a serious man, and almost every hiccup in the school got his attention and had trouble shaking it. Hayes was tenacious, humorless, and spoke awkwardly in long run-on sentences, splitting infinitives and misplacing qualifiers and creating nonexistent words by adding "wise" to the end of them. Lydia, being the tenth-grade English teacher, was one of the few people who noted the grammatical imperfection in his speech. To everyone else, he just sounded like a pompous oaf.

"We have had on several occasions what I consider to be indignant reactions from parents regarding certain subjects which have come up time and again during the course of what ought to be nothing more than a fairly pedestrian health and physical education curriculum."

All eyes turned to Alicia Clay. She remained still, staring stubbornly at Nigel.

"I think the most prudent thing to do at this juncture is turn the floor over to Alicia, who is more cognizant of said matters, and perhaps she can both apprise us of this set of circumstances as well as shed some light on them, motivationwise."

Lydia pinched her lips to stop a smile. She noticed a few other teachers doing the same.

Alicia Clay stood up and faced the room. She was a striking woman, several inches taller than Nigel, which was only one of the reasons he disliked her. Her skin was a beautiful pale brown, and her hair was short, neatly shorn off at the scalp, accentuating her strong bone structure and large, intelligent eyes. She wore gold hoops in her ears, which swayed slightly as she surveyed the audience. She caught Lydia's eye and her face twitched, which could have been interpreted as a wink.

Looking at her, Lydia was certain that Alicia was indeed a product of royalty, of the men and women who were kings and queens of African tribes before they were taken from their homes and forced into the galleys of slave ships. She was the product of pure and careful breeding, tainted only by the white blood that had invaded her gene pool in past decades, toning her skin down to the color of weak coffee.

Rick Gunther had once challenged the notion of enslaved royalty during a heated debate in the faculty lounge.

"The kings and queens weren't victims of the slave trade. They instigated it. They were slave traders themselves. They participated in the roundup. The collection of slaves by white settlers could not have happened without their willing participation."

"That's no more a valid argument," Alicia countered, "than saying that Americans participated in Nazism by ignoring it for so long."

"The Egyptians didn't ignore slavery. They invented it."

"That's a vile and misleading assertion. I hope to God you're not teaching your black students that they are responsible for the slave trade."

"No, of course not. I teach from the textbooks assigned to me by the school board. Like everyone else employed by the public school system, I teach revisionist history. Fairy tales. Whatever makes people feel comfortable. The truth is the last thing I'm allowed to teach."

"Rick, I have no doubt you do everything in your power to keep your students happy and comfortable. Particularly the ones with double-X chromosomes."

Rick had bailed out then. An abundance of rumors circulated about Rick and his female students, any reference to which made him clam up immediately. Both he and Alicia fell into the category of controversial teachers, each eliciting more than an equal share of angry phone calls from parents. This common nerve was the only thing that kept them on speaking terms.

The real difference was in their handling of such complaints. Rick shied away from it, while Alicia rose to each challenge with consummate assurance. Alicia was fearless.

Now she stood in front of the room, ready and eager to explain her position.

"There have been some complaints from parents," Alicia admitted, "concerning a series of lectures I gave last February. As I'm sure you're all aware, February is the month which is devoted to African-American history and awareness. This particular edict has been handed down by the federal government, upheld by state and local government."

"Time is a factor here, Alicia," Nigel prompted, but she ignored him.

"During that month, I felt it was appropriate to incorporate into my lectures on health and physical fitness those African-American citizens who have devoted their lives to furthering the health and welfare of all Americans. I gave lectures on everyone from Jackie Robinson to Jesse Owens to Martin Luther King Jr. and Spike Lee. Frankly, I fail to see how anyone could object to this, but I'm willing to address the challenge. Parents have accused me of instigating racial disputes. They have claimed that such subjects are inappropriate. How can we separate history from physical and mental health? How can we believe that denying such information to our students is beneficial in any way? The general health of our African-American students, who comprise just over fifty percent of the student body, is very much dependent upon positive self-image. Likewise, the white students stand to gain a great deal from learning the history of struggle experienced by their classmates. My lectures are an effort to erode the racial barrier. Is that pertinent to physical and mental health? I say it is vital to it. I do not apologize for my actions, nor do I deem them destructive or gratuitous."

With this Alicia was clearly finished, but she remained standing, creating an awkward moment.

Only Nigel was bold or stupid enough to challenge her.

"What about Malcolm X? How does he figure in the health lecture?"

Alicia didn't flinch.

"He was an important figure in the Civil Rights movement."

"Maybe so. But a couple of days after your lecture on this important figure, several students came to school to find 'White Devil' spray-painted on their lockers."

"In my class," Alicia said, her steady tone barely reflecting her effort to keep it that way, "I made a point of saying that such a reaction was inappropriate, on the level of a white student deciding to join the KKK after seeing the Ken Burns documentary on the Civil War. Which was required viewing in the senior history class."

At this she shot a look at Rick Gunther, who stared resolutely at his Nikes.

"As teachers we merely put the facts out there," she maintained. "The reaction to them is something we cannot control."

A slight murmur arose from the crowd.

"Well, look, Ally," said Nigel, shamelessly employing the nickname used only by her closest friends, "far be it from me to interfere with the pursuit of knowledge. But likewise, I'd like to arrive at school without having to return a dozen irate phone calls from parents."

"So don't return the calls," Alicia suggested.

A titter spread through the room and Nigel smiled tightly.

Martha Dawson stood abruptly. "May I say a word about Quality-Mart?"

This evoked a mild groan from the audience, and a look of dread on Nigel's face. Martha Dawson's word had a tendency to expand into something more like an evangelical sermon.

"Well, I'd hoped to move on to vending machines," Nigel said wistfully, knowing the chance was now slim.

"As we all know, this weekend is opening day, and I trust that everyone will be participating in the boycott."

There was no stopping Martha on certain subjects. Before Quality-Mart was a threat, she gave equally impassioned speeches about imposing a dress code on students whose current attire she deemed "disrespectful and unholy." Likewise with their language, haircuts, magazines, and the "fraternizing in the halls," which included any degree of physical contact.

Martha had been teaching too long. Her patience had worn thin. Her capacity for change had been severely strained. It had actually taken a physical toll. She was gaunt and unsteady on her feet (except when standing to lecture to a captive audience). Her mind was starting to show the strain as well. She had trouble remembering things, like the Christian names of faculty members. As a result she called everyone, male and female, by their surnames, as if she were in the military.

"I'd like to alert everyone to the fact that I will be present at the opening ceremonies, in the capacity of collecting names of all the prominent townspeople who patronize the event. So you should all be aware that if you do see fit to violate the boycott, your name will be recorded."

"Now hold on," said someone in the crowd.

Lydia shot to her feet. "Mrs. Dawson, you're establishing a blacklist?"

Martha looked genuinely confused. "No. The names of whites will be taken as well."

Nervous laughter erupted. Martha smiled uncertainly.

"No, what I mean is . . . you can't do this," Lydia persisted. "It's wrong. It's unconstitutional. What do you intend to do with that list?"

"Why, circulate it, of course. I'll submit it to the local paper, and post it on the bulletin board. How does that interfere with the Constitution?"

"You can't do it," Lydia said breathlessly. "It violates a thousand statutes I can't recall at the moment."

"Crane," Martha said primly, "you are still relatively new to this town. Perhaps up North you don't have the same sort of standards that we do down here. In Fawley, we answer to a higher law. We answer to God's law."

"Sorry, but God's law still takes a back seat to the Supreme Court."

Someone in the audience gasped. Someone else muttered, "That's right."

"Maybe you're not aware that I'm a member of Milton Memorial Methodist Church," Lydia surged on. "But that's irrelevant. It does not mean that I condone this sort of vigilantism. It's a free country, and Quality-Mart is going to open, whether you like it or not. Let's keep our heads about this thing. It's just a store."

Martha sniffed. "Just a store which sells firearms and alcohol."

"Both of which can be legally purchased in town."

"Not by me, Crane. Not by me."

Lydia had to bite her lip, along, she was certain, with several other faculty members. Many were the days that Mrs. Dawson arrived at work smelling like a still. And many were the Mondays she called in sick with what most of her colleagues had taken to calling the "Smirnoff flu."

"What you do is your business," Lydia said. "And what everyone else does, short of committing a felony, is theirs."

"Take it up with Jesus," Martha Dawson suggested.

"What if He showed up at Quality-Mart? Would you take His name down?"

"Blasphemy!" Martha shouted.

"Now hold on," Nigel interrupted. "We've really exhausted this subject. It's not school business."

"It's everyone's business," Martha said. "This establishment will be the downfall of this town. Not that it has far to fall. Perhaps you do not care about this place, Crane, but I do. My ancestors founded it. My grandfather brought the first post office here."

Now Martha was off on another favorite subject, the lengths to which her relatives had gone to put Fawley on the map. Nigel saw the danger and tried to interrupt, but Martha was a formidable force.

"So don't you come here, Crane, and tell us how to run our business in Virginia. You are an outsider, an interloper."

"I'm from Virginia, Mrs. Dawson. Born and bred."

"*Northern* Virginia," Martha all but shrieked. "Northern Virginia most certainly does not count."

"George Washington lived in northern Virginia," Lydia said, now feeling a little impish.

"Is this where we've all arrived? Do we now let strangers from the North tell us how to conduct our lives? Are we back to the days of Reconstruction? I do not abide by Crane's rules. I do not know her God."

Nigel moved in, eager to put a stop to a faculty meeting gone tragically wrong.

"Let's adjourn now. We'll get to vending machines next week."

But his efforts at peacemaking were in vain. Mrs. Dawson's knees had buckled and she was clutching her chest.

Dr. Rivilla rushed to her side. A Cuban immigrant, Dr. Rivilla understood the most rudimentary English, but she certainly knew how to interpret catastrophe in any language. She knew the laws of math and physics like the back of her hand; beyond that she could only relate to physical demise. She claimed to be a medical doctor in her native country of Cuba, and occasionally students and teachers alike would sidestep the usual medical channels—basically, the bored school nurses—and go straight to her for advice.

"Heart attach," Dr. Rivilla mispronounced, feeling Martha's pulse and her brow. "Call the ambulance."

A disorganized attempt was made, but before anyone could contemplate the mechanics of CPR, Martha was on her feet again, shooing her concerned colleagues away.

"Don't be ridiculous," she said. "There are no heart problems in my family. We all die of cancer."

This was obviously the last word on the matter. Nigel officially declared the meeting adjourned.

5

DANNY CRANE WAS the sales manager of Howard J. Mecklin & Co., the only commercial contracting firm in the county. On paper, it sounded like an interesting position. He met with clients, made bids, studied blueprints, approved and disapproved the plans, kept all the contractors to their schedules. Some days he visited the building sites. That was his favorite part, observing all the activity, watching the men in hardhats meticulously measuring, sawing, hammering, pouring concrete, sandblasting. He envied them their serious, unimaginative task of putting things in place. It struck him as a grown-up version of the games he'd enjoyed as a child. Erector sets and Tonka toys and sandcastles. He longed to jump in and join them. Occasionally he resented whatever forces kept him at a distance—his education, his suit, his knowledge of numbers. He was prevented from joining the fun because he knew too much.

Though it was strictly out of line, he sometimes shed his jacket and pitched in with the smaller jobs, such as hoisting the lumber or driving in a nail or two. The subcontractors eyed him suspiciously. Danny had put in his years of hands-on labor, but to the workers he would always be a suit. He had crossed an invisible line and could never return.

Sometimes when he drove past their buildings—the Bank of Virginia downtown, or the County Health Complex on the Greensboro Road—he felt a shock of pride, mixed with humility. He had built those structures in a broad sense; in a stricter sense, he'd done nothing at all.

This duality of purpose kept him confused. Was he a builder or not? Was he responsible for the work, or did he merely prevent it from going wrong?

Danny had a fantasy. He thought more and more each day about resigning his position and going back to sandblasting bridges. Sometimes he dreamed about it, and in his half-dazed state in the morning he'd find himself searching for his hardhat. Embarrassed by such longings, he'd throw himself into paperwork and end up doing more than was required. On such days, Howard Mecklin would smile approvingly and say that it was just a matter of time before he received his rightful promotion to vice president. The words sent him into a tailspin of panic and into a slump that would set him back for weeks.

Lydia knew nothing of Danny's fantasies. She knew less and less of his interior life lately. He kept his weaknesses locked up, terrified that if she discovered them she would renounce her vows and go directly back to her promising life in northern Virginia. It wouldn't take much. The specter of her parents was always hovering, reminding her of all the fine things she had sacrificed to marry him. He knew that Lydia's parents considered her marriage a phase. They treated her as if she were in the grip of some sort of cult; they held on to the hope that she would one day recover her senses. Their greatest hope was his greatest fear, for he sometimes viewed his marriage in similar terms.

The day he slipped the ring on her finger, he remembered thinking (or was it praying?), Just give me five years. Five years with this woman who is too good for this place, certainly too good for me. Let me have that much time.

Danny had no idea what his life was about, where he was going, or what he should reach for. But he knew that he wanted Lydia. In fact, he marked the day that he first set eyes on her as the day he understood what it was to want something. Now he was learning what it meant to keep it.

They had been married for three years, so he could not escape the feeling that his time was running out. Perhaps it was a self-fulfilling prophecy that he now suspected Lydia of losing interest. He sometimes caught her staring at him with what he could swear was disillusion. On the bad days it seemed more like distrust. He made love to her nearly every day. It was the only way he could think to reaffirm his commitment to her, to express his desire. Danny had never been good with words.

Love was hard for him. Abstract concepts had always made him feel confused and incapable. If the world functioned completely on those terms, Danny was certain he would be considered abnormal, dysfunctional. In school he had discovered that the universe divided neatly into two parts—ideas and numbers. Ideas paralyzed him. Numbers soothed him with their rigidity, their unforgiving nature, their unflinching absolutes. One plus one always equaled two—of this there could be no doubt, no impassioned debate.

He was an excellent math student. He felt more than a flair for it. He felt something like a calling. It was like a religion to him, a sanctuary, a place where everything fell into order. When he got into higher maths, he recoiled at the abstracts, the creative interpretations, theorems and logarithms, the notion of irrational number systems and infinity. But he took comfort in the knowledge that even though some mathematical equations had yet to be solved, there was universal acceptance that solutions did exist. It was numbers, after all, and numbers did not harbor gray areas. There was no judgment, no morality to numbers.

Despite his fear of the arts, he still confronted them. He read voraciously, less out of interest than of a desire to make literature work on a numerical plane. He felt determined to define it, boil all abstract notions down to science. This usually proved impossible. He found himself moved by literature, and the emotions made him feel uncomfortable, fluish. He often suffered a stomachache for days after a good book. The abstracts gripped him; the notions of love and jealousy and hatred and forgiveness made his head swim. When they were first married, Lydia tried to form a book group. The first three meetings were canceled because of his sudden illnesses.

He dreamed of a logical world. This board here, this nail there, this pipe fitting in that. Oh, what a place, where everything fit, piece by piece, brick by brick, without wonder.

Lydia was sitting at the kitchen table, her lesson plans spread out around her, listening to Ella Fitzgerald singing the *Cole Porter Songbook*. Show tunes were an interest that she and Rex shared, though they rarely discussed it. By reflex, the music made the muscles in Danny's stomach tighten. He could see Rex waltzing across the den with an invisible partner.

Lydia's pen tapped out the rhythm on the tabletop. Next to her elbow were a dozen or so empty Hershey's Kisses wrappers. She must be getting her period, Danny thought, but knew better than to say it.

"Hi, honey," he said, leaning over for a chocolate-flavored kiss. It still felt funny, after all this time, calling her "honey" or any sort of pet name. It didn't fit her. She didn't mind, but to him it never felt right.

Lydia said, "I'm teaching D. H. Lawrence to my sophomores this year, and they can fire me if they don't like it."

"Lawrence, Lawrence," he said, loosening his tie. "The guy who lived in the desert?"

"That was T. E. Lawrence. D.H. was in love with his mother."

"Who was T.E. in love with?" he asked. He kissed the nape of her neck and her back straightened.

"Little Arab boys," she said. She pressed her cheek against his shirt. "You smell like wood."

"I was on site for a while today."

Lydia said nothing to this. Danny was aware of her silence.

"Let's get pizza," she said.

"Okay, I'll pick one up."

"Pick it up? Where are you going?"

"It's Friday."

"Oh," Lydia said.

On Fridays after work, Danny did his mother's grocery shopping. It had started a few months earlier when she asked him to pick up a quart of milk. Now it had evolved into a full list, complete with coupons. Somewhere along the line, his mother had suddenly and inexplicably stopped driving. She claimed it was because her eyesight was deteriorating, though Danny noticed she had not given up sewing, working crossword puzzles, or scouring *People* and *Redbook* magazines cover to cover.

"Do you mind?" Danny asked. "It won't take long."

"It's not that. I just think it's a little . . . indulgent."

"She can't drive, Lydia."

"She won't drive. There's a difference."

"Every family has its idiosyncrasies. Look at yours."

"My family isn't idiosyncratic. They're just cruel."

She unwrapped a Hershey's Kiss and popped it into her mouth. Danny smiled, watching her.

"What's irritating," she said, cornering the candy on one side of her mouth, creating a bump in her cheek, "is that you all go to such great distances to normalize your behavior. Nobody ever says, Gee, I wonder why Rex is still living at home, or why Kyle keeps trying to kill himself, or why Rita and her daughters haven't left home since your Uncle Pike died. You all just accept it, as if it's the way everybody lives."

"First of all," Danny said in an even tone, hoping to avoid a fight, "you're talking about the extreme members of my family. I mean, Kyle is nobody's idea of a model citizen."

"What about Rita?"

"She and the girls are shy."

"They are agoraphobic, Danny. They are housebound."

"Joyce got out."

"Yes, and she's regarded as the strange one."

Danny shook his head, opened the fridge door, then closed it again. Ella Fitzgerald sang, "You're the top, you're the tower of Pisa . . ."

Danny said, "You knew about my family when you married me."

"I did not," Lydia said. "I certainly didn't know they were going to get worse."

"So what difference does it make to you if my aunt and cousins never leave home, or if Kyle kills himself, for that matter? You're not responsible for any of them."

Lydia turned in her chair and reached up for his hand. He gave it to her. She ran her fingers across his palm, feeling the hard skin.

"They take you away from me," she said.

"No they don't. No one can."

He pulled her up and kissed her.

"I'm jealous," she whispered. "I don't have anyone else."

"You don't need anyone else," he said, and wrapped his arms all the way around her.

The Food Lion was not crowded. It was the night before the big Saturday opening at Quality-Mart, so everyone was home, saving their money. Danny moved quickly up and down the aisles, the wheels on his cart squeaking loudly in the empty store. He searched for Pepperidge Farm soups, Uncle Ben's Wild Rice, 1 percent skim milk, Graham crackers and Eggo frozen waffles.

He thought about his conversation with Lydia and wondered if she were right, if he constantly made excuses for his family. The trouble was, he just had a different idea about how it all worked. Lydia honestly thought that family could be chosen or rejected, that you could put them all back on the shelf like damaged goods. Her parents had demonstrated a similar attitude when they disowned her. Danny had never seen things that way at all. He did not think family was to be evaluated and analyzed. He thought family was to be endured.

Still, he was starting to feel weighed down by them. By his mother's grocery shopping, for example. Would he be doing this every Friday night for the rest of her life? And would he be bickering with Rex forever, pleading with him to act more like a man? Danny sometimes felt each family member's problem was taking up a space inside him, leaving less and less room for himself.

As he turned the corner of the frozen food aisle, he saw Kyle. At first Danny thought that he had somehow managed to conjure his cousin, like a hallucination. But there he was, thin and shivering, staring into the freezer, as if somewhere amid the chicken pot pies, fish sticks, and frozen pizzas, lay the answer.

Danny's first instinct was to run away. It was an instinct that had been with him ever since he'd met Lydia. But Danny could not abandon his cousin. There was too much connecting them, too much history. Lydia could not understand this. With any luck, she'd never have to.

Kyle was in his usual disheveled state. His ash blond hair was down to his shoulders, uncombed, and his gaunt face was smudged with a few days' growth of beard. He wore a green fatigue jacket over ripped jeans. The clothes seemed to swallow him. He was getting skinnier all the time. Danny wondered if he was doing coke again. If so, he should definitely turn around or else he'd get hit up for money. But before he could make a move, Kyle had found him.

He grinned like a kid. "Hey, Danny. Hell's bells, I was just thinking about you."

"Thinking what?"

"Wondering why you hadn't been out to my new place. It's been a coon's age. Hey, how's married life?" he asked, as if Danny were a newlywed. As if they hadn't seen each other in the emergency room less than a week ago. "Feel any smarter?"

"I don't think marriage is supposed to make you any smarter."

"Well, it ain't made you any prettier."

Kyle pulled a cigarette out of his shirt pocket and lit it.

"You can't smoke in here, can you?" Danny asked.

"You can till they say you can't." He took a long drag, then said, "What are you doing here?"

"Getting groceries."

"Wife's got you on a short leash, huh."

"It's for Mama, actually."

"Shit. Two short leashes. Hey, I heard you were out to the hospital the other night, when I had that wreck."

Danny stared at him. Kyle didn't remember. He wondered how many of those rescues Kyle had forgotten. Maybe he genuinely didn't know how many times Danny had tried to save him.

"Yeah, I was there."

"Shit, I was so fucked up." Kyle laughed, the way they both used to laugh about drinking beer in junior high.

"You're lucky you weren't hurt," Danny said.

"Yeah, well, that depends on who you ask."

Kyle took a long drag of his cigarette, studying Danny and grinning. "Come on home with me. I want to show you where I live."

Danny hesitated. Kyle read his expression and laughed.

"I ain't gonna kidnap you or nothing. Take a look at the place and be on your way. Or call the wife and invite her if you want to."

"Lydia's busy."

"Now, isn't that a treasure? A busy wife. She's some sort of career woman?"

"She's just a teacher."

"I like that. She's shaping the minds of our youth. Far be it from you to interfere with that. Truth is, she could probably use a break from you."

"All right," Danny said suddenly, abruptly. He felt sixteen again, afraid of being teased by Kyle, accused of being scared of women. "Just let me pay."

Kyle followed him to the checkout with a six-pack of beer and an assortment of frozen foods.

"Let me get that," Danny said on a whim, and Kyle didn't argue.

"Kyle, put that damn cigarette out," said the cashier.

"Brenda, don't pick on a man with a plastic leg."

"It ain't slowed you down none."

"Hey, you know my cousin Danny?"

"We only graduated high school together."

Danny smiled, though he had no memory of the woman, outside of her association with Food Lion. He often found he had huge gaps in his memory when it came to his high school years. "Selective amnesia," Lydia called it.

Kyle limped out to the parking lot, carrying one of the grocery bags, while Danny struggled with the other three. When they'd reached the truck, Kyle tossed his bag carelessly in the back and extracted the cigarette which had been smoldering on his bottom lip.

"Let me show you the best thing about this," Kyle said. He pulled up his pant leg to the knee, revealing the plastic leg. Then he extinguished the cigarette butt on his calf, leaving a round black mark just below the knee. It looked so much like a bullet hole that Danny had to glance away.

"It's strange, isn't it?" Kyle said. "It's like that foot was cursed. Now that it's gone, I feel like I can start over. I feel like it's all behind me now, Danny."

Danny stared at the parking lot, the cars blurring and running together like paint on a canvas.

"What do you reckon they did with that foot?" Kyle asked. "Ever wonder about that? Do they just throw away the limbs they cut off? Put them in a Hefty bag? Or is there some kind of garbage disposal for amputated limbs? If I'd been conscious, I'd have asked for it. I'd have had it stuffed. Too bad you didn't think of that."

Danny coughed. He was trying to think of some way to escape.

Kyle said, "You were probably just as happy to see it go. Considering."

Danny shivered. "Damn, it got cold all of a sudden."

Kyle fished another cigarette out of his pocket, staring hard at Danny. "Does that wife of yours know the story? About me and my bad leg?"

"Some of it."

Kyle nodded, flicking his lighter. The wind bounced the flame around but didn't extinguish it.

"They say they'll love you for better or worse, but why push your luck?"

Danny swallowed and tucked his chin into his jacket.

"Tell you what, Danny, the night they cut my leg off, I was downright relieved. I could have cried for joy."

"You were half dead, Kyle. You didn't feel anything."

"I had one of those near-death experiences. I was watching everything from a distance. I saw Mama crying over me. I saw your daddy talking to the doctor. I heard you tell them to go ahead and saw it off."

"Bullshit," Danny said.

"No, I mean it. And I saw this bright light, and then I heard this voice saying, 'Damn, boy, you're too mean to die.'"

Danny laughed. Kyle socked him in the chest, too hard.

"Had you going though, didn't I?"

6

KYLE'S PLACE WAS a trailer out in the middle of nowhere, about five miles from the main road, near something that might have been a pond at one time but now was more like a stagnant mud puddle. A mangy dog crawled out from under a bush and snarled at them when they got out of the car.

"Shut up, Syphilis," Kyle said. The dog stopped growling but still showed her teeth.

"Nice name for a dog."

"It's just her nickname."

The trailer was an old model, beige with brown trim, resting on cinder blocks. The door almost fell off in Kyle's hand. The inside was incongruously well kept. The walls were freshly painted, the windows were dressed with gingham curtains. The furniture was old but clean. The television, a brand-new Sony, was on though no one was watching it.

Kyle said, "I lifted that from the Best Buys in Greensboro."

"Bullshit."

"As God is my witness. I worked there for two weeks. Got some nice stereo equipment, too. And a Cuisinart. Then I got fired, but not for stealing. For my attitude. Is that a hell of a note? Man's got a plastic leg and a police record, and it's his attitude that does him in. Too bad they couldn't amputate *that*. Do you think maybe the day is coming when you can get an attitude transplant?"

"Anything's possible."

"Shit, that's what you think. I applied for a job out at the Quality-Mart. Had a good interview, too, with some kid who called himself the assistant manager. Graham Mundy was his name. What kind of faggot name is that? That's a guy who gets out of the shower to piss. Looked fifteen years old, this kid. Hadn't had his first wet dream yet, and he's going to tell me what? But I played nice and he tells me I'm as good as in. Never heard from the fucker again. You believe that shit? So it's not like I ain't tried to work, but if some snot-nose kid wants to turn me down, it just makes the state pay me more."

Syphilis tried to sneak through a crack in the door, but Kyle kicked her down the wooden steps.

"Get on. She don't like you in here."

Danny had little time to wonder who "she" was. A door at the other end of the trailer flew open and a woman emerged, walking as if someone had lit a match to her heels.

"That don't mean I want you breaking her neck," she said, moving past both of them, out the door. Danny watched her through the window as she called out to Syphilis and scratched her lovingly behind the ears. The dog was understandably skeptical.

After a few moments the woman returned, going directly to the kitchen, still not looking at either of them.

"You behave or I'll give her your supper," she said, her back to Kyle.

Kyle said, "We got company."

"I see that. What we ain't got is food enough for three people."

"I won't stay," Danny said.

She turned around at last. Her face was a pale oval, her chin jutting out in a permanent gesture of challenge. Her thin, dark hair fell to her shoulders, wispy bangs scattered across her forehead. Her eyes were deep set, gray and quick. She reminded Danny of some black and white photograph he'd seen, a Dorothea Lange subject. The Dust Bowl mother with the shoeless children gathering at her waist. Looking at her made him feel uncomfortable, exposed.

She was small, with sharp edges and hollows. She wore a white T-shirt with no bra, a silver heart medallion falling between her breasts. When she saw Danny staring at it, she picked it up and rubbed the heart against her lips.

"Amanda," Kyle said. "This is my cousin Danny Crane."

Amanda nodded, scrutinizing him.

"You were some hotshot baseball player, weren't you?"

"A long time ago."

"I think I saw you play back in high school."

"Amanda went to Carver," Kyle said. "She's from Wycombe County."

Danny nodded, searching for a response.

"You still live in Wycombe?" he asked.

"I live here," she said. "But I still go see my mama now and then."

"Amanda's a waitress at the Green Lantern," Kyle said.

"Oh, really?" Danny said. The Green Lantern was a restaurant out on 29 that attracted businessmen and vacationers passing through, and a few locals on birthdays and anniversaries. "Do you enjoy that?" he asked her.

"I just can't wait for the sun to rise."

After this, the conversation seemed to die. Kyle had become interested in the local news. He put his good leg up on the coffee table and unhitched the false one, tossing it across the room like a shoe.

"Get me a beer, babe, if it don't hurt you any," Kyle instructed her.

"It don't hurt me. It's your liver."

She reached in the fridge, took the last can of beer and threw it at him. "Where's the groceries?"

Kyle jerked his head toward the door.

"You could have at least brought them in."

"I could have done a lot of things."

"I'll help you," Danny said.

She shrugged and he followed her out. She didn't speak until they reached the car. She moved awkwardly, determined and defensive at once. She was one of those people who was always out of reach of anything—a touch, a glance, a kind word.

"It's good you're related to Kyle," she said. "I don't have to explain him to you."

"I probably know him as well as anybody. And I still don't know him at all," Danny said.

"He ain't no big mystery. He's just mean."

"You like that in a man, do you?"

"Never met any other kind, except weak. Weak is worse."

They walked back to the house with the groceries, not speaking, the half-dead grass rasping under their shoes.

He ended up staying for dinner, cold ham and fried apples. There was more than enough, since Kyle chose to drink his dinner on the couch, in front of the game shows. Amanda ignored him and ate in silence. Danny struggled to make conversation, asking questions and receiving monosyllabic replies.

After a few beers, Kyle's personality predictably took a turn for the worse. He developed a combative attitude toward the contestants on *Jeopardy* and delighted when they missed a question.

"There you go, hot-shit English professor. Not so damn smart, are you?" he grumbled at the set.

"We've got brown sugar pie for dessert," Amanda said, her gray eyes falling on him like a threat.

"I'm full," Danny said, sensing a need to escape but not wanting to offend her.

"It's good. I brought it home from work."

"I'm sure it's wonderful, but I need to get back. My wife's probably wondering what happened to me."

"Oh yeah," she said, lighting a cigarette. "Kyle told me you had a wife."

"Damn faggot, that's what you are," Kyle informed the English professor. "You don't know sports from shit. You're a fucking Graham Mundy."

"Kyle, we got company."

"Danny ain't company, he's family."

Danny stood and stretched, feeling a tightness in his chest. He felt desperate all of a sudden. He wanted to run from the room. He wanted to blink his eyes and find himself back home, Lydia greeting him at the door with open arms.

"Thanks for dinner," he said, heading to the door.

"Don't forget it, college boy. You're family, and nothing you ever do can change that," Kyle said.

Walking out to the truck, Danny could hear the theme music of *Jeopardy* and the whir of the garbage disposal. Looking around, he could detect no other sign of life. Even Syphilis had disappeared. The bare tree limbs bowed in the wind, cutting eerie patterns against the night sky.

As he opened the door he felt a presence behind him and turned, sucking in a breath. Amanda had materialized behind him, like a ghost.

"You left this," she said, holding his jacket.

"Thanks."

"You'll come back, won't you? Bring your wife."

"I will."

Amanda smiled knowingly.

"Kyle can't help himself. It's all on account of his hard life."

"What hard life?"

"His daddy and all."

Danny felt his throat tighten.

"What about his daddy?"

She looked at him. "Well, you know. Getting murdered by a black and all."

"The man was exonerated. It was self-defense."

"Yeah, well. We know the truth, don't we?" Danny stared at her. Those eyes were so cold and flat, like granite. And if there was an emotion in them, it was not visible to the naked eye. It was hard to fathom what she knew, and whether knowing it had influenced her at all.

Driving home Danny stared at the dark, bare landscape and wondered why every moment he spent in the presence of Kyle felt like a betrayal.

7

ON OPENING DAY at Quality-Mart, the parking lot was overflowing. By eleven o'clock there was a line to get into the store. The weather had turned again, and people shivered in the brisk March wind, sipping from Styrofoam cups of coffee provided by the store. A local band played bluegrass music. Clowns passed out balloons to unhappy children. County deputies circled on foot, waiting for the inevitable.

The store itself looked vast and unfriendly, cut against a landscape of cedars and maples and oaks, the only inorganic thing along the straight stretch of highway. It reminded Lydia of a prison she'd seen once on a trip across the state with her parents—a stark brick building appearing out of nowhere. It was a sudden shock of civilization in a lush wilderness, and it made her feel lonely just watching it shoot past. Quality-Mart had the same effect. Despite the full parking lot and forced gaiety, the pushing and shoving and shouts of recognition among neighbors, the place felt desolate and—though Lydia hated to admit it—foreboding.

A small group of protesters stood at the door, carrying signs that promised gloom and doom, not to mention the wrath of God. Martha Dawson was at the center of that commotion, her notebook and pen handy to take names. Lydia caught her eye and flashed a smile. Martha took a moment to glare at her before scribbling.

"I'm on the blacklist," Lydia announced triumphantly.

Joyce looked at her and struggled to smile.

"We shouldn't be here," Joyce said.

"I'm kidding," Lydia said. She noticed that Joyce was sunken into her coat, as if she wanted to be swallowed up by it. "Are you cold? Do you want my scarf?"

"No, I'm fine."

Bringing Joyce to this had been a crazy idea. Lydia knew she was making a mistake by pursuing it, but she didn't want to come to opening day alone, and she knew Danny wouldn't come with her. There was no chance of dragging Dee along, either, though she desperately wanted to come.

"I swear to God, I'm ready to put on a wig and a false nose and go," Dee had declared that morning on the phone. "But John would leave me over this one, Lydia. I'm head of the by-God boycott committee."

After hanging up with Dee, Lydia called Joyce as a last resort. She'd mentioned the outing to her before but knew that Joyce wouldn't go unless pushed. Pushing Joyce proved to be only a matter of saying, "Come on, it'll be fun. I'll pick you up in an hour."

Lydia wasn't sure of the reason behind her need to attend Quality-Mart opening day. Part of it was curiosity, certainly. But there was something much larger at work. As much as she enjoyed Fawley, she felt a constant need to defy it, to fight against its customs and convictions. Danny had an easy explanation for it. He felt that defiance was a part of Lydia's personality, and that she could only be happy in a place where she was swimming against the tide.

"Fitting in is a sort of surrender to you," he'd accused. "That's why you married me instead of the Hamster."

He had a point. Marrying Ham had seemed very much like a surrender. It reeked of comfort. She had yearned for a quiet life, but that was different, in her mind, from a complacent one. Lydia had always been proud of her restless nature, and she encouraged it in others. This, perhaps, was why she had insisted on bringing Joyce to Quality-Mart. She felt that Joyce could benefit from a little dose of rebellion.

Joyce was only mildly nervous when she first got in the car with Lydia, but the fear seemed to build on itself. She looked small and frail now, shivering in her nylon parka. Her face was red from the assault of the wind; by contrast, her scar had turned an almost incandescent white. Lydia was fond of Joyce and always tried to see her in the best light, but there was no denying how ugly she was. ("Unfortunate," Lydia's mother would say, a euphemism she used on everything from poverty to alcoholism, anything she perceived as a weakness in others.) Joyce did have a fine, straight nose and warm brown eyes with full lashes. But her mouth was unnaturally narrow, and the scar was so inescapable. It dominated her face to the point that it was hard to see anything else. Joyce's apologetic posture, and her ubiquitous squint, did nothing to improve matters. Joyce behaved as if her impairment were an unfair burden on the rest of the world; she felt guilty about inflicting it on others.

"We can go," Lydia suggested, sensing her discomfort. "Why don't we go home? We can come back another time."

"No," Joyce said. "We've waited this long."

"Honestly, Joyce, I don't even want to buy anything. I'm a looky-loo. Let's go get some lunch."

Joyce was considering it, and Lydia was hoping she'd say yes. Suddenly she'd lost her desire to go inside Quality-Mart and to see people filling their carts with discounted items they didn't need. She realized, to her dismay, that Quality-Mart could only be fun with Dee, whose irreverent asides would take the edge off the pathetic nature of this event. With Joyce, Lydia suddenly no longer felt like the detached, ironic observer. She felt like a participant, a patron. For a quick, frightening moment, Lydia saw with unwelcome clarity the darker side of this bucolic existence.

She found herself thinking of Camille, as she often did. She and her former best friend had fallen out of touch. So much so that Lydia could no longer picture her in anything but a bikini, which was what she was wearing during their last meaningful excursion, the one to Myrtle Beach, when she'd first met Danny. Now she imagined the swimsuited Camille walking through the parking lot saying, "Jesus Christ, what do these people hope to find in there? The Holy Grail? Lydia, these people would crawl across broken glass for a Weber grill."

Lydia did not smile when she thought of Camille. Their separation had not been a happy one. Not acrimonious, either. Just a slow, dull dissolution, like spring snow melting into a gray puddle. They had run out of things to say, and ways to avoid the lack of connection, the polarization of their choices.

"I should have known you'd be first in line," someone said. Lydia looked up to see Rick Gunther approaching them. At first glance, she mistook him for a student in his torn jeans, varsity coach's jacket, and gleaming Nikes. Lydia was always surprised to see her colleagues out of standard teaching attire. The clothes they chose to wear in their leisure time always seemed slightly uncharacteristic. But then, she was certain they felt the same way about her.

Rick was absurdly handsome and looked younger than he had any right to. He was approaching forty, yet the only wrinkles in evidence were the laugh lines around his eyes. They were green and laced with thick lashes, and when he smiled he possessed an air of innocence that nothing in his personality could support. Lydia did not trust Rick's charm. But then, people with charm did not expect to be trusted.

"I wasn't the first in line," Lydia replied. "Otherwise I'd be in there grabbing markdowns instead of shivering in the wind. You know Joyce, don't you?"

"Sure," Rick said. "I shop at Oliver's like everybody else. Highway robbery, I might add."

Joyce's face managed to turn an even deeper shade of red.

"We have competitive prices," she argued.

"Competitive with New York City, maybe. If you don't watch, this place here is gonna sink you."

"Well, they don't have fresh produce or meat, and if y'all would rather have frozen food there's nothing I can do about it."

Rick laughed. "I'm a bachelor. That's all I eat."

"Excuse me, mister, you can't just break in line like that," said a fat woman in line next to Lydia.

"I'm just talking to my neighbors," Rick said.

"Well, I drove all the way up here from Roxboro, and you're not my neighbor, so get yourself at the end of the line."

"Ma'am, I just want to talk to my friends," he said.

"Why don't I just talk to that security guard?"

"Go ahead," Rick suggested.

Turning to her companion, the woman said, "This is why I never come across the state line. Virginians always have thought they were better than anybody else."

Joyce said, "Not everybody else. Just the fat California hicks."

Lydia and Rick stared at Joyce, who was looking directly and un-apologetically at the stranger.

"You're why we didn't want this store in the first place," Joyce went

on. The woman was momentarily too stunned to reply. Clearly, she had
her doubts about snapping at a woman with a facial disfigurement. But
her slightly less obese companion had no such qualms.

"Well, then what are you doing here?" the other woman retorted.
"Why don't you go home and make more room for the rest of us?"

Lydia was actually formulating some puerile response, something to
do with the amount of room they were taking up, when she was approached by a woman dressed like a firecracker.

"Would y'all like to sign up for a Ford Explorer?" she asked, handing
Lydia a flyer that read, "A cracking good deal!" Lydia looked at the piece
of paper, so disoriented by what was happening around her that she
thought the firecracker lady was actually giving away cars.

"Hey, we're going somewhere," Rick announced.

All prior issues were forgotten as the line moved and the people in it
were caught up in the force of its purpose. There was no getting out or
turning back. They bumped each other, chins and shoulders and thighs
thumping together, until they were propelled through the automatic
doors. Once inside, the shoppers froze as if confused by the realization
of their goal.

"It's big," Joyce said.

It was, in fact, enormous. Lydia felt a sudden rush of familiarity. She
had spent most of her youth exploring large structures, from the Springfield mall to the Smithsonian, and she was certain that no man-made
structure could surprise her again. But this did. The layout did nothing to
obscure or deny its scope. It wanted to project its largeness; it was as if
it hoped to defeat its customers. There were no barriers or corridors or
clearly marked divisions within the warehouse-type building. Just end-
less racks of clothing, shelves of whatnots, glassed cases of jewelry and
electronic equipment. The bottleneck at the door consisted of shoppers
too overwhelmed to embark on their long-awaited journey. It spread before them like the land of Oz, glistening with promise and power. And
they stood staring, wondering what it could possibly mean, knowing that
with all its seductive choices, it contained absolutely nothing that they
needed, and everything that they could desire.

Lydia and Rick and Joyce moved through the aisles as if they were
walking through a zoo or some sort of living museum. They watched the
people hunched over the sale tables, sifting through the flawed clothing and
chipped dinnerware. They walked past vast offerings of power tools and

talking dolls and silk plants, scatter rugs and throw pillows and kitchen gadgets. It was oddly mesmerizing. After a few seconds, Lydia actually began to believe she could use an electric skillet or a potpourri jar.

Joyce shook her head and said, "Jesus."

Rick laughed. "That's probably the only thing they don't sell here."

But he was wrong. Just past the bathroom fixtures they were confronted by a large display of religious statuettes and colorful editions of the Bible.

Joyce fingered a cheap porcelain ceramic of the Nativity. Lydia picked up a gold-plated crucifix.

"Who would buy this?" Lydia asked.

"Christ is spinning in His grave," Rick said. "I don't think He ever imagined Himself to be the bluelight special."

"I think He'd like it," Joyce said quietly.

"Why's that?" Rick asked.

"Jesus wanted to walk among the people."

"Okay," Rick admitted, "but I don't think he ever expected to have rhinestone eyes."

Joyce laughed, and the Nativity slipped. Rick reached out to grab it and his hand closed around Joyce's fingers. The statuette fell and shattered on the ground.

"Oh God," Joyce said.

"Don't worry about it," Lydia said.

"I broke the Lord," Joyce said.

"No, I broke it," Rick said, leaning down to collect the pieces.

"It's okay," Lydia said, seeing a look of panic descend on Joyce's face. "It'll heal itself."

Joyce looked horrified, but Rick began to laugh.

"In three days it'll be good as new," he agreed.

An angry young man in a red smock raced toward them. A button on one side of his chest announced, "I'm here for you!" The other badge identified him as Graham Mundy, the assistant manager.

"Someone's gotta pay for this," Graham announced. He could not have been more than twenty, and was possessed of a self-righteous anger far beyond his years. To say that he took his job seriously was a masterpiece of understatement.

"Who's going to pay for this?" Graham persisted.

"Maybe Jesus can," Rick suggested. "He's paid for everything else."

"I am not amused," Graham said.

"I don't think you've been amused in a long time, Graham," Lydia said.

Joyce recovered long enough to unzip her purse, but Rick was faster. He pulled out a rumpled twenty-dollar bill and shoved it at the clerk.

"I gotta fill out a report," the clerk said.

"How about you take this and we'll forget it ever happened?" Rick said.

Graham Mundy pocketed the bill and said, "Y'all go look at the shoes or something y'all can't smash up."

They took his advice and turned in the direction of the clothing racks.

"Oh, look—isn't that Nigel Hayes?" Rick asked.

Lydia turned in time to see the slim, slightly hunched figure disappearing behind a display of Dustbusters.

"Was it?"

But before she could confirm the sighting she felt a hand on her elbow, and turned to find herself staring directly at Inez Milton, who was guiltily clutching an armful of bath towels.

"I thought that was you, Lydia," Inez said in a half-whisper. "I won't tell if you don't."

"Tell what, Inez?"

"It's just that my towels are all worn out and the ones at Leggett's are so expensive."

"You don't have to apologize to me."

"Hi, Joyce. We haven't seen you at church lately," Inez said, smiling, putting a hand on Joyce's arm. Inez treated everyone with mercy, withholding judgment, as if she were running for office and could not afford to exclude anyone's vote. But she was not gaining any ground with Joyce, whose whole body stiffened at Inez's touch.

"I've been busy," Joyce said.

"Yes, well, my towels are so worn out," Inez repeated. "We'll see you this Sunday, I hope."

They waved to her and stood frozen in place for a moment, forgetting their purpose.

"Where are we going?" Rick asked.

"Shoes," Lydia suggested, and they went off, searching.

The shoe department was vast, taking up most of the back part of the store. Many of the shoppers had gravitated there, waving bargains at each other across the aisle.

"Real leather!" a woman called out triumphantly, holding loafers in the air like an Olympic torch.

Rick and Lydia got caught up in the commotion. It was hard not to. The shoe aisle was particularly lively, promoting the feeling that the right pair of shoes could solve anything. They tried on several, parading them in front of slanted floor mirrors. Rick slipped on a pair of cowboy boots while Lydia clacked across the tiles in a pair of red patent-leather high heels. Joyce sat on a bench, attempting to smile. She was still suffering over the broken Nativity.

"Put these on," Rick suggested, offering her a pair of black satin pumps with stitched-on pearls. Joyce stared at him and shook her head. "Come on, they're you."

He pulled off her sensible brown lace-ups, as she kicked in protest. Lydia watched, fearing that Joyce might have reached her limit. She felt like breaking in to protect her, but as Rick kneeled at Joyce's feet and peeled off her sock, something else began to happen. Joyce's bare foot emerged, and it was beautiful. Thin and sleek, its nails white and perfectly sculpted. Lydia wondered if she weren't trying to will the image, to imagine at least one part of Joyce's anatomy to be perfect. But as she caught the look on Rick's face, she knew she had not imagined it. Joyce's foot was alluring. Lydia stood still and watched as Rick stared at this perfect thing in front of him. But what was more amazing was Joyce's face, relaxed and waiting for whatever came next.

Rick took the black satin pump and slipped it onto Joyce's foot. It fit perfectly, the heel sliding in with a whispering sound, a moment so perfectly timed it was as if they expected some magical transformation to take place. Trumpets might sound and Joyce's face might suddenly rid itself of its history. Rick raised his eyes as if in anticipation of such an event.

"It's perfect," Rick said. He repeated the pattern with her other foot and Lydia watched, feeling her breath catch in her chest. The act was so intimate, she felt as if she were watching something sexual and she had to fight the impulse to turn away. Joyce stared into Rick's eyes, then stood, walking across the floor in the black satin pumps. The clicking sound was mesmerizing. She moved gracefully to the back of the store, past the families pushing sneakers onto their children's sweaty feet, until she reached a full-length mirror on the far wall. There she stood, studying herself in the mirror. Her eyes avoided her face and fell with complete conviction on her feet. She was thinking what Lydia was thinking, and certainly what Rick, with his frozen expression, must be thinking. If everyone looked down rather than out, if eyes were trained to judge from the ground up, Joyce would defeat them all.

"They look great on you," Lydia said. "You have to have them."

Joyce laughed nervously and slipped them off, embarrassed by her momentary lapse of humility.

"They're twenty-nine dollars, and I have nowhere to wear them," she said.

"I want to buy them for you," Rick said.

Joyce turned to him abruptly, as if she had forgotten he was there. "That's ridiculous. Why should you buy me some shoes?"

"I'd just like to, that's all."

"Lydia, let's go," Joyce said. She grabbed her old shoes and walked in her bare feet toward the front of the store. Lydia could see that Rick was honestly confused by Joyce's reaction. Was this the only way he knew how to communicate with women? Had he relied on charm so long that he did not know how to provide anything else? Lydia did not think so. She thought that his desire to do something for Joyce was sincere. She just could not imagine what had motivated it, other than his surprise at seeing Joyce's foot, a notion too absurd to entertain, but for the fact that she herself had been strangely affected by it.

"Yes, we'd better go," Lydia said. "I'll see you at school."

Rick did not say anything. Lydia walked away, pushing through the maze of clothing racks and sports equipment, and eager shoppers who bumped her as they maneuvered their carts through the aisles. She suddenly felt panicked, as if she were becoming one of *those* women, obsessed with Corelle ware and fireplace sets and disposable razors on sale. She could not find the door fast enough.

"Goodbye and come back," said the firecracker lady.

Joyce was already at the car, lacing up her shoes.

"What's wrong?" Lydia asked. "Are you okay?"

"I got a little rattled in there," Joyce said.

"Yes, it was pretty hideous."

The air inside the car was close, stale, and warm. It was comforting after the cold wind in the parking lot and the cavernous feeling of Quality-Mart. As she was buckling her seat belt, Joyce said, "What are *you* afraid of, Lydia?"

Lydia was caught off guard. She felt certain that no one had ever asked her that question outright, and that she had never contemplated it in such specific terms. The first thought that came to mind was unnerving, because it was a fear she had not been able to name until she found herself in the aisles of the Quality-Mart, watching all those people desperately throwing merchandise into their baskets. She was afraid of being common.

She hesitated to say this to Joyce, because the fear was still so embryonic, and because she worried that Joyce would interpret it as an indictment of her character. So she decided to stick to something easy.

"Oh, I don't know," she sighed. "Age. Death. The usual stuff."

"Really?" Joyce said, sounding genuinely surprised. "Are there really people who are having such a good time here they don't want to leave?"

For a second Lydia thought she meant here, at Quality-Mart. Then she realized the reference was broader, encompassing the planet, consciousness, life.

"I suppose," Lydia replied.

"Are you?"

"Sometimes."

"What I would like," Joyce said slowly, deliberately, as if someone had asked her that specific question, "is one day on earth when I didn't feel completely ridiculous."

Lydia felt panicked to come up with an honest and reassuring response. She knew that Joyce was talking about something beyond her own experience, a concept so personal and intense that it had no real hope, or even an intention, of being understood. Still, Lydia felt compelled to reply. She was raised to reply. She could not let a serious, unappealing thought hang out there to dry.

"Rick was trying to be kind," Lydia offered.

Joyce did not look at her.

"People shouldn't have to try," she said.

8

DANNY WAS NOT there when she came home from Quality-Mart opening day. He was not there as suppertime approached, and after calling his parents (they said he hadn't been there all day), Lydia decided to go out for dinner at the Red Fox Inn, a barely respectable place just outside of town, near the Texaco station. She felt a mild degree of discomfort among the kids (the staff rarely checked IDs) and the older, potbellied truck drivers passing through town. She would have felt much more uncomfortable at Fawley Square, where everyone in town could see her alone, and instantly start spreading rumors about her. No matter how dysfunctional the marriage, in Fawley couples did not eat out independently of one another.

She had a grilled cheese sandwich and beer and three cigarettes, a habit she did not particularly enjoy, but she felt the need to do something destructive whenever she was annoyed with Danny. He had been late the night before, too. Was this the beginning of the end, the husband who came up with a thousand excuses for coming home late? Had they slipped into some bizarre, older-than-its-years marriage pattern, where they no longer felt the need to answer to one another?

Whenever there was the slightest hiccup in their marriage, Lydia had a tendency to leap ahead to divorce, to the dramatic unraveling of a doomed union. She knew it was because her parents had predicted a disaster that she felt the compulsion to deliver one. Small problems other couples might put down to ordinary differences Lydia immediately elevated to the level of prophecy fulfilled. Danny was aloof and evasive, terrified of responsibility, her mother had diagnosed after all of an afternoon in his presence, their one and only meeting. He will do nothing but disappoint you. And if you think that band on his finger assures anything, you are living in a dream world.

Lydia knew, in the rational part of her brain, that her mother was expressing some frustration of her own, some disappointment in her own marriage that was not readily apparent. Her parents had seemed the picture of marital bliss. She could not recall a single incident of raised voices or doors slamming or nights when her father did not come home. He worked late, often, but her mother always waited up for him and no argument ensued that she was aware of. There had been dark, low mumblings behind the bedroom door occasionally, but they always emerged smiling, speaking respectfully to one another. Then again, there didn't seem to be a great amount of passion between them, and this was the thing Lydia had vowed to find in her own union. She would endure the fights and the screaming she never witnessed, if it meant that the other side was strong evidence of affection she had never observed between her parents.

Sometimes Lydia feared that she forgave Danny too much in an effort to defy her parents. It was true, he was aloof and evasive, but she romanticized that tendency. There was something exciting about having to chase after a husband, trying to extract emotion, or at least information, and coax him out of his moods. Thus far, she had always been successful. But on ordinary nights, such as this, when she felt it was reasonable to expect her husband to come home, she had difficulty fighting that annoying voice in her head saying that this was wrong, she deserved better.

"All interesting men are difficult," Camille used to say, justifying her string of tortured romances with unfaithful companions. It was one of the few philosophies Camille espoused with which Lydia agreed. She felt women were far too eager to find comfort and stability. She wanted her relationship to be alive, electric, turbulent, which she had found, though not in the way she expected. Her relationship continually kept her on edge, not because Danny was such a maverick, but because his behavior was thoroughly unpredictable, unfathomable in its own quiet way. He was an enigma because of what was missing, the details he deliberately left out of his own story.

Like those pills she had found in his drawer a while back. Sleeping pills. Ativan, she seemed to recall. But she couldn't remember if the bottle was full or empty. She wished she had counted them so she could check again and see how many he had taken. It didn't really matter, did it? Thinking back, she was vaguely aware that he had some difficulty sleeping. He often stayed up later than she did, and she was conscious of him tossing and turning in bed, but she didn't analyze it. Plenty of people had trouble falling asleep. She remembered her own bout of insomnia back in law school, when she had come to rely on two Benadryl tablets a night. But she knew what that was about. She hated law school and the fear of following the wrong path churned inside of her every night. The minute she dropped out she had no trouble sleeping at all.

So it wasn't the pills that worried her so much as Danny's need for them. What was keeping him awake? Did he suffer from a similar fear, that he was heading in the wrong direction? And if so, did that mean he distrusted the course of his marriage? That didn't seem likely. She felt confident that he loved her—perhaps even adored her. He rarely said so, but she could tell in the way that he looked at her, the way that he made love to her almost every night, always with enthusiasm, never by rote. What other demons could he be struggling with, and why couldn't he reveal them to her?

As she finished her second beer, Lydia was conscious of an anger growing inside her like a virus. It surprised her, the sudden attack. I sacrificed everything for him, she thought. I gave up everything. He should know that. He should, he should. . . . But she could not name what it was she expected.

She paid the bill and drove home, feeling wide awake and eager, as if she were heading to some sporting event. She wanted the game to start. She wanted to play. She wanted to know the score.

Danny drove in around ten o'clock, stomping mud off his work boots before coming into the house. Lydia ignored him at first, waiting for him to volunteer an explanation. She stared blankly at the television while he moved around the kitchen, pouring himself a beer. He sat down on the couch next to her and stared at the TV for a few minutes, a dull courtroom drama that she knew could not possibly interest him.

"Where've you been?" she finally asked, when it was clear he had no intention of speaking.

"Out to the Brendel site."

"Why?" she asked. "It's Saturday night, for God's sake."

"They've been having trouble with the plaster. It keeps buckling in the rain. I think we might have to replace a subcontractor."

"But what does that have to do with you?"

"It's my deal," he said simply, sipping his beer.

"But you're not a construction worker. Let the subcontractor go there."

"It gives them a sense of security to see a suit out there. It was a big fuckup, the plaster work. I'm trying to make the developers feel good about their investment. It's the whole ethos behind the business. We don't just disappear behind the walls once the contract is signed."

"That's not the way other contracting companies work."

He nodded. "Which is why we've survived the recession."

"Well, is that where you were last night? At the Brendel site?"

Danny took a long sip of his beer, wiped his mouth with his sleeve and said, "I was at my mother's."

"I called there."

Another sip of beer and Danny crumpled the can. The fact that he could be missing for hours and reticent about where he'd been frightened Lydia, not because she thought he was having an affair, but because she knew perfectly well he wasn't. His behavior was more complicated than that. In fact, if she had found lipstick on his collar, she would have been enormously relieved.

Danny waited. He let a protracted moment of silence crawl past, during which time he stared resolutely at the shrunken can. He looked dark, as if a shadow had passed over him. When he did this, deliberately manufactured silence and dared Lydia to break it, she honestly felt there was something dangerous about Danny. That kind of cold, hostile patience worried her. It was what made soldiers sit in the trenches, or predators sit in wait for their prey, without blinking or twitching a muscle.

Usually this tactic wore Lydia down. She would break in with another, equally demanding question. Or, more often than not, she would apologize.

Tonight, she would wait.

"I had to go to the grocery store," Danny finally said.

"You were with Kyle, weren't you?"

"I hate that I can't tell you when I go to see my own cousin," he said.

"So do I."

"Okay, so I saw Kyle. What do you want to do—call the lawyers?"

"I just want you to be honest with me."

"You hate Kyle."

"So you lie to me in order to avoid hearing how much I hate Kyle?"

"No, I lie to spare your feelings. I know the whole business upsets you so I can't see the point of rubbing your face in it."

"Okay, let me get this straight. You lie to me to avoid confronting my feelings."

"Stop it," he said, pressing his fingertips to his neck, as if checking his pulse. "I hate it when you analyze me."

"Oh, I see. You hate the feelings and you hate the logic. That pretty much takes care of both sides of the brain. What part of me do you like? My legs? My haircut?"

"Lydia," he said, now pressing his fingers under his ears, "you're too hard on me. You expect too much. You want me to turn my back on my family. . . ."

"That's what *I* did."

"Well, maybe you're stronger than me."

"Don't give me that self-deprecating bullshit. You can't have that escape route. What the hell are you doing? Why are you *poking* at yourself?"

His fingers were now prodding his armpits.

"It's my glands, all right?" he said. "I think they're swollen."

"When did this start?"

"I don't know. A month or two ago."

"Danny, you don't have swollen glands for months. You have them for a couple of days and then you collapse from something like mono or Hodgkin's disease."

He sighed. "I'm going to bed."

Lydia fumed. This was Danny's specialty—opening up the lid of a variety of disasters, then walking out. He was a leaver. He walked out on fights. He sometimes abandoned significant statements mid-sentence. When she questioned him, he stared stubbornly at the wall like a four-teen-year-old who'd been asked to name names.

She stood for a long time staring at the door, thinking she might get in her car and drive away. But this had never been in her nature. She had to see a thing through.

Danny was asleep when she came into the room. Lydia sighed, staring at him. This man was too confusing for her. On calm, uneventful

nights he tossed and turned in the bed, his eyes staring at the ceiling until gray light seeped through the curtains. Tonight, after a bitter argument,
he'd dropped off as if he'd run a marathon.

Lydia dressed for bed and sat down beside him.

"What's going on with you?" she asked.

He jerked awake and stared at her, his eyes full of sleep-panic, struggling to recognize her.

"What?" he said.

"Danny, you scare me."

"What time is it?"

"The way you act, it's frightening."

"That's ridiculous."

He opened his arms and reached for her. She gently pushed him away.
He turned his face into the pillow.

"I don't understand the things you do. This thing with the glands, do
you really think you have something?"

He shrugged.

"And going out to building sites. And hanging around with Kyle."

He sat up and fluffed the pillow behind him, ready to take her on now
that Kyle had been mentioned.

"Don't try to understand that one, Lydia. Some things are just a matter of history. You honestly think I don't know what Kyle is? I know it
better than anybody. But there's a bond between us. There's a connection. It's beyond the rules."

"Why?"

"You know why. Because of his father, Uncle Pike. I promised him I'd
look out for Kyle."

"But Kyle was a child then. So were you. Both of you should be able
to look out for yourselves now."

"It doesn't work that way."

"Why not?"

"Because it doesn't," he answered angrily. "Let me have some unwritten rules, Lydia. Let me have some irrational moments."

"I do. I let you have them all the time. It's just that you're having so
many of them lately. I feel like I don't even know you."

He hooked his arm around her abruptly, kissing her hard on the mouth.
Lydia pushed him away and wiped her mouth with the back of her arm.
He stared at her as if he had been mortally wounded. She knew it was a

cheap shot, but she couldn't stand the way he used sex to avoid emotion. "High-class problems," she could imagine Dee saying. But when he did that, when he seduced her to shut her up, Lydia felt as if she were being buried alive.

"You're going to talk to me if it kills you," she said.

"What!" he shouted. "What do you want to know? Christ almighty, Lydia, you think you have to regurgitate your every emotion. People are not supposed to confess everything. People are supposed to have a certain amount of secrets."

"That's bullshit. I don't . . ."

"I know you don't! That's my point, I wish you would. Keep something to yourself for once and let me do the same."

"Great, and then we can have a marriage like your parents'."

"See, you've got a real talent for this. You can bring my family into anything."

"They're in everything, Danny. They're in you. Can't you see yourself carrying on the tradition of silence? They don't talk about anything. They systematically shut out the world. Your mother won't even drive to town. And your Aunt Rita and those girls, they won't leave the goddamned house."

"Stop trying to save everybody, Lydia, some people just want to get along, they don't want to be better than they are."

He pressed his fingers to his neck again. Lydia reached up in a rage to grab his hands, but he grabbed her arms first and pushed her back on the bed. She lay still, frightened and excited, knowing that this was going to mean something, that whatever happened next could change her life.

Danny covered his face with his hand, but he didn't cry. He didn't move for a long time. Finally, through his fingers he said, "I love you. My God, you're all I ever think about. What else do you need to know?"

Lydia couldn't answer. She felt ashamed at her disappointment. It wasn't quite enough that he loved her. It was probably enough when she met him, but then she hardly knew him. She knew that he was thoughtful and quiet and mysterious, that when he spoke she understood him, and he made her laugh. She knew that he lived this simple life, but that his character was anything but simple, and she believed that her marriage to him would be a journey, a process of unlocking all these doors. But what she had never considered was that once she unlocked them, she would not like what she found.

Worst of all, Lydia realized, was that she had invested her belief in some divine aspect of their relationship. She had been certain she would be rewarded for trusting her heart. She believed that magical things would happen to them. But now, if only ordinary things were going to happen to them, did she have the strength to stand it?

He sat waiting for her to answer his question, and when she didn't, and instead lay breathing up at him like a frightened rabbit, he lay down and turned on his side with his back to her.

In all of her years of marriage, this was the first time that Lydia had truly felt alone. Danny could not defend or protect her. He was not on her side, and if he wasn't, who was? Certainly not her parents, or her older brother, Eric. She was never close to him, but lately she found herself wanting to talk to him. He had taken sides against her when she married, and his resentment of her ran even deeper than her parents'. He wrote her a letter shortly before the wedding and accused her of destroying the family. Subsequently, he'd refused to return her phone calls. She thought of him, living in Alexandria and practicing law in the city, his wife Carolyn making the home perfect and taking care of their son, her nephew, whom she'd never seen, not even in a photograph. She tried to picture him sometimes. He was at least two by now. Zachary. It was a ridiculous name. Why were these affluent, upwardly mobile people intent on giving their children names that belonged to cowboys and pioneers? Who were they fooling? Zachary would go to St. Albans and eventually Harvard or UVA. He would be a lawyer or a doctor. But he would never pick up a shovel or round up cattle or build a barn, as any self-respecting person named Zachary should do.

Did Zachary look like Eric? Did he get his sharp nose, his long eyelashes, his blowsy cheeks? Or did he have Carolyn's thin hair and fair skin—was he wispy and fragile, like his mother? Or perhaps he looked something like Lydia. Perhaps he shared her wide mouth, square jaw, her thick hair. It frightened her to think that Zach might have something in common with her, and she could not be there to claim the connection.

She could not think of her nephew for long. It made her head roar. It made her want to drink. She thought instead of people she might have on her side, like Dee or Joyce. She and Dee certainly had some kind of relationship. They had a similar sense of humor, a kind of irreverence

about the lives they were leading, as if it were all a kind of benign hoax.
But there were times when she felt that Dee was leading her on, that Dee
really bought in to all the things she claimed to resist. In a strange way,
she felt set up by Dee, as if her neighbor were drawing all of the cynicism
out of her in order to use it against her. This was ridiculous, she knew.
Ever since her family turned against her, she was suspicious of anyone
who claimed to like her.

That was why she trusted Joyce. Joyce did not claim anything. And
Joyce was too meek to possess an ulterior motive, or even to harbor a
strong judgment. Joyce was like a character in a bad play. She was exactly what she was written to be—no levels, no room for interpretation,
no interior life. But this was not the sort of person Lydia wanted to de-
pend on. In fact, Joyce turned Lydia into someone she did not want to be.
She found herself playing the role of the manipulator, always trying to
trick Joyce out of herself. To her, Joyce was like the proverbial Englishman who, if awakened by surprise, would speak like everyone else. She
kept thinking she could sneak up on Joyce and shock her into action. But
there was no surprise to Joyce. The facade was not a facade. It was who
she was, as if the effort to pretend that she could cope was all there was
to her. The effort to survive was her character.

Why did she want to save Joyce? Why did she want to save anyone,
when she herself could use plenty of salvation?

These thoughts exhausted her and she drifted off to sleep, just as she
was, her head at the footboard, her legs hanging off the side of the mattress.

It was a light, stressful sleep, and for a while she dreamt of Quality-
Mart, the grotesque clowns passing out balloons to dull-eyed children.
And in her dream, each balloon caused the children to lift up, float up to
the stratosphere, while their parents watched with dull surprise. In her
dream she chased after the children, grabbing at their shoelaces. She
screamed at the parents to help her, but they only watched. Then the
clown handed a balloon to Joyce, and an innocent smile spread across
her tortured face. She waved as she, too, began to lift upward. Lydia
lunged for her and Joyce continued to wave, saying, "It's okay, Lydia. It's
what I want. Let me go." She stayed still and watched Joyce growing
smaller, thinking, This is right. Let it happen. Then suddenly she looked
at the clown and saw that behind the white pancake makeup, the oversized mouth, the downturned eyes, was the face of Kyle. He grinned
sadistically at her. His hand reached out, offering her a balloon.

"I know you're not a clown," she informed him.

"But you're the only one," he said, laughing.

There was the sound of a gunshot, and the balloon deflated and Kyle was suddenly falling toward her. She tried to run and couldn't.

Suddenly she was awake, sitting up in bed, her breath coming hard and fast. Danny slept peacefully. She reached out and shook his shoulder, gently at first, then harder. His eyes popped open and he stared vacantly at her, with no sense of time or place or meaning.

"Tell me about Kyle," she said.

Danny sat up. "Did the phone ring?"

"No. I want you to tell me the story. Of him and you and Uncle Pike."

"I've told you before," he said, flopping back down on the pillow.

"Tell me again."

"If I tell you again, can we go to sleep and not fight anymore?"

"Yes."

She waited. He stared at her and sighed, crossing his arms behind his head. In a monotone he started, like a weary parent who had told the fairy tale once too often and could not drum up the energy to make it come to life. Beside him Lydia listened, like the child who wanted to hear it again and again, until the story made sense.

"Within an hour after Uncle Pike died, there were at least a dozen versions of how it happened. I heard them all, and there were only two things everybody managed to get right. Uncle Pike was dead, and a black man had killed him.

"I was thirteen when it happened, a month younger than Kyle. I was a good athlete; he wasn't. I was already starting to get a beard and he wasn't. It's crazy, but I think that was a factor. He had to make up for that with his behavior, so he was wilder than I was, which to him was a sure sign of masculinity. Whatever the reason, by the time he was thirteen, Kyle was bad. Not just mischievous. Bad, like you'd imagine evil to be. Not a mood or a fit, but something inside him that could not be disconnected."

"Tell me," Lydia said, clutching her knees, staring at his face, striped by the moonlight shining through the blinds. This was the point where she always stopped him. This was the point where Danny sighed and there was a thick pause.

"I could tell you stories, but I'm not sure they'd sound convincing.

Things he did to cats, stuff like that. His fearlessness. I swear to God, he jumped off the track inches from a train once. Me and a bunch of guys were standing there. All the way home we couldn't talk. One of the guys pissed in his pants, I found out later. I just kept having nightmares about it. It was the first time Kyle tried to kill himself. And I didn't understand it, but somehow I knew that was what I had seen.

"By the time he was thirteen, his own mother was scared to death of him. So were his sisters, the ones we just call the girls. The slew of hens, Kyle used to say. Joyce wasn't so afraid of him, though. She just detested him."

"What made her different?" Lydia asked.

"I don't know. She was the oldest, maybe. She was scarred. Emotionally, I mean. The thing with her face happened later."

"How did it happen?"

"I don't remember. Something about the venetian blinds. I was too young to understand it."

"So she hated Kyle already."

"I can never remember a time when Joyce was speaking to him."

"Go on," Lydia said. "Tell me about Pike."

"Uncle Pike thought Kyle could do no wrong. Uncle Pike was the kindest man you could ever imagine. Just like Daddy but without the temper. I never heard him raise his voice once, except when Kyle almost turned a tractor over on himself. He wasn't allowed to drive it, see, and he hopped up there and started turning a corner before anybody could stop him. That thing wobbled, and Uncle Pike took off like he had a fire under his ass. When he caught up to Kyle he jerked him off the tractor, knocked him two blocks, yelling to high heaven. Then he picked him up and carried him all the way back to the house.

"It was like every hope in the world Pike had was connected to Kyle. He took him to the tobacco fields, took him to the pig barn on slaughtering day, took him to church, took him to poker games. Took him hunting—that was the big one. The only thing Kyle was better at than me; he could shoot. One reason was Pike started taking him as a kid. Most boys couldn't go until they were twelve. It was an unwritten rule. But Kyle was out there when he was six—not shooting anything himself, but watching it all. Sometimes I wonder if that had something to do with it."

"How could it not?" Lydia asked. "A six-year-old kid, watching all that bloodlust. I mean, that's what hunting is. Don't give me the meat-for-the-winter story. Those people want to kill something."

"Well, I don't know about that. But I was never crazy about hunting myself. I couldn't stand the way the deer would look up at you, those seconds before dying, like, 'What did I ever do to you?' Riding back in the truck, I always thought about the ones that got away."

"So then Rex got sick," Lydia said, urging him along. She knew all the salient moments in the story, the turning points, the epiphanies.

"Rex got sick," Danny said, pausing to yawn. "When I was twelve. Rex and I weren't all that connected. Six years is a big age difference, especially when you have nothing in common. He was always weird, you know, collecting stamps and gardening, making pottery, cooking. He had an Easy-Bake oven, I swear to God. I tried playing baseball with him. He was scared of the ball. And you know, when I was twelve, anybody who didn't like baseball was from Mars. Then he got meningitis."

"And you felt guilty."

"It was more than that. It was the first time it ever occurred to me that people my age could die. I knew he could die—I knew he probably would. To this day the doctors say it's a miracle he survived. My mother was a wreck and my father was in denial, and I was left to fend for myself. So Kyle came down and stayed in my room the whole time he was in the hospital. Every morning when my eyes opened, before I could think about my brother dying, Kyle was up and suggesting some outrageous activity for the day. Firecrackers in bottles, shooting windows out with our BB guns, shoplifting, hitchhiking, chicken on the train tracks. He led me to trouble, and I welcomed it because that kind of danger kept me from thinking about what was really at stake.

"That went on for what seemed like months, but was probably about three weeks. Then Rex got better. He came home from the hospital and Kyle went back to his house. But we stayed close after that. I felt this loyalty to him. It's hard to explain."

"But Kyle kept on getting in trouble," Lydia said, filling in part of the story.

"Yeah. It wasn't just trouble, though. It was meanness. He was *cruel*. One thing I remember—it won't sound so horrible but it was. We were coming out of the drugstore one day, and there was a group of black men hanging out on the corner. There always was, and we never paid much attention. But this day, for no reason, Kyle went up to them and asked for a smoke. The men just looked at him, too surprised to refuse him. They seemed old to me then, but I guess they were about my age now, maybe even younger. One of the men had half an earlobe missing. He was the one who gave Kyle a cigarette. He gave one to me, too. Kyle stuck his behind his ear. I just held mine, not knowing what to do with it. I never did like to smoke, being a jock and all. Then Kyle said, 'Why aren't y'all working?'

"'Nobody's hiring,' the guy said.

"'Hell, Tawnee Mill's hiring left and right,' said Kyle. 'They got fifty positions to fill and they pay ten dollars an hour to a floor sweeper. Anybody can sweep a damn floor.'

"The guy said he hadn't heard about that, but Kyle kept insisting it was true. He told them that people would start lining up at six o'clock the next morning. Those men looked at him, and I swear their faces came to life the slightest bit, a little twitch of hope, or something. Then we turned away and left them standing there. After we'd gotten a few steps away Kyle said, 'That's how dumb a nigger is. He'll believe anything.' Then he threw his cigarette into the ditch. When I asked him why, he said, 'You think I'm gonna put that thing in my mouth?'

"I thought about that for a long time, remembering the way those men looked at him, like they wanted to believe him. They wanted to trust a white kid, but they knew it wasn't any use. And that night, I sat in the dark in my room and smoked that cigarette. I felt like I owed it to them."

Danny turned on his side now, looking at Lydia. He ran his finger along her shin. She didn't move. She was afraid the story would stop. She knew this was the hardest part.

"It was just an ordinary day in June," he said, "right before my birthday. I was going to Kyle's house to show him a magazine, this picture of an air rifle I wanted. I wasn't allowed to have a real rifle till I was sixteen, but this was the next best thing. I took the shortcut through the woods, like I always did. When I was just about to the house, I heard screaming. I started to run. By the time I got there, Aunt Rita and the girls were forming a semicircle, all of them screaming and wailing. I saw Uncle Pike's car peel out of the driveway and go tearing off down the road, spewing gravel. It seemed like it took me a month to get there. When I did, I saw Kyle sitting in the middle of the semicircle, clutching his leg. I kept asking what happened, but none of the girls could stop crying long enough to say. Finally Kyle looked up at me, and I'll never forget it. He grinned and said, 'A damn nigger shot me. You believe that?'

"It wasn't a bad wound. One shot to the foot. There was hardly any blood. I called my folks and they came down to the house. My father took Kyle off to the hospital. The rest of us sat around the living room in dead silence, waiting. We didn't even know what for. Kyle and my father got back to the house around dinnertime. Kyle had a cast on and he was showing everybody his walking cane. It didn't even seem to bother him that Pike had gone chasing after the person who shot him and still hadn't come back. And the funny thing? Once Kyle was there, it was like nobody else cared either. All the attention was on him. When the policeman came to the door around eight, we all just stared at him. We couldn't imagine what he was about to tell us."

"What did he tell you?" Lydia asked.

Danny thought for a moment. "He said Pike had been shot. Dead. That's all. The details came out later. A lot of it didn't come out until the trial. Some of it still isn't all that clear, but what we know is this: This black man, named Tom Fitzgerald, was riding down Snake Path Road, going toward Route Forty-eight. That was where most black people around here lived in those days. Anyway, Tom and his wife were coming home from grocery shopping. They saw Uncle Pike's car come up fast behind them. Pike laid on the horn, and Tom Fitzgerald waved for him to go around. But Uncle Pike didn't want to. He kept bumping the car, pulling beside it, trying to force it off the road. Finally Tom Fitzgerald got scared, so he pulled off to the side. Uncle Pike came up to the window, screaming something about his boy getting shot. He started trying to open the door, but Tom's side was locked, so he headed around to the side where Tom's wife was sitting. That's when Tom got scared. His wife was five months pregnant at the time. So he reached into his glove compartment and pulled out a thirty-eight that he kept for his family's protection. He'd never had to use it. Until Pike opened that car door and laid a hand on Tom Fitzgerald's wife. Then he fired four times, and it was all over.

"None of the family went to the trial. We only knew what we read in the paper. The trial itself got a lot of media attention. Tom Fitzgerald waived a jury trial—he knew there was no such thing as twelve impartial people in the county. The judge acquitted him. Called it self-defense. Tom Fitzgerald left town two days later. Smart move. He wouldn't have lasted here a week. The judge had to leave town, too. The facts sometimes get lost in hysteria, but the one irrefutable piece of evidence was that the bullet they pulled out of Kyle's foot wasn't from a thirty-eight. Uncle Pike had the wrong man. So given that, it was reasonable for Tom Fitzgerald to respond the way he did."

"That's new," Lydia said.

"What?"

"The stuff about the bullet. You never told me that. I guess I always thought Tom Fitzgerald could have done it."

"No," Danny said.

The other thing he'd never told her was that none of the family had attended the trial. Lydia could not imagine why. Wouldn't they be curious? Wouldn't they want to know the truth? Lydia knew that if anyone she loved were ever murdered she'd be right there for every second of the trial, going over every detail, making sure nothing was overlooked.

"So who do you think really shot Kyle?" Lydia asked, as she always did. Danny's answer was always a version of the same thing.

"It could have been anyone. You don't have to work hard to make enemies in this town, and Kyle worked hard. A lot of people hated him, and they weren't all black. The whole story seems like folklore to me now. If I hadn't been there for some of it, I'd be tempted to believe it never happened. The fact that he doesn't even have that leg anymore makes it seem all the more unreal."

"Isn't that a weird coincidence, him losing that leg?"

"Well, that's another story."

"Did it ever occur to anybody around here that if they didn't treat guns like pets, like something anybody has a right to own, then all this mess could be avoided?"

Danny looked at her as if she were speaking in tongues.

"No," he said. "It didn't."

She felt embarrassed. She was missing the point, after all, but the story always made her feel irrational.

"All right," she said. She was too tired to talk about it anymore.

The telling was always cathartic, particularly for Danny. She saw the shape of his body change as his shoulders relaxed and his breathing slowed. She felt close to him again; she understood his struggle. He wanted to escape them all, as much as she wanted to leave her own history behind. But it was impossible. Families lived inside, like radiation, hibernating in the cells. They knew too much. And because of that, they could not be abandoned.

9

GRAHAM MUNDY FELT pleased with himself as he did the books. It had been a stellar opening day—they'd cleared close to a quarter million, which exceeded the expectations of anyone in the Quality-Mart organization. Somehow, he felt personally responsible. He realized he was only the assistant manager and that he'd spent most of the day reorganizing the displays and keeping an eye out for shoplifters. But at least he'd had the good sense to take this job. At least he knew a good situation when he saw it. If he kept up the good work, he'd be a manager in no time, and maybe he'd even open up his own franchise, and then his ex-girlfriend, Lisa, would be sorry she'd dumped him for that real estate agent from Charlotte. When he took the assistant manager job at Quality-Mart, Lisa said it was a nowhere job and he had no vision. He couldn't wait for her to read about the big opening day in the news. Maybe he'd even get a mention. One of the ladies from the local news had interviewed him, so it was possible that he'd end up on television. Imagine Lisa's face when she saw that. Imagine her staring at the screen with those dark blue eyes, twirling a strand of black hair around her forefinger. Maybe she'd get regretful and teary. His mother always said Lisa wasn't good enough for him, but his mother didn't see her finer points. His mother didn't know what it was like when she kissed him and whispered silly nicknames in his ear. But those were the things he was trying to forget.

Around 11 P.M., Graham told the night manager, Carl, to go home.
Carl was a hard-drinking, boisterous guy who enjoyed ordering people
around but displayed no patience for the more intricate aspects of the job,
like bookkeeping. This was Graham's strong suit, and he knew Carl
would put up no argument when he volunteered. Besides, nobody saw
Graham as a threat. They saw him as shy and reserved; what they
couldn't see was the need that propelled him, that drive to prove himself.

Not that the day already hadn't offered plenty of opportunities. Graham had had to break up several fights at the sales tables, accost shoplifters, and intervene when one of the cashiers had an anxiety attack.
He'd worn every hat that day and had done it with grace and dignity. He
had a mental image of himself moving through the place like Eisenhower
through Europe, taking control wherever it was needed.

He realized suddenly that he was hungry. The only thing he'd had to
eat all day was a sausage biscuit at nine o'clock that morning. He was
thinking about going to the 7-Eleven and getting a burrito when he heard
strange sounds from outside in the parking lot. Graham knew that Ferris, the sixty-year-old security guard, was out there keeping watch, although there wasn't much to watch for, since the armored truck had
already left and the only money in the safe was a little over two thousand
dollars. Ferris was a sweet old man but not the sharpest knife in the
drawer, so there was no telling what could be going on. Graham analyzed
the sounds after he heard them. It sounded like the cry of a cat, something guttural and muted, followed by a quick popping sound. What
could that be? Maybe Ferris had knocked over a trashcan or walked into
the Dumpsters. His eyesight wasn't all that good. Or maybe he'd had an
encounter with some raucous teenagers from town. Even though Graham
was only twenty-three himself, and it had not been long ago when he was
guilty of silly youthful indiscretions, he felt he'd passed through some
barrier to maturity and now had the right to hold forth. He'd tell those
kids a thing.

He stood, yawned and stretched, and headed out to the parking lot.

Outside, the night was thick and dark. A fog had moved in, obscuring
the moon and diluting the fluorescent streetlights. The landscape before
him seemed flat and ordinary. He suddenly felt depressed as the cool
night air hit him, and it occurred to him for a fleeting second that Lisa
was right, and despite all his delusions of grandeur, he was just a sales
clerk posing as something else.

That was when Graham saw Ferris lying on the ground, the short coat of his blue uniform flapped open, a scarlet stain spreading like ink across his shirt. Graham's first thought was that Ferris had had a heart attack, and that his heart had actually exploded in his chest. But it didn't happen that way, did it? Graham struggled to remember CPR. His knees felt like rubber. His chest constricted and he suddenly recalled the asthma attacks from his childhood, and the realization that no one on earth, not even his beautiful mother with the piled-up blond hair, could provide him with enough air to breathe.

That was when he heard the voice.

"Give me the money," it said.

"What?" Graham asked, trying to make out the shadowy form. "There's no money. It's all gone."

"Don't fuck with me. I want it," said the voice.

"Well, just calm down. Come with me in the office. We'll work something out."

"Fine," he said.

They walked into the store and all the while Graham was sure he'd be able to solve this. He'd never met a problem he couldn't solve. He knew the gun was there, and he knew Ferris was lying out there on the asphalt, but he could not feel the danger. He felt certain that logic would introduce itself. Graham had his whole life to live, after all, and so did this man, and surely they could reach some kind of agreement.

Graham's hands were steady as he opened the cash drawer. The bills sat in the slots, looking small and endangered, and he felt the need to defend the lack of wealth.

"The truck was already here," he said. "We had a real good day but they took it all."

"Like I give a shit," said the man. "Hand it over."

"Okay, but just don't hurt me."

The man seemed unconcerned with his pain. Graham started counting out the cash. Somewhere in the distance, a siren howled. Graham looked up, startled. The man stared at him.

"Did you call the cops?"

"Honest to God, no."

The man laughed. "What makes you think God is honest?"

Graham smiled, because he didn't know what else to do. And then, suddenly, he decided to talk. He said, "Look, maybe you and I could strike a deal. We could work something out. You don't have to go around shooting people. You could get a job. I could give you a job. I'm the manager."

The smile on the man's face faded, and the look in his eyes turned into pure, clean rage.

Graham heard the click of the gun being cocked. All he could think of was how foolish he looked, standing there in his red coat. He was going to die this way, looking foolish and scared, and everyone would know his last moment was one of panic and despair. He should have joined the Air Force when he could; he should have died overseas like his cousin Al, who got shot down in the Gulf War, and whose body was never found. So he died with all that grace and all that perfect memory. And no one got to see that look on his face.

"Lisa," he said, and then it felt like something was splitting his chest apart, like a crowbar prying out his heart.

10

THE NEWS WAS everywhere and nowhere. It didn't make it in time for the morning paper, and even the morning news crew missed it. Looking back later, Lydia could swear there was no specific instance when she was made aware of what happened. No where-were-you-when-Kennedy-was-shot type of moment. Just a sudden awareness and a sense of confusion that fell over the town like an unpredicted snow.

Two people murdered at Quality-Mart. The sound of it buzzed and floated around, through telephone wires and down the street, spinning and going nowhere, like something caught in the wind. The names of the victims were not being released, pending the notification of the next of kin.

There had been a flurry of phone calls—from Danny's mother and Dee and Mrs. Hurley next door. Lydia couldn't honestly remember which came first, or how she felt when she heard the news. The only thing she recalled with great clarity was Danny's reaction, which was uncharacteristic. He actually went pale and had to sit down. It took a few moments for him to speak, and when he did he said, "I should have known. I should have seen it coming."

"What?" Lydia questioned. "How could you? How could anybody?"

"The whole thing felt like trouble," he went on. "I was nervous about it. I should have done something when I could."

Lydia stared at him, clutching her coffee mug next to her chest for comfort. He looked slightly crazed, and his words were bordering on incoherent. What the hell was he talking about? He was the one who told her the story about the interstate, how everyone predicted doom and had been disappointed. He was the one who dismissed his own involvement in the building of Quality-Mart. Now he felt responsible? He saw it coming?

"Danny, you're not making any sense," she said. "What on earth does this have to do with you?"

He stared at the floor for a moment, his eyes roving back and forth as if he were reading the tiles. Then he looked up and slowly his face came back to life. He even smiled.

"Boy, it gets to you, doesn't it? I kind of lost it for a second."

"Yeah, you kind of did."

He stood up and shook his head, as if to rid himself of some unwelcome voice inside it. "It's just so strange, how everyone was predicting this."

"Nobody was predicting murder, were they?"

"You know what I mean. They all thought something bad would happen there."

"It's a bizarre coincidence," Lydia said, "not the wrath of God."

"I know."

"Stores get robbed all the time."

"Not around here."

"Well, maybe times are changing."

He looked at her and said, "This is the biggest news since Uncle Pike."

Lydia studied his face. She could have sworn there was a degree of disappointment in there, as if he did not want Uncle Pike's tragedy to be surpassed.

"You're late for work," she said.

He kissed her and held her next to him longer than usual. She closed her eyes and smelled his smells—soap and shaving cream and the starch in his shirt. He felt warm and his heart was beating fast against her chest.

"Have a good day at school," he said.

He had never said that to her before. It sounded strange, as if he were talking to a child.

"You have a good day," she said, "playing in the dirt."

"No chance. I've got paperwork up to the ceiling."

She watched him walk out to the truck and then, for the first time since she'd moved to Fawley, she moved through the house, locking all the doors.

She went into the bedroom and opened the nightstand by Danny's side of the bed. Rummaging through the debris, she located the bottle of pills and held it up to the light. It was empty. It scared her, and then she reminded herself that it might have always been empty. She had not taken the time to count the contents. Maybe the bottle was old. She looked at the date—it had been prescribed over two years ago, which might have been good news if they hadn't been married then. She sifted through the contents of the drawer and came up with nothing surprising. Whatever Danny had been worried about, obviously he was over it now.

She closed the drawer and reprimanded herself for her suspicions. All the drama was occurring outside her house. She did not need to create more.

She showered and dressed and poured herself one more cup of coffee, which she planned to savor in front of the TV before she left for work. But as she was about to sit down, she saw a cop car pulling into the driveway. She watched from the window as Les Carlisle got out and moved toward the front door, hat in hand, looking cautiously around him as if checking for strangers or hostile dogs. She opened the door before he could ring the bell.

"Hey, Lydia, got a minute?" he asked, shaking his hair away from his forehead. Les was a kid, still swimming around in his twenties. He possessed no recognizable social skills, let alone an ability to intimidate. Still, Lydia was conditioned enough to let the uniform unnerve her.

"Les, come in," she said. "I've got to leave for school in a minute. Want some coffee?"

"Oh no, ma'am. I had about ten cups back at the station. I been up all night, as you might imagine."

"Yes, I'm sure it's been a rough night."

"So you heard."

"Rumors, yes."

"It's all true, I'm afraid. Two dead, no suspects. The thing of it is, we had a unit on the scene fifteen minutes before it happened. They left 'cause the payroll was all counted and in the armored truck. There was only two grand left in the register and the assistant manager was just putting it in the safe. Nobody thought to stick around, since all the big money had been delivered. What we didn't count on was the robbers didn't know the big money was gone. They were stupid, like most criminals are. But you could say we were stupid for not allowing for that."

He hesitated, as if he wanted Lydia to reassure him. She couldn't. She thought his statement was solid and had no interest in contradicting it.

Les cleared his throat and ran his fingers through his thin blond hair. He'd be bald by the time he was Lydia's age. She wondered if he knew that, if he were taking any steps to prevent it. The way he shifted on his feet and attempted to straighten his posture made her feel he was trying to flirt with her. She was mildly depressed when she realized he had no such intention, that he viewed her as an elder and was trying to appear more mature.

"Well, I won't keep you," he said. "Is Danny here?"

She shook her head. "He left an hour ago."

Les nodded, running his thumb across his lip.

"He was here with me last night, all night. We were in bed by ten."

Les stared at her blankly, then threw back his head and laughed. It was a nervous, booming laugh which rattled off the formica.

"Well, there goes our prime suspect." He laughed some more, until he noticed her thin, tight smile. "No, I'm not really here on business. I was just asking 'cause we occasionally get up a poker game on Friday nights and we lost a couple of guys lately and I wondered if I could deal him in. I mean, I hope you aren't opposed to that kind of thing. We just play for small money."

"I don't mind," Lydia said, "but Danny usually does his mother's shopping on Fridays."

"Mrs. Crane isn't sick, is she?"

"Oh no. She just doesn't like to drive."

Les made a clicking noise with his tongue and said, "It's a shame when folks get like that. Old, I mean."

"She's not really old. She's just nervous."

He nodded. "The whole family's a little on the nervous side, aren't they? I mean, Joyce down at Oliver's. And all those girls who live with their mama. Now Kyle, he's not nervous. He's just mean as a snake."

Lydia smiled tightly. She distrusted Kyle as much as anyone, but she felt enough loyalty to take offense at Les's remarks.

"I'll tell Danny you came by. Is there anything else?"

"Well, yes, ma'am, there is. Since I'm here I might as well put it to you. We're asking around, you know. Talking to people who were at opening day, wondering if they saw anyone suspicious."

"How do you know I was at opening day?"

"We've got a list. Martha Dawson took some names. You know her?

Sure you do, she works at the school. Well, she was there recording names of everybody in town who showed up."

Lydia nodded. "It's a pretty long list, I'll bet."

"Yeah, well, we're not going to get through all of it. She put a star by your name because she said you stirred up a fight in the parking lot."

For a second she couldn't imagine what he meant. Then she remembered Joyce's altercation with the fat woman in line.

"There was an argument, yes. Joyce exchanged words with a woman from North Carolina. I don't think that's a particularly interesting lead."

"No, I guess not."

Lydia took a sip of coffee and stared hard at the officer. He looked at his shoes.

"But you'd be surprised," he said. "We get some of our most promising leads just talking to folks." He took out his pad and a pencil, as if such leads were imminent. Then he stared at her, waiting. Lydia couldn't think of anything to say.

"How long have you been on the force?" she asked, feeling as if the tables had been turned and it was her job to interrogate him.

"Three years," he admitted. "But . . ."

She waited for the rest of the sentence, the statement which might mitigate his youth, but even Les was at a loss as to how to substantiate himself. "I've known your family forever, though."

She was confused, wondering how this kid could know anything about her family. Then she realized he was referring to Danny, to her family in Fawley. She suspected that Les was on the verge of insulting her. She had tolerated his remarks about her in-laws and Kyle, and she found it hard to dispute them. It was true that Sally was jittery, and Joyce was withdrawn, and it was certainly odd that Aunt Rita, Pike's widow, still had all three of her girls living with her. But she wasn't sure how this could be any of Les's business, or how it related to his poker night or the murders at Quality-Mart.

"That Kyle," Les said. "He's a one, isn't he? I stopped him for speeding once and he pulled a hunting knife on me. Pointed it right at my neck."

"Did you take him in?"

"Oh, hell no. Everybody knows what Kyle is like."

"Maybe if someone took the initiative and held him accountable for his actions, he wouldn't be like that."

"Well," Les said, clearing his throat, sticking his pen behind his ear, "I'm not really here about Kyle. He's not a suspect either."

Lydia said, "The men who were killed, were they locals?"

"Oh no. The security guard was from Martinsville. And the manager was from Greensboro. Related to Charles Mundy, you know, the big Cadillac dealer?"

Lydia felt the blood drain from her face. She wasn't sure why the news hit her so hard. The image of Graham Mundy flashed before her, the angry young man wearing the badge with the solicitous message, who berated them for breaking the Nativity. She saw his pale pink skin, his chapped lips, his pocked nose, all those details she had no idea she had retained. Would she have teased Graham had she known? Was that the last unpleasant encounter of his life?

"Matter of fact," Les went on, "the investigation isn't even in our jurisdiction. But we're helping out where we can. There's the chance the murderer could be from Fawley, but nobody thinks it's very likely."

"I wish I could help, but I can't," she said, glancing at her watch. He was going to make her late. And she wanted to escape him. She did not want to have to explain why she felt so breathless, why the coffee cup was shaking in her hand. She wanted to calm herself, reason it out, remind herself that she'd had nothing to do with Graham's death, that her sarcasm had not killed him, and she could not have foreseen his death.

"Anything you could tell us would be a help," Les said. "You know how cops always say that in the movies, but it's true."

"Honestly, I didn't see anything suspicious at Quality-Mart. I saw a lot of locals there and I guess that's kind of suspicious, given how everyone was supposed to be morally opposed to the idea. But really it's just human nature."

"Yes, ma'am, you're right about that. Well, if you do think of anything, you'll give us a call, won't you?"

"You'll be the first to know."

She escorted him to the door, which was really only a matter of walking a few feet.

"How's Danny doing anyway? His job going okay?" Les asked.

"Fine, as far as I know."

"It's funny, everybody thought he was going to be some big shot. A star ballplayer or a politician or something. I guess he just has a taste for the simple life."

Lydia smiled. "Life with me is anything but simple."

"Really? You strike me as real easygoing. I mean, I know you're from up North, but you seem real normal."

"Thank you."

He pushed the screen door open, then paused, studying her.

"Why were you at Quality-Mart anyhow?" he asked.

"What?"

"I mean, you're real active in the church and everybody knows their stand. Weren't you on the boycott committee?"

Lydia bristled. Les was not a member of Milton Memorial, so this information could only have come to him through gossip or investigation. Either venue was equally troubling.

Suddenly she didn't find Les's young, peach-fuzzed face so disarming. There was something in his eyes, a determination marked by a strong, even dangerous sense of righteousness. She saw with perfect clarity that the good-old-boy thing was just an act, that he hadn't really come about the poker game, and it had all been leading to this moment. Les had wanted to confront her about her attendance at Quality-Mart. Her heart began to speed up and she felt irrationally afraid, as if Les really could take her off and lock her up and no one would ever come to her rescue.

She was, after all, the outsider.

"What difference does it make?" she asked him.

"No difference," he said. "It just struck me as odd."

"Why? There were a lot of people at Quality-Mart. A lot of people from the church, too. Inez Milton, for one."

"It's not a big deal," Les said, grinning.

"It is to me. It's a very big deal to be harassed by the cops because I went shopping."

"I don't think you can call this harassment, Lydia."

She stared at him. His grin never faded. He was making fun of her. She saw in that moment how much he disliked her, and it rattled her. She crossed her arms. She swallowed, trying to conquer the lump in her throat. And then the anger came, hard and familiar.

"Oh, really, Les? Well, let's see. You walked into my house, failing to identify yourself as a police officer, under the pretense of inviting my husband to a poker game. Gambling is illegal in this county, is it not? You then began to interrogate me without my consent and without identifying just cause for said interrogation. You made speculations against members of my family without justification, and now you're making, I believe, some kind of implication about my attendance at Quality-Mart? Should I call an attorney before this goes any further?"

"Lydia, we don't operate like that around here. You see me all the time at Fawley Square. You really need me to pull out my badge and show you that I'm a cop?"

"Let me explain something to you, Les. I'm going to be late for work because I took the time to talk to you. I hate to be late for work. And I hate that the reason you're here to talk to me is because you're working off the names on a blacklist recorded by someone whose sense of rectitude is only exceeded by her taste for eighty-proof vodka. So when you're ready to treat this as the serious situation that it is, and approach me on a professional basis—you know, with specific leads, that kind of thing—then I'll be happy to answer any and all of your questions. Okay?"

Les shook his head, his smile still in place. "You'll excuse me if I can't get all impressed by your legal mumbo jumbo. I know you're educated and all, but I've got a job to do. Like finding the murderer of two innocent people."

"Oh, *innocent* people," she said. "That's a different story. Now, how did a couple of Quality-Mart employees get to be innocent, when just a day ago they were considered to be evil?"

Les ignored that. He went out the door, letting it slam behind him, walking with a full head of steam. Lydia followed him and he increased his pace, as if she might be pursuing him. When he was standing next to his police car, which obviously gave him a sense of security, Les said, "You never have caught on, have you? You haven't figured out how we live around here."

"Oh, I'm starting to, Les."

"I'll be back," he said.

"I'm not going anywhere," she answered, and the sound of it made her feel trapped.

He drove away and she stared again at the remnants of her coffee, feeling petty in her triumph. Why did she constantly take these people on, as if there were any doubt who would win? Graham Mundy was a prime example. Did humiliating people with less advantage enrich her life?

"An easy victory is not worth having," her father always claimed. "A lopsided win diminishes both parties. Always remember that, Lydia."

"But I disagree, Daddy," she'd said, because Camille was standing nearby. "Any victory is worth having, and the easier the better."

Camille had laughed, that cool, lusty laugh that, once she'd evoked it, made Lydia feel smart. And it scared her to think that somewhere in her every intention, there still lurked the desire to make Camille laugh.

But there was more to it. There was that look in Les's eyes, the naked contempt, for no reason she could imagine except that she did not belong. She was not one of them. Suddenly, being the outsider was not so amusing. And suddenly, she realized she knew nothing about these people, about how deep their convictions ran, and what they might do to defend them.

11

W HEN SALLY SAW the news about the two dead men on TV, her first, unfiltered thought was, "Well, at least they distinguished themselves."

She immediately felt bad about that. She then tried to put herself in the place of the families, to imagine what it would feel like if it were Danny or Rex or Nelson lying dead in a parking lot. She couldn't picture it. She tried to hate the killer, but that was hard too, not knowing who it was. She just kept seeing Tom Fitzgerald, the man who shot Pike.

The newscasters told all about the victims: their goals, their achievements, their hobbies, the churches they belonged to. The old security guard had been the horseshoe champion of the county two years in a row. The assistant manager had been a decorated Eagle Scout. Their accomplishments were small, but on TV they sounded very important. And then Sally wondered what anyone would have to say about her if she ever got murdered.

Sally Crane was Nelson Crane's wife, Daniel and Rex's mother. She was Ruth and Samuel Hines's daughter, several people's cousin, innumerable people's friend. It bothered her that she could not be defined outside her associations with others. She had fantasies about creating her own identity. When she watched *Oprah,* she imagined herself as a guest on her show. It was hard to imagine what the topic might be. "Women who've given everything to their families." "Women who fear they might die without making a mark." "Women who wonder what the point of life is." She'd never seen such topics discussed on *Oprah,* so she was sure they weren't pertinent to the human condition. Still, it did not stop her from imagining what she might say.

"Well, Oprah, I got married at nineteen and had two boys. I put all my energy into raising them. My oldest son, Danny, is married, but he and his wife don't come over as often as they should, and they aren't even thinking about children. Rex, my youngest, is more problematic. He doesn't seem to want to leave home. Don't get me wrong, I love having him. But I'd like him to have a life of his own, too. I keep thinking, did I do something wrong? He had meningitis as a child, and maybe I over-protected him."

"What is it you're really worried about, Sally?" Oprah would ask in that caring but incisive way.

"Well, I'd just like to know that I've done something important."

"Don't you think your children are important?"

"Well, of course they are," she'd say because she would be on national television and all her relatives would be watching. But the truth was that she wasn't at all sure her children were important. They had not made any particular mark. They had not even achieved the most ordinary goals, like supplying her with grandchildren. She could see how Beethoven's mother, or Steven Spielberg's mother, might say they were worth all the idiosyncrasies and worry, but she had yet to see any remarkable fruits of her labor. The most she could say was that she had kept them alive—the most basic requirement of a parent.

"Well, that's something," Oprah might say, placing a caring hand on her shoulder.

"Then there's the other matter with Danny," Sally would say, feeling more relaxed. "We all thought he'd be something big. He was so tall and handsome, such a good athlete. And smart? He could say the alphabet backward when he was six. And he could add huge sums without a pencil and paper. He went off to college and got a degree, and he played semipro baseball for a while, then came back home and went to work for Mecklin, which is a big commercial contracting business."

"Yes, I've heard of it," Oprah would say. (This *was* Sally's fantasy, after all.)

"Well, he was being groomed to take over the business, but he's still just a sales manager. Which is a shirt-and-tie job and I shouldn't complain in these hard times. But we all just expected him to do more. I mean, we thought he was going to be famous. A star ballplayer, like Cal Ripkin Jr. or somebody. We thought we'd be reading about him in the news. Now he's just like anybody else. Which is fine for an ordinary person, but Danny was never ordinary."

At this point Oprah would have to take a question from the audience. A thin young woman with short hair, wearing a sleek business suit and bold earrings (looking not unlike her daughter-in-law, Lydia) would say, "Mrs. Crane, is this really about wanting your son to do more? Or is it about wishing you had done more?"

Sally had trouble getting past that question. Oprah announced a commercial break and never did come back.

Whenever that question surfaced in the audience, and it always did, Sally went numb and wanted to end the program. It reminded her of a segment she had seen once several months back when one of those New Age feminists who'd written a book about why women were so unhappy in the modern world had said, "The whole conflict between men and women stems from the simplest lesson we all learn as soon as we can understand language: men make things happen; women wait for things to happen to them."

She went on to illustrate this idea by way of countless fairy tales.

"Take 'Snow White,' for example. The child is run out of town and nearly killed because of the inescapable fact of her own beauty. She then moves in with seven men—seven short men, which in societal terms, makes them eunuchs—and starts cleaning up after them. She talks to the animals and cleans and cooks. But most of all she waits. What does she wait for? Some tall prince she's glimpsed once in her life. But her waiting pays off. Even in death this man finds her and brings her back to life.

"And then there's Cinderella. She lives in this terrible matriarchy and when the ball comes around, the women are all painted as crass and evil because they actually *do* something. They get ready for the ball. Cinderella's dress is made for her by her animal friends. Note that a good woman is always able to communicate with animals. So her dress is torn to shreds by her sisters and Cinderella boo-hoos and waits until a fairy godmother shows up and makes her another dress. I mean, how many dresses does this woman get?"

At this point the audience had hooted with laughter and Sally had sat still in her chair, clutching the remote control, confused and riveted.

"So she goes to the ball and without doing much of anything, gets the prince. Then she loses him, and the glass slipper, and she waits until he comes around again and finds her. But Cinderella was at least the most active of the bunch. At least she *went* to the ball. Which compared to Sleeping Beauty is a great feat. Sleeping Beauty literally sleeps until something spectacular happens to her."

It had been a lively audience, and the applause was met with equal indignation from women who swore that the fairy tales were harmless and enchanting and had not ruined their lives at all. Sally had sat there watching the whole charade, wondering where she stood on this issue, and could not come up with an answer. They were just stories, after all. She'd never believed them for a minute. But looking back over her life, she could see she'd done an excessive amount of waiting. Even as she watched the show she was waiting. Waiting for her husband to come home and rescue her from the boredom, from the ridiculous turn her life seemed to take whenever he stepped out the door.

Despite her fantasies, Sally still felt she had a grip on things until the Quality-Mart murders happened. Long after she heard the news, she had to stop and wonder if it were real or something she'd seen on an afternoon talk show. Even after she'd fully digested the fact that it had happened to her (or at least to her community) she couldn't escape the feeling that any minute, talk show producers would be on her doorstep, wanting to gather details for an upcoming episode. In fact, in the days following the murders, Sally felt oddly happy and hopeful. It was a change; it was special. Maybe her life wasn't going to be a slow decline, lived out in her armchair. Maybe something was going to happen to her.

She recalled feeling the same way when Pike died. She did feel upset, because she liked him, but buried underneath was some hope that this might be a catalyst, the moment when her life would take a sharp turn and go somewhere else altogether. It didn't happen. In fact, things had gone drastically downhill since Pike's death. Nelson had been so devastated by it, he'd thrown himself into his work, coming home later and later every night, and he never felt like going out or taking trips (not that there was anywhere to go). He'd all but abandoned his gardening, which used to be his favorite hobby. His once thriving garden now consisted of a few tomato plants and some sprigs of mint.

The Quality-Mart murders had nowhere near the same effect on Nelson. He didn't even seem to care very much. He clucked his tongue when he watched the news, shaking his head in that solemn way he had. But he didn't have much to say on the subject. Nelson had been indifferent to Quality-Mart from the beginning.

Some people did not regard the murders as bad news at all. They felt vindicated to the point of gleefulness. People in her own church (of which she was still a member but never felt the energy to attend lately) seemed to have gotten a second wind from it all. The night the news broke there was a vigil in the fellowship hall, which she'd heard was more like a party, with lively chatter and plenty of rich desserts. Martha Dawson was on the local news, smiling a calm and almost beatific smile at the reporter. "Well, it's what we all expected," she said into the microphone. "We didn't expect it so *soon,*" she added, as if this were a nice little bonus.

The mother of the assistant manager came on TV, in her sweat suit, with matted hair, chapped lips, and swollen eyes. She said, "Graham never hurt a soul in his life. Why would anyone want to kill him?"

Sally wasn't the only one who questioned why the woman couldn't have put herself together a little better. A touch of lipstick and a comb through the hair would have made all the difference. Everyone knew she was the wife of Charlie Mundy, the big Cadillac dealer. Were they expected to believe she didn't have anything in her closet, or was her lack of concern for her appearance supposed to accentuate her grief? Sally had no idea what she would do under those circumstances, but she thought she might try to dress herself up better out of respect for Danny. (It was only Danny who ever died in her fearful imagination. Rex had already defied death, so she figured he was safe.)

They even interviewed the assistant manager's ex-fiancée. She was a small, mousy-looking girl with dyed black hair and big blue eyes, which were red-rimmed from crying. She talked all about how brilliant Graham was, how kind he was, how he was the gentlest soul on earth. If he was so wonderful, Sally thought, how come she was his ex-fiancée instead of his wife? She knew it wasn't entirely fair to place value judgments on dead people, but it struck her as odd how flawless people became once they died. When they were alive, they were just like anybody else—basically good, but chock-full of annoying little habits. It was the same way with Pike. He turned into a saint once he died, but Sally couldn't help remembering how cold he was to his daughters and how easy he was on Kyle. All of that was conveniently forgotten the minute his heart stopped beating.

But what good did it do to think of these things? She ought to just let it all go and feel sorry for the victims. That's what Oprah would do, after all.

The day after the murders, Danny and Lydia showed up for dinner. Danny looked tired and too thin. Lydia always looked that way, so there was little to notice about her. The only indication that her life had been interrupted was the absence of earrings, which always seemed to dangle around her chin. She still wore that strange makeup, a pale powder and dark red lipstick, which had the effect of making her look like she was made out of porcelain, like one of those keepsake dolls always being auctioned on the QVC channel. Her hair was another mystery. Blunt cut and stick straight, it always seemed too long in the front, dangling in her eyes. The rest was shorn off at the nape of the neck. It seemed to Sally that Lydia only wanted hair where it was least practical.

Sally had once tried not to be so critical of Lydia. Danny was clearly devoted to her, and she did come from one of the finest families in Virginia—the Hunts of Fairfax County. Buildings were named after them. Lydia had gone to all the best schools and vacationed in Europe. But after spending some time in Lydia's company, and hearing about her crazy parents (disowning their own child, no less), Sally decided that rich people really didn't have any more sense than the rest of the population.

Rex set aside his models for the day and came down to have dinner. Sally noticed, with a vague sense of discomfort, that her son was too well dressed. She knew that it was odd for a mother to complain about her son's attention to hygiene and fashion. In fact, most mothers had the opposite complaint, and she experienced her share of that concern with Danny. He had liked to wear ripped jeans in high school, still didn't shave on weekends, and his hair always looked slightly uncombed. But she realized, now that Rex was in full-blown manhood, that she sorely missed those complaints. The untidiness, the disregard for his appearance was directly tied in to Danny's masculinity. Her carping at him had been an exercise, a thing that a mother was supposed to do, even though she never expected a normal man to change his habits at the behest of his mother. There was something oddly disconcerting about a man who put on a shirt and tie for Sunday lunch, who insisted on wearing French cuffs with pearl-inlaid cuff links at a casual meal, who shaved incessantly, al-

ways smelled like the cosmetic section of a department store, and dried
his hair with a blow-dryer and a styling brush. (She'd once found hairspray in his bathroom cabinet. It was men's hairspray, at least—she tried
to count her blessings.)

Rex spent a great amount of his limited income on clothes, which
might have made more sense if he ever went out, or if all these efforts
were an attempt to impress women. But Rex had no social life to speak
of. These concerns seemed to go deeper; his fashion sense seemed directly related to his own personal belief system. As it was Sally found
herself unnerved by a young man who understood designer labels.
("Calvin Klein is showing seersucker for spring," he declared recently.
"You've got to admit that's chancy.") He claimed that anything but cotton or silk irritated his skin. "One day, Mother," he repeatedly told her, "I
will get you to understand the importance of natural fabrics." It was
Sally's opinion that a man should not even understand the concept of natural fabrics, let alone place a value on it. But she knew, too, that this was
a problem that Oprah or anyone else with a psychological background
would not have any sympathy for. This was Sally's problem and she tried
hard to overcome it.

Rex immediately positioned himself beside Lydia. He seemed fascinated by the girl, and that always gave Sally some hope. He couldn't possibly be *so* odd, given how drawn he was to Lydia. He sat right up under
her and stared at her, taking note of her every move. When Lydia let a
tiny piece of salad fall off her fork, Rex descended on her lap with a napkin, wiping vigorously at a stain on her skirt.

"That's linen, isn't it? It'll stain like the dickens," he cautioned. "Don't
dare wash it, it'll shrink to high heaven. Do you have Woolite?"

Lydia said she did. Rex was a little too relieved.

"Well, I suppose that's the end of Quality-Mart," Nel said as they
worked on the dry meat loaf (Danny liked it that way) and mashed potatoes. "I can't say I'm sorry to see it go. Even though they did advertise
some good prices on the Weed-Eater. I've been meaning to get a Weed-
Eater. Now I guess I never will."

"You can order them from a catalogue," Danny said. But Nelson just
shrugged, as if that required a monumental effort.

"Those poor mothers," Sally said. "That's all I can think about. Their
babies killed, for how much money did they say, Nellie?"

"Two thousand dollars. Wasn't much."

"The security guard was in his sixties, Mother," Rex said, stifling a yawn.

"I don't care, he's still somebody's baby. Or father. He mattered somewhere to somebody," Sally said passionately, as if the issue of the guard's self-worth had been challenged.

"I wonder if they have any suspects," Danny said.

"All they know is it was a black man," Sally said.

Lydia looked at her, pressing her ruddy lips together. Oh, here it comes, thought Sally.

"Who said that?" Lydia asked.

"I read it in the paper. There was an eyewitness."

"To the murders?"

Sally nodded. "Somebody lived across the road."

"Oh, and from across the road in the middle of the night, they could see it was a black man?"

"They saw his car," Sally said, struggling to be patient.

At this Lydia actually threw her head back and laughed. Rex smiled, chewing on his napkin, a nervous habit. Sally wanted to swat at him, but she was too afraid of what Lydia would say. A very unpredictable girl was her daughter-in-law.

"Please, tell me what a black man's car looks like," Lydia said, catching her breath.

Danny, who was staring hard at his plate, mumbled, "They do tend to drive similar cars."

At this Lydia's jaw literally dropped, and Sally was actually a little surprised herself. Danny would usually stand by Lydia if she said the moon was cheese.

"You must be joking."

Danny said, "Look, the cops are grasping at straws. I guess they'll take any lead. You can't blame them for that."

"Uh-huh. And if someone said the car looked just like a white man's, you think they'd be running every white name on the computer and rounding up every white guy off the street?"

"What makes you think they're doing that?" Danny asked. "You think the cops are out persecuting all the blacks in town? It doesn't happen like that."

"It doesn't? What if a white guy had shot Kyle? Would Pike have chased every white person in town off the road?"

There was a gasp. It took Sally a few seconds to realize it had come from Nel. Nel wasn't the gasping type. He was sitting as still as a rock, as if he'd succumbed to a rigid faint.

Lydia actually turned red in the face—Sally had no idea it was possible for her daughter-in-law to blush.

"I'm sorry, that was an insensitive thing to say," Lydia said in a calm, even voice.

"It was true, though," Rex said.

"But a white man didn't shoot Kyle," Sally said. She could see that Lydia wanted to come back with some uppity remark, but she didn't dare. Her quick tongue had cost her her courage.

"Let's just drop it," Danny said.

They struggled through their dinner for a few tense moments until Lydia excused herself and went to the bathroom.

"Look, Lydia has strong opinions," Danny said, attempting to put forth an explanation.

Nellie nodded, saying, "People from D.C. have a whole different idea about blacks."

Danny pushed his plate away, much of his food still untouched. Sally glanced at her son's plate and worried. There wasn't much that could get in the way of Danny and his appetite. Maybe he was starting to see that his wife wasn't the right partner for him. Sally did not like the idea of divorce, but better that than a lifetime of unhappiness. Danny was young. He could start over.

"Anybody seen Kyle around?" Danny suddenly asked, his fingers drumming quietly on the tablecloth.

"Would anybody want to?" Rex questioned.

Sally said, "What made you think of Kyle?"

He shrugged. "I was just wondering about him."

Nel said, "If Pike could see what the boy has become, he'd be heartbroken. He'd never get over it."

Sally said nothing. She bit her tongue to keep from speaking the truth. Pike would never be able to see any bad in Kyle. If he came back tomorrow, he would think Kyle was just fine.

Lydia returned. Her cheeks were pinker than when she left, and her lips were outlined and colored, a deep, solemn red.

"Feel better, honey?" Sally asked.

Lydia nodded and looked as if she wanted to say something else. Before she could, Sally jumped up and went for the lemon chess pie she'd made that morning between phone calls about the murders. Despite the distractions, the crust had come out perfect.

That night there were snow flurries. A cold front had moved in unexpectedly, dashing everyone's hopes for an early spring. Sally decided to walk down to Rita's house to make sure she and the girls were okay. She was afraid Rita had turned off her gas too soon, like many people in town. Sally pictured poor, frail Rita shivering away in that badly insulated farmhouse, her daughters hovering around her like kittens in an oversized litter, fighting for warmth. Nel neither discouraged her from going nor volunteered to go with her. She left him sitting in front of CNN, writing checks for bills that should have been paid weeks ago.

Sally and Nel didn't talk much anymore, and it worried her. She wondered if they'd run out of things to say to each other. Or maybe they'd never had much to say, but the boys provided a distraction. Sometimes she could pull Nel into a conversation about Danny. That was, after all, his favorite subject. They would sometimes talk about his days as a baseball player. Nel was crushed when Danny dropped out and didn't go on to the big leagues. But, as always with his eldest son, he made excuses. Put the best face on things. "It's just as well," he'd said at the time. "Pro ball's a hard life. High divorce rate. Drugs. You name it. He'll probably have a better life right here in Fawley."

But sometimes, late at night, she would come into the den and find him flipping through Danny's scrapbooks, stuck on the baseball pages, just sitting there staring.

About Rex, Nel said very little. Sometimes Sally caught him observing his younger son with a look of benign curiosity, as if he were watching a zoo animal. Even in the days when they thought Rex was dying, Nel watched him with the same sort of detached concern. If Rex had died back then, Sally suspected that Nel would have accepted it without much anger, as if Rex had always been some sort of aberration of nature, and his existence on the planet had always been questionable. Sometimes, even now, she felt Nel looking at Rex as if he were a comet which had somehow survived the ozone layer and now deposited himself on earth, an unwanted reminder of all the forces beyond their control.

Nel liked control. He disliked surprises, any sort of change. The two of them still lived in the house where Sally had grown up. Her father had left it to her in his will. Nel balked at the idea at first—there seemed something unmanly about living in the woman's house. But it was nicer than anything they could afford in those days, and the farmland was rich and fertile. Not that Nel was a farmer, but he did enjoy gardening. Furthermore, Pike and Rita lived on the neighboring farm. Nel loved the idea of being right next door to his brother. He thought it would be good for Danny to have his cousin Kyle close by. So a few months before Rex was born, they moved in and stayed.

There was only one house separating theirs from Rita's. It was a tiny little clapboard house situated between the open stretches of farmland. She knew it used to be the slaves' quarters back in her great-grandparents' day, and later, when she was growing up, it belonged to the sharecroppers, the Perkinses. Ernest Perkins was a little boy her age and they played together until the age when it became inappropriate. When Sally was in the fifth grade, Ernest died of the flu. It just took him overnight, so the rumor went. Sally's own mother had argued that Ernest's parents hadn't fought too hard to keep him. They had eleven children, and they could use one less mouth to feed. Looking back, Sally sometimes realized that the things her mother said were not particularly nice. Everyone credited her for being candid, but Sally was still haunted by the image of Ernest wasting away in his bed while his parents went on about their business.

She saw that image again when Rex got sick. She spent every night at the hospital with him, for fear that if she didn't she'd be as bad as old Mrs. Perkins, letting her son go out of lack of concern. Even now she sometimes thought it was her constant vigil that had kept him alive.

She saw the image of Ernest again when Kyle nearly died that time. Kyle had nearly died a dozen times, but the one she remembered most clearly was the car wreck five winters ago when he lost his leg. She remembered how Rita had acted in the emergency room. The way she almost seemed willing to let him go. No, not willing—hoping.

Sally walked quickly past the old Perkins place, trying not to look at it. She knew that it had been converted into a cute little two-bedroom home. She knew that the Murphys lived there now, that young couple who moved over from Roanoke. He worked at the Goodyear place, and the wife was a cashier at the Food Lion. Normal people living normal lives. But to her, the ghost of Ernest Perkins persisted, and she never failed to see his starved and lonely face at the window.

As soon as Sally stepped into Rita's house, she realized her concern for their welfare had been more than unwarranted—it was downright silly. The house felt like a Turkish sauna. In fact, Rita was wearing a short-sleeved cotton housedress and terrycloth scuffs. Her three daughters were similarly dressed, huddled around a raging fire in the fireplace, working on a jigsaw puzzle.

"No, I've got the furnace turned up high as it will go," Rita said as Sally began to shed layers of clothing. "Pike always warned me against turning off the gas too soon. He said the temperature can drop out of nowhere and the pipes will freeze, and then you've got real trouble."

Rita applied this borrowed philosophy to almost everything. She asked Nel or Danny to change the oil in her car at least once a month. If they dared to suggest she was being overcautious, she'd say, "Okay, let the oil get low and the engine seize up and crack. Then you've got real money troubles."

Rita spent a large amount of her limited income trying to avoid real money troubles. But Sally couldn't imagine what Rita might do with her money if she didn't spend it in an attempt to avoid disaster. It wasn't like she was going to treat herself to anything.

"How are you girls doing?" Sally asked. She sometimes had trouble keeping her nieces' names straight. Joyce was not a problem—she was the one with the scar, the eldest, the one who'd moved out of the house. She was also the only one who resembled Pike. She and Kyle had inherited Pike's sharp nose, hollow cheeks, ash blond hair, and thin top lip. The rest of the girls looked like Rita must have done in her various stages of development. Dark, moon-faced, suspicious and afraid, bordering on beauty but succumbing to that bland midwestern look. Rita's family was from Iowa. How any of them ended up out here was still something of a mystery. Rita never talked about her family. It was as if she didn't have a history until she met Pike.

The remaining girls were called Rosalie, Imogen, and Lucy. Immy, the one with the ugliest name, happened to be the prettiest, but when their heads were bowed and their faces obscured by shadows, Sally felt incapable of picking her out.

"We're fine," one of them answered without looking up from her efforts.

Sally sat on the couch and accepted a cup of coffee gratefully. It was less than a half mile walk to Rita's house, but on a night like this, fraught with cold and distant tragedy, it had felt like quite a journey. The coffee was fresh brewed from a percolator that always seemed to be warming on the stove. Rita was never without coffee. Why had she worried about her? Sally wondered. In her own peculiar way, Rita seemed to have a much better handle on life and its capricious nature than she or Nelson did.

Two sips into the coffee Sally realized she had not come down here to comfort Rita. She had come to comfort herself. There was something strangely appealing about Rita and the girls' cloistered life. Like the stories she'd read as a child of pioneer families, everything seemed complete within this basic example of civilization. What did anyone need beyond family, a fire, good coffee, and a jigsaw puzzle? She thought of Nelson at home scribbling out checks to corporations in distant cities and she thought how disconnected life was, how much of it had become about answering to people they didn't even know.

"How are the boys?" Rita asked, sitting on the couch beside her, wringing her hands. Rita had always wrung her hands, way before Pike was killed. It created a dry, rasping sound, and Sally was surprised there was anything left of those fingers, the way the constant motion seemed to whittle away at the skin.

"They're fine."

"No grandchildren yet?" Rita asked, like someone who hadn't seen her nephews in years. Maybe it had been a few years since Rita had seen Rex. Danny, on the other hand, had a habit of dropping by occasionally to fix things—a leak in the kitchen sink, a screen door that was loose on its hinges. And since Danny was the only one likely to produce grandchildren, the question seemed all the more inappropriate. Did Rita think she could have missed an entire pregnancy and birth?

No, Rita didn't think that, of course. Rita was fishing for gossip. And Sally realized, with a slight start, that she had come down here seeking the same thing. Rita was more of a slave to the television than either she or Nelson, and if there had been a break in the Quality-Mart murders, Rita would know.

"No, no grandchildren," Sally said. "That daughter-in-law of mine is so liberal. She probably doesn't believe in babies. Probably thinks they're unconstitutional. Only way Danny will get her pregnant is to hit her over the head with a rock first."

At this the girls giggled and Sally felt proud of herself for eliciting any sort of response.

"Sally, you're going straight to hell," Rita said with an interested smile.

"No, I mean it. I got a lecture from her tonight from something I said. I heard the murder suspect they were looking for was black and she just flew right off the handle and all but called me a racist."

"He was black," one of the girls spoke up. "That's been confirmed."

Rita nodded. "It came on the news. They're close to arresting somebody. But who's surprised by that? What does Lydia think, that black people aren't capable of that kind of thing? Just remind her of what happened to Pike."

Sally just nodded. It would have killed Rita to hear what Lydia had said about Pike's murder. Some things were better left unspoken.

Borrowing from Nelson's philosophy, Sally said, "People from D.C. don't think like we do. I guess they get all this liberalism bred into them. Her father is some kind of liberal lawyer up North. She can't help herself, really."

"She's pretty, at least," one of the girls said.

"Lydia? She looks like one of those dolls on the home shopping network. I sometimes feel like pinching her to see if she's alive," Sally said.

The girls giggled, and even Rita smiled. In spite of her desire to criticize Lydia, it made Sally feel good to know her family thought her daughter-in-law was pretty. What would Danny be thinking of to marry an ugly girl, with all his looks and promise?

"There's no accounting for taste," Rita said. "Pike always said, pretty is as pretty does."

"She doesn't do pretty, that's for sure. She doesn't know I know this, but she was at the Quality-Mart opening day. A friend of Martha Dawson told me."

"She's got original ideas," Rita said by way of an explanation. "Danny could have done a lot worse. At least he's got somebody."

Sally took this as a veiled criticism of Rex and was trying to think of a way to respond when there was the sound of a car pulling up in the graveled driveway.

"Is that Nellie?" Rita asked nervously.

"I wouldn't think so."

The girls all looked up as Rita hurried to the window. Rita stood very still, watching. Finally she let the curtains drop and said, "It's Kyle again."

The girls all panicked at once. One of them stood abruptly, knocking a few pieces of the puzzle onto the floor.

"Mama, you don't have to let him in, do you?"

"He won't want to come in. He never does." Turning to Sally, she said, "He does this. Parks in front of the house and just sits there looking at it. Sometimes he stays all night but he never does get out."

"Well, what on earth is he up to?" Sally questioned.

"Since when does anybody know what Kyle is up to? Ever since Pike died he's been like a tornado. No way of knowing which direction he'll go."

Sally pulled the curtain back. "Rita, he's getting out. And there's somebody with him."

"Mama, please, don't let him in. Say it's too late."

Rita stood rooted to the ground, wringing her hands at an accelerated pace. "Sally, can you tell him we're going to bed?"

"Rita, I can't lie for you."

"We are going to bed!" Immy announced. She headed off down the hallway, and the other two followed like ducks in a row.

The doorbell rang and rang. Sally and Rita stood looking at each other until finally the door opened and Kyle poked his head in.

Sally looked at his boyish face, the sad eyes and the stringy hair, the thin mustache clinging to his top lip, and she wondered how the family had managed to turn him into such a monster. Then she had a terrible thought. She thought she would rather have Kyle as a son than Rex. At least Kyle had the nerve and the energy to be mischievous. Having a troublemaker for a son would be so much easier to explain than this curious figure who seemed to have checked into her home like a guest at a luxury hotel. She would not have to make excuses for Kyle. She would simply bemoan her plight, throw her hands up in exasperation and say, "I can't do anything with him." That was a fairly common, almost boastful, complaint among mothers. Rex was another matter. She constantly felt the need to explain him and the effort to do so was wearing her out.

"Mama, you still up?" Kyle asked.

"Why, yes, honey," Rita said in a shaky voice. "Come on in out of the cold."

They both stood frozen in place as Kyle walked in, pulling a girl by the hand. She was young and thin and pale, straight dark hair falling around her face, wearing bell-bottom jeans and clogs and a peacoat. At first glance, Sally thought she was a teenager. But as they both walked into the light, she could see that the girl was at least as old as Kyle, possibly older.

There was another thing. What a relief it would be to see Rex dragging a woman into the house. How happy she would be to worry about Rex getting some woman into trouble. How she longed to give him lectures about birth control. But warning Rex about unwanted pregnancies seemed about as sensible as warning an Eskimo about sunstroke.

"Y'all burning the midnight oil?" Kyle asked. "Hey, Aunt Sally. What are you doing here?"

"Checking on your mother."

"Why? She having wild parties again?" Looking at the unfinished puzzle, he asked, "Where are the peahens?"

"They were tired, I reckon," Rita said nervously. "Y'all take off your coats and stay awhile."

"Hell, I feel like taking everything off in this damn place. No wonder everybody's so skinny in this family. Sit in here and sweat off a whole person," Kyle said. His words were lazy, slurred. He was probably drunk, though Kyle was usually a lot more animated and jerky when he had too much liquor in him.

The girl stood beside him, stonelike, staring at her feet. There was a weird half-smile on her lips, like she was remembering a joke someone had recently told her.

"Mama," Kyle said, after he'd thrown his coat onto the couch. "I want you to meet Amanda Jean Pierce, the woman who changed my life."

Amanda glanced up then, her cool eyes connecting with Rita's.

"Well, if anybody's life needed changing, it was yours," Sally said abruptly, unreasonably. She was not trying to criticize Kyle. She was, in fact, trying to make him laugh. She succeeded. Kyle threw his head back and Amanda's smirk grew into a full smile. She looked pretty when she smiled, even though something about her remained vacant and fragile.

Kyle said, "This here is Danny's mother. Now you see where Danny gets his wit."

Amanda's eyes fell on Sally, who felt exposed by them. Just looking into them made her feel empty, as if this strange girl had the power to drain something out of her. The eyes were a remarkable color, a dirty gray, like rainwater. Sally felt funny about eyes that did not take on a definite color—sharp blue or glassy green or deep brown. Eyes like Amanda's always seemed in between strong shades. It made her feel that the person was not complete, had not finished forming. Amanda's eyes were open to interpretation, making her seem unpredictable and dangerous.

This was a ludicrous notion, since Amanda with her slight form and taut smile was clearly incapable of hurting anyone.

"I've met Danny," Amanda said.

"Oh, really? Well, Danny has a way of getting around," Sally said.

"He's the only person Kyle truly loves."

If Rita had a reaction to this, it appeared only to be one of relief, perhaps reassured by the notion that Kyle could love anyone.

"Have y'all eaten?" Rita asked. "We've got some leftovers."

"I don't want any leftovers," Kyle said. "But I'll tell you something, it just skins my hide to think I've got something to celebrate, and nobody in town knows what it is."

Sally quickly dismissed the idea that it could be Kyle's birthday. His was July 12, exactly a month later than Danny's. Maybe he was about to announce his engagement. She wasn't sure how that news would be greeted. Sally looked to Rita, who only stared at Kyle with the temptation of a false smile perched at the edge of her lips.

"What is it, honey?" she asked with a tremor in her voice.

"My first kill."

They just stared at him, afraid to ask.

He said, "Exactly twenty-four years ago today I shot my first deer."

Rita shook her head. "No, honey. You couldn't have. It's not deer season."

"Mama, it don't have to be deer season to shoot a deer."

"Well, I remember your first kill and that was definitely well within season."

"Maybe it was the first kill Daddy told you about. But he took me out when I was ten just to practice. I had a doe in my sights and I just pulled the trigger. Clean shot to the head."

"A doe?" Rita gasped. "Kyle, for goodness sake, it's a crime to shoot a doe even in season. I don't believe a word of this."

"Don't worry, Daddy gave me a walloping. We took her out and buried her in a shallow grave. But he never did tell you, and for all his yelling at me, I knew he wasn't too mad. He was pretty impressed with it. One shot, the deer was down. And it was my first time out."

"I just don't think that's anything to be proud of," Rita said, wringing her hands, the raspy sound filling the room.

"Here's what y'all peahens don't get," Kyle went on, sounding drunker now. Sally could see the outline of a flask inside his coat pocket. "A man appreciates the killer instinct. Daddy might have given my backside a strapping, but deep down he was proud that I could do what had to be done. He was proud that I wouldn't back away from the challenge. And when he died, all the courage in this family went with it. Hell, he'd cry his eyes out if he could see what y'all have turned into. If he knew he'd left behind a whole brood of scared women, he'd just take a running jump off a cliff."

"That's enough, Kyle," Sally said.

"Danny's got it," he said, rounding on her. "He's got the courage, but he fights it. Love has gone and turned him soft. But not me. I found myself a woman who's got more courage than I do. And I'll never leave this bitch because she puts me in my place."

Amanda tucked a strand of hair behind her ear, remarkably unaffected for someone who'd just been referred to as a bitch.

"Let me fix you something to eat," Rita said, which was her answer to any conflict.

"We ain't hungry, Mama."

To everyone's surprise, Amanda said, "What have you got?"

"Some leftover chicken, black-eyed peas, and applesauce."

"I'd like some peas," Amanda said, moving away from Kyle.

"It'll only take me a second to heat them up," Rita said, heading toward the kitchen.

"No, Mama. She don't need anything. She eats like a pig."

"Well, it must be a runt pig then 'cause she's no bigger than a minute."

"We didn't come here to eat no damn food. We came here to say this was the anniversary of my first kill."

"Black-eyed peas are good luck," Amanda said quietly.

"We don't need no luck. We got all the luck we can use."

Suddenly and solemnly, Amanda bowed her head and began to cry. Sally and Rita stared at her, too stunned to respond. Kyle whipped an arm around her.

"There you've gone and done it. Amanda's sensitive, and she's shy. Here you thought I'd never meet anybody, Mama, and I've gone and found myself a woman who's shy and sensitive. What do you make of that?"

"I make that she's hungry, Kyle, and you ought to let her eat."

"I can feed her on my own. All my life you tried to tell me I couldn't do nothing. Well, this I can do. I can take care of my woman. Say good night now."

Amanda was still sniffling when she went out. Kyle paused in the doorway and turned to them, grinning.

"Hey, what do y'all think about this Quality-Mart murderer? He sure grabbed the headlines, didn't he?"

"I think he's a sick individual," Sally said.

"Well, I'd like to shake his hand. That assistant manager he shot? Turned me down for a job. If you ask me, he got what was coming."

"Oh, Kyle," Rita said, shaking her head. "Don't say that."

"Too late. Not taking it back, either. Good night now. Sweet dreams."

And he was gone. Rita and Sally stood in silence as the car outside started up and spit gravel until it squealed across the blacktop.

"What did I do to deserve him?" Rita asked.

"He's just running his mouth," Sally answered. "He's not as bad as all that."

Rita seemed to cool right before her eyes. Too late, Sally remembered the warning that her husband had issued many years back, right after Pike had died. Nellie had said, "If you want to be friends with Rita, commiserate. When you start to cheer her up, put the best face on things, you lose her. Her grief is her badge, and she'll fight you for it."

Rita thanked Sally for coming, her tone now hard and distant, implying she did not appreciate it at all.

Sally's walk home seemed longer and colder than it had before, and part of its chill lay in the realization that she was in no hurry to get where she was going. Rita's life seemed preferable to her own, full of need and mystery and unanswered questions. The only questions left in her life were those whose answers were unworthy of the suspense. She longed for some element of surprise.

She even envied Rita's nerves and jitters, envied the fact that Rita would spend this night and many more surrounded by her daughters, waiting for the next unhappy surprise. How curious, Sally thought as she walked past the Perkins house and tried to peer inside through the thin sheers on the windows. How odd that we spend our lives trying to avoid surprise, trying to get everything to fall in line. Only to discover that the thing that kept us interested in life was the "what next." She felt, sadly, that her life had straightened out like the road before her, and there would be no more unexpected turns.

12

AFTER THE MURDERS, everything at Fawley High School changed. Nigel suddenly invoked several random emergency measures, such as a mandatory dress code for the boys (no bulky jackets, no backpacks, and absolutely no "I Survived Quality-Mart Opening Day" T-shirts). He ordered extra security for the hallways and parking lots. And he called a special devotional assembly in the morning, during which the Reverend John Evans spoke.

Lydia sat in the audience with her colleagues, quietly fuming. John stood up there preaching to the kids about God's vengeance being swift and terrible, how the killer would have his day in the court of man as well as the court of Christ, and so on until Lydia's ears began to ring and her head pounded. Leaning over to Rick Gunther, she whispered, "Has anyone in this county heard of separation of church and state?"

Rick shrugged and said, "I wouldn't bring it up just now."

"Sssh!" Martha Dawson hissed in Lydia's direction.

It was during these wild, off-kilter days that Lydia began to question the turn her life had taken. She felt out of step with everyone around her. She knew the murders were frightening and unnerving; she understood the town's impatience to catch the killers and see justice meted out. Yet it all struck her as unnecessarily harsh, the sense of panic and despair. Shouldn't they be reassuring the kids instead of stirring up their fear?

Her own students were restless and angry, pissed about having to throw themselves back into work after the tragedy. The murders had given the whole school a festive feel, as if it were the day before Christmas vacation and no one could be expected to concentrate. They behaved as if Lydia was being disrespectful, almost cruel, when she launched into her lecture on Thomas Hardy.

"Who can care?" Jenny Mathers, the auburn-tressed head cheerleader questioned, dabbing at her eyes. "I mean, this is horrible and it happened to *us*. It's not some story. It's real."

"Hardy is real, too," Lydia tried to argue. "And maybe his observations of human nature can help us understand our own circumstances."

"But I don't want to understand. I just want it not to have happened. Not here," Jenny said, and she began to cry in earnest. Then the portly, bespectacled Rachel Rivens put her arm around her best friend, patting and shushing her, while glaring at Lydia. Quietly, she waited the moment out. Then she began drawing a map of Hardy's West Country on the board. Behind her she could hear low, angry mumblings. She could feel the looks and the gestures boring into her back.

The mood persisted for days. The more her students resisted, the sterner Lydia became, giving difficult pop quizzes with no bonus questions, and spontaneously assigning research papers that even she was going to live to regret. The last thing she wanted to do was read a dozen lazy pursuits of the fatalistic implications in Victorian literature. Why was she being like this? Should she take the time to comfort her class? She couldn't, because for the life of her, she could not see the connection between these moon-faced children and the dead men. Their sorrow was baffling to her. It was spoiled and indulgent. Why shouldn't tragedy happen in Fawley? Violence was everywhere. These kids never seemed especially concerned, or even aware, that there were two thousand murders a year just four hours up Interstate 29. But two dead on the Greensboro Road and they were stricken with grief. Did they honestly think they were protected? Did they think crime was for other people to worry about?

Lydia knew this was not fair. So she had grown up in a violent city— that did not mean everyone should have to. But she disliked the extreme nature of the reactions around her. Slowly, as she knew it would, the concern became insidious.

Rumors were everywhere. The men had been caught, they were sixteen years old—no, fourteen—and on drugs, of course, and black, certainly, and already they were going to be released on a technicality. The truth was, the investigation wasn't happening. It seemed to have stalled after the announcement that two "young African-American men" were responsible. The newscasters reported it sardonically, with thinly veiled disgust at having to refer to a couple of murderers in politically correct terms. The police seemed to lose interest shortly after. There was nothing surprising about that, nothing challenging, either. It would simply be a matter of harassing every black man under the age of forty from here to Greensboro.

The black kids at school were nervous, Lydia observed. How could they not be? Everyone regarded them a little differently. Did they know something? Were they related to the killers? There were fights in the cafeteria, in the halls, in the gym. No one ever said so, but everyone knew the nature of the disruptions.

Then there was the deification of the victims. Photos of the two dead men were flashed up on the TV screen at regular intervals. Graham Mundy was shown at his high school prom, wearing a badly fitting tuxedo, his ex-fiancée smiling beside him in a mint green gown with a bushy carnation sprouting from her shoulder. The security guard, a grandfather type, was depicted at a family picnic, tossing horseshoes, his stomach bulging over his belt. Couldn't they have found more dignified photos? Lydia wondered.

"They want to capture them in moments of repose," Danny had replied. "It makes them more sympathetic."

"But the victims don't need sympathy. They didn't *do* anything. It's the murderers who need sympathy. Are you telling me an entire Christian community can't figure that out?"

"Take it up with John Evans," Danny had replied.

Danny, Lydia observed, was uncomfortable discussing the murders. Whenever it came up, he got irritable. When it came on the TV, he switched the channel or left the room. She couldn't blame him much for that. She found it harder and harder to watch the news coverage. She was actually repulsed by the outpouring of concern for the dead people's families. She hated seeing the neighbors and friends being interviewed on TV, weeping copiously and declaring what remarkable people they were, how the world would suffer without them. Lydia thought grief should be a personal and private thing, something which had no business being sold on television, wedged between the sports and aspirin commercials. And anyway, this did not look like grief. It was looking more and more like proselytizing.

Lydia had always disliked the superiority of pain. Violent death did not, by itself, elevate the importance of individuals. If anything, it diminished them. It diminished the entire human race each time someone's life ended stupidly. The only remarkable thing about this crime was how unremarkable it was. Two very ordinary, not particularly gifted or significant, people were snuffed out for no particular reason. One newscaster called the victims "heroes." How so? Lydia wondered. She had met Graham Mundy, and there was nothing heroic about him. He was officious and shrill and had an inflated sense of himself. This did not mean he deserved to die, but it certainly did not mean he deserved to be called a hero.

What was even more troubling to Lydia, was how puffed up everyone else became in the wake of the tragedy, as if the deaths had somehow improved the status of every individual in town, given them a new sense of importance, whether or not they were directly related to the victims. Simply by virtue of the fact that they recognized the murders to be a bad thing, they were superior.

"And God help us if they actually bake a casserole or say a prayer or wear a ribbon," Lydia ranted on to her husband, despite his reluctance to discuss it. "Then they want a by-God Nobel Prize. You should see Martha Dawson, strutting around school like some Ursuline nun. She wears black every day. She's in mourning, for God's sake."

"I don't understand why this makes you so mad," Danny shot back at her.

It was past nine in the evening, and she was heating up his dinner in the microwave. He had come home late again, disheveled and distracted. She wanted to say she was focusing on this so she wouldn't have to interrogate him. But that would have defeated the purpose.

"Because, Danny, it scares me when people start feeling righteous. Something bad is always lurking around the corner of virtue."

"Only you could come up with that."

"I'm serious, you watch. They're already baying for blood."

"Who?"

"Everybody. I saw a man-on-the-street interview on the news. Asking ordinary people what they thought should be done to the criminals when they were caught. Hanging, firing squad, electrocution, lethal injection.

Dismemberment got a mention. Oh, Mrs. Pickeral from the bank—the sweet lady who always says 'God bless' after she counts out your money? She said they ought to harvest their organs while they were alive and donate them to people who needed transplants."

Danny could not resist a smile, but he refused to comment. Instead he pretended to focus on the sports page while his free hand kneaded the glands in his neck. Watching him, Lydia started to feel that she was the one who was having a little bit of a breakdown. Did any of this make sense, or was it paranoia? Perhaps the community was having an appropriate response to a terrible tragedy, and it was she who was losing touch with reality.

As if he could hear her thoughts, Danny looked up and said, "Honey, let's just try to ride this out. Every now and then the town loses its mind collectively. It can't last forever. When they catch the guy—"

He stopped, mid-comment, as if he didn't want to finish the thought.

So Lydia finished it for him. "When they catch him, it'll just get worse. Can you imagine what they'll do to him?"

"Maybe they won't catch him," Danny said quietly, as if he were hoping.

That Friday marked the end of a long, fitful week, and Lydia was relieved to have it over with. She decided to skip the faculty meeting, as she was certain it would be nothing but more discussion of the murders and how they, as citizens, could help the police in their investigation. The day before, Martha Dawson had actually recommended they take up money and hire a private detective. Lydia was close to the breaking point, and she knew she could not resist saying something sarcastic. It was best just to remove herself from the mix.

When she pushed the bathroom door open, she was glad to find Alicia Clay there, one of the few faculty members who had not tried her patience lately.

"Are you having as much trouble with your classes as I am?" Lydia asked. "We're at least a week behind and I can't see them ever getting interested in nineteenth-century literature again." She rummaged in her purse for her lipstick and awaited Alicia's answer. There was none. Looking up, she saw that Alicia was crying. The sight of it left her speechless. She had seen Alicia take on the entire school board without flinching, defending her ideas with grace and humor. Now, to see her face streaked with tears, her bottom lip quivering, Lydia actually felt dizzy with dread.

"Alicia, what—?"

"I've been asked to resign," Alicia said.

"What the hell for?"

"I don't think it's for being too pretty, do you? I hate to get all Angela Davis, but it's for being black, let's face it," Alicia said, wiping mascara away from her eyes with a paper towel. "Well, no, that's not accurate. For being black and unapologetic."

"But that's ridiculous. Take them to court."

"Oh no, they can substantiate their complaint. They can say it was because I took a detour from the assigned curriculum, which of course I did. But who can expect to hold a class's interest by teaching them about gum disease? Who can keep a health class limited to muscle building and flossing? This is not what I became a teacher for. This is not why I went into debt getting a master's degree."

"It's this goddamned Quality-Mart thing," Lydia said. "They're so fucking paranoid. I knew this would get ugly."

Alicia said nothing to this. She just kept wiping at her eyes, looking for stray mascara, giving herself a goal.

"Well, maybe it's a good thing," Lydia attempted. "Maybe you should take this opportunity to pursue something better."

"In Fawley? Like what?"

"You don't have to stay here."

"My parents are here, my sisters. And of course my kid. You know I'm divorced and I've got joint custody with my asshole husband, so I can't move more than twenty miles away. That doesn't even get me to Greensboro."

Alicia stared at her hands as she wound the tattered tissue around her forefinger. "You know they're saying a black kid is responsible for the murders. Or two kids. Or twelve. But they were black. That detail never changes. And now they're saying that I contributed to the problem. Believe that? It was my fault, indirectly. Not that it was one of my kids. But I stirred things up with my controversial lectures. It's subliminal, they say. It has a cumulative effect."

"Well, that's ridiculous. It doesn't make sense."

"Oh, you want this to make *sense*. Lydia, this is a different world. You never did work that out. You can't come down here ranting about the

Constitution and statutes and violations of civil liberties. They don't give a flying fuck about the people's rights. You don't demand, or discuss, or confront down here. What you do down here is *behave*. What is it that white folks say to their babies? 'Stop that crying or I'll give you something to cry about.' There you go, that's how it works. And listen up, girl. When they finish with me, they're coming after you."

Lydia smirked. "Let them."

"O-kay," Alicia sang skeptically.

"Look, Alicia, I'll speak to Nigel about you. If he won't reinstate you, I'll threaten to resign."

"Don't be stupid. Fall on a sword for me, and all you'll find is your unemployed self with a knife through your heart."

"Oh God," Lydia said, leaning against the tiles, staring up at the corked ceiling. "I know Martha Dawson's behind this."

"Everybody's behind it, Lydia. There's no conspiracy. Conspiracy means that somebody opposes your point of view, that you've got to work outside the system. Down here, this *is* the system. Oh, God, shut me up before I turn into a Spike Lee movie. I gotta go pick up my daughter now."

She walked to the door, then turned, and over her shoulder she caught Lydia's face in the mirror. Their eyes locked and Alicia smiled. "It's so stupid, the idea that I could encourage anyone to hate white people. Look at me. I've got so much white blood in me I could be Strom Thurmond's love child."

"Don't give up," Lydia said.

"Oh, sweetheart," Alicia said. "You folks say the cutest things."

Lydia came home from work wanting a beer. She went straight to the phone and called Dee.

"Get over here on the double," Lydia said, kicking off her shoes, staring out her window to see if the neighbors were around. She always felt watched in the afternoons.

"Why, what's wrong?" Dee asked.

"I don't want to drink alone. If I drink alone at four o'clock, I'm an alcoholic."

"Alcoholics go to meetings. And I've got the saints with me."

Lydia could hear the boys in the background, screaming and pummeling each other.

"Bring them over."

"Okay. Just let me turn on the Crock-Pot."

The minute Dee stepped into her kitchen, though, Lydia was overcome with a sense of self-restraint. In light of all that was happening, could she really trust Dee? One thing the week's events had taught her was that she did not really know these people. She did not understand the motor here. Their connection to Fawley came first; it overshadowed every other relationship. She thought of her lectures on Thomas Hardy's *Return of the Native*. The main character is not Eustacia Vye, she told them. The main character is the community of Egdon Heath. They had written it down, without question, without interest. Because they knew exactly what she meant, and they had no idea that there was another way to be.

"So let's have it," Dee said, once the boys were engaged in a game of roll and tumble on the front lawn and Lydia had opened another long-neck Bud.

"Have what?" Lydia asked, stalling.

Dee appeared honest, trustworthy. She wore an oversized sweatshirt and ripped jeans and sneakers. The plain silver cross hung in the hollow of her throat. She wore no makeup. Her look was unpretentious; she was hiding nothing. But Lydia could not escape the suspicion that Dee was on the other side, looking for quirks in her neighbor's character that she might be able to report back to the congregation.

"What's wrong with you and Danny?" Dee persisted.

Lydia couldn't speak for a moment. She didn't know where to start. Perhaps with the most telling sign of trouble, the fact that he was spending more and more time on building sites. It was happening almost every day now. He came home and hurried to their bedroom to change his clothes, hoping she wouldn't see the mud-spattered shoes and specks of sawdust on his suit.

It was during these wandering phases that Danny started to do other strange things. The insomnia, for instance. She was now conscious of him tossing in bed all night. Sometimes she'd wake at 3 A.M. to the distant murmur of the TV and the shadowy light playing across the carpet in the hallway.

He obviously wasn't taking the Ativan anymore. She had sneaked another look at the bottle in his nightstand drawer and found it to be empty. He had not refilled it. And because he hadn't, he didn't sleep.

Then there was the preoccupation with various parts of his body. The glands, most obviously. But there was something going on with his stomach. He constantly lifted his shirt to stare at his midsection. She used to question if he was worried about his weight, but once he'd admitted to her that he thought he had a rash. He'd asked her to look at it, and she found herself staring at his flat, white stomach, seeing nothing but a thin trail of dark hair leading from his belt to his navel. Her insistence that she could see nothing like a rash seemed to anger him, and he scratched hard at it, leaving red streaks like tire marks across his skin.

Then there was the preoccupation with his fingers. It had taken her a while to register this. The flexing, the bending, it was more than a nervous habit. He stared at them, at the tips, bringing them close to his eyes and blowing on them, as if to put out some invisible fire. This was nowhere near as amusing as the stomach rash. This seemed so illogical that she dreaded asking about it. But he did it so often that she finally had to give in.

"They tingle," he'd admitted to her. "It's like pinpricks."

She would have laughed, if she hadn't felt so terrified.

"Come on, Lydia. You got me over here, now tell me," Dee insisted.

"I found these pills," Lydia blurted out, "in Danny's sock drawer."

Dee raised an eyebrow; she was not disappointed.

"What was it? Valium?" she asked.

"No, nothing like that," Lydia said. She did not want to tell her about the Ativan because that phase was apparently over. But there was something else, something she had found that morning, when she had succumbed to another fit of snooping.

"It was homeopathic stuff," Lydia admitted, recalling the bottle she had located beneath his winter wool socks. An innocuous bottle with a rainbow on the label. "It said 'A natural remedy for anxiety and stress.'"

Dee waited. She was expecting more. When Lydia failed to supply it, Dee said, "So he's feeling stressed."

"Yes, but what *about?*" Lydia said, and immediately regretted the desperate tone in her voice.

Dee shrugged. "Maybe his job is harder than you think it is. Howard Mecklin has a reputation."

"But Howard hardly has anything to do with the company anymore. It's supposed to be in the hands of Ben and Danny. I don't know, Dee, it's just a strange thing. Danny's not someone who buys into homeopathic medicine. I didn't even know you could find it around here."

"So what do you think?" Dee pressed her. "Do you have a theory?"

Lydia was on the verge of explaining a difficult thought. It came down to this—she had made a point of marrying a man whose understanding of life was pragmatic and concrete. His perspective did not encompass anything that floated on the periphery of science. She had married him because he was so stable and so sure of the source of that stability. One plus one always equaled two with Danny. Now she had to confront the possibility of living with a man who had started to invest in the abstract, who believed in magic formulas and unseen forces.

Oh, but that was just a hundred-dollar explanation for something so simple, so elemental. The fact was this—at the end of the day, after taking on the world and asserting her wide range of beliefs, Lydia wanted to feel safe. And Danny was scaring her.

Before she could articulate any of this, a wail erupted from outside. But Dee did not move. She was too intrigued.

Lydia shook her head and stared at her beer bottle, at the white and red label that was starting to curl up from condensation. She hadn't been much of a drinker in college. She hadn't done much in college except study and try to play out her parents' expectations. William and Mary had been the perfect place for someone who was serious about work. If the sheer brain power around her and the demands of her professors had not been enough, the legacy of the school would do the rest to remind her that this was no place to play. Thomas Jefferson had studied here. Christopher Wren had designed one of the buildings. There were traditions to be upheld, and all forms of escape needed to be left behind.

Her life up to this point had been devoted to seriousness, to logic and reason, to enlightenment. Perhaps that was the reason any degree of disorder, any event that could not be rationally explained made her tremble and turn to beer.

"Tell me about Danny," Lydia said. "What was he like before I met him?"

"What's to tell? He's the same guy. He was a star. Everybody wanted to be like him."

"Did he ever talk about his glands?"

"His what?"

One of the boys appeared at the door, his chubby face streaked with dirty tears.

"Mommy, Matthew's not sharing," he complained in his small, duck voice.

"Sharing what?"

"The rocks."

"Mark, the world is full of rocks. He doesn't have to share."

"But you always have to share," Mark insisted, his tiny voice full of a passionate desire for justice.

"Work it out. I'm busy."

"You're poopy," Mark announced with complete authority before disappearing.

"Tell me again why you don't want to have kids," Dee said. She reached into her purse and extracted a wrinkled pack of cigarettes. "Don't look at me like that. And if you tell John, I'll deny every word."

Lydia inhaled the scent and wanted to smoke. "I feel like calling my parents," she said.

"That is a big mistake," Dee said decisively, pointing her lit Marlboro like a finger.

"I know, but when Danny checks out like this, I need someone to rely on."

"Checks out? He's taken some vitamins. That's what it amounts to. Those pills are like ground-up tea and basil leaves. Seriously, let him have that peculiarity."

"You don't understand, Dee. When he does these weird things, I can't talk to him. He gets mad if I mention it, but I can't not mention it, so I just have to shut up or go in another room. I'm completely alone."

"You have friends. You have me."

Lydia pinched her lip. "It's not the same. I didn't leave my whole way of life, my family, everything . . . I didn't leave that for friends. I ditched it all for Danny."

Dee leaned forward and squeezed her arm. "And you were right."

Lydia struggled to smile. She hesitated to bring up this last point, but why not? It was, after all, the most important.

"Then there's Kyle," she said.

Dee took a long drag on her cigarette and nodded, as if she finally understood. "Well, that's another matter. When Danny and I were pretending to date, we had lots of discussions about Kyle. See, I think Kyle is a walking disaster and Danny would be better off pretending they were just casual acquaintances. But there's some kind of connection because of Pike's death."

"Tell me about that."

Dee shrugged. "I only know what everybody in town knows. Kyle was shot, and Pike went chasing after whoever he thought it was. But he got the wrong guy, which is kind of an embarrassment. Everybody liked Pike, and nobody likes to admit he died a foolish death. But he did. He squandered his life."

"Who do you think shot Kyle?"

"Oh, who cares?" Dee said, then looked as if someone had just slapped her on the back. "Did I just say that? It's the beer. Christ, forget I said that. It's just that everybody in town hated Kyle then."

"But not now?" Lydia asked.

"Nobody thinks about Kyle anymore." She plunked her empty beer bottle on the table and said, "I'm ready for another."

Lydia went to the fridge, pausing to look out the window at the boys. They were sitting on the grass, staring out at the empty street, temporarily at a loss for ideas. Lydia thought how frightening it must feel to have children. Two little people who were starting from scratch, who did not know anything at all, and were relying on the tall ones to explain it to them.

"So what did Les Carlisle want?" Dee asked abruptly.

"How did you know about that?"

"Lydia, I can see your house from my kitchen window."

"He wanted to talk about Quality-Mart. Because I was there on opening day. He's working off a list of names that Martha Dawson composed on Saturday."

"It's such a waste of time anyway. They're never gonna catch that guy. John's sure enjoying the whole thing, though. It's good for business. I haven't seen him so energized since the Baptist preacher got run out of town for embezzling."

Another screech of discontent rose up from the lawn and fell on Dee's indifferent ears.

"Should I go see about them?" Lydia asked.

Dee sucked her cigarette down to the filter and said, "Here's the big lie. That having children fulfills you somehow, like every moment in their presence is a little piece of magic. Like you suddenly don't mind being needed every second, demanded and unappreciated. It's a weird thing that happens. You love them to death and you resent loving them because your life is never your own again. For three years I've just felt like a rusty anchor for two little brainless boats. Children want to go out to sea. Your job is to rescue them. You're like a lifeguard, without pay, without medals. You don't even get a mention in the paper."

Another wail erupted, and Dee shot up, as if she possessed the ability to distinguish an important cry from an insignificant one. She went to the window and looked out.

"Matthew's got a microscopic cut on his foot. Alert the authorities."

Dee stubbed out her cigarette and went outside. Lydia watched from the window as Dee stood over Matthew, inspecting his wound. As she watched, Lydia wondered what she would be doing right now if she had married Hamilton Crider, who had come into his significant inheritance and now lived in Cleveland Park, in a house featured in *Architectural Digest.* Lydia had never cared much about houses. She always felt uncomfortable in her childhood home in Georgetown, an historical landmark which occasionally attracted the curiosity of tourists. As a little girl she'd looked through the bay window at all the sightseers collecting in front of her house. They were plain and badly dressed and sometimes overweight, and yet she envied them. Their lives seemed so purposeless. They had nowhere to be, no demands made on their time, let alone their lineage.

"Oh, those sad people," her mother used to say whenever she caught Lydia staring. But those people didn't seem sad to her. Reasonably handsome men would throw their arms around badly shaped women in tent dresses, as if they were genuinely surprised at their good fortune. Those people had discovered some secret happiness that went deeper than anything she could imagine. They delighted in ice-cream cones and T-shirts and postcards, and staring at the houses of complete strangers. So odd, it seemed to her, that they'd gaze at her house, as if they wanted to trade places with the people inside it.

We're the sad people, Lydia remembered thinking at the time, though she couldn't understand why back then. Now she knew. They were the ones who had no other lives to envy, no daydreams about winning the lottery, no concept of a heaven that might reward them for their suffering. Her family would never make a pilgrimage to Iowa and stand outside the farmhouses, wondering what it would be like to trade circumstances. What those tourists sought could be achieved. They could win the lottery or receive an unexpected inheritance and buy whatever satisfaction they felt was missing. But what was missing in her family's life could not be so easily obtained. They could never realize the value in wishing for something else. They did not understand that hoping for more, better, easier, was a kind of glue connecting the human race. It was the thing all those people had in common, not having enough. All her family could do was cling defensively to what they had, and pity anyone who wanted it.

She watched through the window as Dee picked up Matthew and held him tight, pushing his sobbing face down onto her shoulder. She rocked her son from side to side, kissing his tousled hair. I'm never going to have that, Lydia thought as she stared at them. It made her sad, knowing it so soon and so completely, but it was a fact. Lydia couldn't take care of a child. She had to take care of her husband.

13

DANNY HAD ALWAYS assumed that crazy people had no idea they were crazy. The few truly unbalanced people he'd encountered—like Hubble, the alcoholic artist who walked around muttering to parking meters, and old Mrs. Jones, who often wore her pajamas into town and pushed her groceries around in a baby carriage—seemed unaware that they weren't playing by the rules. He suspected that the slide into insanity was similar to getting drunk, where the world started to seem a little bizarre but the brain adapted to the new surroundings without question, until all judgment was gone. But now he was starting to wonder if that was how it happened. Maybe you could feel it; maybe it felt more like the flu, where you were conscious of something being wrong but you couldn't say what. And then you just knew. You woke up one morning and said, Oh, I'm losing it. I'm coming apart.

That was how he felt. Unhinged. As if parts of his brain were separating, like paper in water. His thinking was scattered. Notions rolled around in his head like marbles. He could not control their direction. Those were the bad days, where he felt entirely uncertain about what he might do next. He told himself every morning that he was going to pull it all together, and yet he felt incapable of controlling his impulses. He did things he did not want to do. And if being unable to determine one's actions was not insanity, then what was?

He thought about other women. Jan, his secretary, and Lori Marshall, the female construction worker they had just hired, and sometimes Dee. Sometimes he thought of Amanda. His meeting with her had been brief and unsettling, but it didn't interfere with his desire. He didn't want to sleep with any of them so much as take them away to a distant location and tell them all his problems. He knew in his heart that he didn't want these women at all, that he only wanted Lydia. He wanted her more than he wanted his next breath. Yet he could not pursue her, could not reassure her. He saw the way she watched him, as if he might suddenly burst into flames. Perhaps she could see it, too, his gradual descent into some other place.

But those were just the bad days. On the bad days he couldn't sleep at all and he wanted pills. He couldn't get Ativan anymore, and the vitamins he'd ordered from a magazine didn't seem to do much at all. He couldn't escape himself.

He was able to function for the most part, so he could not seriously be losing his mind. The other possibility was just as unlikely, and somehow, oddly, more comforting. The other possibility was that he was dying.

Exactly how he was dying was a hazy sort of idea. It was a rare and thoroughly devastating illness. It invaded his body like a drug. His stomach itched and his fingertips burned and his tongue felt funny. There were boils on his gums and he felt fluish all the time. He'd taken three AIDS tests and was forced to accept the negative results—how could it have been otherwise? He was at absolutely no risk for AIDS, yet it seemed the perfect explanation for these nebulous symptoms.

Terminal cancer seemed another likely possibility, but Dr. Steen, who'd taken care of his family as long as he could remember, assured him there was nothing unusual in his symptoms except for slightly high blood pressure which could, of course, be attributed to his anxiety.

"Tell me what's really going on," the kindly gray-haired man had implored after Danny's third visit in as many months.

Danny knew no way of answering him except to say that he felt weird, that amorphous sort of imbalance that cancer patients seemed to experience shortly before their devastating condition was diagnosed.

"There's nothing wrong with you that a nice vacation wouldn't take care of. Caneel Bay in the Virgin Islands. It was my late wife's favorite spot on earth. Wanted to have her ashes scattered there, but my daughter said no. Anyhow, you look into it."

Danny promised he would.

But he hadn't, of course, and the only thing that seemed to relieve his anxiety was work. Not office work, but standing outside a construction site, staring up at a skeleton structure, so simple and undemanding, asking only that logic be imposed on it. He spent more and more time among the builders, and it was not going unnoticed by his boss.

Ben Mecklin, the boss's son, had taken him out for a drink a few nights ago. Ben was a good guy, someone who, unlike Danny, was graced with social skills and a phlegmatic detachment from the pressures of work. He put people at ease. If a site was falling behind in its deadline, if rain were delaying the progress or if subcontractors were becoming sluggish or spoiled, Ben settled it by organizing a cookout or a company softball game. Ben thought the way to good business was through throwing the workers a bone. Ben never seemed to notice that such benign acts of courtesy just made the workers behave more irresponsibly, thinking that the boss felt an allegiance to them in spite of their sloppy performance. Like spoiled children, they were being rewarded for bad behavior. Personally, Danny believed that his approach was more effective. The workers took the job far more seriously when he appeared on a site. They spent less time on lunch, and seemed to perform better in an effort to impress him or, when Danny joined in, a desire to show him up.

Danny and Ben had been good friends in the old days, when both were on the line, part of the construction crew. Danny only worked summers, between college semesters, but Ben was a full-time employee. Ben seemed to appreciate, in those days, that Danny brought none of his college smarts to the task. He pitched in, got up as early, worked as hard, and left as late as anyone. It was this devotion to the task that had caused Ben to recommend Danny's full-time employment to the company.

He and Ben had formed a strong attachment. They told each other everything, they shared tastes in music and movies, cars and motorcycles and women. Their discussions of women, of course, were always abstract. Models, actresses, or local girls who paid no attention to them. Once they started dating seriously, all discussions were off.

Danny liked Ben and found it difficult to accept the ways in which he had changed after he had taken over the mantle from his father. Suddenly Ben was a businessman, someone who, while he pretended to sympathize with and understand the workers, really looked down on them. He had spent his whole life waiting to boss people around.

The first year Danny had spent in the office, he went to Ben asking what they should get the subcontractors for a Christmas present. Danny's ideas consisted of a nice bonus or extra vacation time, but Ben said, "Come on, we'll give 'em a ham and they'll be slobbering with appreciation. These are simple people, don't overdo it."

This exemplified Ben's attitude toward the work force. Any complaint could be answered with a quick fix, a superficial nod to their concerns. Ben had never grasped, or had not retained the knowledge, that these people were just like them, and what they desired was some significant understanding of the value of their work. This, Danny believed, was something he gave them every time he appeared at a building site. But it was not something Ben appreciated, and it had all come to a head quite recently.

"Daddy is worried," Ben had said as they sat drinking vodka and tonics at Fawley Square. Ben was baby-faced and highly strung, his eyes perpetually darting around the room when he spoke. He always wore a suit and he never took off the jacket, even after work. Danny remembered the days when he and Ben worked together in construction, two kids in ripped jeans and T-shirts, sweating and spitting into the dirt. That seemed like yesterday, and here they were, two businessmen sipping cocktails, acting like the men they used to make fun of.

"Daddy thinks you're not serious about the business," Ben said. Danny found it unsettling to hear a grown man talking about his Daddy. It made him feel sorry for Ben, for reasons he couldn't name.

"How could he think that? I've never cared about anything else. Except my wife," he added, as if Lydia might be listening.

"Well, you don't spend much time in the office and you're not drumming up much business, and that's what he really needs. He thought you were someone who could help expand the business."

"It doesn't matter how much the business expands if the operations aren't secure. The workers make the business."

"Yeah, well, I guess that's the university speaking," said Ben, who was more than mildly resentful of Danny's education. "Daddy says the buyers make the business, and the buyers want to see us expanding."

"Okay, so we'll expand. But only at a practical rate. I don't need to warn you of the danger of overextending. We take on bids without having the available labor to see it through, suddenly we're juggling and hedging, and nobody's happy. The subs are tired, the work is sloppy, the clients are shortchanged. It's the fastest way to make a company go under. Like any other business, you can't sell what you don't have."

"Danny, put aside the economics bullshit for a minute and admit the truth. Your priorities are off. Your allegiance is to the workers, not the company. Everyone knows it, and we think you should just admit it and let us deal with it. If you're not a company man, come clean with it."

"This company is my whole life. I was hired to bring my understanding of economics to the table, and I can't discuss economics without placing a premium on the labor. I won't sell them out. If that's what you want, then you might as well fire me. Are you firing me, Ben?"

"Don't overreact," Ben said. "You're my friend and I know what makes you tick. You're scared of testing your true talent. Give in to it, Danny. Admit that you're an office man and not a builder. Office work, like it or not, is compromise and manipulation. The more bids we get, the more work the laborers will have, and they all want to work. I do appreciate your economic skills, I just think you misuse them. Say you make a bid and say you can start the first of the month and finish in three more. So you're a month late starting and two more finishing up. The client will grumble, but he'll tolerate it. In the end the work is done, and if a sub or two storms off in a huff, you replace them. You've still got your deal, and the workers are interchangeable. You gotta take advantage of the hard times. You know that. Come on, you and I can do great things with this company if you'll just commit to it."

"I don't believe people are interchangeable," Danny said.

"Well, you've got to work on that. It's the difference between a successful businessman and one who just keeps the mill grinding. Daddy wants to break out into the national—hell, the global—market. We're never gonna do that by protecting the labor. That's what the steel industry did, and now nobody's working in that industry. So what was accomplished there?"

Danny thought about arguing, but he felt the very real threat of being fired as he stared at Ben's nervous, twitching smile. A grown man who talked about his Daddy was capable of anything. So he bought the next round of drinks and swore his performance in the office would improve. He made a silent vow to himself that at least for a week, he'd avoid the building sites. He and Ben spent the rest of the evening talking about the NBA playoffs, trying desperately to locate some common ground.

The threat had stayed with him, though, and he'd tried to make good on his vow. He went about his business, struggling to keep his secret, like someone trying to conceal a drug habit. He recalled the days when Kyle was using coke. He would come to Danny for money, acting all jittery and sniffing incessantly and rubbing at his nose. And when Danny questioned his habit, Kyle would act wounded and deny it vehemently, swearing on the soul of his dead father. Danny felt he would do the same—in fact, did do the same whenever Lydia questioned his strange behavior. He did what the addict did; he turned it on his accuser. "What do you think of me, that I'm coming unglued?" he'd challenge bitterly. "That I'm losing all my judgment? Is that what you think? I appreciate your faith in me." Lydia would get hurt then and go in another room, and Danny felt like drawing a bath and drowning himself in it.

Occasionally memory would revisit him, like an intruder. It would break in through an open window, usually drunkenness or exhaustion, some sort of emotional neglect. Kyle's bleeding foot and the girls' screams and the look of rage in Uncle Pike's eyes as he raced out of the yard. And in those moments he would think that what was haunting him was not the threat of death, but of life. The possibility that he would just go on and on this way, living like a successful thief, in nervous triumph, waiting to get caught. He'd live and live and grow old and die, knowing what he knew.

But what did he really know, except that Uncle Pike's death was foolish and wasteful? Everyone knew that. Danny possessed a minor detail, a fragment of truth that would not change anything. So he was obliged to keep it. He was doing what he had to do.

The hardest times were the times spent in the presence of his family. Recently he had considered resurrecting Lydia's suggestion and declining the weekly invitation. But he was afraid such a step might be misinterpreted—or rather, he reminded himself, be interpreted correctly.

For some reason, the Quality-Mart murders made him even more anxious. Fortunately, he could use the excuse that everyone in town was using, that the sudden tragedy had thrown him off course and made him feel disoriented.

Two Sundays after the murders, his mother was even more uptight than usual when they arrived for lunch. She burned the roast and forgot to put the biscuits in the oven. When the damaged meal finally appeared on the table, she was too distraught to eat any of it, and sat sipping a cup of coffee while the rest of them picked at their plates, shoving the contents around like the remains of a fire.

"I just don't understand it," Sally said. "I just don't see how this could happen to us. I mean, everyone was warning us, but who could have really seen it coming? Every night we have to go to bed knowing there's a murderer out there. Or *two*."

"There've always been murderers out there," Lydia said. "I think what scares everybody so much is the anonymity of the deaths. The fact that we didn't really know the men who died, and we don't know who killed them. It's the big question mark."

She stopped abruptly, as if she had more to say but she registered Sally's alarmed expression.

"Always been murderers?" Sally questioned. "In Fawley? I don't think so. You're confusing us with Washington, D.C. This has always been a safe, wholesome place to live."

Lydia swallowed her food, waited a second, then said, "Well, I was thinking of Pike. I mean, that was a murder."

Danny dropped his fork with a clank. He glared at his wife. Why must she always bring up Pike? Didn't she understand the effect it had? She seemed to realize too late, and she gave him an apologetic look. He made no effort to reassure her.

Sally said, "Pike's death . . . that was a freak thing. You can't compare it."

"No," Lydia said. "You're right, I can't. I'm sorry."

"Jesus, Joseph, and Mary," Rex suddenly piped up. "Murder this, murder that. Can't we talk about anything else? Did anyone happen to notice that the dogwoods are blooming?"

Nelson's attention was snared by this. He looked up from his plate. "Where?"

"Everywhere. The one over on Gray's Road, next to the funeral parlor is in full bloom."

"The pink one?" Nelson asked. "I don't believe it."

"Drive by and look for yourself."

"But it's too early," Sally said, a note of panic in her voice. "They'll freeze."

"Well, write your congressman. I don't know what to tell you, Mother. Incidentally, this roast is roughly the consistency of rawhide."

"I know, I cooked it too long, but with what I've had to deal with lately . . ." Sally didn't finish that thought, and no one asked for an explanation.

Rex picked up a magazine and started to read. He hummed as his eyes scanned the pages. Nelson glared at him. There was no mistaking that look of broad disapproval, as if everything about his son was touching an exposed nerve.

Danny stared at his brother in a similar fashion. Rex was wearing a pink lamb's-wool sweater over a woman's print shirt. It looked obscene.

" 'Night and day,' " Rex suddenly sang out. " 'You are the one . . .' "

"This isn't a goddamned nightclub," Nelson said.

"Really?" Rex said. "And yet it's so festive."

"Don't be an asshole, Rex. And what are you wearing?" Danny asked evenly.

Rex glanced down, then up at his brother. "This sweater cost more than your living-room set."

Danny felt an irrepressible rage toward his brother, who'd once threatened to die and now treated that second chance at life as if he had been given standby tickets to an opera.

"God let you live so you could be a man," Danny said.

"Oh, really? You've spoken to Him lately?"

"No arguing, all right?" Nelson implored. "I work hard all week and I deserve a little peace and quiet."

But Rex ignored him. "I mean, let's talk about what being a man means, Daniel. Does it mean playing baseball for a living? Or failing to play baseball for a living? Does it mean wearing a hardhat and whistling at women? Please, enlighten me on the male perspective."

"Rex," Sally spoke up, "you know that is one of my old sweaters and I've asked you not to wear it many times."

"Why not? It's virgin wool, Mother. As rare a commodity in the fabric family as it is in the human population. Although in Joyce's case, it would be quite redundant."

"Okay, that's enough," Nel said, pushing his plate back.

Suddenly Lydia spoke up. "I think Joyce is doing just fine."

"Do you?" Rex asked, leaning closer to Lydia, resting his chin on his fist. "You know something we don't? Please tell. We must talk about something besides the Quality-Mart murders before I implode."

"I just think she's a lot more balanced than you give her credit for," Lydia said. She was still eating her roast, long after everyone else had given up. "At least she got out of that house."

"Yes, she moved all of two miles away."

"Which is more than you've done," Danny spoke up.

"I just hate families that bicker at the table," Sally said, staring for-lornly at her plate. "It's like white trash."

"Well, Mother, we're not exactly registered with the First Families of Virginia," Rex said.

"And speaking of people not losing their virginity," Danny said abruptly.

Rex turned to him with an eager smile.

"Oh, now," Rex said, "are you asking? Because I'm more than will-ing to divulge all."

"Jehovah's Witness," Nel said, his face turning red. "There will be no smut talk at this table. What the hell has this place turned into? Eat your food, Daniel."

"No, he doesn't have to," Sally said. "It's all such a disaster, I can't blame anybody for not eating it. Lydia, honey, you really don't have to finish that roast."

"But I like it well done," Lydia said, and smiled at her mother-in-law. "Really, ever since I was a kid I've liked it cooked off the bone. It's per-fect."

Danny felt like crying. He swallowed hard at a lump in his throat. Un-der the table he put his hand on her knee. She smiled at him, without looking up.

"How's the insurance business, Nel?" Lydia asked. She was trying her best to restore order. Danny felt grateful. She took his hand and moved it further up her thigh, under her dress. His breath was fast and uneven. He had an erection.

"Horrible," Nelson said. "Couldn't be worse."

"Don't be so negative. You just wrote a nice accident policy for Martha Dawson," Sally said.

Nel nodded and said, "She's crazy. She thinks her children are trying to kill her, so she makes me write out these specific terms saying that in the event of suspicious death, even if it appears to be natural causes, only the church and her Siamese cat will benefit."

"What children?" Lydia asked. Her eyes were fixed calmly on her father-in-law, even as she maneuvered her husband's hand toward her crotch.

"Oh, she's got some stepchildren," Nelson said, "from a marriage two decades ago. Martha's under the illusion that she's got some money and her family is after it. Actually, she's got nothing and her stepchildren live in Baltimore and don't even send her a Christmas card."

"That's sad," she said. As Danny's fingers crept between her thighs, she suddenly clasped them together, trapping him.

Danny bit his lip and smiled. He was thinking of how they'd laugh once they were in his truck, on the way home. She'd put her head on his shoulder and he'd drive and fiddle with the radio while she kissed his neck.

"Oh, God help us!" Aunt Rita shrieked, tearing into the house abruptly.

Lydia relaxed her thighs and Danny sat up straight. His erection deflated like a slashed tire.

Rita's hair was wild and loose. Her eyes were glassy. One of the girls was following her—Danny was hard pressed to say which one, but he might have put money on Lucy. She was the youngest, not quite thirty, but she looked every bit as old as her mother. They shared the same expression, their shoulders slumped, their chins tucked and trembling.

"He's gone," Aunt Rita was saying.

Nelson threw his napkin down and said, "What has Kyle gone and done now?"

The girl said, "He shot up the kitchen with a rifle. Broke half our dishes. Then he took Mama's car and went."

"Jesus Christ," Nel said.

Nel grabbed his coat and cap from the hall rack. Danny felt his aunt's solicitous stare. He resisted looking directly at it. He wanted to stay put. He wanted to touch Lydia again; he wanted to feel the soft, secret skin inside her thighs.

"Come on, son," Nel said. "You're the only one who can talk to him."

"I don't know where I got this reputation for being able to talk to Kyle."

"He loves you, Danny," Rita reminded him, as if this put him in some sort of special category, as if earning Kyle's love had afforded him a kind of entitlement.

"Why on earth do you people keep going after Kyle? Every one of you would prefer it if he'd fall off the planet," Rex said, scraping Danny's uneaten food onto his own plate. "If he wants to get lost so bad, let him stay lost. But then, if Kyle went away our family might face the horrible possibility of becoming normal. I suppose we can't let that happen."

"I don't think there's any danger of that," Danny said, "as long as you're around."

Rex actually laughed at that remark, but Sally went pale and frowned at her older son.

"Please, you two, don't we have enough problems?" she pleaded.

"Oh, Mother, we can never have *enough* problems," Rex said, shoveling a heaping spoonful of cold mashed potatoes into his mouth.

Danny stared at his brother and fought back the anger. It was wrong to hate Rex—it was like hating a bobtailed cat or a lame dog. But somehow Danny blamed Rex for his unholy alliance with Kyle. If Rex had not gotten sick, everything might be different. He might not now feel obligated to leave the dinner table, and his wife, and go chasing after a man bent on destroying himself.

Well, he didn't have to go. He could start now the process of distancing himself from Kyle. He could stay put, and in doing so he could choose to protect his life rather than his past.

He looked at Lydia. She was smiling at him.

"I'll wait," she said.

Rita's car was an old Plymouth Fury that, despite the meticulous attention given to its lubrication system, leaked oil like a cow pissing on a flat rock. Nel and Danny got into the pickup truck and followed the trail of black ooze, all the way down old Route 29, onto the Chalkpit Lane, over to the Snake Path Road, a winding mess of asphalt that earned its name by twisting irrationally through a barren stretch of farmland all the way to Wycombe County. It was a treacherous route even for a careful driver. Danny had lost several school friends to its radical turns over the years. Kyle did not stand a chance.

Rounding one of the sharpest twists, unoriginally known as Dead Man's Curve, they saw the Fury, its nose touching a tree, a thin mist of white smoke rising above the hood.

"Son of a bitch," Nel said.

"It's not as bad as it looks," Danny said.

The wreck seemed staged, Danny thought as he got out of the truck and headed toward the Fury. Its nose was slightly crumpled against the trunk of the enormous oak tree. If Kyle had really been doing any sort of speed on that turn, the car would have folded accordion-style, and there would be no need to call an ambulance.

When Danny approached the driver's side, he saw Kyle sitting behind the steering wheel, wide awake, staring at the windshield and tapping his fingers on the dash. His other hand clutched a can of Miller, and he seemed to have just picked this place to park and think things over.

"Hey," Danny said, tapping on the window. Kyle smiled when he saw his cousin and rolled down the window.

"Hey yourself."

"What happened?"

"Damn brakes blew out on me going sixty."

"Bullshit, you'd be dead."

"Kyle Crane defies death once again. How many lives you reckon I got left?"

"Too many," Danny said.

"Ha!" Kyle threw his head back and laughed.

"No shit, Kyle, what really happened?" Danny asked.

Kyle hesitated, then jerked his head in the direction of the passenger seat. "Get in."

Danny threw a look toward his father, who was waiting in the truck, his face strained with worry. Danny gave him a thumbs-up to let him know everything was okay, then obeyed Kyle's order and got into the car. He was surprised to discover that the radio was on and Kyle's fingers were actually tapping out a beat on the dashboard.

Kyle said, "One minute I'm driving, the next there's a goddamn tree in front of me. Things happen too fast around here."

"You're lucky you didn't kill yourself."

"Lucky for who?"

"Kyle, if you really wanted to die you know how to get that done. You want to live forever, and I swear there are times when I think you might."

"Now wouldn't that be a hell of a note? Sometimes I think about it, Danny. I mean, eventually evolution is gonna get there, isn't it? Somebody's going to crack the immortality thing one day, and we've got it figured that it's going to be somebody good. Now why would we think that? Jesus Christ was the son of God and he couldn't do it. I figure the first immortal's gonna be a bad guy. 'Cause, see, the rest of you fools want to help people, take care of each other. But every time you do that, it makes you weak. Hell, no. To live forever you gotta look out for yourself."

Danny said, "Why would you want to live forever?"

"Just to prove a point."

Kyle laughed, a drunken laugh that went on too long.

Danny said, "Let me ask you something. And I want you to tell me the truth. Are you doing coke again?"

Kyle's expression was one of genuine bewilderment. "Coke? Hell, Danny, where would I get the money for that? Shit, I can't even afford a joint."

Danny said nothing. He waited.

"No, I'm through with that. She wouldn't let me get away with it, anyhow."

"You mean Amanda?"

"No, I mean Syphilis. Shit, yeah, Amanda. She keeps me in line. She's a real honest girl. You know she's never took a single drug? Smokes like a Turk, but that's it. And get this—she's only fucked eight guys. Not counting her stepfather, which she couldn't help. Single digits, man. She's practically a virgin."

Kyle sucked in his breath and stared out the window, away from Danny. "That's just what you don't get about me. Cocaine? That was the easy part. Getting my leg sawed off? A breeze. Now I've got something worse. Now I've started to care about somebody. I swear to God, it's gonna kill me."

His lip quivered. Danny shifted, feeling uneasy.

"Where were you headed, Kyle?"

"Where was I headed. Now that's the million-dollar question. I don't think I've ever been headed anywhere. You're the only person who ever thought I was headed . . ."

His voice broke off and he started to cry. Danny was startled; he couldn't ever remember seeing his cousin cry. Everyone had commented about how dry-eyed he was at Pike's funeral. It was an act Danny really did not believe Kyle was capable of. Seeing it now, Danny did not feel the sense of hope that he knew he should have, the realization that Kyle did have emotions and was willing to share them. This only made Danny want to look away, as if he were seeing something pornographic. Kyle's weakness was much more unsettling than anything Danny had ever seen, more troubling than that bloody lump lying under the sheet.

If Kyle could feel remorse, then he had a chance. And the chance was so small, so buried beneath the years of damage and confusion, it had almost no hope of surviving.

Danny put a hand on Kyle's arm. Kyle flinched and stared at Danny with sudden clarity, as if he'd just woken up.

"I'm scared shitless," he said. "They're gonna come for me."

"Who is?" Danny asked. His chest tightened and he could feel that strange tingling in his fingertips.

"They're gonna blame me," he said.

"Look, Uncle Pike's death was a freak thing. You can't let it haunt you this way. I struggle with it, too. But we've both got to get past it."

Kyle shook his head vigorously. "No, not that. The murders. At the Quality-Mart. They're gonna say it was me, and I need you to stand by me."

Now Danny felt cold all over. He started to shiver, even though the air in the car was warm and close. The sweat on his brow started to congeal and he felt sick, as if a sudden flu were descending on him.

"Why would they blame you?" Danny asked.

"Because I was out that night, driving around. I was in a foul mood and I couldn't stand just sitting in front of the TV set. I talked Amanda into going for a ride with me. But we had a fight and she got out of the car. I just kept on riding. I remembered that the place had opened that day, and I thought I'd ride out and see what was going on. But I didn't know how late it was and it was closed when I got there. I sat in the parking lot and drank a beer. And if somebody saw my car, it's all gonna be over with. Who on earth would stand up for me?"

"Don't be ridiculous. They're looking for a black guy. Or two. And anyway, somebody would need a lot more proof than seeing your car in the area."

Kyle laughed and wiped his nose with his sleeve. "Since when? Hell, they got nothing and they're just blaming it on a black guy 'cause nothing else makes sense. They'll take anybody they can get, and nobody on earth would miss me if I did forty years. What I'm saying is, you have to stand up for me, Danny. Say I was with you."

"Kyle, I can't lie."

Kyle stared levelly at him. "I think you can."

Danny sighed. "Look, if it comes to that, I'll take care of you. I won't let them blame you. Nobody will blame you."

Kyle smiled, a quivering, childish smile. "That's what my daddy used to say."

Danny patted his cousin's arm, which felt awkward, but it was the only thing he could think to do.

Kyle said, "I wouldn't care so much if it was just me. But Amanda's in the picture now. She's the only thing I care about. She's the only person since my daddy who has seen some good in me. Can you get her for me? Can you bring her back?"

Danny hesitated, and Kyle buried his face in his hands and his shoulders shook. He cried like a girl, making lowing sounds and sucking in jagged breaths. It was the worst thing that Danny had ever seen. Suddenly there was a tapping sound and Nel's face appeared at Kyle's window.

"Everything all right in there?" he asked.

Kyle's emotion disappeared like a trick of the light. "We'll be right with you, Uncle Nel. You just make yourself comfortable."

Danny made a flicking motion with his hand, and Nel backed off.

"You have to get her for me," Kyle said, turning back to Danny. His face was as pink as an Easter egg.

"I don't even know where she is, Kyle. I only met her once."

"She's out at the Green Lantern. She works there."

"That's back out on Twenty-nine."

"I know. I missed a turn. Please, Danny."

"What do you want me to tell her?"

"I gotta have her back. If I don't get her, I'll kill myself."

"Kyle, don't make threats like that. It's not funny."

Kyle lunged across the seat and grabbed a fistful of Danny's T-shirt. "I know I talk a lot of shit, Danny. But I've got to have her. She's the only thing I've done right. When you think about all the bad things I did, just look at her and you'll know I can do something right. You know that, don't you, when you look at her? I saw you looking at her that night at my house. You're half in love with her yourself. You know she's worth having."

Danny pushed him away. It made him uncomfortable to think Kyle had picked up on that. It was an exaggeration, though, to say he was half in love with her. He knew it was nowhere close to that. It was something stranger, more unsettling. He did not know how to explain it, even to himself.

Kyle leaned even closer to Danny and said, "If I have her, maybe I can get my life going. Maybe all the other stuff in my life won't dog me. Maybe it's all we need, Danny, just one person who loves us no matter what. Somebody who's seen all the ugly stuff and doesn't care. You found that, didn't you?"

"I think so," Danny said.

"God, she's something. Lydia. She'd jump off a bridge for you. She'd get burned at the stake for your sorry ass. You appreciate that, don't you?"

"Sure I do," Danny said dryly, not because he didn't appreciate it but because he wasn't sure of it. These days he wasn't even sure she'd be there in the morning when he woke up, let alone die for him. Lydia was too smart; she had too much promise. She'd never throw her life away for anybody, least of all him.

Kyle collapsed against the seat and stared at the roof of the car, at the peeling layer of blue vinyl, the stuffings leaking out like entrails.

"Let's get you home," Danny suggested. "My father'll drive you back. I'll take my truck out to the Green Lantern."

Kyle finished off his beer and crumpled the can.

"What would you say if I told you I'd done it—I'd shot those people?"

Danny went cold again. Here was the moment. Kyle could confess to him now, and what would he do with the secret? He didn't want to own it. Didn't want to get near it. Please God, he prayed skeptically, don't let me hear it. But his prayers always felt empty, even blasphemous. He knew God wasn't buying it. To him, God was like a loan officer at the bank, smirking at his humility, poised to ask, Yes, but what will you do for me? And Danny always came up short. He had no collateral.

"You didn't do it," Danny said, hoping his saying so would put an end to it. "You didn't kill those people."

"I know, but if I had."

"Kyle, there's no point in discussing hypothetical situations."

"I like to think you'd stand by me. Because I've done that for you. That's what family is for, isn't it? Blood's thicker than water and all that."

"I guess," Danny said quietly. "Now, come on, let me go get my father. And I'll go find Amanda for you."

Kyle stared at the dashboard for a long time, then shook his head.

"Oh shit, never mind," he said. "She's not worth it."

The Green Lantern was empty. The waitresses were clearing up after the Sunday dinner rush. When Danny stepped inside, he saw Amanda over at a table in the corner, folding a napkin in the shape of a party hat. He walked toward her, and she looked up at him with no sign of recognition.

"Are you late for lunch or early for supper?" she asked.

"I'm neither one. I'm here about Kyle."

She stared down at the napkin. Her face was much as he remembered it, pale as bleached flour. Her lips were the color of raspberry jam, with chapped, railroad tracks of dry skin across them.

"When do you get off work?" he asked.

"I just have to finish these napkins." She worked on the square piece of linen as if it were a piece of art. "Know why we do this?" she asked.

"No."

"Because people when they come to restaurants don't like to know that someone else was sitting at the table just minutes before. So you set the table and fold the napkins in such a fussy way that it makes them forget that anyone else could have ever been there."

"Really?"

She nodded. "It's all a part of restaurant psychology."

"I never knew there was such a thing."

"Neither did I. But the manager here went to college. He learned this stuff. That's why we have to refill the catsup bottles, so nobody will suspect that anyone was ever here before them. And the color red? You see it a lot in restaurants. Red is supposed to make people hungry. No one ever uses blue in a restaurant because that makes them calm. They don't want to eat when they see blue. And if you want a high turnover rate, you put lots of windows in the restaurant, so people can see the world going by and remind themselves to get back out there in it. In your nicer restaurants, it's dark and there aren't so many windows."

"That's fascinating."

"No, it's not. It's bullshit. Like here, where we expect a big turnover, the waitresses are supposed to say, 'Can I get you anything else?' That's supposed to make the customers understand that they need to leave. But in a nice restaurant, you just say, 'How is everything?' Someday I'll work in a dark restaurant and say, 'How is everything?' It's something to shoot for."

"Kyle is looking for you," Danny said. He was afraid that if he didn't speak up he could pass an entire afternoon discussing restaurant psychology.

Amanda stiffened and stood tall at the mention of his name. Her collar bones jutted out at sharp angles. Her waist was so small, he thought he could fit his hands completely around it. Her dark hair shone in the afternoon light, but it looked thin, too, as though, if he touched it, it might fall out in his hand. Everything about her looked fragile, yet when her gray eyes fell on him he felt afraid.

"Kyle knows how to find me," she said.

"Well, he met with an accident."

For the first time her face registered concern.

"It's all right," Danny said. "My father took him home. He's dealing with it."

"Your daddy doesn't like him."

"Where did you hear that?"

Amanda smirked and put her napkin down. It was complete in its intricate design and matched the others. She stared at it admiringly. Danny got the feeling that she was willing to stare at it forever.

"Do you need a ride somewhere?"

"Don't try taking me to Kyle," she said.

"Okay. Wherever you want to go."

"Let's just ride for a while."

Amanda whipped off her apron and followed Danny into the parking lot, without ever informing anyone she was leaving. He wondered if he were getting her into trouble, but he sensed that trouble was something Amanda was no stranger to. She was involved with Kyle, after all. How cautious could she be?

"You and Kyle must have had a fight," Danny said, once they were inside the truck. The engine sputtered before starting, as if it objected to the union of its passengers. Finally it gave in, and he pulled the truck out onto 29.

"Two nights ago," she said.

"What was it about?"

"Our fights aren't ever about anything."

"But there must have been some point to it."

She laughed. "Only educated people think there's a point to things."

"I'm not that educated."

"You went to college, didn't you?"

"So what?"

She was quiet for a moment, then said, "How come you didn't try to do better?"

"Better than what?"

"Well, you were some hot-shit ballplayer. What happened?"

Danny swallowed. "I sustained a knee injury."

"Christ, Magic Johnson got AIDS. He still went to the Olympics."

"Maybe I just wasn't good enough," Danny admitted. It was the truth. It was the thing he never talked about. He gave it all up because he knew he couldn't do it, couldn't perform the way he was expected to. And he'd tried to cut his humiliation short. Still, there were days when he wondered about what would have happened if he'd stuck it out. Oddly enough, he knew that if Kyle had been given the opportunity, he'd have seen it through, out of sheer obstinacy and determination. Danny always felt eager to quit. Quitting made him feel peaceful and relaxed, at least in the beginning. He savored the calm that came after scaling back, after admitting that he wasn't what people thought, that he was less than he seemed. Then the shame and anxiety came. But first, and for a long while, there was the tranquillity of failure.

"Still," Amanda said, "even if you couldn't have made it as a ballplayer, you could have done better."

"Better than what?"

"Working in construction."

"I don't work in construction. I'm a sales manager."

"At a construction firm."

"Contracting."

"Those words mean something to you, I guess."

"I like my job," Danny said defensively. It was partly true.

Amanda said nothing. She stared out the window at the scenery moving past. This part of old 29 was a deserted path. Before the bypass was built, it had connected Fawley to the civilized world, taking farmers into Greensboro to sell their wares. If it had remained as the main artery, all manner of attractions would have cropped up. Gas stations and minimalls and fast-food restaurants. But the bypass had been built, and the old artery toward civilization remained undeveloped. Huge stretches of neglected land, state-protected forests, and lone houses built and inhabited by either the poorest or the most reclusive members of society. Whenever Danny drove along these roads, he was forced to picture Fawley as it might have been when his father was a child— no connection to the outside world, but this paved stretch of road, leading through the trees and promising, but never revealing, something better.

"I wish you'd tell me where we're going," Danny said.

Amanda looked at him. "I haven't decided."

"Well, Kyle sure talks like he wants to see you. I'm not advising you either way, but he sounds sincere."

"Pull the truck over," she said.

"What?"

"Just do it."

Danny pulled the truck over to the soft shoulder and cut the engine. Amanda smiled and jerked her head in a solicitous gesture.

"Come here," she said.

"What for?"

"I want to show you something."

Cautiously, Danny moved across the seat. As he got closer, he noticed her smell. All the smells of a Sunday afternoon—lilies and roast beef and oil-soaped wood. Danny wondered if Amanda was about to touch him. He wanted it to happen, he wanted to feel what he was certain was the cold and bony touch of her slender hands. But she didn't do that. Instead, she swept up her hair and pulled back her ear.

"Look," she said.

He didn't know where to look. But she pulled again and he saw the skin behind her ear—a network of black laces protruding along the white, smooth surface. His memory raced back to childhood injuries and he knew he was looking at stitches. Quite a few of them, in fact. Eight, maybe ten.

"What happened?" he asked.

"He almost pulled my damn ear off."

"I didn't realize that was possible."

"Neither did I. And I don't think it was his plan. He just grabbed me there and threw me across the room. The thing was flapping against my face like a donkey's ear. Kyle took one look at it and passed out cold."

Danny felt like doing the same. Amanda laughed and rubbed her thumb along her lip, as if recalling a fond memory.

"He gave me this, too," she said, holding up her arms in the light. There was a string of plum-colored bruises around each wrist, like bracelets.

She dropped her hands into her lap and said, "Still want to take me to Kyle?"

"No."

"Then take me back to the Lantern. My mama'll come and pick me up."

"I can take you to Wycombe County."

"I don't want you to. I'd feel grateful."

"No harm in that."

She smiled. "It's the worst feeling in the world. It's why Kyle hits me, you know. He feels grateful."

Danny drove her back to the Green Lantern. He didn't know what else to do. Taking her to Kyle was no longer an option, and she had no intention of letting him drive her to her mother's place. Still, he stopped in the parking lot of the restaurant, feeling that he should make one more effort.

He asked the question before he wanted to. He said, "Where was Kyle on the night of the murders?"

Amanda barely glanced at him. "He was with me. For a while. We went out riding, and we fought, and he pulled the car over and pushed me out. I walked home and fell asleep. He came home sometime in the morning. Why?"

"Just curious."

She smiled. "Bullshit."

"I just felt like I had to ask the question," Danny said.

"Do you feel better now that you've asked it?"

Danny shrugged. "I wasn't expecting to feel better."

Amanda looked out the window for a long moment, then turned back to him.

"My stepfather used to come into my room at night. He said, whatever you do, as long as you don't tell, it's not bad. When it gets bad is when you send it out in the world, where it can hurt people."

There was laughter somewhere in her voice.

He looked away from her. He couldn't stand it anymore, those unfathomable eyes. He could not imagine what she knew.

"You don't have to stay with him," Danny said, without conviction. "There are places you can go for help."

"But that's the problem, isn't it? He's where I go for help."

Danny sat in the truck and watched as she walked toward the pay phone, her arms crossed against her chest, shielding her from the wind. When she was beside him, she seemed so strong and certain. It was only from a distance that he could see how small she was. She was a tiny shape, moving across the gravel, with her hair whipping across her face and all the odds in the world against her.

14

JOYCE'S APARTMENT WAS a simple, uncomplicated place. It was also a shrine to indecision. The furnishings made no statement and offered no argument. A plain tweed couch and matching armchair, a glass coffee table, and a wide bookshelf, only one shelf of which was occupied by books. The books themselves could not be disputed—encyclopedias, book club editions of a few classics, a Time-Life series about space. There was a small television, a VCR, and a radio. The remaining open area was occupied by gewgaws, glass figurines of ballerinas and animals, and a few pieces from the Dickens Village collection. The one photograph she displayed was one of herself on her high school graduation day. She was fond of it for a couple of reasons. One was because it didn't look like her. She stood in her black cap and gown, clutching her diploma to her chest, and her expression was decidedly sardonic. It was a characteristic she did not believe herself to possess, yet there it was, captured in full Kodak color, a woman who thought that such a ceremony meant nothing, and her participation in it was obligatory. Of course I graduated, said the easy, crooked smile. So what? Who doesn't?

The other thing she liked about it, which was not visible to the eye of any observer, was that Danny took it. She knew that the taker of the photograph had everything to do with her expression. She was communicating with him, sharing in his own private knowledge that this was all somehow a hoax, that given her background, which he shared, graduating from high school was no more a step forward than falling out of a moving car. She had escaped, but where did that escape take her except to a hard landing on cold, unforgiving asphalt?

She never expected anyone else to see the meaning of it all, and no one ever did. In a way, Joyce thought of it as a photograph of Danny, and for that reason she valued it beyond measure. Danny was the only person she cared to recall from her entire history.

Joyce loved her apartment for many reasons, but one of them was that it carried not even a shadow of her former life. A detective could scour this place and never come up with a worthwhile clue about the person who occupied it. The identity of her place was its lack of identity; it was the life she had always strived for. Many a night she had relaxed on the couch in front of the TV, thinking, Anyone could live here. It was an accurate representation of nothing in particular, and she had spent most of her life trying to free herself of her particulars. It wasn't an easy task, being devoid of opinion or attitude. She did not feel that way, but she could live that way, and she could hope to reinvent herself. She could create a completely malleable person, a chameleon who shamelessly adapted to her environment for purposes of survival.

It took her a few years to get the place exactly as she wanted it, a safe haven, a sanctuary of neutrality. It was only after she felt she'd achieved that goal that she began to take lovers. It was something she'd contemplated doing for a long time. She had never intended to be a virgin until she was thirty; she had no idea it would take her so long to escape herself. But she knew she would never feel comfortable becoming intimate with a man until she had exorcised her past. The last thing she wanted to do was let a stranger in on her secrets. She did not want to confess or explain anything. She was horrified by the notion that, in a moment of weakness, mistaking sex for love, she might start trying to communicate her story to someone. That could only lead her down a terrible path of self-pity, melodrama, a desire to be saved. No, she could not for a second allow sex to become some kind of act of attrition. It needed to be a cool and logical act, the fulfillment of a physical need rather than an emotional one. She wanted to experience sex the way the more adventurous girls in high school had—a guiltless act that cost them nothing emotionally, that did not require an apology or an explanation any more than taking a shower or flossing their teeth.

Sometimes, she thought, she really wanted to experience sex the way that men did. Men did not bring any sort of history or personal invest- ment to the act. And why should they? Why should anyone? The body did not require it. Joyce had read several books on the subject, and she was very much disturbed by the accounts that stated it was not uncom- mon for women to burst into tears or hysterical laughter at the point of orgasm. The books never mentioned men responding in a similar fash- ion. So what could that mean? That women could see the whole business for what it was? This is what all the pain and worry and self-scrutiny has been about? This is *it?*

Joyce wanted nothing to do with the typical female response. She did not want to laugh or cry or even feel contemplative about it. She wanted to fall into a deep, uncomplicated sleep when it was over, knowing she had completed a normal and evolutionary act. And she knew that achiev- ing that response would take some work.

Her first lover was someone from out of town, a traveling insurance salesman she'd picked up in a now defunct bar in Greensboro called the Miami Room. Miami was represented by a few neon palm trees on the walls, and the tropical shirts sported by the waitresses and bartenders. The insurance salesman, who called himself Gil (she always suspected he had lied about his name), was a stiff, unimaginative fellow with a re- ceding hairline and ragged fingernails that he had chewed off down to the quick. He smelled like Dentyne and lied about being married. She could see the indentation, a white band of skin on an otherwise tanned finger. She didn't care. It did not fit into her scheme to worry about some wife in a distant state. And she did not perceive herself as a threat. She did not want any woman's husband for an extended amount of time. When the insurance salesman got out of bed the next morning, he had made some attempt toward pretending he'd see her again.

"I have several clients in this area," he'd said, straightening his tie in her mirror. "I could make an excuse to get back here next weekend."

"Don't," she'd said.

"Why not?"

Raising herself up on her elbows, she'd leaned into a shaft of sunlight. "You probably didn't get a good look at me last night. Look now."

He stared at her face for a long moment, trying to decide whether or not he had any sort of reaction dwelling secretly inside himself. Then he shook his head.

"I don't care about that. It relieves me in a way. I don't have to apologize for this," he'd said, pinching a tiny roll of fat around his midsection, then sweeping his palm against his forehead. "Or this."

"Don't come back, Gil. If we meet up again, that would be fine. But don't come looking for me."

He had seemed even more relieved by her statement because he could see that it contained no hidden plea. She was releasing him, and that sense of freedom made him want her more. He had come back, several times, encountering her at the same bar. After it closed, she never saw him again.

But that was fine. She had found that lovers were not difficult to acquire. Most were from out of town. She visited the nightclubs in Greensboro fairly regularly, finding herself free of the worry that accompanied her during the day. When she walked down the streets of Fawley, she felt obligated to maintain some sort of persona. She had to be somewhat predictable, and this was what set the alarms off in her brain. But when she went into a nightclub, she knew her connection to the people within it was fleeting. There were no expectations. She did not have to account for herself.

She never wondered, as these strange women on TV or in magazines seemed to, what was lacking in herself that she needed to participate in these emotionally bankrupt relationships. In fact, each affair seemed to fortify her. Each time she woke up next to a virtual stranger she felt invincible. I have done this unthinkable thing, she thought. And yet, nothing has happened. No plagues, no biblical judgments, no scarlet letter, no terminal illness. I am here, as I was, only stronger. Because I have proven them all wrong.

It had been quite some time since Joyce had had a lover. She did not mind. She could go months without thinking about sex. Strangely, her job seemed to supply what was missing. It seemed to offer a similar dynamic—the anticipation, the possibility of failure, the thrill of victory, the quiet that followed each successful transaction. She was actually relieved to come home to an empty apartment. She did not have to make conversation, did not have to apologize for watching television or eating cereal for dinner. She liked the quiet, the stillness, the lack of expectation.

Joyce had no desire for any kind of company, not even pets. She had brought a cat home from the pound once, but their relationship lasted less than a week. He was a stupid tabby thing who met her at the door in the evenings, mewing incessantly. She hated the way his round gold eyes stared up at her, wanting her to supply whatever was missing in his life. She did not like the feel of him curled in her lap. She felt inhibited by his affection.

When she took him back to the pound, the woman behind the desk glared at her. "We'll probably end up putting him to sleep, you know."

"Whatever you think is best."

"You can live with that, knowing you're the difference between him living or dying?"

"I think so, yes."

I've lived through worse, Joyce wanted to say. She did not think of the cat again for a long time. But lately, she woke up in the middle of the night, imagining his cry. She felt haunted by him. She woke up in the morning with the feeling that she had murdered someone. After a while, she realized it was just a cat, and she couldn't even be sure he was dead. Maybe someone else had taken him home. Still, it was an eerie feeling that followed her around, the idea that she had killed and could kill again.

One night, as she was watching the news, she realized where it was all coming from. The anchorwoman had used those very words to describe the Quality-Mart murderer or murderers. (They still didn't know how many people were involved.) Whoever had done it, she said, was still out there. He killed once and he could kill again. Joyce felt panicked, as if she were responsible, as if they were looking for her.

She recalled her encounter with Graham Mundy with complete clarity. She could see every detail of his face. She could remember his anger, out of proportion to the crime she had committed. She remembered how loud his voice had sounded, and the way people had started to stare. And she remembered a surge of violent hatred toward him. She even remembered wanting to kill him.

But you didn't, she reminded herself, over and over. And wanting to kill someone was not against the law. Neither was breaking a ceramic Nativity. She had not cursed anyone. She had not caused anything. It was all an accident.

That was disturbing in its own way, the idea that she had no real effect on people, or on the order of things.

• • •

Wednesday evening Joyce suddenly got the urge to go to church. She had always disliked church. She could not see the point of pursuing the affection of a God whose obligation it was to love her anyway. It had been a while since she'd gone, but she dimly recalled a peaceful feeling she encountered after going to a service. She may not have been convinced, but simply by virtue of her being there, her doubts were forgiven.

Of all the services, the Wednesday evening "gatherings" were the least objectionable. The sermon was short and casual, and they sang a few hymns and later socialized on the steps and the lawn outside. But what appealed to her most was the knowledge that Danny and Lydia would be there. Ever since the murders, she had felt a strong desire to talk to Danny. She wasn't sure why. Maybe she relied on him to reassure her. Maybe if Danny told her it wasn't her fault, she'd believe him. Danny struck her as a tortured soul, distant and perplexed, and because of this pain she recognized in him, she trusted him. She knew he had to understand her on some level. He seemed to like her, and she knew it wasn't just because he was related to her. He had no time at all for her sisters, and very little for her mother. He had loved her father and he seemed to harbor some attachment to Kyle. Not that he was fooled by him, though. Danny didn't seem to be fooled by anyone. He just accepted people or not, on their own terms.

And he was so handsome. As a youngster, she was always attracted to him. As a child she used to ask her mother about the possibility of marrying her cousin.

"Don't be ridiculous," Rita would always answer. "You'd have retarded children."

"I don't want to have children," was Joyce's reply.

"You can't love your cousin that way. Not that he'd love you back. Danny is going places. He'll marry someone special."

Danny had married someone special, and Joyce had matured enough to understand why it could never have been her, even if they hadn't been related. But she still loved him and valued his attention, on the rare occasions when she subjected herself to it.

Church had already begun when she slipped in and hurried over to the back pew. It was tricky, because the back pews were always the most crowded. It was odd the way people arranged themselves in a sanctuary. Unlike a movie or a theater, the crowd got thicker toward the back. The first few rows were practically empty, and anyone who dared sit in them was a bit suspect. They were the exhibitionists, the brazenly pious. They were monitoring the reverend, waiting to catch him in a mistake.

Then, too, people preferred to sit at the back in case John Evans went on too long and they felt the need to slip out. Not that John wouldn't notice. He saw everything. Joyce could feel his eyes landing squarely on her as she tiptoed in, and she could have sworn he stopped his sermon until she was comfortably situated. She felt some heads turn, and she noticed Lydia, three rows ahead, smiling at her over her shoulder. Her fingers flickered in a wave, but Joyce didn't dare respond. She felt John might stop the whole service, like a teacher, and ask if Joyce wanted to share anything with the congregation.

A sudden feeling of anxiety descended on her; her ears rang, and she could not hear a word of John's sermon. She was dimly aware that he was referring to Quality-Mart, for the word "murder" came up again and again. She was grateful for the roar, like a tornado, inside her head. She didn't want to hear any more. She didn't want to know. She felt hot. Sweat sprouted on her forehead and her hair felt glued to her scalp. She couldn't even look at the woman beside her, but she detected by shape and smell that it was Sissy Burnette. Sissy was fleshy and always reeked of cigarettes and Doublemint. She could hear her jaws working furiously on the gum, as if she were trying to bring it back to life.

Finally they stood and sang "Just a Closer Walk with Thee." They remained standing as John spread his hands and gave the benediction: "Now may the peace of God which passeth all understanding rest with you and abide with you forever more. Amen."

Now, how is that possible? Joyce wondered. How can a peace which is beyond understanding rest with anybody? Wouldn't a peace which was perfectly comprehensible be easier to swallow?

As people crawled over her, Joyce stood still and waited for Danny and Lydia to pass by. She flinched as Sissy put a hand on her shoulder and said, "It's so good to see you here, Joyce. We've missed you. You're in our prayers."

"Okay," Joyce said. She could not imagine what on earth people were praying for on her behalf. She didn't even pretend to pray for Sissy, or for anyone.

When Danny and Lydia walked up she stepped out and smiled at them, and realized to her horror that she had nothing to say.

Lydia came to the rescue. She touched Joyce lightly on the sleeve and said, "You look so nice in that dress. Green is your color."

"Oh, thank you," Joyce said, a little too enthusiastically. Lydia's praise washed over her and comforted her far more effectively than John Evans's benediction. She tried to think of a reciprocal compliment, but it seemed silly to comment on Lydia's appearance, which was always perfect.

Danny stood at a respectful distance from his wife, his hand touching the small of her back. Joyce wondered what it would feel like to have a man touch her in that respectful way. She averted her eyes, ashamed of her interest.

She followed them out onto the lawn of the church. It was cool again, suddenly, and they all tried to pretend they weren't shivering as they huddled close together on the grass.

Even in the dim glow of the street light, Joyce could see that Danny did not look well. His face looked drawn and his eyes were a little puffy, as if he needed sleep. He was fidgety, too. She noticed that he kept running his fingers along his neck, and occasionally worked them under his armpits as if checking for a foreign body. She noticed Lydia staring at these peculiar gestures. Lydia, who never seemed rattled by anything, crossed her arms tightly over her stomach and sucked in a breath. Clearly, Danny's behavior disturbed her.

Danny said, "I never got to congratulate you, Joyce."

"On what?"

"Your promotion. Assistant manager? That's great."

"Oh well, it's just work. I mean, it's not like your job."

At this Danny smirked and said, "It's not like I'm curing cancer or anything. My wife is the real star of the family."

"Right," Lydia said. "I'm busy sending a whole generation of sanitation workers and unwed mothers into the world."

"Come on, your class got the highest score in the county on standardized tests this fall."

"Yeah, I know, but it doesn't impress them at all. They'd rather get the highest score on the latest video game."

"You're too hard on yourself," Danny said, abandoning his own anatomy for a second, long enough to put an arm around his wife. She leaned into him and smiled up at his chin. Joyce looked at her feet, blushing.

Lydia said, "Not nearly as hard as my students are on me. They hate me for conducting class. They all want to take the month off to recover from Quality-Mart."

"Please, I think we've heard enough about that to last a lifetime," Danny said.

"Have they caught anybody?" Joyce asked. She didn't want to discuss it, but she feared her refusal to do so would betray her own guilt.

Lydia shook her head. "They're still looking for the ubiquitous black teenagers."

A quick wind whipped up and they all moved a little closer together, bowing their heads, waiting for it to pass.

"So much for early spring," Lydia said.

"It's just a cold snap," Danny reassured her. "Can't last."

Lydia glanced over her shoulder and said, "There's Dee, waving at me. I'm gonna go say hello."

She walked away and as they watched her move across the grass, Joyce felt suddenly nervous, the way she did at high school dances when she found herself alone with a boy she had a crush on. She desperately wanted to think of something to say to hold his interest. Danny smiled at her and resumed the odd inspection of his neck.

"What brings you out here?" he asked.

Joyce shrugged. "Oh, I don't know. I felt like doing something constructive."

"How's your family?"

Joyce felt slightly defensive when he asked that, as if he were deliberately making a distinction between his own life and hers. As if he didn't own those people, as if they belonged exclusively to her.

She said, "You probably see more of them than I do."

Danny shook his head. "I pulled Kyle out of another car wreck the other day. No big deal. Nothing new. I got a glimpse of your mother. She seems real edgy. She's lost some weight."

Joyce sighed. There was nothing she could say about that.

"Do you ever talk to her?" Danny asked.

Joyce shook her head. She wasn't sure how she felt about that admission. She sometimes missed her mother, the way one might miss warm weather in the middle of winter. It was a nice idea. But it didn't solve anything.

"She never got over me leaving," Joyce said. "She's waiting for me to come back. And I'm never going to. I'm never going back there."

"You're right," Danny said. "You're right to stay away."

A moment of thick silence passed between them. Now Danny's fingers were exploring the area around his ears. Joyce wanted him to stop. She wanted him to be calm. Danny had always been the most capable, the most rational person in her life. This agitated manner of his was making her feel as if her entire universe were on the verge of coming apart.

"I've been wanting to talk to you," he said suddenly, spitting out the words. Joyce was surprised by them. She wanted to encourage him, but she felt the safest thing to do was wait. Finally he dropped his hands to his sides and said, "I've been wanting to talk to you about Kyle."

Joyce felt rigid. There was nothing on earth she wanted to talk about less than Kyle. Why was Danny doing this to her? Why was he acting strange and saying things she didn't want to hear?

"No," she said, shaking her head. "I don't want to."

"I know. It's hard for me, too. But I need to know if you're thinking . . . the same thing that I am."

Her father's funeral was the last time she'd seen that look of desperation on Danny's face, as if he were on the verge of shouting out something, just because he couldn't stand knowing it anymore, mulling it over, by himself.

"Joyce," he said, "tell me something."

She stood still and waited.

He paused, looking up to the sky as if it might supply him with the right words. "Have you noticed anything strange about Kyle lately?"

Joyce let the question settle in the air. The ambient chatter around her seemed to grow dimmer and she felt detached, as though, if she screamed, no one would hear.

She said, "Danny, I never see Kyle anymore. I never want to see him again. I couldn't even tell you what he looks like these days."

"He looks the same," Danny said. "He *is* the same. Except that he has a girlfriend."

Joyce tried to picture that, some woman wanting to touch him, to sleep with him. Some woman who felt safe turning off the lights with him in the room.

"Who is she?" Joyce asked.

"Her name is Amanda."

He didn't speak for a moment. He was busy staring at his fingers. Joyce thought he might leave it at that. She hoped he would. He touched his fingers to his lips, then blew on them.

"But tell me," Danny went on, "have you heard anything about Kyle lately? Has he been getting into trouble?"

Joyce laughed. "I don't think of him that way, getting into and out of trouble like a bathtub. To me, he *is* trouble. It's not a temporary condition."

Danny didn't smile. She felt stranded in the conversation now. She shouldn't have gotten into it. She should have refused.

Danny said, "Ever since this thing at Quality-Mart . . ."

His voice broke off. He couldn't finish the sentence. He knew he didn't need to.

Joyce felt relieved. Things were suddenly becoming clear to her. Images moved into focus, like reception clearing on a TV screen. She understood now what the distant dread had been about, that sense that she was somehow responsible for Graham Mundy's death. It wasn't because she broke the Nativity. It was because she was related to Kyle, and that Kyle was somehow to blame.

She said, "Oh, Danny."

The relief was lifting, as quickly as it had descended, and now she felt fear creeping into her body like a sickness.

"I know it's farfetched," Danny said. "But that guy, that Graham Mundy, he turned Kyle down for a job. And he's been acting so strange. The other day he started crying. I'd never seen him cry in my life."

Joyce shuddered. She hated that image; she wanted it to be gone.

"Please," Danny said. "Tell me I'm crazy."

Joyce stared at him, at the moonlight falling on his face, at his lips moving, so slightly, as if he were praying. He wasn't crazy. He was smart and solemn and perfect. When was it going to be over, she wondered? When was Kyle going to leave them alone?

"Danny," she said. "They're looking for a black man, aren't they?"

"Yes, but that's just a guess. It doesn't mean anything."

"I think it means everything."

He looked at her. "What? What are you saying?"

Joyce said nothing. She waited for him to understand.

Danny said, "We can't do this. We can't protect him. We can't just keep quiet, can we?"

"We already have," she said. "All our lives."

Lydia appeared then, like an apparition, placing her hand on Danny's shoulder. He actually jumped, and they all laughed nervously.

"Let's go," Lydia said. "I've had enough religion for one evening. We'll give you a ride, Joyce."

"Oh no, I drove. I'll be fine."

Danny did not look at her again. He slipped his hand into Lydia's and they walked away. Joyce felt ashamed of her resentment, as if she had been spurned by a lover with whom she had shared one wild, irrational, intimate moment that would connect them forever.

Joyce drove home along the quiet streets, feeling rattled, wondering if a butterscotch sundae at Dairy Queen would help her forget. She suspected it might, but she definitely did not want to see any more neighbors tonight. Church had provided her with all the exposure she needed for the evening. So perhaps a better idea would be to drive out to the 7-Eleven and pick up a quart of Häagen Dazs. Or even better, a six-pack of beer. Before she reached the turn-off, she witnessed a sight which made her forget her plan. A car was stalled in the right lane, just after the stoplight. The hood was raised, and someone hovered under it, gazing at the engine.

Joyce had no intention of stopping, but she couldn't help it. The car had swerved left, blocking the lane which would allow her to move around it. She pulled to a stop and blew her horn, realizing seconds later how pointless that was.

The man under the hood looked up at her. His face was barely recognizable in the shadowy light. It took her a moment to realize she was staring at Rick Gunther.

She had not seen Rick since their encounter at Quality-Mart. She did not see much of Rick otherwise, except when he stopped in at the store for Stouffer's macaroni and cheese. She had never really liked Rick, mainly because of all the rumors she'd heard of him and his female students. Some of them she knew to be true. She'd seen him in town, talking on the street corners with young girls. The girls would smile and flip their hair and he'd gaze off in the distance, as if their attention didn't matter. And the more it didn't matter, the more they'd flip their hair.

As she stared at him through the glare of her headlights, all she could think of was him slipping that black satin pump onto her foot. It had been a horrifying moment for her. It was not especially lessened now, by the sight of him toiling over his steaming engine.

It was too late, though. He had spotted her.

"Hey," he said, coming around to her open window.

"Hey yourself."

He looked at her dress and said, "Going to church?"

"I've been."

He nodded, running his fingers through his dark hair. "Know anything about cars?"

"I can recognize them in a lineup."

Rick laughed. Joyce's heart raced. It did not sound like her own voice. It sounded like something Lydia would say.

"I think I've blown a gasket," he said.

"That sounds serious."

"Well, if I've cracked the engine it's serious enough to keep me from retiring."

"When were you planning on retiring?"

"No time soon. Would you give me a ride?"

Before she could answer he had moved around on the other side and opened the door. He slid into the seat next to her, smelling of the outdoors and engine parts. Somewhere, under all that, was the scent of cologne.

"Where do you want to go?" Joyce asked.

"South of France, all my life. The beaches are topless."

"I don't have enough gas."

"Your place, then."

"Mine?"

"I live in the apartments on Franklin Road, which is quite a distance. If you live close by, I'd just like to call the Auto Club."

"I live at the Elmwood Apartments, two blocks from here."

"Perfect," he said, settling into the seat as if it were an easy chair.

Joyce drove, conscious of her manner, coming to full stops at the stop signs and looking in both directions. She could feel Rick looking at her, like a driving instructor.

"Where are you coming from?" she asked.

"Doesn't matter," he answered. "The Auto Club never asks where you're coming from, only where you're going."

"The Auto Club's not asking. I am."

"Do you really care?"

"Not at all. I'm just making conversation."

Rick laughed. He chewed on a fingernail as she turned onto her street. "How come you didn't let me buy those shoes for you?"

"I don't need any black pumps."

"They looked great on you."

"I don't need to look great."

She turned the car into the parking lot of her apartment building. There was a small gathering of black kids around a pickup truck, the thumping bass of a rap song echoing off the building.

"You like living here?" Rick asked.

"It's usually quieter than this," she lied, afraid to admit she found the sound of their nocturnal activities soothing. She liked to know that people around her were getting on with the business of living. That way, she could be assured they were paying no attention to her. Indeed, they did not glance in her direction as they got out of the car.

When she unlocked her door and let Rick in, she felt relieved at the sight of her apartment, devoid, as always, of anything approaching her personality. It was perfectly sterile. Rick moved into the living room, looking around, as if searching for secrets. Joyce was proud of herself for not providing any.

"There's the phone."

Rick picked it up and dialed as she went into the kitchen to make tea. By the time she emerged with two steaming cups, he was flopped on her tweed couch, leafing through *Newsweek.*

"Is everything okay?" Joyce asked, setting the tea down in front of him. He picked up his mug as if he expected it. He felt no need to thank her, and for that she felt grateful. The last thing she needed was a man pretending that a mug of tea mattered.

"Yeah, they're coming here. They'll take me to my car. Do you live here alone?"

"Of course. Why?"

"It's so settled," he answered. "I mean, everything is in its place, like you're not expecting any surprises."

"I'm not."

"You could get married or something."

Joyce laughed, sipping her tea. "I don't think so."

"Why, because of your face?"

Joyce stalled, her lips pressed to her cup. No one had ever confronted her that way before. Her face was the unspeakable subject.

"No, not that. I won't get married because I don't want to be."

"Why not?" Rick asked.

Joyce shrugged. "I've never seen it work."

He stared at her, holding his mug in two hands. "Neither have I. Isn't that strange? People keep doing it anyway."

"Well, I'm sure it works for some people," Joyce said.

"Like Lydia and Danny?" Rick asked.

"They seem happy," she admitted.

"Everybody seems happy. That's the whole point of marriage, isn't it? To seem happy." He took a sip of his tea, then said, "Sometimes I think that the point of marriage is just the point of life, to get as many good years as you can. Then you move on. I don't know, you're talking to a confirmed bachelor. Male-female relationships seem doomed, in my estimation."

"Why?" Joyce asked, glad for the warm cup of tea she held next to her face.

"Because we always want different things. Women want to be loved indefinitely, without question. Men want the question. They want the mystery. You can't have both. So men stay married as long as their interest will hold. Women stay married forever, even after it's over."

"I don't know," Joyce said. "I've never been there."

"But you want to be. You all behave as if it's the final act of life. Once it's achieved, you don't expect anything else."

"Why do you keep saying 'you'? I've never been close. I can't even have a cat. I just want to be alone."

"Me, too. But there's always that hour, in the middle of the night, when you wake up feeling restless and incomplete. You realize at three A.M. you're going to die. And you wish you had something to grab. You wish you could touch another person and say, 'This can't be it, can it? There has to be more. It can't be the slow decline to nothingness.' If marriage serves any purpose, that has to be it. Having someone to grab when it all gets too scary."

"I don't want anyone to grab me," she said.

"What about someone to hold you?" he asked, his voice softening. "Everyone wants that."

The doorbell buzzed. Rick jumped, spilling his tea.

"How did they get here so soon?" he asked.

Joyce rose and went to the door. It wasn't the Auto Club. It was her neighbor, old Mrs. Winston, requesting them to keep their voices down. Joyce reassured her and sent her away.

"Were we loud?" Rick asked.

"No. But she's not used to hearing any noise in my apartment."

"So how much can she hear?"

"When you're old you can hear a lot of unwanted sounds. You can hear people living. It's got to disturb you."

Joyce sat down on the carpet and tried to ignore the way Rick was staring at her.

"If it weren't for that thing on your face, you'd be pretty," he said.

"My father used to have a saying. You can put kittens in the oven, but that don't make them biscuits."

Rick stared at her. "What the hell does that mean?"

"You figure it out."

Rick thought for a moment, but she could tell he wasn't really thinking about her words. Finally he said, "What is it about a scar that scares people?"

"People don't like anything ugly."

"But you're not ugly. You're just disfigured."

"You have such a way with words," she said. It was exciting her, the way he talked, so unapologetically. Not like all her benign lovers who acted like it didn't matter. But when they kissed her, they kissed her neck. They wouldn't go near her face.

"How did it happen?" Rick asked.

"It doesn't matter. It won't change anything."

Rick put his mug down and leaned forward on the couch. "Okay. Here's a secret. You know where I was tonight?"

"You don't have to tell me."

"At Cindy Wettenhall's house. She used to be a student of mine. She's gorgeous, this nineteen-year-old goddess. Her skin is so soft, it's like rose petals. But when I touch it, I feel like I'm going to disappear. There's nothing beyond it. I feel helpless when I'm with her."

"Why?"

"Because she doesn't get my jokes. But why should she? She hasn't lived. She hasn't experienced anything. It's God's big joke that the most desirable women are those who have not experienced anything. It's like He's saying, You can have this flesh but you're not going to be happy with it."

"I don't think that's God's joke at all. I think that's man's joke."

The doorbell buzzed again. Joyce rose and opened the door to find a surly Triple A mechanic standing there.

"So where's the car?" he asked.

Rick stood and went to the door.

"There is no car," he said.

"I just got paged."

"So just get lost. Okay?"

Rick slipped him a bill, the size of which Joyce was unable to see. He closed the door and Joyce stood beside him, feeling afraid.

"Why did you do that?" she asked.

"I don't feel ready to go home," he answered.

"When will you?"

"When we finish talking," he answered, and went back to the couch. She stood by the door, wondering.

Rick flopped on the couch again, putting his feet on her coffee table. Fortunately, Joyce had no real feelings about her furniture, so she didn't have to ask him not to do it. It would have been pointless anyway. Men did not understand the concept of preserving other people's belongings. As far as Joyce was concerned, a man's disregard for property went back to one simple and elemental moment in his development: the freedom to pee outside.

This was a theory Joyce had concocted over the years. The Peeing Outdoors Theory. The first time she saw her brother whip out his penis and whaz on the hydrangeas, she knew that the sexes would never be equal. The message was subtle but inescapable—the world did not want to know about her bodily functions. She must reveal them in secret, get rid of them, cleanse herself of them. But men felt no such shame. They were spared the embarrassment of their natural impulses. More significantly, men were given the message at an early age that the world was theirs to piss on.

Figuratively speaking, Rick was pissing on her coffee table, and the damage was far too done for her to try and combat it now.

"Do you want me to drive you home?" Joyce asked.

"No, not yet," he said, resting his neck against her sofa cushions. "I'm having a good time."

"But you can't stay here."

He didn't seem to hear her. She was starting to worry because tomorrow they were going to receive a large shipment of frozen foods, and she needed to be at work by eight.

Suddenly Rick asked, "Are you a virgin?"

Joyce was too surprised to be angry. "That's a very personal question."

"Of course it is. Who cares about impersonal information?"

Joyce was busy trying to find a way to avoid an answer when he said, "I don't think you are."

"Why?"

"Because of what happened at Quality-Mart. I mean, with me and your foot. Feet are very private. And they're usually hideous-looking. I have been with some stunningly beautiful women whose feet looked like hell. Like a gorilla's. Yours was perfect. And when I touched it, I could just tell that you'd been touched before."

"That's not very compelling evidence."

"Okay, what else? You're funny. Generally speaking, virgins have no sense of humor. It's like they don't discover irony until they get laid. Why is that, I wonder?"

"Because," Joyce said, "until women have sex, they don't get the joke."

"So who's the guy?"

"What makes you think there's only one?"

He grinned and nodded. "Good. I was right."

Joyce sipped her tea. She felt foolish. Here she sat, priding herself on her inscrutable surroundings, and she had willingly given up her most private information. Despite her intentions, Rick was getting to know her. He was making her surrender information.

"Have you ever been in love?" he asked.

"No," she said. She couldn't seem to stop herself.

"Yeah, me either."

"So why do you keep going after these women?"

Rick stared at his cup for a long moment. Joyce was sure his tea was long gone, so perhaps he was reading something in the pattern that the leaves had left behind.

"I guess I don't want to grow up," he admitted. "I guess I hate the idea of losing my hair and getting glasses and all that. Most people have a sense of what they do, what they're good at. I'm good at being young."

"But you're not young."

"I know, and sometimes I think I'd just as soon be dead. It's like the point of my life is over. People are born to do a certain thing, and once that goal is achieved they should just walk out onto the ice. It's like professional athletes. Once they retire, they've lived out their usefulness. You read these stories about how they go on to invest in a business or do charity work or something, but deep down you know they're just waiting out their time. They've finished their work. They're treading water."

He sighed and shook his head. He smiled at her, looking slightly embarrassed. "I don't know what I'm saying. I'm not a kid anymore and I should just get over it. I should move on. Right?"

Joyce shrugged. "I know people say that life is about moving on. But to me, it's always been about hanging on."

He sat up and moved to the edge of his seat again. He looked genuinely startled, as if she had just identified the meaning of life.

"Oh my God," he said. "That's really it, isn't it? I'm honestly trying to do the right thing. It's bad enough that I'm sleeping with students. But it's a struggle just to confine myself to seventeen-year-olds. Sometimes I want to do something worse. What people don't get is that I'm trying to be *good*. Do you know what I mean?"

Joyce nodded. "Some people start from a lower point."

"Oh my God," he repeated.

Joyce felt exhausted. She didn't want to talk anymore, but she couldn't find a way to end it.

"Do you think we get punished for the things we do?" he asked her.

"You mean on earth?"

"No, later. In heaven. Or hell, or whatever. You go to church. You must believe."

"I believe in God," she said. "But I don't think He's benevolent. He's more like some bored kid, acting up all the time. Like He's got too many toys to play with so He doesn't take care of them."

She hesitated to look at Rick. She could feel him staring at her. She could feel him wanting to say something to her, something extreme and confidential. She didn't want to know his secrets. She didn't want to reveal any more of her own.

"You should go home now," she said.

"I can't. I sent the Triple A guy home."

"I'll drive you," she said.

"You'd have to drive back alone. And it's not safe, this late."

"Well, you can't stay here."

"I'll sleep on the couch. I'll be gone before you get up. You'll never know I was here."

She wished that were true. But she would never forget that he was here, and that she had told him so many things. She had given up a part of herself. She could not get it back.

"Do whatever you want," she said, standing up. She walked away from him, toward her bedroom.

"Joyce," he said.

"What?" she asked, her back to him.

"Don't move."

For some reason, she obeyed. She heard him get off the couch and walk toward her. She could feel him right behind her and she had no idea what he was about to do.

"Look at me," he said.

Slowly, she turned. He reached out and touched her face, his fingers landing softly on her scar. It didn't hurt, but she recoiled just the same. He was so close she could smell the tea on his breath.

"Sleep well," he said.

He leaned forward, and before she knew it his lips were against hers. She pushed him away, and he looked surprised.

"I just wanted to tell you something," he said.

"Tell me later," she answered and walked away.

She left him there, standing in her hallway, surprised at being abandoned. Once she was safely inside her bedroom she touched her lips with her fingertips. A thousand things could happen between now and her deathbed, and this is what she'd remember—the feel of Rick Gunther's lips against hers. Sloppy and chapped and full of curious intentions.

Joyce took off all her clothes and pulled the comforter up around her chin. She shivered, her limbs knocking together. Her teeth were chattering. She thought of Rick lying on her couch and she shivered harder. She thought of Danny and all the curious things he had said to her on the church lawn. Why had she gone out tonight? She knew better than to do that, to expose herself to that kind of danger. She was right to avoid the world because whenever she ventured out into it, she collided with all its contradictions. How did people do it, day after day? How did they fight all these little wars?

Somehow, she fell asleep. She dreamed about frozen foods. She was standing knee-deep in Stouffer's entrees, wondering where to put them. Her feet were cold. Ice was melting between her toes, making them wet. And when she woke up she realized that the sensation was real. Someone was in the room with her, licking her toes.

She sat up and saw Rick kneeling at the end of her bed, fondling her feet, kissing them and rubbing them against his cheek.

"What are you doing?" she gasped.

"I just want to see your feet," he whispered.

"You're out of your mind."

"They're so beautiful."

"You're crazy."

She tried to push him away, but he moved onto the bed and lay on top of her, whispering in her ear, "Don't move."

"Rick, you don't have to do this," she said.

"Yes, I do," he whispered, his lips moist and desperate next to her ear.

"What I mean is," she said, pausing to catch her breath, "just let me say something."

"Don't say anything." He was still dressed, and his heavy, fully clothed body pressed down on her like a vise. His belt buckle was digging into her stomach. She wished she could believe he was drunk, but he was fully conscious and smelled of nothing more potent than Lipton's.

She tried to move, but he was too strong for her. She pushed against his chest but her efforts only encouraged him. He entered her before she could stop him. And once he was inside, there was no going back.

"Oh God, oh God," he said. She tried to reposition herself. She could not really feel him. She could only feel the belt buckle digging into her. He interpreted her every move as an attempt to resist him, and that made him push harder. Without warning he came, his body turning rigid, then collapsing. He rolled off of her, and Joyce thought, my God, this is why he sleeps with teenagers, because he's so bad at it and they're too inexperienced to know.

"I'm sorry," he said, lying on his back, one hand on his chest, panting up at the ceiling.

She wanted to say, No kidding. But she stayed silent. She made no effort to reassure him, to tell him she would have consented, given the chance. She felt he was enjoying his shame.

"I shouldn't have done that," he said. "I'll never forgive myself," he said.

She doubted that. She suspected he had forgiven himself long before he had done it.

15

ABRUPTLY, THE PROFILE of the Quality-Mart murderer changed. The coroner's lab report had come back from Charlottesville, stating that some microscopic skin fibers under the security guard's fingernails were that of a Caucasian. Lydia scoured the article in the *Fawley Register,* under the bold headline: MURDER CASE TAKES UNEXPECTED TURN.

"Hmm," she said, "but is the DNA analysis as reliable as the black car theory?"

"I don't know why you take such delight in this," Danny grumbled at the breakfast table, stabbing angrily at his cornflakes.

"Oh, hang on. The whole town has been treating this like a block party, and *I'm* the one who's accused of enjoying it?"

"Lydia, you are. Admit it. You love it that the cops were wrong. White guy, black guy, orange guy, who cares?"

"You're forgetting the possibility of an orange woman."

"The point is, two people are dead."

Lydia stared at him. His complexion was a shade lighter, she could swear, and slightly gray, almost the color of ash. Was this case really getting to him so much, or was it something else?

"Are you feeling okay?" she asked.

He issued a sarcastic huff and shook his head. "Yeah, I'm great."

"No, I mean, physically."

At this he raised his eyes and stared at her as if she had suddenly started speaking Portuguese. He slid his chair back and reached for his jacket.

"Danny, I want you to talk to me," she said.

"No, you don't. You don't want me to talk about my problems. You just want me to be happy."

Lydia found herself laughing involuntarily, by reflex.

"Is that such a crime?" she asked.

"It's not a crime, but it's a form of pressure," he said. "I'm completely aware that I can't bring my problems home to you. You have to know that everything's going to be all right. There's not a person on earth who can promise you that. Least of all me."

"Danny, that's not it. I just want . . . I just want . . ."

She found it impossible to finish that sentence. Danny nodded.

"Yes," he said. "You just want."

He walked out of the room, and it took her a while to realize he had actually left the house. She stood and ran to the window, watching as the truck pulled out of the drive.

Her nose touched the glass as she stared at the bare trees, lifting and bowing in the wind. She felt as desolate as the landscape. She felt there was a place she had avoided all her life—being alone, looking at an empty road under a seasonless sky, afraid to turn around. And here she was at that place. She had, without knowing, arrived.

She called in sick at work. She spent the rest of the day in her housecoat, flipping through magazines and half-listening to the shrill voices of the daytime talk shows. Sometimes she glanced up and stared at the fat, pale faces with great slashes of red lipstick across their mouths and earrings dangling like air fresheners, and for a split second she wondered where she was, what she was doing here. Fragments of law school came back to her, writs and precedents and statutes, hurling at her like detritus from space. For one protracted moment she looked out the window and wondered if it were possible to miss your life. To miss it, like a train. To stand on the wrong platform, to go east instead of west and never realize it except for that nagging feeling that something was off. What if she had done this? What if her life, the one she should have chosen, were carrying on without her? What if there were some inexplicable gap in someone else's life—like Hamilton's or Camille's—that she might have filled, that might have made everyone's existence happier or easier or more consistent?

It was absurd, and she knew it; as irrational as believing in fortune cookies or horoscopes, and yet something about it was truly haunting. Lydia could not escape the feeling that she was in the wrong place. And the reason she had never really understood Danny's family or her colleagues or Fawley as a concept was that she simply should not be here. She had been hurled out of her own universe like a meteor. She had somehow gotten off course.

Finally she fell asleep and stayed that way until a slate gray evening light settled across the room. She woke with a start and hurried into the shower. She slipped on a simple black sweater dress and had just finished putting on her makeup when Danny came in.

"You look nice," he said, standing in the doorway, loosening his tie. "What's the occasion?"

"Oh, nothing. I just felt like dressing up. I thought we might go out or something."

The thought seemed to paralyze him. He looked around the room as if he might find a reason to say no.

"I hate it when we fight," she said.

Now he looked perplexed. "Did we fight?"

"This morning."

"Oh." He shrugged, as if he'd forgotten it.

She moved over to him, her heart pounding, and slipped her arms around his neck. He smelled like an office, thank God. Ink and paper and Xerox machines and coffee. She buried her nose against his shirt.

"Danny," she said, her forehead pressed against his chest, "I've been thinking all day . . . and I know there has to be a reason I married you . . . and that you married me. A good reason that we took a chance like that. We're smart, rational people. We couldn't have just jumped into this on a whim, could we? So I want to hang on to that."

He pushed her away slightly, just so he could see her face.

"Lydia," he said, "what's happened?"

"Nothing. I'm trying to reassure you. I'm just saying I don't think it could be a mistake."

"Whoever said it was?"

"I don't know."

"Oh Christ," he said and pulled her close to him. He held her so hard her breastbone began to ache, but she didn't want him to let go.

"I love you so much," he said.

She started to cry into his shirt and when she pulled away she could see she had left lacy mascara marks across his chest, like spiders.

"Listen," she said, unsure of what might follow.

"I've resigned my position," he said.

Lydia stared at him. What could that mean? Surely nothing bad, because he was smiling at her. He was giving her that crooked boyish grin which she rarely got a chance to see.

"What position?" she finally asked.

"In the firm. I'm not a sales manager anymore. I'm going back on the line."

Her stomach dropped. She felt the need to grab something, but the closest thing was Danny and she was backing away from him, slowly but deliberately.

"What does that mean?" she asked.

"I'm going back on the line," he repeated, with no noticeable difference in his inflection.

"I don't get it," she said.

"I'm going back to building. It's what I've always wanted to do."

"You're going to be a construction worker?"

"I've always been a construction worker," he said. "This idea that I'm someone who does paperwork is ridiculous. It's been making me miserable. I've always done my best work out there with the guys. You know, the material. I need to be hands on. I need to build something, Lydia. Crunching numbers and approving blueprints, that's not constructive. That's not about building things. I can't be the guy who arranges cutbacks and bullies the workers. That job is about stopping things, or at least slowing them down. I need to make things happen. And the only way to do that is to be right out there, with the hammer and nails and concrete."

Lydia felt dizzy. She pressed her palm to her forehead.

"You got demoted?" she asked.

"No, not at all," he said. "I requested it. I told Howard and Ben that I'm not cut out for office work. They were okay with it. Honestly, they were kind of relieved."

Lydia couldn't speak. She couldn't because there were so many voices resounding in her head—her parents, Camille, Hamilton, everyone from her old life, all talking at once, wanting to be heard.

"Are you worried about the money? Because with overtime, it's about the same. And now that I'm in the union, I get more vacation time. We could visit your family this Christmas."

"Danny," she said incredulously, "I don't have a family. You . . . you are it."

"Well, we could have a baby."

"Oh God," she said. She sank onto the bed and stared at the flowered pattern until it all ran together.

"What is it?" he asked. "You don't want to be married to a blue-collar guy?"

"That's not what you are."

"That's what you're scared of, isn't it? You're ashamed of it."

"No, Danny. It just doesn't fit, that's all. I can't explain it. It doesn't feel like my life. I feel more and more lost. Like I just took a wrong turn and got here by mistake."

She looked up. He was staring at her, stoically, waiting.

She said, "I don't care what you do. If you're a guy in a hardhat, okay, that's what you are. But I just feel things are going backward. Do you know? All around me. Everyone's in retreat. I guess I always thought life was forward motion. I thought we'd be thinking bigger instead of smaller. Wanting more instead of less."

Danny let a moment pass before he responded. When he spoke, it was with an edge of excitement that made him seem slightly disconnected.

"I had this moment of clarity. I was reading this article in Dr. Steen's office, and it was—"

"What were you doing in Jerry's office?" she asked.

"It was nothing. I thought I had something, but it wasn't anything. The point is, I read this article about a scientific experiment they do with rats. A rat is smart—its instincts are very similar to a human's. They're persistent and they know how to second-guess. They have incredible nesting and survival instincts. Anyway, they did this experiment where they put a rat in a maze with a piece of cheese at the end. They let the rat find the cheese once, then they took it away. The rat went back and back and back, looking for it. But finally, it gave up. It didn't go back for the cheese."

Lydia stared at him. She had no idea what to say.

"It learns, Lydia. It learns not to waste its energy on the impossible. But people aren't like that, the article said. People keep going back and expending their energy on things which are unlikely or even impossible.

So in a way, rats are smarter. They're superior. They learn better than we do."

It took Lydia a second to find her voice.

"Danny," she said, struggling to maintain control. "How can you talk to me about rats? People aren't inferior to rats. People find cures for diseases, and paint paintings and build restaurants. Rats eat tinfoil, Danny. That's how fucking stupid they are. Did it ever occur to you that's why we're standing upright and driving and voting and not living in people's garbage cans . . . because we don't give up? Precisely because we don't learn that lesson?"

Danny shook his head and grabbed at the back of his neck. "I don't know, Lydia. I felt so good about this decision, but now that I've talked to you about it . . ."

"Oh, I've ruined it?"

"Yeah, you kind of have."

She sighed and pulled at a string on her dress. "This is all so wrong," she said quietly.

"Lydia, listen to me. It's not wrong. You said it yourself. It *can't* have been a mistake, us getting together. And anyway, we are in it together and we've got to do our best. That's what I'm trying to do. I'm trying to get rid of the other stuff that's bothering me . . . the stress, the worry . . . so I can just concentrate on you."

"You shouldn't have to concentrate on loving someone, should you? I'm just asking, Danny, because I don't know."

Before Danny could respond, the doorbell rang and they both recoiled, as if they'd been shot by the same bullet. It made them laugh, joylessly. Without speaking of it they went downstairs, their hands brushing against each other as they moved.

Les Carlisle stood in the doorway, his police hat pushed firmly onto his head. He stood straight, trying to look as official as possible. The sight made Lydia smile. Les avoided her eyes.

"Danny, Lydia, sorry to bother you."

"No bother," Lydia said. "Can I get you some coffee?"

"No, ma'am," he said, stepping into the living room. "I just need five minutes of Danny's time."

"Danny's?"

"It's a family matter, Lydia."

"I'm his family."

"It's unrelated to you," Les said firmly.

Danny gave her shoulder a squeeze. Lydia felt irrationally rejected. She wanted to hear, even though she was certain Danny would tell her later what it was about. Still, she disliked being sent to the kitchen like a child during a grown-up party. She sat in a chair and chewed on a fingernail as she strained to hear their low voices in the living room. She knew it couldn't be a death. Les would have announced that in front of her. She wondered if he might actually be speaking to Danny about her own behavior during their last encounter.

"You got to do something about your wife," she could imagine him saying. "You better fix her wagon or we'll fix it for her."

She opened a Diet Pepsi and fumbled in her purse for a pack of cigarettes. She lit one and squinted through the smoke at the hands on the clock, which seemed stuck. In the next room the voices droned, sounding ominous, like the voices from inside a doctor's office.

Her cigarette had burned down to the filter when she heard the door close and Danny came into the kitchen. He gave her a curious smile.

"You're smoking now?" he asked.

"What did Les want?"

"It was about the Quality-Mart thing."

"What about it?"

"Oh, you know. Have I seen anybody, do I know anything? Now that it's a white guy, they have to start all over."

He opened the refrigerator and stared at its contents.

"What would you know about it?" she asked, grinding out her cigarette.

"Well, not a whole hell of a lot," he admitted, finally grabbing a beer and popping the top as he turned around. "Like I didn't know you were there on opening day."

Lydia froze, uncertain how defensive she should be. Did it really matter? She couldn't tell from his expression.

"I thought I told you that," she said.

"With Joyce? That you definitely didn't tell me."

"Does it matter? Jesus, Danny, do I have to account for my every move?" She was trembling slightly as she reached for the pack of cigarettes. Danny's eyes followed the motion.

"Well, you certainly seem to want my itinerary on an hourly basis," he said.

"That is not true."

"Am I at the building site, am I with Kyle, am I shopping for my mother . . . ?"

"Stop it, Danny. You know it's not like that."

She struck the match hard and as it touched the end of the cigarette she caught her husband's expression. He was staring at the wall, and he was, unmistakably, terrified. He closed his eyes and rolled the can across his forehead, as if engaged in some sort of bizarre praying ritual.

Lydia said, "Jesus Christ. He wanted to talk to you about Kyle."

Danny said nothing; he kept rolling the can across his forehead.

"They think Kyle did it," she said.

"No, they don't. They just asked some questions."

"But why would they ask if . . ."

"It's a small town, Lydia. Anytime something goes wrong, they look to Kyle. It just makes sense. The guy's got a history of trouble. They have to eliminate him as a suspect, that's all."

"Have they?" she asked.

At last he stopped rolling the can. He took a long sip from it, then poured the rest down the sink.

"Danny, have they eliminated him as a suspect?"

"Yes," he said.

He walked out and left her sitting there with her cigarette burning. She no longer wanted it, but she felt too stubborn, or embarrassed, to put it out.

16

REX BEGAN TO bring home a friend. For a long time, Sally couldn't see anything unusual about it. He was an older man from the library who appreciated chess as much as Rex did, and they sat for hours in the living room, staring at the pieces, moving them silently around the board. They hardly talked to each other. They listened to classical music. When chess was over, they'd examine Rex's models or his stamp collection, then pour themselves a cup of tea or a cocktail and sip them in the kitchen while Sally cooked. They talked about things that didn't interest her. Books and art and politics. The talk swept around the room like a breeze. She was aware of it; it changed the atmosphere. But she did not feel affected by it one way or another. It was just nice to have some company while she peeled potatoes.

It was Nelson who was bothered. He began to talk to her about it in bed at night. Sally was a little bit unsettled by his sudden interest in discussing something with her. They used to talk about the kids when they were young, discussing their grades or their friends, imagining what line of work they'd go into or what they'd be good at. Nelson always thought Rex would be an advertising man, for no particular reason she could fathom. But he used to buy him books about advertising, and he'd have friends who knew people who knew people in New York call him and advise him on how to break in. Rex tolerated it all with a sense of amused detachment, as if his father were the child whose wild imagination needed to be indulged.

Danny, Nelson had decided long ago, was going to be a ballplayer, and he was very nearly right. Nelson had never quite recovered from Danny's failure to go on to the majors. For years he denied the knee injury and kept saying that Danny would "bounce back." But when it became clear that it wasn't going to happen, he settled for the idea of Danny as a doctor. Again, he bought Danny books on the subject and encouraged him to ask Jerry Steen about medical school. Danny didn't show any interest in medicine. Oddly, Danny didn't show any real interest in anything. All of his interests were mild, easily forgotten, more like moods. Even when he was playing baseball, and people from colleges were coming to scout him, and later when the scouts came from the major leagues, Danny could not get excited. He didn't play any better or worse knowing that those people were in the stands. He played exactly the same, as if nothing at all were at stake.

"The boy's got self-confidence," Nelson used to say. "Nerves of steel."

But Sally didn't think so. She didn't think Danny had any nerves at all. Danny's whole approach to life was like sitting at the dinner table. He knew the next course was coming, so he waited. He was never surprised.

And things did come to Danny. The athletic scholarship, his job, his wife. Things and events found Danny. He let himself be discovered. Which was admirable, she supposed, except she knew that Danny would be just as calm about being left. Danny was a charmed boy, but there was something a little worrying about a person who did not, or could not, struggle.

The last thing Sally could remember Nelson wanting to discuss in bed was Danny's decision not to go to medical school, a decision he'd officially announced only a few years ago. Well, of course he wasn't going to medical school, Sally thought at the time. He was thirty years old then and had never shown any interest in medicine. Nelson seemed genuinely surprised and disappointed, though.

"Surely he can't mean to work at Mecklin for the rest of his life," Nelson had said. "Where's the opportunity there?"

"He'll find what he wants to do," Sally reassured him. "Just give him time."

They had given him time; they still were, as far as Nelson was concerned. He harbored a notion that Danny was still making plans, still waiting to spring his surprise career on them. As for Rex, it had been years since Nelson had waited for anything from him. With Rex, Nelson just closed his eyes and hoped for the best.

"I don't like this person," Nelson said one night in bed. "This library person, he smells like books."

Sally looked up from *Good Housekeeping.* It took her a moment to understand what in the world Nelson meant—something he'd seen on the news, or the cover of her magazine?

"And what's the fruity accent he's got?" Nelson persisted, and that was when it fell into place.

"Oh, you mean Mr. Grafton. He's English."

"What the hell is an English person doing in the Fawley Library?"

"He works there, in the stacks."

"Stacks of what?"

"Nelson," she sighed. "Don't you even know what your son's job is? Don't you understand library science?"

"I don't care about his job, I just want to know what an Englishman is doing in my house every damn night."

Sally felt alarmed now, so unusual was it to hear Nelson care enough about something to swear. Why did it matter to him that Rex had a friend? She was cheered by it. She hated thinking of her son spending all of his time alone, huddled over some model of a Spitfire or the *Cutty Sark.*

Now that Nelson mentioned it, though, Mr. Grafton did seem a little off. Sally had tried hard not to see it, but it was there. It *was* strange to have someone in Fawley calling the bathroom the "loo," and the trashcan the "dustbin," and requesting hot tea with cream. "Oh, I could go for a cuppa," Mr. Grafton would invariably say as they wandered into the kitchen. (Rex, however, did not break the tradition of a glass of Scotch as the sun descended.) But the fact that Mr. Grafton was English was really the least of it. He was older, at least in his fifties, with thick gray hair and deep crow's feet. He dressed in a curious way. He wore vests and scarves (waistcoats and cravats, he called them), and rings on at least two fingers. Not wedding rings, but crests, large bulking things with writing on them, like party invitations. He was painfully thin and slumped when he talked or listened, his arms encircling his midsection as if he'd been struck by a cramp. When he laughed, he threw his head back to reveal a mouthful of gapped, yellowed teeth. And he smoked a pipe.

The reason she didn't worry much about Mr. Grafton was that Rex didn't seem particularly interested in him. As soon as he left the house, it was as if he were never there. Rex didn't mention him, and all that remained was the dull smell of pipe smoke and an empty teacup. Sally just always assumed he was someone that Rex put up with, someone to play chess with because there was no one else—the way she felt about her friend Betty Kirk, someone who bored her but who was always available for lunch, bridge club, or sales.

Nelson's concern sent off all manner of dormant alarms in her brain. What kind of man was her son? If she weren't related to him, would she find him distasteful? She tried to imagine what the psychologist in the *Good Housekeeping* advice column would say about such a situation.

Dear Dr. Joyce Brothers,
I have a twenty-nine-year-old son in good health, with above average intelligence, who works part time in the local library and still lives at home. He's a polite person with good hygiene. He takes great pride in his appearance and stays up to date with politics and literature. However, he doesn't seem to have a lot of friends. He doesn't date, and his only companion is an aging Englishman from the library with whom he plays chess in the afternoons. I wouldn't describe him (my son) as shy or withdrawn, yet he seems to have no interest in socializing or striking out on his own. He doesn't eat a lot and does his own laundry (in fact, he often does mine!), so it's not as if his presence in our home creates a financial problem. Should I be worried about this?

Signed,
Conflicted in Virginia

Her letter was easy. The reply was a bit more difficult to imagine. First she imagined the response which would help her sleep:

Dear Conflicted,
Relax. There is no standard definition of what is normal and what is not. If your son is living a fairly responsible life (holding a job, not taking drugs or behaving in other self-destructive ways), there is no reason for you to be concerned about his lifestyle. There are plenty of so-called normal adults who are trapped in unhappy mar-

riages, committing adultery, and abusing substances in order to deny their misery. Just be thankful that your son has found a way to make himself happy. And congratulate yourself on the fact that he feels so content and secure in his home that he has no desire to leave it.

Sincerely,
Dr. Brothers

But the other possibility loomed large in her mind, and she forced herself to reckon with it:

Dear Conflicted,
Part of our job as parents is to raise self-confident adults who can fend for themselves. It is not normal for a grown man to live at home with his parents if he is not hampered by some physical or mental handicap. We are by nature social creatures. The refusal to establish a separate identity from our parents and forge a new life with friends of our own choosing is indicative of a person with a serious developmental impairment. I strongly recommend counseling for your son as well as yourself.

Good luck,
Dr. Brothers

Neither response seemed completely accurate, and neither could solve the dilemma of how to answer her husband's concerns. Sally had always felt it was her obligation to reassure people. When her children cried she picked them up, wiped away their tears and told them it wasn't as bad as it seemed. She provided a similar role in her husband's life. She rubbed his back after a hard day at work, and even at the height of the recession she told him that the insurance business would swing back, and that he couldn't allow himself to be depressed. He was a smart man with a good business sense. Things would work out; he would be victorious in the end.

But was he? The insurance business had never regained its heyday, and now as he entered his sixties, he couldn't even think of retiring. They could not live on his savings, and he was only earning enough now to allow them to live from one paycheck to another. He had devoted his whole life to his work and it seemed to have no intention of rewarding him for those efforts. She tried to keep that in mind whenever he got grumpy. It had to be hard, realizing your whole life's work added up to nothing. It was no wonder he put so much stock in his sons. They were his only hope.

She tried to think of how to answer Nel's question, because he expected to be answered. He lay in bed beside her, the candlewick bedspread pulled up under his chin, his round, ruddy face turned toward her like the face of a puppy, wanting reassurance.

"Mr. Grafton is very polite," Sally said, hoping her approval of him would carry some weight.

"Well, a lot of people are polite, but I don't want my son entertaining them in my home. It's not normal for a grown man to be bringing home other men like playmates."

"Rex gets lonely. I can't see the harm in him passing the afternoon with one of his colleagues."

"He doesn't bring home any female colleagues."

"The only woman in the library is Justine Becker, who weighs two hundred pounds and has an illegitimate baby. Frankly, I'd rather have Mr. Grafton drinking tea in my kitchen."

"He drinks tea?" Nelson asked, as if this detail were particularly alarming. "Hot tea?"

"He's English."

"Why the hell would an Englishman come to Fawley?"

"I don't know, Nelson. He's been here for several years now. People know him. I'm surprised you don't."

"Why would I? I don't go in the library."

"Well, if you're so curious, why don't you ask him what he's doing in Fawley?"

"I don't want to know."

"Then drop it."

"Jesus Christ," Nelson said, turning away from her and wrapping the covers around himself like a cocoon. "Things were never like this before," he said, his back turned squarely toward her. "Danny never brought any Englishmen home with him. What the hell is happening to this family?"

Sally put her magazine aside and said, "Remember when Rex was sick, and Dr. Steen took us aside and told us to prepare for the worst? You said, 'He's going to die.' And Jerry said, 'There's that, and then there's the possibility that he'll live but his mind will be affected.' I remember distinctly what you said. 'I don't care if he ends up playing Tonka toys for the rest of his days, just save him.'"

Sally stared at her husband's back, which was so still she thought he might have fallen asleep. Finally he sighed, causing the covers to lift like a cloud.

"I *wouldn't* mind Tonka toys. What I mind is some old fart with an English accent."

"But that's not the point, Nellie. You said then that you'd love him no matter what he became. Now you're complaining about his friends."

"Friend, Sally. If he had more than one, maybe I wouldn't be complaining."

"Let's just count our blessings," she coaxed.

"I don't have a daughter, so I don't want to be entertaining male suitors in my house," Nelson declared.

"But don't you want him to be happy?" Sally asked.

"No, I do not. Not if being happy means he thinks he ought to be wearing a skirt. I'm too old for this kind of thing. I can't go opening up my horizons at sixty-two. Hell, if my bosses found out about this, I don't know how much longer I'd be employed."

"I'll talk to him," she said, the way she always did. All through their upbringing, Sally promised to restore peace after a meaningful conversation with her sons. Usually the issue at hand was no more serious than cleaning their rooms or taking out the trash or improving their grades. She tried hard now to believe that talking to Rex involved nothing more serious than that. But the truth was, if Rex really was on the verge of finding himself more interested in men than women, all of her efforts to dissuade him would fall on deafened ears. She knew now that such lifestyle choices were often a result of some genetic quirk of the brain. She could not talk him out of it.

"I'll take care of it," she said anyway.

"Good," Nelson said, and seconds later he was snoring, reassured by his belief in his wife's restorative powers.

Jerry Steen's office was crowded. Sally sat amid a cluster of cold- and flu-infected patients, who were expelling mucus into handkerchiefs and tissues, some wiping their noses on their sleeves. The flu had come late to town and Sally felt grateful that it had, until now, skipped over her home. She tried to keep her distance from the others, sitting all the way across the room and covering her mouth with her handkerchief. She felt grateful when Grace, the austere head nurse, called her name.

"Worst time of year," Grace said, slapping the blood-pressure cuff around her arm. "People think they're safe, but they aren't. They even stop taking their vitamins. You're taking yours, aren't you?"

Grace talked in a deep, scolding voice. She didn't believe in pampering patients. Sally's arm ached as the cuff inflated. She bit her bottom lip and nodded to the vitamin question.

Actually, she didn't believe much in vitamins. Nelson hated them, for one thing. When she tried to take a One-a-Day he accused her of pill popping, one of those expressions from the sixties that still haunted him.

Grace ripped off the cuff and said nothing about Sally's blood pressure, just jotted a number down on her file. Sally thought about asking, but then Jerry Steen walked in. He was wearing street clothes—a madras shirt, khakis, and white tennis shoes. Though she'd known Jerry most of her life, it worried her a little to see him without his white doctor's coat. Foolishly, she imagined that Jerry could not legitimately call himself a doctor without that coat, and that his judgment might be skewed in the absence of it.

"Sally Crane," he said. "Where does the time go?"

"Oh, I don't get out much these days."

"Danny says you've stopped driving." He was looking at her chart as he talked to her. She couldn't imagine what all was in there. Decades of small complaints, flu shots, three pregnancies, one miscarriage. It was only when she saw Jerry that she ever recalled that miscarriage, which was more like a bad period. She was only six weeks along; she had a hard time thinking of it as a lost baby, maybe even the girl she'd always wanted. It embarrassed her to be in the presence of someone who could open a chart and review all of her weakest moments.

"Yes," she said. "My eyes aren't so good anymore."

"She doesn't have a fever," Grace said, a bit critically, before leaving the room.

Jerry sat on his stool and put his hands on his knees. He was handsome for his age, with thinning white hair and clear blue eyes. In fact, he was one of those rare people who looked better as they got older. As a young man, he was not handsome at all, on the verge of being fat, with blowsy cheeks and eyes that all but disappeared behind thick brows. As he moved into old age, those characteristics suited him, as if his face had been patiently waiting all these years to hit sixty.

Sally wondered if he were having an affair with Grace. At least, that's what the whole town wondered back when Louise was alive. Now that Jerry was a widower, whatever he got up to with Grace couldn't be called an affair exactly. Sally didn't hear so much talk about Jerry's back-room antics these days. They weren't nearly so interesting if they weren't adulterous.

"Are we checking your eyes today?" he asked.

"No, I'm not really here about my eyes," Sally said. "In fact, I'm not here about myself, Jerry. I'm worried about my son."

Jerry nodded, as if he were expecting this. He rubbed his chin thoughtfully and said, "Yes. He does have some problems. Though they aren't physical. Rest assured of that, he's healthy as a horse."

"You think he's got mental problems?"

Jerry stood and paced away from her, as if this issue required deep concentration. "Psychosomatic illnesses are not exactly mental problems. They start in the mind, but the symptoms themselves are quite real. It's all a result of stress."

Sally felt confused. "I don't think Rex has any stress."

"Rex?"

She felt momentarily confused, as if Jerry had forgotten who her children were. How could he forget Rex? He delivered him and treated him for meningitis. He was the one, in fact, who had told them to start calling relatives. As long as she lived, she would never forget that moment, standing there in the hospital waiting room, feeling stunned by the news. And embarrassed. This emotion was more acute in her memory than any other, the utter humiliation of having to call her family and tell them her son was dying. She felt her one, perhaps her only obligation to her children was to keep them alive. To let a child die was to fail. Even now, she blushed at the memory of it, of having come so close to letting her family down.

"Yes, Rex," Sally said. "You didn't think I meant Danny, did you?"

"Actually, I did."

"What's wrong with Danny?"

"He thinks he's dying. He's not, Sally. He's got absolutely nothing wrong with him. I'm sure it's just a phase."

"What kind of phase?" She felt alarmed. Phases were for adolescents, weren't they? People didn't have phases after they left home and got married. Danny had not even had them as a teenager.

"He's fine, I promise. Tell me about Rex," Jerry said, trying to distract her with a placid smile. "Is he feeling all right? I've barely seen him since he was ill. What's he doing these days?"

"Nothing," she admitted. "He's living at home and working at the library. But he's got this friend, and I'm a little concerned about it."

"What kind of friend?"

Sally attempted to explain, offering a brief explanation of Mr. Grafton, trying to illustrate Nelson's concern without putting too fine a point on it. Halfway through her explanation she felt very silly indeed and wanted to run out of the room. But Jerry was blocking her path, standing in front of the door with his arms crossed over his stomach, nodding as she talked.

"I don't think it's anything to worry about," Jerry said.

"Do you know Mr. Grafton?"

"No, I don't think I do. But let's say your worst fears were true. If Rex were a homosexual, there would be nothing I or you or anyone else could do about it."

"But it might be my fault."

Jerry shrugged. "People don't think that way anymore. Scientific evidence suggests it's genetically predetermined."

"I know that," Sally said a little impatiently. After all, she had seen this subject nearly exhausted on daytime talk shows. But Jerry could not possibly understand exactly what she needed from him, which was some sort of answer to take back home, something to reassure her husband. She should have known she would not find that here. She did, in fact, know it. But all the way during the bus ride to his office, she had expected some sort of solution. Not necessarily a remedy, but an answer. Something that had gone wrong back in the old days when he was sick. If Jerry had been able to tell her where she had gone wrong, she might at least have been able to go back home and tell her husband that the illness was to blame. The misstep they had taken was so long ago, there was no hope of correcting it. Then Nelson might settle down, might not get so worked up whenever Mr. Grafton came into the house. Things could be smoothed out. Her life could be settled again.

"But isn't there something I could do?" Sally said, staring at the floor. It was a hard thing to talk about, eye to eye. "Isn't there something I could say to him?"

"Well, no. You could try to encourage him to have safe sex. You could buy him some condoms."

"Oh my God!" Sally said, her head snapping up. "I don't think he's doing that. I mean, Mr. Grafton, his friend . . . he's so elderly. He's my age. He's *genteel*."

Jerry nodded. "Well, if Rex is not sexually active, you don't have much to worry about. Here's what I think you should do. Go back home and do some housework. Clean the oven. Wax the floors. My wife always used to find some difficult chore whenever she wanted to calm herself down."

Sally wondered what calming down Louise Steen had ever required. Always so dull and unimaginative. Always the worst player in the bridge club. Louise did not seem to possess the power to think ahead, to imagine what her partner might have in mind. She could not tell interesting stories to save her life. She could not even tally the score. They used to refer to her (behind her back, of course) as the dummy. They might as well have had a doll sitting in for Louise. What on earth had Jerry Steen been thinking to marry such a woman? No wonder he got up to something with Grace.

But perhaps some men were satisfied with that. Perhaps they did not want any sort of trouble when they came home. And a woman with opinions was trouble. Her own daughter-in-law was evidence enough of that.

Sally had once had opinions. She couldn't remember them very clearly, but she had some distant recollection of clashing with Nelson over ideas about how to raise the children. Where had all her ideas gone? She wasn't sure she missed them very much. She wasn't sure that ideas were even supposed to endure. Perhaps that was the whole point to living this long—ridding oneself of all those difficult notions.

She considered Jerry's suggestion about housework. She supposed she could go home and wash the windows or clean out the closets, two chores that nagged at her like indigestion. But Sally had never really felt an affinity for housework. It always felt like something she was doing in place of something else. All her life, she had hurried herself through each task, as if she were desperate to move on to something more interesting. But at the end of each day she just collapsed in the easy chair with her sewing and the *TV Guide*. Even now she felt that this chore, sitting in an office with Jerry, was taking up valuable time. But had her time ever been valuable? Had there ever been something else, something better to do?

"There just aren't enough hours in a day," she used to tell her husband when he came home from work. But the truth was, there were plenty of hours in a day. There just weren't enough good ones.

"There's nothing I want to do," she said abruptly to Jerry. She felt immediately sorry. She felt embarrassed, as she had all those years ago, when Rex got sick. She hated the sight and the sound of her own weakness.

Jerry smiled, to her surprise, and sat down on the stool again.

"Now listen," he said, taking her hand in his. She felt odd about it, but didn't know how to object. "Your life is far from over. There are a million things you could do."

"Name one," Sally said.

"Your two o'clock is threatening to leave," Grace announced, sticking her head in the door.

"I'll be right there," Jerry said.

"I took the stitches out of that Pierce girl. You want to see her?"

"Not unless she wants to see me."

Grace went back out. Sally looked away from Jerry, her hands trembling slightly as she gathered her things.

"I'm sorry, I've taken up too much of your time," she said. To her surprise, Jerry reached for her hand again.

"You know how hard I tried to save Pike," he said.

"Pike?"

He nodded. "I was the one who worked on him. All those years ago. I never forgot it."

Again, without warning, Sally felt embarrassed. All this history, all these hiccups in the course of her life. Why did she feel that normal lives did not include death and illness, secrets and tragedies? Why did she feel that somewhere in the world, people were existing free from such shameful drama?

As if he read her mind, Jerry said, "And I'm sorry about that thing with Rex. When I told you he was dying."

"Oh, but he was dying," she said, trying to sound cheerful. Jerry smiled appreciatively. "I mean, you couldn't have known. Nobody could. We were all prepared for it. But he pulled through. God works in mysterious ways."

"When he works at all," Jerry said.

Sally went out without asking what he meant by that. She wasn't sure she wanted to know.

As she was coming out of the office, she saw a young girl waiting at the bus stop. She looked vaguely familiar. Her thin, dark hair was pulled back in a braid, revealing a sharp, pale face. Her eyes were scanning the ground, as if she were deciphering some code on the sidewalk. Sally glanced down but saw nothing. Looking back up, she noticed a pale pink ridge behind the girl's ear. For some reason, Sally felt compelled to talk to her.

"Are you waiting for the Thirty-seven?"

The girl raised her eyes to her. They were a strange, stormy gray. She blinked them rapidly and in that second, Sally remembered her.

"Amanda," she said. "Isn't that your name?"

The girl blinked again. "Who are you?"

"I'm Sally Crane. I'm Kyle's aunt. We met at Rita's house, a while back."

"Oh, okay," the girl said flatly, as if the recollection neither pleased nor disappointed her. "Sure, yeah. Do you have a cigarette?"

"I don't smoke," Sally said, though she wished she did so she could offer her one. She had the strangest impulse to give the girl something.

"Were you seeing Dr. Steen?" Sally asked.

"Supposed to. I just had some stitches out, so the nurse did it. She said it didn't matter if I got a scar 'cause it's behind my ear. Just don't cut my hair short. You believe that?"

"Well, Grace doesn't have the best bedside manner."

"What's the Thirty-seven?" Amanda asked.

"Oh, I was talking about the bus."

Amanda looked down the road, then back at Sally. "I wasn't waiting for the bus. I was waiting for Kyle. He said he'd come back for me, but I think he took off. The bastard. Why do I put up with him? I swear to God."

"I'm sure Kyle has his good points," Sally said.

Amanda shook her head, rubbing her thumb along her bottom lip, as if she were contemplating sucking it. She had such a young, frail face. Yet something in her eyes made her look old. Next to her, Sally felt awkward and naive, as if she had a lot to learn.

"Sometimes I say to myself, get the hell out," Amanda said, staring straight ahead, as if she weren't talking to Sally in particular. Actually it had a lyrical sound, as if she were reciting a poem. "I say, get out before he does something really bad. Maybe he already has, I don't know. And, yeah, he does knock me around, and I'm smart enough to know that that's not going to get me anywhere good."

She turned toward Sally at last, with a smile tucked in one corner of her mouth. "You know what's so weird? People like me and Kyle, we're just like anybody else. We really think good things are gonna happen to us. We think we're gonna win the lottery. We think we're gonna get a good job and buy a house and have a baby. We don't get it, that we're not going anywhere. Sometimes I get it, like right this minute, staring at the street and knowing that bastard has gone to a bar and I'm gonna have to hitchhike home. I get it, that my life is gonna end in a gutter or something. What I want to know is, how come you can't hang on to that? How come I won't know it an hour from now when I need it?"

She finished the question and stood staring at Sally as if she really might have the answer. But Sally felt shocked to the core and she knew that if she allowed her lips to part, something like an animal's cry might come out, something strange and desperate. So she pressed her lips together and waited and prayed for the 37 to come.

Suddenly there was the screech of tires and Rita's old Plymouth Fury pulled up across the street. Its hood was still smashed in, the headlights shattered. Kyle sat behind the wheel, drinking a beer. He waved cheerfully at the two of them.

Amanda shook her head slowly, then smiled at Sally, as if they were sharing a private joke.

Sally wanted to shout as the girl walked across the road. She wanted to reach out and pull her back and save her from all those years of pain and deception and God knows what-all Kyle had in store for her. But she let her go without saying a word. She watched as the girl opened the door to the crippled car and climbed in next to Kyle. They waved again, and the car coughed black fumes into the air as it drove off, disappearing behind a bend of twisted oaks and plain, familiar houses.

17

D ANNY WAS HAVING a dream. He came in and out of it, opening his eyes long enough to reacquaint himself with reality before succumbing again. He did not resist the dream. He wanted to go there.

It was a real moment from his life, but it only visited him in his sleep. It was the night Kyle nearly died. There had been many such nights, but none so clear as the night they cut off his cousin's leg. The phone had rung in the early hours, as it so often did. But Danny was alone. It was long before he met Lydia. He was working in construction at Mecklin and his mornings came quick, shortly after five. He got up and went about his business before he was fully awake. The room was cold and damp. It was morning but it felt like the dead of night. When the call came, he was lacing up his work boots.

"What?" he said into the phone.

"It's Kyle," his father said.

"What about him?"

"He's not going to make it. Get down here."

Danny felt strangely relieved as he drove to the hospital. He knew that Kyle was not going to make it. Kyle was never meant to make it, and he knew his life was in a sort of holding pattern until Kyle eventually did himself in. He had promised Pike that he would look out for him, but even as he promised it he sensed that Pike perceived it as a short-lived assignment. Kyle was one of those people who would not be around to bother people for long. Perhaps if Pike had known how long his son would go on defying death, he would not have burdened his nephew with the task of seeing him through the close calls.

Danny came into the emergency room feeling tough, ready for whatever he needed to face. Danny had a great stomach for disaster then. He did not recoil at the sight of blood, even when it was Kyle's. And that was all he could see when he walked into the emergency room, a bloody sheet with something resembling Kyle underneath it.

His father was there, talking to a young doctor off in a corner. Danny approached them bravely, throwing no more than a casual glance toward the form which used to be his cousin. Kyle was dead as far as Danny was concerned. His emotion would come later. Now there were details to contend with.

He was vaguely aware of Aunt Rita standing by the body, holding the hand of the corpse and making small, invisible designs on it with her index finger. He wanted to grab her and tell her to let it go. But Rita was not conscious of him, not conscious of anything but Kyle's lifeless hand.

"Danny, thank God," his father said when he walked up. The young doctor looked at him, as if he were expecting some sort of alien creature and was thrown off by the appearance of an average guy.

"He's dead," Danny said.

"No, he's not dead," said the doctor, who could not have been much older than Danny but seemed to think he was. The doctor was angry, and the anger lent him an air of authority. "But he will be soon if someone doesn't intervene."

"What's going on?" Danny asked, feeling irritable about Kyle's half-dead status. As usual, Kyle could not get things done the normal way.

"They need to operate, and Rita won't give her consent."

"What's wrong with him?"

"He's chewed up inside," said the doctor, seemingly proud of his poetic diagnosis. "That leg has to go, and even then we're not sure it'll do the trick. But nothing's going to happen unless someone gives the word."

"Rita's not thinking straight," his father admitted. "Can you talk to her?"

Danny shrugged and walked away from them, approaching Rita with the same kind of casual fearlessness he had felt whenever he and Kyle had gotten into trouble for breaking a window or setting off firecrackers. Talking Rita out of trouble had never been much of a problem when Pike was alive. It was all about assuring her that Pike would never find out. Danny could not imagine what his mission entailed now.

"Aunt Rita, how's he doing?" Danny asked, moving up next to her. She was a small woman who always seemed lost in her clothes. That night she was wearing a wool cardigan over her nightgown, giving her the appearance of one of those poor souls hanging around on street corners with baskets full of empty Coke bottles.

"Danny," she said, stroking Kyle's pale, bony hand, the ubiquitous inch of dirt and motor oil still under his fingernails. "He always loved you so much."

"Yes, we're like brothers," Danny said, hoping she couldn't detect the lack of emotion in his voice.

"I mean Pike. He thought you were the best thing. He said, 'Kyle will be okay as long as Danny is around.'"

"He's going to be okay," Danny said, staring at his cousin's face. It was streaked with blood, starting to turn black as it coagulated.

"They want to cut off his leg," Rita said, lowering her voice almost to a whisper, as if imparting some bizarre information.

"Well, that wouldn't be so bad, would it? Kyle's not an athlete or anything. He'd do okay with one leg."

Even as he said these things, Danny wasn't sure. Who could live with one leg? Most people, probably. Could he take responsibility for relieving Kyle of a limb? One thing he felt certain of was that Kyle would want to live. Kyle fought for his consciousness as valiantly as anyone he'd ever known.

Rita stared down at her son's hand, as if the sight of it were mesmerizing her.

"But here's the thing, Danny. Pike always loved this boy so much. There was nothing on earth he ever loved as much as Kyle. And I just keep thinking, wouldn't I be doing Pike a favor? To send him his boy? Wouldn't that be a nice gift?"

Danny felt cold all over. He looked across the room and met the doctor's gaze, whose look was one of complete contempt.

"Uncle Pike wouldn't want it," Danny said to Rita, turning back to her.

"Oh, but I think he would. He must be lonely up there, Danny."

Danny pried his cousin's hand away from Rita's iron grip. Kyle's hand was cold and clammy. He recalled those nights Kyle spent in his brother's bed, and all those days they had spent together playing chicken on the train tracks and stealing magazines from Whitman's Drugstore.

He recalled them, not fondly, but in an effort to remind himself of why
he must fight for Kyle's life. Because at the moment, and despite the doctor's look of disgust, Danny felt himself wanting to agree with Rita.
What good would Kyle do on earth? Weren't there some people whose
inclination toward self-destruction was less a folly than an act of gen-
erosity? Kyle might know, on some level, that he needed to rid the world
of himself.

The trouble was, Danny did not believe that Pike was in heaven or that
Kyle would go somewhere and keep him company on a bank of clouds. He
thought Kyle, if released, would free-fall into blackness and become a part
of the family legend. The no-good son, the violent boy, the wasted life.

How peaceful it would be to let Kyle go. He could start to live without looking over his shoulder. He would be released. But not yet. He had
not finished paying his debt.

"We have to save him, Aunt Rita," he said. "Let's give him a chance."

She looked at him, as if she were thoroughly exhausted. She threw her
hands up and gave an exasperated sigh, as if they were arguing over
whether or not to buy a new rug.

"Whatever you think," she said.

"Sign the form," Danny had said.

She'd signed and the surgery had been performed, and two days later
Kyle was sitting up in bed, swearing at the doctors and at the television,
and treating his new chance at life like a curse he'd been born to endure.

The first thing Kyle had said to Danny was, "Did you let them cut my
goddamn leg off, Danny? I'll get your ass for this. You'll rue the goddamn day."

Sitting up in bed, his IV dangling from his wrist, he pointed a trembling finger at the center of Danny's chest and said, "I own you now."

Danny only shrugged. It wasn't much of a threat. Ever since Pike had
died, he was aware of Kyle's hold on him. Because of the secret, because
of what they both knew and never told. Because they and only they understood the futility of Pike's death, the complete and utter senselessness
of it. Because of this knowledge, Kyle had owned him for a long time. It
felt like forever.

The dream was accurate; it did not incorporate surreal or disconnected
elements. It was like watching a reel of his life played back. It could have
taken a moment or all night. It could have started from the second the

phone rang and ended when he sat up in bed, breathing hard, sweating.

Lydia was on the phone, which meant she had responded to the sound before he had, something that had never happened before. She stood naked, the phone in one hand, struggling to put her robe on with the other. He was aroused by the sight of her, even in his moment of confusion and fear. Oh, thank God, he thought, his heart thumping so hard it ached. Thank God she's here and I want her.

"Slow down," Lydia was saying. "You've got to stop crying. I can't understand you."

"Kyle's crying?" Danny asked, scrambling out of bed.

"It's not Kyle, it's some woman."

"Rita?"

Lydia shook her head. "Amanda, and she wants you. She says you're the only one who cares."

With this Lydia thrust the phone at him. Danny stood holding it, wondering if the urgency lay in explaining to his wife who Amanda was, or hearing Amanda's complaint. Lydia walked away, relieving him of the choice.

"Oh God! Oh Christ!" Amanda was screaming.

"It's Danny, Amanda. Tell me what's wrong."

"He's in there and he's dying."

"In where?"

"The hou-ou-ouse," she moaned.

"The trailer?"

"Fuck you!" she wailed. "Fuck your whole family, you never cared about him!"

"Where are you right now? Amanda, I have to know how to find you."

"I'm at Carter's. The Texaco station."

"Stay there."

"No, I'm going back for him. And you should go, too. He's your family."

"I'll be there," he assured her, but she had already hung up.

He pulled on jeans and a shirt, tucked his boots under his arm and headed for the front door. Lydia was standing in the hall, completely dressed, smoking.

He said, "That was Amanda. She's . . ."

"I know who she is."

He nodded. He didn't ask how she knew.

"Stay here. I'll be back."

"What is it this time?"

"I don't know, but she sounded hysterical. He's in the trailer. I don't know, maybe he tried to kill himself. God knows what else he has up his sleeve."

"I'm going with you," Lydia said.

"No."

"Forget it, Danny. I'm in this."

Lydia's presence in the truck was distracting to Danny. Usually he used this time to think of what he would say to his family members, how he'd calm Aunt Rita, get the facts from his father, consult with the doctor, and, if Kyle was conscious, issue firm but cautious admonishments to him. But his wife's presence wasn't the only unusual circumstance on this evening. He had to keep reminding himself he wasn't going to the hospital, was in fact heading for Kyle's trailer, and had no idea what he'd find when he got there.

Long before he made the turn onto the deserted road that led to the trailer and saw the pale, golden nimbus floating toward the clouds, he knew. A fire. What else but a fire? What was the only embarrassing catastrophe Kyle had not yet inflicted on his family? No self-respecting, no-'count country hellion went to his grave without setting a fire.

Danny felt his whole life had been leading to this moment. He was instantly transported to his youth, getting up in the middle of the night to chase fires with his father. If the alarm rang more than three times, the whole family rose, as if awakened by an alarm clock, and started putting on coats over their pajamas. Without speaking they would all climb into the car, and his father would drive to the firehouse and follow the trail of water left behind by the leaky truck. It was one of the few family outings to which no one objected, an interest they all shared, a common hobby. No one questioned it. It took many years for Danny even to ponder his father's interest in chasing fires. Perhaps it was Nelson's frustration at never making the volunteer fire department. (There was a long waiting list, and they preferred young men without families.) Perhaps it was simple voyeurism, morbid fascination. Something exciting to break up the monotony of their lives. All these things could be counted as valid factors, but Danny suspected something else.

Fires did not happen to good families. He knew they could technically happen to anyone, but as a general rule they happened to poor people, careless or neglectful people. People whose electrical wiring was faulty, who fell asleep or passed out drunk with lit cigarettes. People who were trying to keep warm with space heaters or charcoal grills. Sometimes it was a business, a barn or a warehouse, but the genesis was no less sophisticated—arson, bums, failing businessmen trying to collect on insurance. There was definitely an indignity to fires. Where there was smoke, there was usually an irresponsible, wayward type, someone who had tried to veer outside the normal strictures of society. And failing all that, if the victims had indeed come by their fires honestly, they would soon be pathetic enough. They'd have collections taken up for them at church. They'd have jars with their names on them in the drugstore, the supermarket, the library. Soon enough they would be tromping around in other people's clothes.

And so, Danny thought, his father liked to follow fires so he could gaze on with a sense of grim satisfaction, knowing he'd done better than that, knowing that whatever else had gone wrong in his life, he had not allowed hearth and home to go up in smoke.

"Jesus Christ," Lydia said as they made the turn, and the orange mist rose up out of the trees. "Do you see that?"

"Yeah," Danny said. He was prepared, and the sight of what lay before him was only surprising in that it was slightly less fierce than he imagined. He had pictured flames shooting up toward the sky, but all he saw was this thick sepia smoke, with the occasional spark shooting toward the stars.

They were nowhere near the first to arrive. Danny wondered how he had slept through the fire alarms—he usually woke by reflex, the way he had as a child. Two fire trucks sat a few yards back, and firefighters in yellow coats were running back and forth empty-handed, as if they didn't know where to start. There were two police cars, as well, and a crowd of onlookers. Where had they come from? Kyle was miles away from any neighbors, so Danny could only assume they had come from the same place from which his family had once come—people from town, driving out to witness someone else's misfortune.

Danny parked the truck as close as possible and jumped out of the cab. Lydia was right on his heels as he ran toward the crowd. A firefighter stepped in his path.

"There's nothing to see here," he said.

"I'm family," Danny said, short of breath. "That's my cousin's place."

"Well, there's nothing you can do for him."

Danny thought, Good, this is good. It's right for Kyle to die in a fire. So much more original than a car crash. So much more fitting his personality. Here I am, he thought, standing in the presence of another family legend, the story that will be passed on to future generations. Your late cousin Kyle, the one who died in the fire.

It took him a few seconds to recognize Amanda. She was standing among the others, holding Syphilis close to her chest, petting her and kissing the mangled fur. She watched the sight before her with detached interest, like watching a play-off game without caring about the outcome. Just watching for the sake of the sport.

"Amanda," he shouted. The noise around him was deafening. The murmur of the crowd, the rumble of the fire engines, the quick, static bursts of the two-way radio. Then, of course, the dull rumbling of the fire, digesting the trailer. Everything was gone; it was hard to imagine what it was burning now. Just atmosphere, maybe. Just the residue of Kyle's life.

"Amanda!" he shouted, louder. She turned and gave a slow smile, as if it were a chance meeting at a family reunion.

Then her face changed and she ran toward him, Syphilis bouncing against her chest. As she reached him, she began to cry.

"Is he dead?" Danny asked.

She collapsed against him, crying into his shoulder. He embraced her and the dog, who made no attempt to object. He could feel the bony animal shuddering against him.

"We had a fight and I went out. I don't know what I was thinking. I knew he was too drunk to leave him alone. I took the car keys with me so he wouldn't drive. I never figured on this."

She wept some more and he continued to hold her. Lydia was standing next to him, watching with her mouth slightly parted. She had not adjusted to all this yet, had not prepared herself the way he had during the long drive.

"But he's in there," Danny said.

Amanda stood back, straightening her posture and trying to regain some dignity. Her face was pale, gray around the edges from soot. Danny's question seemed to irritate her. Her eyes turned cold and she blinked languidly, as if she were suddenly bored with the whole business.

"Of course he's in there," she said. For the first time she looked toward Lydia. "Is this your wife?"

Danny made a brief introduction and to his surprise, Lydia smiled and put a hand on Amanda's arm.

"Are you okay?" Lydia asked.

"Of course I'm not fucking okay. My boyfriend is a pile of ashes. He could be a bastard, I know, but nobody deserves this. Do you have a cigarette?"

Lydia fished a pack out of her pocket.

"Is it a good idea to smoke right now?" Danny asked.

"I think it's a fucking excellent idea," Amanda said.

Lydia lit her cigarette, then lit one for herself.

"You seem pretty cavalier about this," Danny said to Amanda.

"What does that mean?" Amanda asked, taking a drag off her cigarette, then blowing the smoke next to Syphilis's ear. "What's cavalier, a hundred-dollar word for don't give a shit?"

"Kyle is dead, and you're just . . . I don't know . . ."

Amanda shrugged. "What do you want me to do, run in there after him? What are these, Marlboro Lights? They're so weak, I might as well just breathe the air."

"I'm not much of a smoker," Lydia admitted. "But are you okay? You're not hurt?"

"I'm fine." Amanda smiled at Lydia then said to Danny, "She's pretty, all right. Smart too, I'll bet. How long have you two been married?"

"Jesus Christ," Danny said, then moved past them toward the flaming wreckage. He was amazed at how far he was allowed to get before someone stopped him. He could feel the heat on his face, a sweat breaking out all over his skin. He was almost at the door when another firefighter, a black guy, grabbed him.

"Hang on, cowboy. Where the hell do you think you're going?"

"My cousin's in there," Danny said.

"Then your cousin's long gone. I'm sorry to be the one to break the news to you." He wiped the soot away from his eyes and squinted. "Danny?"

"Yeah?"

"Marcus Whitehead. I was on the baseball team with you. Shortstop. I sucked."

"Oh, right."

"Jesus, I'm just now putting it together. That's Kyle in there?"

Danny nodded. He suddenly had a picture of Kyle's fake leg melting in the heat, the plastic and metal oozing and running together like molten lava. Kyle helped him practice baseball, he pitched for hours on end, never asking for a turn, knowing it was Danny who had a future in the sport, knowing he was only there to help service that dream. Kyle had devoted much of his life to the cause of his cousin. And now he's gone, Danny thought, and I did nothing, and I feel nothing.

Marcus put a hand on his shoulder.

"Oh, man, I'm sorry."

"He could have been better. He just didn't know how to pull himself out. I hate that he's ending up like this, that he's gonna die an asshole."

"Aw hell, Danny, if he'd lived he'd of still been an asshole. Try not to take it so hard. Some lives just go that way. It's worse when it's some-body who didn't deserve it. He did this to himself."

"I don't think so," Danny said, his voice wavering. He could feel the soot building up on his own face now, and as the tears slid down he imag-ined them leaving white streaks. But he felt no embarrassment. He wanted to keep talking, as if he needed to convince someone of Kyle's worth. "I think he had a lot of help getting here. Nobody can do this much damage by themselves."

Marcus nodded, rubbing his chin, pushing back his yellow fireman's hat as if he needed a moment to concentrate.

Danny said, "He was a great hunter, you know. Much better than me. He could sit so still in the woods. It was like he could almost stop breath-ing. And he'd sit there forever, as long as it took, not moving to cough or scratch an itch. His reflexes were so sharp. I saw him take down a buck once, a twelve-pointer. Brought it down before I even saw it. He knew, he had an instinct."

"He was a killer," Marcus said.

"No, he was a survivor."

"Well," Marcus said, pulling his hat back down, "not anymore, he isn't."

Amanda was hungry. She said she hadn't eaten for days and she looked as if she was telling the truth. When Lydia took her arm, Danny had the sensation that it might break off in her fingers. So because he could not think of a reason to say no, he took them in search of food. It was late, but Danny had no sense of time. He didn't care.

Kyle was dead. Finally dead. He was having a hard time getting his mind around it. But he didn't want to tell anyone just yet. He wanted to think it through. He didn't see the point of waking up the family to give them the news, when in only a couple of hours they'd be getting up any-way. Let them have one last good sleep, then the tragedy could begin. And it would last, Danny knew, for years to come. His family would mourn Kyle's loss as deeply as Pike's. Somehow, the troubled souls caused the most grief when they went. Because, Danny suspected, no one could take solace in the notion that Kyle was in heaven. No heaven that any of them dared believe in, anyway.

"What's open this late?" Danny asked, once they were all inside the truck and moving aimlessly down the dark road.

"I can make omelettes," Lydia said.

"Quality-Mart," Amanda said.

"What?"

"They got an all-night diner there. Just opened last week. It's not in the store, just right next to it."

"Wait a minute—that place is still open?" Danny asked incredulously. "After everything that happened?"

It had never occurred to him, even for a second, that Quality-Mart would continue to operate after the murders. He recognized in himself a ridiculously naive notion that the place would shut down out of respect for the dead. That the place would recognize its own evil and run away in the night like a thief. But how could he think such a thing? Millions of dollars had been pumped into the place. Of course it was still there and probably always would be.

"Yeah, it's doing okay," Amanda said. "I was thinking of getting a job there myself. I mean, when Kyle was around I couldn't. He wouldn't even let me go near it 'cause he said it was cursed. But he was just pissed 'cause they didn't give him a job."

The truck seemed to take itself out to Quality-Mart. Danny wasn't even aware that he knew the way, but suddenly they were pulling into the vast, empty parking lot. He stopped in front of the annex, which was a fifties-style diner with a long soda fountain and red booths and neon lights advertising soft drinks and beer in the windows. It called itself, simply, The Diner. It seemed so out of place next to the enormous warehouse of a store, like a plane hangar, a monument to the decade of no style or substance, just product, and lots of it. And beside it, the little quaint tribute to simpler times, better days.

They got out of the truck without speaking and hurried across the parking lot, their eyes darting across the shadows, trying to detect the spot where it happened. Nervously they looked, as if the bodies might still be there, or at least traces of blood. Danny was relieved when they got inside the diner.

They sat in a booth. Music was blaring but only one other couple was in there, leaning across the Formica table, arguing. The waiter allowed Amanda to bring the dog in. Syphilis sat under the table, whimpering, as Amanda slipped her scraps of hamburger and french fries.

Amanda ate voraciously, as if she had not seen real food in months. In between bites, she talked about Kyle.

"The thing nobody got about him was that he wanted to be good. Every night in bed he used to say to me, 'Amanda, tomorrow is another day. And as long as there's another day, I've got another chance.' He had this idea that he wanted to live up to his family's expectations. I said, Kyle, what expectations? Your family is a bunch of cripples. 'Not Danny,' he'd say. 'Danny is a star. Danny fooled them all.' You don't mind me telling you this?"

"Not at all," Danny said, cutting into his rubbery fried eggs. He was thinking of how to handle things, when to break it to his family and how to arrange the funeral. He knew he'd be burdened with all those decisions. Rita would fall apart, as usual, and his father would go into a funk of despair. His mother would be energized. Nothing excited her like a tragedy, some horrible predicament that needed to be solved, some sort of chaos that required ordering. He decided he'd let his mother do as much work as she wanted to. She could pick out the casket and decide what hymns needed to be sung. A church funeral would be ridiculous— what could the pastor say about Kyle? But he knew that suggesting anything else would be like suggesting a burial at sea, or shooting Kyle's remains into space.

"Do you have another cigarette?" Amanda asked Lydia. Lydia plopped the wrinkled pack down on the table and Amanda fished one out gratefully. "Kyle always said you'd married well, Danny. He was right. I think he was half in love with Lydia, and who could blame him?"

"He hardly knew me," Lydia said.

"But he loved the idea of you. This smart somebody from somewhere else, who loved his cousin enough to settle down in this hellhole. You don't mind me calling it a hellhole?"

Lydia just smiled.

"My whole life I've just felt like I was dumped here," Amanda went on. "Like God didn't care enough about me to put me someplace important. The thing me and Kyle had in common was, we both caught hell growing up."

Danny looked at her with dull surprise. "What do you mean? Kyle had everything. Everybody catered to him."

"Not how he told it."

"Then he's a liar."

"Was a liar," Amanda said evenly. She picked up the ketchup bottle and spanked it until a big red dollop fell out. "Anyway, let's just say we'd both seen hard times. He liked that about me. You know that story, don't you?"

"I don't know anything about you," Danny said.

"My mama was the fortune-teller. She told every man's fortune in the county and then some. The people who came out there? Lord, half the police force. Teachers. Preachers. You name it. I grew up with all these secrets, you know. I have the dirt on folks."

She grinned at them and Danny felt threatened. He did not want to hear the names. He didn't want to know her secrets.

"So then she goes and marries one of them, some Orkin man or something. He always smelled like bug spray. He started doing me at about fifteen. He paid me at least, I'll give him that. But it was fucked. I got pregnant, and when I tried to undo it, things got messed up. So I won't ever have a baby. Kyle liked that about me, too. You'd be surprised, some men don't go for that at all. I mean, they don't want you to get knocked up, but they like knowing you could."

Danny felt a headache coming on. He had downed his food too fast and now it settled in his gut like rocks. Syphilis was curled up on his feet, and every time he shifted the dog issued a plaintive wail.

"Where will you go now?" Lydia asked Amanda.

She shrugged. "Where I was when Kyle met me. No place. I'd sleep with a friend sometimes, or at the restaurant or in my car. When I had a car."

"You're homeless?" Lydia asked.

Amanda thought about it as she chewed. "I don't have a home, if that's what you mean."

"Well, you'd better stay with us for a while."

Danny looked at his wife as if lightning had just struck and caused her brain to misfire.

"No," Danny said, too shocked to remember his manners.

"She's got nowhere to go, Danny. She can't sleep on the street."

"There are shelters and stuff. And she's got parents."

"Excuse me, can I break in here? I don't want to stay with you. Thanks all the same," Amanda said.

"Well, you're at least staying with us tonight," Lydia said.

"Are you doing this to get back at me?" Danny asked.

"No, I'm doing it because where I come from, we don't like the idea of people we know wandering the streets."

"We don't know Amanda."

"Excuse me again," Amanda said. "Lydia, I see you're trying to do the decent thing. But what Danny's trying to tell you is good folks don't take in white trash. On account of how it *looks,* you know. How it looks is a big thing around these parts."

But that was not it, even though Danny was content to let Lydia think it. The one advantage to losing Kyle was losing all that history along with him. Amanda had too much knowledge. She'd represent his past in human form, lurking around corners like some mythical creature of conscience, like the furies.

"Well, it's not only Danny's house," Lydia said. "And I don't give a damn about how it looks, so you're staying with us tonight."

Amanda grinned, smoking her cigarette. She slid her eyes over to Danny and gave him one of her cold, knowing smiles. "She's a hard lady to argue with. But who knows that better than you, huh?"

They drove back to the house in silence. Amanda sat next to the window and smoked the rest of Lydia's cigarettes. Syphilis lay under Lydia's feet, whining and chewing at the upholstery. At one point she peed and Danny let the window down to expel the aroma, a sharp smell of ammonia and garlic, which made Amanda laugh.

"Oh God, she ate the spaghetti I threw out last night."

Danny felt sick by the time he pulled the truck into the driveway. It was almost morning, a thin layer of sunlight accumulating along the horizon. He had to go to work in an hour. For the first time he wished he were back in the office and had the luxury of showing up closer to eleven, claiming personal tragedy, rather than standing on a beam, shivering as the sun crept through the clouds.

They walked up the driveway and saw a figure sitting on the front step, leaning against the doorway, as if he had been there for hours. My father, Danny thought, wanting to know the details. His father would have heard bits and pieces through the shortwave radio. How to explain the rest to him?

"Oh my God," Amanda said.

They stood still, their shoulders touching, staring straight ahead as if they were all having the same delusion. Kyle's voice came out of the darkness.

"Where the hell have you goons been? I near about froze my ass off. Syphilis, get over here, give your daddy a kiss, you mangy bitch."

18

T HE FIRST WEEK of April, the rains began. They were harsh, almost biblical in nature, washing away the early planted flowers and crops, leaving huge potholes in the roads, ruining outdoor weddings and picnics. People in town took the weather personally.

"Where in the world is this coming from?" customers would ask Joyce in the grocery store, as if she had orchestrated the downpour or at the very least had not done enough to intervene. They all saw it as a form of punishment, insult added to injury after the recent tragedies.

"Like we needed this," they'd say. "After the murders and all that. Looks like God could have seen fit to give us a nice spring."

"I suppose," Joyce would reply, though when she felt brave she'd declare that it was better than a drought, which the town had been experiencing last year at this time, planting seeds that were threatened in the ground, in danger of dying before they could take root. People did not respond favorably to her reassurances, though. For the most part, Joyce found, people did not want to be reassured. They wanted to be agreed with. So she tried to do that, even though her heart wasn't in it.

Her heart wasn't in any aspect of her work these days. She was too distracted, thinking of Rick, knowing he was in her apartment, all afternoon whenever it rained because there were no football tryouts. She pictured him moving through her apartment, touching her things, even looking in her drawers. It made her so nervous she could hardly concentrate on the inventory, and actually made a few mistakes when placing orders, which Mr. Oliver wasted no time in pointing out.

"Hell's bells, Joyce, twenty cases of Mountain Dew? I'm lucky if I can move two six-packs. And you didn't even put Wonder Bread on the list."

"I'm sorry, Mr. Oliver," she told him humbly, sitting inside his cramped office. He glared at her from across his desk and she tried to concentrate on the picture of his wafer thin wife and their retarded son, Percy.

"What's going on with you, Joyce? Your head is in the clouds. Are you on some kind of drug?"

"No, sir."

"Are you having some kind of family tragedy? I heard about your brother's accident—is that it? You worried about him?"

"I don't speak to my brother, sir."

"Well, cough up some kind of excuse or I'm gonna think you're losing your marbles."

Joyce looked straight at him, at his hard, pinched face, which had always reminded her of the face of the terrible Pharaoh she remembered from her children's illustrated Bible. And so she had always imagined that a variety of plagues were awaiting him, and that perhaps the burden of his retarded son was part of God's punishment.

In her less creative moments, though, Joyce knew he was just a little bully, so uninterested in other people and their lives that he could never imagine for an instant that Joyce had a lover.

But then, Joyce thought, she didn't really have a lover. Rick was more like a gentleman caller. Ever since the first night, he had not laid a finger on her. He wanted to sit with her, eat dinner with her, watch TV with her. But mostly he wanted to talk to her.

Rick did not talk about his feelings for her. Rick talked about his feelings for everyone else. He had confessed to her that every rumor she'd ever heard about him and his students was true. He found it impossible to resist the beautiful, nubile girls who threw themselves into his path. At the same time, he found it impossible not to confess to her how empty and alone those affairs made him feel. He did not claim to put an end to them; rather he let her know that being with her was what fortified him, gave him the courage to go on. It was a rather confusing contradiction, but Joyce believed that she had lived with worse things. A man who pursued her in an effort to counterbalance the rest of his life was not so horrible. Married men did it all the time. She and Rick had merely managed to invert the normal pattern. The wild, reckless, desirable girls represented the wife who didn't understand him. She, the stolid, unattractive confidante, represented the diversion that fortified him, made him believe in himself again. She offered him the stolen hours. They offered him the old, predictable way of life, the ball and chain, the commitment he felt compelled to defy. With the young girls, he did not sneak. He was rather too careless about his actions, she thought. But with Joyce, he operated under deep cover, sometimes parking blocks away and waiting until after midnight to leave. He would never think of taking Joyce out in public. And she knew he had not breathed a word of this relationship to anyone.

Every time Joyce came home to find him in her apartment, she felt both annoyed and hopeful. He had usually made a mess, left papers sitting on the floor, or dirty dishes on the coffee table. But on the other hand, perhaps tonight was the night he'd want to make love to her again. It wasn't the sex she yearned for so much, because the sex had been pretty awful. It was justification of her hours spent behind closed doors, in his company. Please, God, she thought, let him want to have sex with me because otherwise, I'm just going to have to listen to him talk. Then she knew she would be in danger of becoming the proverbial ear, the agony aunt.

She did not particularly want to know about Rick's weaknesses, his insecurities. She had never been attracted to those things. She had always been drawn to strength, to the denial of emotion. She was not a romantic, and she sometimes feared Rick had mistaken her for one.

"It all started with my mother," Rick had told her a few nights ago, when the rains first began. "I guess that's a cliché. I guess everything starts with your mother."

Not so, Joyce thought. Everything in her life seemed to have started with her father. Her father's rejection of her, Kyle's jealousy over her father's attention, even her sisters' awareness that if Pike did indeed harbor a favorite among the girls it was Joyce, his firstborn.

"She used to sleep with me," Rick admitted. "I don't mean sexually. She just shared a room with me until I was about sixteen. She claimed she couldn't sleep through my father's snoring, so she moved into my room and slept in the other twin bed. It was embarrassing, though. She had all her things in my room. Her clothes and her shoes, her perfume and makeup on my dresser. I was scared to bring guys home with me 'cause they'd see all this female stuff in my room. I remember I tried telling my best friend, Wallace, about my mother sharing my room. He laughed so hard he practically went into convulsions. Then he told everybody, including his parents, who stopped letting him come to my house. It was kinda odd. I was this big football player who shared a room with his mother. So one day I confronted her about it and said it was making the guys not want to hang out with me. That night she moved all her stuff back into Dad's room, but she never treated me the same again. She looked at me like I was a piece of lint. To this day, she won't talk to me about it. And I keep thinking, I was right, wasn't I? Asking her to move out."

"You were right," Joyce told him. She tried to imagine her mother sleeping in a room with Kyle, and the image was so bizarre she could barely entertain it. Her mother had seemed to fear Kyle from the time he could walk.

"And I think," Rick went on, "that's the reason I'm confused about women. I can't sleep with anyone who's remotely like a mother to me."

"I see," Joyce said.

"You're different," he said, and left it at that.

How? she wanted to scream. How am I different, what do you want from me, what are your intentions? But she did not say any of this for fear she would drive him away. And for some perverse reason, she needed him there.

The day that Mr. Oliver yelled at her about her mistakes, Joyce began to get scared. She was afraid that she was jeopardizing her safe and comfortable life for this odd arrangement, and on the way home she considered telling Rick that things had to change. She wasn't sure how to get him out of her life. He wasn't like the cat that she'd taken back to the pound. He was much more difficult to remove because she could not be sure what he was doing there. She did not feel comfortable saying they had to stop—stop what? Talking? And it did not make sense to say to a man, "Start sleeping with me or you'll have to leave."

But something along those lines was brewing in her brain when she walked into her apartment that day. He was stretched on her couch, channel surfing, the remote control and a Coke can resting on his stomach.

"Hey," he said, not looking up, but he immediately began to confess. "I've been thinking, maybe teaching is too narrow an occupation for me.

Maybe I should really try to get into sports. I've seen these commentators and most of them don't know a football from a canker sore. They use terms that aren't even applicable. One time I heard a guy say here comes the full court press! I swear to God he said that on national TV."

Joyce dropped her purse on the floor and took off her raincoat, letting it drip onto the welcome mat.

"We have to talk," she said.

"Sure. I ordered pizza by the way. You're looking a little skinny these days. You getting sick or something?"

"No, I feel fine."

"Cindy Wettenhall is threatening to tell her parents."

Joyce stood there staring at him. He turned off the TV and stood, stretching his long arms over his head. His fingers almost brushed the ceiling. His face was so shocking to her. It was impossible for anyone to look like that, to have such an harmonious arrangement of features. How could God have invested all this perfection in a man like Rick?

"So what happens then?" she asked.

"I guess I get fired. If she tells them it's been going on since she was fifteen, I could get arrested. But I think I talked her out of spilling those beans."

"Why's she doing this?"

"She wants to get married. And as you can imagine, I'm about as far from that as Pluto is from the sun."

He went to the refrigerator and got out a beer. Joyce just kept watching him, standing still in her spot on the welcome mat, her raincoat still dripping.

"Maybe after this I'll finally be finished with girls. Not women, mind you, but girls, because this business is truly fucked."

Joyce stared at him. She had spent too many years protecting herself not to realize what was happening. The imbalance was beginning, and he was getting the upper hand. He was never going to want her, and she was never going to stop hoping that would change.

Finally he looked up at her. She stared at him until he felt uncomfortable.

"What?" he said.

"I want to tell you something."

"What is it?"

She dropped her raincoat, but still did not move from her spot.

She said, "I was thirteen years old. Kyle was nine. I was standing at the window, looking for the UPS truck. It was supposed to bring this dress my mother had ordered for my graduation from junior high school. There was a dance that night and I was hoping it would come in time. I knew it would come in time. Whenever my mother said something would happen, it did. So all I had to do was stand by the window and wait. Kyle had been acting up all day, complaining about me. He didn't want me to get all that attention. So it made him crazy to see me standing there at the window, waiting for my prize. I just ignored him, it was what I did. Then I saw the truck pulling up in the distance. Kyle was standing right next to me. I guess he was holding on to some hope that the truck wouldn't come. And when he saw it, he pushed me hard in the back, and I fell against the window, and the venetian blinds cut into my face, like a knife into warm butter. That's how Daddy always told it, like that description made it more understandable, like it wasn't really Kyle's fault. It was my fault because my cheek was too soft. But what Daddy didn't tell, maybe what he didn't know, was that Kyle kept on pushing me. He held me there, letting the blind dig into my face. I'd pull away and he'd push me back. The blind just chewed up my face like some wild animal. It cut me down to the bone."

"Oh God," Rick said. His face had turned pale but Joyce ignored it.

She went on.

"Daddy told people it was a freak thing. A freak accident. And that night, while I was lying on my bed with fourteen stitches in my face, Daddy was in Kyle's room, reassuring him, telling him not to blame himself."

She finished talking, and then she waited. She waited for Rick to speak, but mostly she waited for the ceiling to crumble or the earth to give way beneath her feet because she had never told anyone this, and now she felt completely exposed, and she was not sure she could survive this moment.

"That's awful," Rick said. "Did he ever apologize?"

She turned and looked at him as if he had just flown in through the window like a bug.

"You don't get it," she said. "My father told Kyle not to blame himself. And so from that day on, he didn't. He didn't blame himself for anything, ever."

Rick thought about it, nodding while he sipped his beer. "That's a terrible story. I hate that."

"He did other things, too, mostly to my sisters. He tied Immy up in the tobacco barn and put peanut butter all over her feet. And after dark, the rats came out."

"Stop it," Rick said. He had turned ashen.

"And my sister Rosalie had this little pig, a runt that Daddy gave her for a pet. Kyle killed it while she was at school and roasted it on a spit, and when she got home he took her out back, saying he had a surprise for her. He pointed a gun at my mother once. She'd told him to take the trash out. I remember he turned to me and my sisters, where we were all sitting at the table, and said, 'Ma, I just wouldn't know where to start.' And then Mama swatted him for saying that, so he went and got his hunting rifle and backed her into the wall with the barrel pressed to her forehead, and she was screaming at him, and we were all crying. And I remember me and the girls just huddled around his feet and begged for my mother's life."

Rick pulled out a chair and sat down. He wiped his forehead with the back of his hand and said, "Christ."

"And then there was the time that Kyle came into my room one night . . ."

"Don't," Rick said.

". . . a while ago, over ten years ago, but it seems recent. He came in with these two friends, all drunk, and he held me down while they ripped off my nightgown, and Kyle said, 'She's not too bad from that end.' He put a pillow over my face so they wouldn't have to see it. I don't know what happened. Maybe they were too drunk, but they didn't do anything to me. They just stood there laughing. I lay there forever, thinking maybe I'd just suffocate, but finally they were gone. The next morning my mother said to me, 'Try locking your door at night.' So I went and packed my things, and that was the last I saw of my home. All I took with me was one of Daddy's old hunting rifles, which I keep under my bed, just in case I ever forget to lock my door."

Rick was staring at her now, and she thought he might cry, which would make things easier. If he cried she would turn him out with no regret at all. But he just kept staring at her, wide-eyed, and he didn't make a move or a sound.

"Now, I want you to go," she said.

"Why?"

"I just want you to leave."

He stood and walked toward her. "Can I come back tomorrow?"

"No, you can't come back at all."

"At least tell me what I did."

Joyce looked down at her feet, the toes of her plain brown shoes curling at the end from the damp weather. She reminded herself of a jester. All she needed was pom-poms and a hat with a bell.

"You're like that dress I was waiting for at the window," she said. "I can have you, but not really. And the price I have to pay for wanting you is too high."

Rick stood still for a moment, and when nothing else happened he went for his coat. It took him a few minutes to find it, to put it on, to zip it up. Then he had to find his umbrella, then his keys, and by the time he was ready Joyce had rid herself of all her pain, and as the door closed behind him, she felt nothing at all.

19

WHEN A NIGHTMARE lives on the periphery for so long, sometimes its arrival is a welcome relief. And anyway, it's the dread which is so exhausting, the fending it off. This Lydia thought as she drove to school, three days after Kyle and Amanda moved in. If someone had ever asked her to describe the worst possible scenario she could imagine for herself, she would not have been creative enough to come up with this. Kyle, the carnival worker, and his anorexic, chain-smoking girlfriend, living in their house, sleeping on the couch, eating at their dinner table, showing no visible signs of moving on.

Furthermore, if Lydia were asked to describe her reaction to such an unlikely event, she would have pictured herself thrown into paroxysms of rage and despair. This did not happen. She embraced the change in her life as, she imagined, someone with a terminal disease might accept the news. Well, I've got it now, what can be done?

No, it was less stoical than that. It was more perverse. She found comfort in the realization that the worst had come, that she no longer had to defend her life choice, to fight off the persistent, haunting reprimands of her parents and Camille. They were right, her life was ridiculous, she had made a huge mistake, and so what? At least she no longer had to wear herself out justifying it all.

I am one of those people, Lydia thought, pulling the car into the parking lot of the high school, watching the dull-eyed students and the yawning teachers heading toward the L-shaped brick building. I am one of those people running up and down the aisles of Quality-Mart, loading things I don't need into my basket. I am storing up. I am hunting—that's what has taken the place of women scouring the forests for sustenance. Now we cruise the aisles of discount stores, looking for things that might keep us alive and please the men. I am playing by the rules now, by God. Just taking my lumps and bearing up. I don't have problems, not the way I once did, like a collection of marbles. My *life* is my problem.

The only obstacle to her complete acquiescence was Danny. Danny was dissatisfied; Danny wanted to struggle against the riptide. He had no interest in giving in to it. So every night he had grumbled to her in bed, "They're leaving here. No fucking way they're staying another minute."

"Danny, they're not going anywhere. They have no money."

"I don't give a shit, I'll let them live on the streets. They're users, Lydia. They'll bleed us dry if we let them."

"So what are you going to do about it?"

"I'll call the police. I'll get Les Carlisle out here to arrest them."

"Arrest them? For what, sponging off their relatives?"

"How can you be so complacent about this?"

"I'm resigned. There's a difference."

She could not think of a way to describe her feelings to Danny. Could not imagine how he would be able to understand that she was actually glad to see Amanda when she came home in the evenings. The pale, doe-eyed girl sat at her kitchen table, watching Lydia cook with her slow, apathetic gaze. Every now and then she'd ask Lydia a question: "What's that spice you're using? Do you have a cigarette? Who cuts your hair?" But most of the time she sat and observed, and the sight of her reminded Lydia of something from Dickens—the phantom children hiding under the skirt of the Ghost of Christmas Present. She had always been frightened and thrilled by that story, and the thing she recalled most clearly was Jacob Marley rattling his chains and screeching, "Mankind was my bus-i-ness!" Lydia felt she had taken on the troubles of the human race in the form of Amanda, the skeletal figure always near her, always hovering. Mankind was her business now.

What would be even harder to explain to Danny was her reaction (or lack of it) to Kyle. He stomped around the house on his plastic leg, leaving a trail of debris—cigarette butts, empty beer bottles, bread crumbs. He sometimes tried to jangle Lydia's nerves, walking into her bedroom unannounced (once catching her half-naked), thumbing through her school papers while he ate, spilling food on them, and attacking her with curious, abrasive comments about her looks, her habits, the way she talked. Once when he saw her reading *Anna Karenina* he said, "Do you really care about that shit, or do you read it to impress people?" And another time when he saw her putting on lipstick in the hall mirror he said, "Prettifying, huh? Scared your boyfriend's getting restless?" He constantly referred to Danny as her boyfriend, to the point that she really wondered if he had forgotten they were married.

Lydia's reaction to Kyle was one of mild annoyance, as if there were a poltergeist in the house, some mischievous character who moved things around and made a lot of noise, but did not possess the ability to inflict pain. She tried to ignore him as much as possible. She did not hope he would go away. She thought that short of divine intervention, Kyle was in her life for good.

She even found herself becoming defensive about him.

"You can't put up with this forever," Dee had said to her last night at the most recent potluck dinner. It was not the quarterly event, but a special potluck called to discuss a couple of urgent matters—closing down Quality-Mart once and for all, and finding the murderer, in that order of importance. It still seemed that the townspeople were much more outraged by the notion of commerce than violence. Yes, it was true that the killer needed to be apprehended, those deaths avenged, but what about the store? What about those discount rates on power tools, which was all but putting Nathan's Hardware out of business? What about the take-out deli they threatened to install, which would certainly cut into Oliver's business? And the diner that was already hurting the Green Lantern? These matters had to be addressed, and if, in the process, suspects were rounded up, more the better.

Despite the urgency, the potluck had only been half full. The rains, no doubt, kept people away. If God wasn't going to give them a nice spring, they could hardly go out of their way to satisfy Him.

"I mean, you can't be serious about keeping them," Dee had said.

"Keeping them? They aren't like stray pets, Dee. They're people who don't have a home."

"They do have a home and it's yours."

"Well, I'm doing a good deed. That should get me some points in heaven."

John, who had been hovering nearby, pretending to collect chairs but really eavesdropping, said, "Lydia, the Lord expects us to be generous, not foolish."

"Excuse me?"

"Kyle is not the most deserving person. If you turned him out, God would understand."

"You know, John, I'm not that concerned about God understanding me. I'd rather hear an explanation as to what the fuck *He's* up to."

"Oh, Lydia," Dee had said, smiling, shaking her head.

But John had remained undaunted. "It's healthy to question the Lord. The only thing God dreads is being ignored."

"Yes," Lydia had said, "that's the reason for a lot of bad behavior."

Dee had not smiled that time. Instead she had moved off to thank Inez Milton for her chicken divan.

When Lydia went into the faculty lounge, she discovered that an impromptu meeting was taking place. Nigel Hayes was there, and a knot of teachers surrounded him, speaking to him in hushed tones. When Lydia walked in, the room went quiet, then Nigel said, "It's only Lydia."

"What's going on?"

"A serious matter, Crane," said Martha.

"Let me guess. Quality-Mart."

"If Crane is going to be disruptive, I vote that she not be allowed to participate."

"Oh, anything but that, Martha," Lydia said.

"Now, let's not start with the contentiousness," Nigel pleaded. "We have enough to discuss without personalizing matters. Let's try to address this thing professionally."

"What's going on?"

"Things seem to have reached critical mass, in the matter of one of our teachers and his relationship to his students, that is to say, extracurricularwise."

"Gunther is fraternizing with the girls," Martha said, her thin lips twitching against a smile.

"Who?" Lydia asked.

"There've been many. But Wettenhall finally blew the whistle."

Lydia did not know anyone by that last name. "Who the hell is that?"

"She's not at the school anymore," Nigel admitted, "which makes it all very murky."

"Murky? I'll give you murky," Martha said. Her eyes actually seemed to be glowing.

"In my country," Dr. Rivilla said, "this happens. My first husband was my teacher, God rest his soul. He loved the young girls, but this was just his nature. He seduced me, it's true. Here we would be arrested. But in my country, we were happy."

"This is not Cuba," Martha snapped.

"That's right, this is a free country," Lydia said.

Martha gave one of her special glares to Lydia and said directly to her, "We are signing a petition to put before the school board to have Gunther expelled."

"There will be a hearing first. We'll let him defend himself," Nigel Hayes said.

"Really, you think that's necessary? It wasn't with Alicia Clay," Lydia said.

Martha said, "Perhaps you think it's perfectly fine that Gunther is having sexual intercourse with teenagers."

"Martha, please, we don't *know* that. Right now it's a rumor," Nigel insisted.

"It's not fine with me, Martha, but it's all speculation. Rick is a good teacher. I don't know about his personal life because I don't ask. He affords me the same luxury," Lydia said.

"So we're not accountable for our behavior, is this what you're saying? What we do in our own time is our business?" Martha spoke right into Lydia's face, as if she thought she could intimidate her. Lydia felt impervious to her anger. What can happen to me now, she wondered, since Kyle and Amanda moved in?

Lydia said, "Here's my problem. This place is starting to feel more like the House Ethics Committee than a high school faculty. I don't feel up to the job. No one ever told me I'd be required to assess the comportment of my colleagues, so if you'll excuse me I won't be signing any petition. Instead, I'll go down the hall and give a vocabulary test."

She walked away feeling strong and proud of herself. But as she taught her morning class, she realized the reason she could not take up the fight against Rick had less to do with her respect for his right to privacy and more to do with her inability to feel sympathy for the girls Rick had supposedly violated. When she looked at the girls in her class, she couldn't help wondering if Rick were sleeping with this one or that one, and not one face made her feel protective or defensive. They did not seem like innocent children. She saw instead femininity in its rawest form, the inherent sexuality of unsophistication. The girls knew they possessed it; sometimes they even used it against Lydia. If they didn't know the answer to a question they would glare at her with contempt for her age, her authority, which made her sexless and therefore pathetic. They would smile, tossing their hair, swinging their long, thin legs, as if to say, So fucking what? I know nothing, but I have everything.

That evening began as any other. There was no reason to think that Kyle would inflict any more harm on them than usual, just the odd insult to her cooking or speculating about Danny's whereabouts, suggesting that he wasn't really working late on the building site. In fact, the only thing that really marked the evening was Danny's unexpected presence. Yet another storm had cropped up, and Danny came home from work in time for dinner. He was tired and dirty, his face smudged with specks of concrete, his hair matted down under his hardhat. He carefully set the yellow hat aside on the kitchen counter, as if he wanted it to serve as a reminder to Lydia. She was married to a construction worker and he dared her to deny it.

Lydia had made meat loaf, mashed potatoes, and peas. Amanda had actually shopped for all the ingredients and prepared them, and helped her shell the peas and mash the potatoes. But when they all sat down to eat Amanda only helped herself to a spoonful of peas and a large glass of beer.

Kyle interrogated Danny about his work. He seemed as annoyed as Lydia at the idea of Danny going back to manual labor.

"Shit, boy, with all the brains in your head, you're pounding nails? What the hell is that about? You're out there keeping company with spicks and niggers."

"Don't say niggers," Amanda suggested.

"I enjoy the work," Danny said, not looking at his cousin. He shoveled his food in, as if he could not wait for the whole business to be over.

"Now what does Miss Harvard University think of her husband in a hardhat? You turned on by that kind of thing?"

Lydia said, "I didn't go to Harvard. And it's Danny's life."

"That's a hell of a note," Kyle said, peas falling out of his mouth like pebbles. Kyle's physical impairment, the missing limb, seemed to inform his whole existence. If he could not have a complete body, he did not recognize the importance of commanding the parts that were left available to him. "Your girlfriend here thinks it's *your* life, Danny. She oughta know better than that. You wanna set her straight, or should I?"

Danny said nothing. He drank his water and stared at Kyle as he swallowed.

"You know your problem," Kyle said, with a mouth full of potatoes. "Danny, your problem is, you married someone who's smarter than you are."

Danny did not respond. Lydia offered Kyle some more meat loaf.

"You're a teacher, aren't you?" Kyle asked her.

"That's right," Lydia said.

"What do you teach?"

"English."

"You mean, how to speak it?"

"No. Literature."

"Literature. Now, that's where some guy makes up a story and puts it down in big words, and some committee of geniuses declares that it's a work of art, so people start pissing in their pants and jerking off over how brilliant it is, and anybody who doesn't get how brilliant it is is generally considered to be an idiot, and they get sent off to work at a gas station. That how it works?"

Lydia stared at her food, pressing her potatoes with the back of her fork, something she used to do as a child.

Amanda said, "The last book Kyle read was the *TV Guide.*"

"Cover to cover," he laughed. "Now, tell me what writers you think are geniuses, Lydia. I'd like to know."

"All the usual people," she said, hoping to end the conversation. She could feel Danny tensing up beside her.

"Think I haven't heard of 'em, is that it?"

"Kyle, give it a rest," Danny said.

"No, come on, throw one at me. Off the top of your head. Not Shakespeare now, that's too easy."

"Dreiser," Lydia said to shut him up.

"That's his first name?"

"Theodore Dreiser."

"Teddy to his friends?"

"I don't know."

"Now what does Teddy Dreiser write about?"

"Kyle, I really don't want to have this discussion with you," she said, getting up, taking her plate to the sink.

"Oh, go ahead," Amanda said. "He's as smart as your fifteen-year-olds."

Lydia turned and looked at Amanda, uncertain if she were siding with Kyle or trying to make peace.

"It's called American naturalism," she said.

"Well, that's my favorite thing in the world!" Kyle said. "But what I mean is, what's it *about?*"

Lydia said, "He wrote about morality."

"Morality," Kyle said, dragging out each syllable, then issuing a low whistle. "That sounds serious. You think I could understand it? Should I give it a go?"

Danny said, "I don't believe it would be your kind of thing."

"Now what would make you say that? You think I'm not a moral guy?"

Danny stood, glowering down at Kyle, and for a second Lydia thought he was about to challenge him. But he finally turned and took his dishes to the sink.

"If you think I'm not moral, that must mean you think I'm immoral. Do you think I'm immoral, Danny? Do you think I'm bad to the bone?"

"I think you're starting to bore me, Kyle."

Lydia said, "Let's just end this, all right?"

Amanda poured herself another glass of beer and said, "Lydia, do you have a cigarette?"

"I don't smoke anymore," Lydia said.

"Oh shit, just my luck. Kyle, give me one of yours," Amanda said.

"Hell no, get your own."

"How about nobody smokes in the house?" Danny suggested.

"Are you saying I set fire to my own goddamn trailer?" Kyle said.

"What?"

"Are you saying that I fell asleep on the couch with a lit cigarette and burned up everything I own?"

"I'm not saying anything like that, Kyle."

"Well, I didn't."

"Give me a cigarette, Kyle," Amanda said, leaning forward. He swatted her hand away.

"Hey," Danny said.

"I did not fall asleep with a lit cigarette even though that's what the bitch told the cops. You know what happened? That whore from hell right there set fire to the place with me in it, passed out drunk on the bed. She tried to kill me."

Lydia sat still. The air felt thick with danger, and she could not see a way out of it. She made fists and let the nails bite into her palms. Across the room, Danny stood equally still, except for his fingers which were flexing, flexing.

Amanda stared levelly at Kyle, taking a long, leisurely sip of beer. When she had finished she wiped her mouth and said, "Come on, one smoke, Kyle. I'll buy you a pack tomorrow."

Kyle fished the pack out of his shirt and threw them at her. She caught them in one hand.

"See, Danny, you and I have a lot in common," Kyle said. "We both got women who are smarter than we are. And that's a fucking nightmare, pal, because you can never turn your back."

Amanda took three drags of her cigarette, rested it on her plate, then stood. She unzipped her jeans and let them fall to the ground. She wore white lace panties, like something Lydia thought belonged on a little girl. She watched as Amanda turned her thigh out to reveal four or five perfectly round red circles that, from a distance, looked like jewels imbedded in her skin.

"See that? Cigarette burns." She turned around and lifted her shirt to reveal her lower back, a dark purple line etched across it. "See that? A two-by-four caught me there."

She reached down and pulled her jeans back on, zipped them up, sat down and picked up her cigarette again. Kyle slowly began to applaud. Lydia watched it all, too horrified to respond. She knew she should do something, say something to stop this nightmare, but nothing came to mind. Finally Danny moved across the room, standing directly over Kyle, and said, "I want you out of my house."

"That right?" He turned and looked at Lydia. "He wants me out of his house."

Lydia found the muscles in her neck and nodded.

"What do you think Teddy Dreiser would have to say about that? I think he'd find that fucking amusing. Being someone who wrote about *morality* and all."

"I want you out of my house, Kyle," Danny repeated.

Without warning Kyle shot up, his nose almost touching Danny's, and screamed, "I want my fucking leg back! You know the leg I mean, don't you? The one you told the doctor to cut off, Danny? That leg? Give me my fucking leg and I'll get out of your house!"

"You were going to die. I saved your life."

"You ruined my life, that's what you did. I have no goddamned life, thanks to you. I gave up whatever pathetic future I ever had to protect you, and don't you ever forget it!"

"Shut up, Kyle," Danny said evenly.

"I've done that for thirty-four years. I did that so you could be a star. Danny the college man, Danny the ballplayer, Danny with the shirt-and-tie job, Danny with the smart, fuckable wife—I gave you all that, and how you thank me is to throw me out of your goddamned house?"

Danny turned and started to walk away. Lydia watched him, glad at once to see him go, because she did not want this moment to happen. For once she thanked Danny for leaving.

"Don't turn your back on me, you bastard!" Kyle screamed. "You killed my father! His blood is on your hands!"

Danny froze in the doorway. Don't let him turn around, Lydia prayed. Let him keep going. But she knew he would turn and when he did he looked at her instead of Kyle. She shook her head slowly at him. This was the moment that she thought would come in a phone call. The moment between contentment and everything else.

He turned toward Kyle and said, "I never asked you to protect me."

"No, you never do ask for anything, Danny. You know things are coming your way. You know people want to save you and you let them. You knew I'd do any damn thing in the world for you and you let me."

With this Kyle sank into his chair and began to cry into the crook of his arm. Amanda watched him with a dull expression, as if she had seen this all before. She knew how it would end.

Danny shook his head mournfully and gazed at his fingers. He brought them close to his face and stared at the tips and blew on them, as if to extinguish once and for all that invisible fire.

Lydia said, "Danny, I don't want to know."

Looking at his fingers he said, "I'm the one who shot Kyle."

• • •

All night, the rain persisted. It hammered down on the roof, the roar of it drowning out all other sounds. Lydia sat in bed and tried to picture what Dee was doing this moment in her house down the street. Arguing with her children, picking up their toys? Making love to John? Praying? What was it that average people did, night after night, to keep themselves sane, to keep their minds from wandering too far?

Danny sat in a chair across the room, running his thumb along his lip and staring at the window. Lydia did not think he would speak at all, or even come to bed. She thought she would wake up in the morning to find him in that same position. But she could not predict Danny anymore. She had lost that ability if she ever possessed it.

"It was Kyle's idea," he eventually said, still looking out the window. "He was showing me his gun. He had ammo in it, and he wasn't supposed to. We were only thirteen. I didn't even have a real gun, just an air rifle. And I knew I wasn't supposed to shoot anything with live rounds in it. But Kyle was goading me. Calling me a chickenshit. Calling me a faggot."

He pinched the bridge of his nose, then looked up.

"I had the gun in my hand. And I wanted to shoot it. I'd gone with my father hunting before, so I knew how it was done. You just aimed and shot and when your catch went down, people congratulated you. There was no shame in killing. No shame. Do you understand me?"

"I'm listening," Lydia said.

"There was a cat. One of Joyce's cats hanging around. A big, fat tabby thing just sitting there, looking at me. And Kyle told me to shoot it. I didn't want to. I didn't want to shoot anything. But Kyle kept calling me a faggot. And I was so scared because of my brother. He was weak. People didn't like him. Even my own father didn't trust him, I could see it. So I would have gone around the world to avoid being like him. I wanted to be like Kyle. Do you get it? I wanted to be like him so much that I knew the only way to prove my courage was to shoot something. So I pointed at the cat. And I shot."

"And what happened?" Lydia asked.

"Nothing. Nothing at all. Kyle said, 'The safety catch is on.' So I took it off and then the gun fired. It fired into his foot. And Kyle started to scream. I threw the gun away. I tossed it over in the bushes. It could still be there for all I know."

"You don't have to keep going," Lydia said.

"And I was just scared shitless. So much trouble ahead. Pike would kill me. My father would kill me. There'd be so much shame. So much hysteria. And I didn't know that Kyle wouldn't die, you realize. I was thirteen and all I knew was that I'd shot someone, and I thought you could die from a foot wound. So when Pike came running up I just stood there waiting for my punishment. I did not get it. I was too young to understand that I could just say the truth and it would be horrible, but it would be over. Everything was so immediate. I couldn't see that it was a turning point. I could not see how, in trying to save myself, I would carry the lie around forever."

"And Pike ran up and what happened?" Lydia asked.

He shook his head. "Everything else is the way I told you. Kyle said to his father, 'A damn nigger shot me, do you believe that?' Kyle didn't even look at me when he did it, didn't even hesitate or stammer, just told the lie and committed to it. He never changed his story, never wavered. And until tonight, he never mentioned it to me again. But it was always there, it was unspoken. I made the deal with him, right then and there. Without saying a word."

"It's not your fault," Lydia said quietly.

"Goddamn it, Lydia, it is. You really don't understand, do you? I wanted to shoot something. I wanted to kill something. Kyle saw that in me, and that's part of what he owns."

"You wanted to kill a cat, Danny. You and a million thirteen-year-old boys."

"I don't know," he said, pressing his hands to his temples. "I can't remember. I shot Kyle. Maybe I wanted to."

"Stop it. I don't believe it. Danny, it was an accident."

"Okay, let's say it was an accident. Let's say it was a stupid thing. Just petty and small and ridiculous. How trivial can it be when it caused two deaths? Uncle Pike and Tom Fitzgerald's baby. And it ruined that man's life. And the judge who had to leave town. Oh Jesus, don't you see how much damage was done? It couldn't have been an accident. That much destruction can only come from—"

He stopped speaking, covering his mouth with his hands and crying into his fingers.

"From what, Danny? The devil?"

He didn't deny it. In fact, she thought she detected a slight nod.

Lydia suddenly felt tired. Out of nowhere, she just wanted to let him believe what he believed and turn over and go to sleep.

"Danny," she said with a great effort. "It is so much more complicated than that. A thousand things led to that moment. And, yes, you did your part. But it doesn't belong to you. And don't even start with the devil, okay, because that is pure bullshit. Every time things get bad people conjure him up, they invite him to the party because they just can't believe that shit happens, and sometimes stupid shit happens, and there's nothing we can do about it."

"But that's just it," he said, turning to her. His eyes were red-rimmed and swollen, making him look mildly possessed. "How stupid it all is. It's the banality of evil."

"Stop using that word. It's ridiculous."

"Lydia, you have to consider the possibility. How else can you explain Kyle, how indestructible he is. And how much pain he's caused. There's no good in him."

"He covered for you all these years. He protected you. That's not good?"

"He protected me so he could control me. No matter how well I did, how great I became, if I played ball or married the woman of my dreams or made a fortune or just tried to have a quiet, happy life—he could take it all away from me in a second."

Lydia shook her head. No wonder this man was so tortured. No wonder he carried that look of doom on his face, the first thing she had ever noticed about him. Because he saw the world in these Gothic terms. He had never seen, after all this time, that they were just ordinary people making extraordinary mistakes.

And what about their marriage? Had he seen her in such terms? She thought of the way they both fell in love, that blinding sense of purpose that defied reason and logic and distance and class. All this time, she was responding to that belief that their marriage would be blessed and sacred and charmed. Because Danny carried these notions inside him, and Lydia must have seen that, and she wanted to believe it. But now she watched her husband wiping his face on his sleeve and she thought that perhaps she had just learned something very important. She had learned that life was just hard, and he still believed it was tragic.

She could not say such things to Danny now, and she knew it. But what worried her more was that she'd never be able to get him to see it, not after he calmed down, not after Kyle had left their house, not ever.

"Let's go to bed," Lydia said.

"There's more," Danny replied.

"No, there isn't," she said. "I'm going to sleep."

"Kyle did it," he said, staring at the ground, unable to look at her. "Kyle killed those men at Quality-Mart."

It sounded so ludicrous that Lydia was not sure she was required to respond. Still, she waited. She had to hear the rest of it.

"He tried to tell me one day. The day he ran his car into the tree and I went after Amanda. He tried to tell me he had done it, but I wouldn't listen."

"What did he tell you?"

"He just kept saying . . . they were coming for him. They were going to get him for it. And he asked me to defend him."

"Kyle is delusional. I'm sure some part of him wants to be responsible, but it's just part of the drama. He can't be responsible for every single tragedy around here."

"I know him, Lydia. He's vengeful. Everything is personal with him. That assistant manager turned him down for a job. That's all it would take. And there could have been other things. He could have been doing drugs again. And then there was Amanda. They had a fight that night."

"Stop it, Danny. Stop doing this. You just can't leave Kyle alone. You want to rescue him so much that you're creating things to save him from."

"I'm not creating it," Danny said evenly. "I *know* it."

Lydia felt desperate, rummaging her brain for some argument, something to convince him he was wrong. Suddenly the thought came to her and she felt hope descend hard and fast, like a panic. She sat up on her knees in bed.

"It can't have been him, Danny," she said. "That night Les Carlisle came here . . . he told you they'd eliminated Kyle as a suspect."

Danny shook his head slowly.

"Yes, they did. You told me that."

Danny said, "They eliminated him because I gave him an alibi. I said he was with me."

Lydia shook her head, the probability of it all floating down on her like ashes, like nuclear winter; she couldn't shake it off. She was dirty. She was in this now.

"You weren't with him," she said weakly. "You were with me."

"I know. But it just came out of my mouth. Les asked me if I could account for Kyle that night and before I knew it, I said he was with me. I'd just been covering for him for so long, I didn't know how to stop."

Without thinking, Lydia climbed out of bed and went to the phone, as if it were ringing. She picked up the receiver and stretched the cord in Danny's direction. From across the room he just stared at her.

"No," he said.

"Just tell them the truth. Then they can investigate Kyle. They can eliminate him on their own, if he didn't do it. And if he did . . ."

"I can't do it."

"Danny, this whole thing is destroying you. It's destroying us."

He said nothing to that. He didn't try to deny it.

Lydia thrust the phone at him and said, "Jesus Christ. Would the great and mighty St. Pike want you to protect a murderer?"

"It's not about Pike," Danny said. "It never was. It's about my family. Tell me, what would happen to them, Lydia? Hell, they fired that teacher Alicia Clay for no reason at all. Because she might have said something to inspire the murderer? What would this town do to the people who raised him and nurtured him and protected him? Hell, my family is hanging on by a thread anyway. Mother and Rex and Rita and those girls— what would happen to them? What would happen to Joyce?"

Lydia was staring at him, listening to all this, the logic of it all settling in, making her feel cold and sick. It was Joyce's name that really got her attention. She could not imagine Joyce sustaining even one more blow.

"So we're just going to live with it," Lydia said. "It's going to be our little secret."

Danny finally raised his eyes to meet hers.

He said, "A secret doesn't get bad until you send it out into the world, where it can hurt people." He smiled weakly. "It's something Amanda told me."

Lydia nodded, as if it made perfect sense, as if Amanda possessed the wisdom of ages, the answer to all their problems.

Lydia's life began to pass before her eyes, as if she were drowning. She thought of all the paths she could have taken that would have led her away from here. She should never have gone off chasing things. She was like those tourists staring into their house in Georgetown. She had looked into the window of Danny's simple life and she had coveted it. She was one of those sad, sad people.

"There's nothing we can do tonight," she said quietly. "Let's go to bed."

Danny nodded. He crawled in bed beside her and put his head on her chest. She ran her fingers through his hair. He was barely breathing against her. Make it all go away, Lydia prayed to nothing and no one in particular. Give me the morning, and a thousand meaningless tasks, and busy work and bored students, so that I don't have to know any of this anymore.

She must have fallen asleep then, must have had her prayers answered, for when she woke, the morning light was streaming in through the shades, pressing down like a demand. She sat up in bed and felt for Danny. He was gone and Syphilis was there. The dog had moved into the room like an innocuous gas and now was crouched next to Lydia's rib, staring up at her with a quizzical eye.

Part Two

1

ON JULY 17, a week before Rex's thirtieth birthday, they caught the Quality-Mart murderer. It had been over a year since the murders, and everyone had given up. The news breathed life back into the town.

He was a young kid, barely eighteen, with long greasy black hair and tattoos all the way up his arms. Sally watched him on TV as they dragged him into the courthouse. He did it all right, she thought. Even though, naturally, he swore up and down that he was nowhere near the place. And they brought in some slick lawyer from up North who said his client's rights were being violated and this was a miscarriage of justice and the system didn't work for poor people, blah blah blah. No, this kid did it all right, Sally decided, staring at his flat, white face. It was in his eyes.

There was a party at the church to celebrate the arrest, but Sally didn't go because it coincided with their own party for Rex's birthday. Rex was a little put out at having to share the spotlight.

"Couldn't they have caught the man next week?" Rex asked. "There's no way my coming of age can compete with this."

The birthday party was a somber affair, pizza and kegs in the Cranes' backyard. But it wasn't the news of the murder that gave it such a strange, funereal feeling. Sally knew exactly why the event was so depressing. She felt that the marking of Rex's thirtieth year on earth was like acknowledging a kind of death. At thirty, they could no longer pretend that their son was going through a phase. They were required to stand back and look at him, and know that this was the person he was, there would be no startling changes in him, no sudden turnaround.

Sally decided it would be a good idea to drink.

She stood under the shade of an oak tree and fanned herself with a paper plate, a smile frozen on her face as she observed the guests and sipped her Chablis.

Danny was calmer without his wife. Everyone noticed it; it wasn't just Sally. Maybe it was grief that made him so peaceful, but whatever reason, it was nice to see him not so fidgety and poking at himself. He just walked around with his arms by his side, smiling a half-smile at nothing in particular. He occasionally turned his head and looked around as if someone had called his name. Sally wondered, watching from across the lawn, if he expected to see Lydia appear. Surely he couldn't still be pining for her. It had been a year since she left without a word. Danny was a good-looking man; he could have any girl in town. Why would he waste his time missing his wife?

"Danny looks handsome," Rita said, approaching her, following her gaze. "Divorce agrees with him."

"He's not divorced," Sally said.

"Well, practically they are."

"Practical only counts in horseshoes," Sally said.

Rita stared at her empty wineglass and said, "How many of those have you had?"

Sally looked down, too, wondering if this were her second or third glass. Funny how they added up. She was never really a drinker before, but she couldn't imagine why.

"Oh, who cares how much I drink," Sally said. "I'm in my own backyard. It wouldn't hurt you, either."

"I have never touched alcohol," Rita said with a huff. "Pike used to always say, drink one glass, then it's a bottle, then it's hard liquor and you've got real troubles."

"Well, wasn't Pike clever. He just had a quip for all occasions."

Rita glared at her and Sally felt herself blush. Was it the wine, making her thoughts roll off her tongue indiscriminately? She didn't really care. It needed to be said. Pike had been perfect long enough.

"I think I'll mingle," Rita said, and moved off. Sally didn't care. She wanted to be alone. The wine made loneliness okay. Wasn't that something?

She watched Nel, who was busy introducing young girls to Rex. He was telling them that his son was a writer posing as a librarian.

"Rex is a very creative person, and any day now he's going to wake up to the fact that he needs to put his ideas down on paper."

"I don't have any ideas, Pop," Rex said, sipping Scotch as he sat reclined on a lawn chair like a Roman emperor, reviewing his troops. Though it was hot and most of the guests wore shorts, Rex was dressed in a navy suit with a starched collar and a silk Italian tie. "You stay around books long enough and you figure out that anything worth saying has already been said."

"He draws!" Nel told the girls. "He draws all the time and makes models, too. I can see him as an illustrator. Children's books, that's ideal. Rex has a children's story in him waiting to get out."

"Yeah, Dad. Sling me a slice of pepperoni."

Rex had made a tape of famous show tunes which played on the portable cassette player she and Nel had given him as a present. The sounds of *South Pacific* and *My Fair Lady* floated out into the humid night, harmonizing with the crickets and cicadas.

" 'Are there lilac trees in the heart of town,' " Rex sang at the top of his lungs, " 'Can you hear a lark in any other part of town?' "

The girls smiled warily at him and backed off. Only Mr. Grafton seemed amused. He joined in several choruses and kept checking on Rex's drink. Mr. Grafton wasted no time in putting away his own share of alcohol, his taste running more toward beer, which he referred to as lager.

Rita's daughters all stood in a clump close to the back door, as if poised to dart inside. They whispered to each other and giggled and chewed the ice in their Cokes. They looked like a bunch of schoolgirls waiting to be asked to dance, Sally observed, instead of women in or approaching their thirties. What the hell kind of family was this? she asked herself. Maybe Lydia was right to leave.

The thought was shocking. She blamed it on the wine.

Rita rejoined her, nibbling on her pizza. She had not fully recovered from the remark about Pike, but she had no one else to talk to.

She nodded in the direction of Danny and said, "Joyce tells me he's depressed. Joyce says he comes by her place every week and picks at his dinner and cries."

"You'll excuse me," Sally said, feeling the need to sway, "if I don't take Joyce's word for it. She has her own things to answer for."

"What does that mean?" Rita challenged.

"It means what it means."

"You don't think Joyce was *attacked,* do you? You've never believed it."

Attacked was the word Rita always used to describe Joyce's predicament. She could not force herself to say rape, which conjured up such nasty images no one wanted to think about it. This way, Joyce could have just been the victim of a sort of imbalance, like someone who had lost an arm-wrestling match.

"That's not for me to decide," Sally answered, staring at the bottom of her glass and suddenly feeling depressed. "But I do think she was a fool to keep that baby, no matter what happened to her."

"You're just jealous," Rita accused, "because I was the first to have a grandchild."

Sally considered this, looking at the tubby little boy lying on a quilt, his limbs flailing as if he were fighting off a swarm of mosquitoes. Looking so stupidly up to the sky, struggling to speak and only emitting a belch. Sally did not really desire grandchildren. Did anyone really like babies? she wondered, watching as people stopped to peer down and coo at him before wandering away. Sally did not become interested in her own children until they could speak. The moment when she could say, "Don't whine," marked a turning point in her life as a mother. She had adored her children once they were able to communicate, but she felt that babyhood was something to be endured.

Even Joyce did not seem particularly concerned with her son. She sat in a lawn chair, gazing up at the trees. Sally suspected that people pretended to love babies because they feared them so much. These little bundles of need, reaching up and demanding, and it seemed their entire purpose in life was to test the capabilities of adults. In a heartbeat, they could expose your inadequacies. If you held them wrong or burped them too fast or made a face that they didn't find amusing, they'd sound the alarm, their squalling serving as a public service announcement to all within earshot—this one's no good! This one can't do it!

Sally vaguely recalled feeling that about her own babies. She felt it now, looking at her sons. Rex, singing into an imaginary microphone, and Danny, finally pausing to talk to a girl half his age. In their own way they were sounding the alarm. There they were, for everyone to observe how badly Sally had done. How comprehensively she had missed the point of motherhood.

Still, Sally was trained to carry on, to ignore the evidence. Suddenly she had an image of the Quality-Mart killer standing there in his white T-shirt, telling the TV reporter he didn't do it.

"This is bullshit, man," he'd said. They'd bleeped out the word but she could read his lips. "They don't have any evidence on me. They just want somebody to take the blame."

Maybe people like that somehow convinced themselves they weren't guilty. Maybe, in a way, that's what she was doing.

She said to Rita, "Well, Joyce has her problems and Danny's got his, but I know that getting rid of Lydia was the best thing he ever did."

"But what's going to become of him now? He's just going to be an unmarried construction worker. He had so much promise, Sally, and now he's just one of us."

"Worse things could happen," Sally declared. "If God appeared on earth right now and said, Sally, your biggest problem is that Danny's going to be a bachelor and Rex is going to stay at home and you're never going to have grandchildren, I'd say, All right, what's the bad news?"

Sally laughed, thinking this was quite a witty retort. But Rita only stared at her, then looked down at her skirt to swipe at invisible crumbs.

"Where's Kyle?" Sally asked suddenly. "Shouldn't he be here?"

"You didn't *invite* him, did you?" Rita asked with a stricken expression. She cast a quick glance over to her girls, who bunched together, heads down, moving like a low cloud across the lawn. "He's not going to show up here."

"I thought he might, since he's living with Danny."

"Oh no, he's not really living there. It's just till they find a place, I'm sure."

"Danny says they aren't looking."

"But he can't live with Danny," Rita said, looking as if she might cry. "Danny couldn't take that."

"He could live with Lydia, he could live with anybody."

"Sally, you were always so hard on her. I don't know what happened there. What got into that girl?"

"Oh, I don't know," Sally declared, with a sigh. She didn't care. She just wanted another glass of wine. She started to head that way, but she saw Danny walking toward her.

"I think I'm going to take off, Mother," he said.

"Take off what?"

"Leave. Go home."

"But we haven't even had the cake."

"I know, but I have to get up at five. And, you know, Kyle and Amanda are at the house. I want to make sure they aren't burning it down or something."

"I wish you'd get them out of there," she said, frowning.

"Short of evicting them, I don't know what to do. Anyway, I got Rex the Harold Arlen collection. I didn't have time to get him a card. So let him know it's from me."

"Do me a favor, honey. Get your mother a glass of wine."

Danny took the glass. "How many have you had?"

"Why do people keep asking me that? Am I a teenager?"

He smiled and kissed her on the cheek. "I guess you've earned some fun."

He walked toward the bar and Sally put her hand to her cheek, feeling strange and sort of winded from the wine and the kiss and the compliment.

That night, she approached Nelson in the bedroom.

"Let's try it," she told her husband. "For old times' sake."

"Try what?" he questioned, rubbing his brow as he got into bed. Nel was no real stranger to alcohol, but it always made his head ache.

"You know, what we used to do."

"Oh, for God's sake, Sally, my head is full of rocks."

"But it's all over now, and we can think of each other."

"What's over?"

"Our children are gone and it's just us."

"Rex isn't gone. He's passed out in his bed, two doors down. He drank way too much. You drank too much too, if you don't mind my saying so."

"I do mind it," Sally said. "I like wine. I never knew how good it was."

"Go to sleep," Nel said. "I've got to work in the morning."

"Please, Nel. I don't get to feel like this very often."

"Sally, we had our turn. We're old. Let's just get some rest."

But she would not let the subject drop, and after enough exploring and coaxing, she got Nel to admit to some distant stirring in himself. They made love, as awkwardly as teenagers, and when it was over, Sally lay in bed wondering if they were doing it right, if Oprah or Sally Jessy would approve.

As Nel snored next to her, Sally wrote a letter in her head.

Dear Dr. Brothers,
I am in my sixties, and my husband and I have been married for forty years. Just recently I discovered the benefits of wine. After three glasses of Chablis, I suddenly found myself wanting to do things I haven't cared about for years. My husband is less enthusiastic. How can I make him see that I want to make up for lost time?
Signed,
Frustrated in Virginia

Dear Frustrated,
Many people in their sixties enjoy a happy and active sex life. There's no reason to expect this part of your life to end. If wine is what it takes to help you realize your own desire, I say more power to you. I enjoy an occasional glass myself.
Sincerely,
Dr. Joyce Brothers

Sally awoke the next morning with a dull pain behind her eyes. Nel was gone already and she lay in bed, with the sticky feeling between her legs, and for a moment she thought she had to get up and see to her small children. It was odd realizing she had nothing to do but lie there, wondering what to do to keep herself busy until her husband came home again.

She finally dragged herself out of bed to face the mess in the kitchen and the trash outdoors. No one had bothered to stay and help clean up. She put on a jogging suit and went out back, picking up empty cups and paper plates like a janitor. Every now and then she thought about Nel, wondering if the evening had changed him, if she could expect a similar performance that night.

But when he came home from work, looking exhausted and defeated, she knew that she could not say anything, could not hope to remind him that she wanted to try it again. Rex was, indeed, still down the hall, and Nel treated his home like some kind of fort, a place in which he could be safe from the invasion of emotion.

They sat together in the den, watching the arraignment of the Quality-Mart murderer. He was wearing a bright orange jumpsuit. He glared at the judge like he wanted to kill him. When the judge asked for his plea he said, "Innocent."

"Not guilty," the judge corrected him.

"Whatever," he said.

Sally wished she had a glass of wine.

The next day she took the bus into town. It had been ages since she'd been shopping on her own. Joyce was surprised to see her when she walked into Oliver's.

"Aunt Sally, what brings you here?"

"Oh, I just needed a few things."

She went around picking up a collection of canned goods—tuna, tomatoes, creamed corn. She bought a pack of Little Debbie Swiss Cakes, Nel's favorite, even though she rarely let him have them. Trying to treat it like an afterthought, she said to Joyce, "And where's the wine?"

Joyce didn't seem surprised by the question. She just said, "We don't sell it. You have to go to 7-Eleven. Or Quality-Mart."

"Oh, of course," Sally said, as if she knew. Nelson had made all the arrangements for the party. He must have gotten the wine from one of those places. The thought of trying to get to either store was overwhelming to her. The bus didn't go there. But she wanted that wine, and she wanted it quite badly.

Sally stared at Joyce as if she might have a solution. But Joyce was just concentrating on scanning the canned foods that Sally didn't really want.

Joyce was a different person these days. She no longer looked worried or apologetic. Her scar was still there, but it was as if she had forgotten about it. She had other things to think about. She had started pulling her hair back, which made her eyes seem bigger and less scared. Someone could actually love Joyce, Sally thought suddenly. There wasn't any rape. Someone had made love to her, and she'd let them.

"It was a nice party you had," Joyce said.

"Well, I was happy to see you there. Family ought to stay together."

Joyce just smiled at the cash register.

"Who keeps your baby while you work?" Sally asked.

"Old Mrs. Winston, who lives next door."

Sally shook her head. "Your mother would sure love to have him. Why don't you two try to make up?"

"There's nothing between us," Joyce said. "Good or bad."

"But why can't you let her take care of that baby?"

"Because, Aunt Sally, this family has not done such a good job of raising boys."

Sally just stared at her, too stunned to reply. Could she really be talking about Danny and Rex, or was it just Kyle? Sally was afraid to ask, afraid of how she might respond right here in the middle of town, with all her neighbors wandering the aisles.

"How is Danny doing?" Joyce asked abruptly.

"Danny? You see him as much as I do. Probably more."

"He still misses Lydia," Joyce said, though Sally hadn't asked. "He just can't get over her. I hate seeing him so sad."

"Oh, I don't think he's sad. I think he's just . . . readjusting. Danny will always get what he wants. He's that way."

Joyce just smiled.

Sally took her groceries and walked out on the street, feeling loose and jittery. She really wanted that wine. She was thinking about it so hard, she almost did not recognize Mr. Grafton.

"My goodness me," he said. "A rare treat to see you away from hearth and home."

She stared at him for a full five seconds before she finally smiled.

"Oh, Mr. Grafton. Where are you going?"

"I just finished my shift and I was actually heading to my automobile. I was hoping to drop in on the birthday boy. Is his excellency at home today?"

"I think so. You have a car?"

"Yes, I am mobile. May I give you a lift?"

"Yes, please," she said, feeling a sense of relief flooding over her, along with an overwhelming affection for Mr. Grafton. "But could we make a stop on the way?"

Mr. Grafton's car was some foreign model, small and boxy, which chugged along the road, emitting black fumes. His radio was tuned to some station Sally had never heard. The news was delivered in from England; they kept calling it the BBC. She didn't want to ask him what that meant. She felt she should know.

Though it was full summer, Mr. Grafton wore a tweed jacket and a turtleneck, which didn't appear to burden him at all. His beard, shot through with white, looked as if it had been snowed on. He smiled at the road as he drove, as if it amused him no end.

"What did young Rex do today? I hope he used his day off constructively."

"He was napping when I left," Sally said. Rex had taken to napping lately, usually after a full day of watching documentaries and building models of the *Challenger,* the space shuttle that had exploded with a teacher in it. Rex had also taken to building models that marked some sort of tragedy, some embarrassing failure. He already had built the *Titanic,* the *Hindenburg,* and the silver Porsche Spider that James Dean had been killed in.

Something about these activities obviously exhausted him.

"Oh, I suppose it's age," Mr. Grafton said. "He's no longer a spry young boy!"

Sally struggled to smile. "He's only thirty."

"Yes, I'm afraid I was being facetious. Thirty, what a wonderful sound. How would you like to be thirty right now?"

I wouldn't, Sally thought, not for all the tea in China. She was surprised by that thought, for she sometimes found herself longing for youth. But now, knowing what she knew, all those disappointments and tragedies awaiting her, all those wrong turns and lost opportunities spreading out before her, she had no desire to go back and try to navigate it all again. Perhaps she wouldn't mind being someone else, some other thirty-year-old woman. So perhaps it was only her own youth she did not desire.

Mr. Grafton shifted gears, grinding them slightly, and said, "No, thirty would not be such a treat, would it? So much the middle ground. As your Dorothy Parker once said, 'People should either be young or dead.' Ah, the elusive Quality-Mart," he said as they approached it.

Sally said nothing as he turned the car into the parking lot. She had never seen anything so big. No wonder someone had gotten killed here. There was too much to reckon with; it could make a person crazy. She could see that skinny, black-haired young boy standing alone in the dark parking lot, believing that he just didn't have a chance in a world like this.

Mr. Grafton parked the car near the front and sighed, staring at the building. He said, " 'Ah, love let us be true / To one another! For the world, which seems to lie before us like a land of dreams, / So various, so beautiful, so new, / Hath really neither joy, nor love, nor light, / Nor certitude, nor peace, nor help from pain; / And we are here as on a darkling plain / Swept with confused alarms of struggle and flight, / Where ignorant armies clash by night.' "

Sally said, "That's very nice. Did you make it up?"

"You flatter me. That was Matthew Arnold," he said. "And this is our very own Dover Beach. Now, what are we in search of?"

"White wine," she said.

"Oh, how adventurous of you. Let's not waste time."

They went into the store. The doors opened automatically with a mechanical swish, one after another, until they were in the big room, full of sale tables and elaborate displays and glass cases and red-smocked people handing out flyers and a voice sporadically breaking through the loudspeaker, telling them what to buy. Sally vaguely took note of the offerings—kitchen gadgets and cameras and TVs and racks of colorful clothes. In some other life she was interested in those things. Now, she wanted wine.

"Excuse me," Mr. Grafton said to a young girl in a red smock. "We are looking for the comestibles."

"Did you try electronics?" she asked, looking perplexed.

"No, my dear, edibles. Food, drink, sustenance."

"Oh, that's aisle seventeen, next to the far wall. Did you want some coupons for Huggies?"

He took the flyer. "What a wonderful country this is," he said. "I can never get over it."

Sally was already walking toward aisle seventeen.

They found some bottles of Chablis on sale for six ninety-nine. Mr. Grafton knew about wine and he recommended spending a little more, so Sally settled on a chardonnay for ten dollars. She took two bottles and really wanted to take another. Mr. Grafton read her thoughts and picked up two more. "Never know when company is coming. Best to be prepared."

Sally felt nervous as they went to the checkout counter. Here she was, so far from home, in the company of a strange man and buying four bottles of wine. But the girl behind the checkout counter didn't seem to care, didn't even glance at them even after Mr. Grafton handed her the money and said, "This is a fascinating establishment."

She just shoved his change and receipt at him and waved the people behind them forward.

Riding home in the car with Mr. Grafton, Sally felt awkward and embarrassed, as if she'd revealed some hideous weakness, and his knowledge of it gave him power, and that power was, in its own way, appealing. It was exactly how she felt after having sex. She blushed and concentrated on breathing.

Finally she said, "I'll write you a check when we get home. For the wine, and for the gas."

"You will do nothing of the sort. But you will, I hope, share a drink with me."

"You like wine? I thought you preferred beer."

"Mrs. Crane, I prefer whatever is going."

Sally felt better about drinking now that she had Mr. Grafton with her. His lack of reaction to her little hobby made her feel as if this were normal behavior. In every home all over the country, people were taking a few glasses of spirits in order to face the evening.

The house was quiet when they came in. Rex was still upstairs sleeping. Sally knew this because the kitchen was exactly how she had left it—slightly messy, dishes in the sink, newspapers on the table. If Rex had been in there, he would have tidied it all up.

Sally found the corkscrew and gave it to Mr. Grafton. She had no idea how to open a bottle of wine. He did, though. He worked with dexterity and ease, like a surgeon. She watched him admiringly. He pulled and the cork popped out with a delicious sound.

He poured them each a glass and for a moment they just stood there and stared at them.

"Go ahead," he said, gesturing. "White wine doesn't really need to breathe."

She took the glass and sipped it. The wine didn't taste as good as she remembered. It was acidy and left a thick feeling at the back of her throat. She felt deflated, but after three more sips it tasted better. The room suddenly felt warm and cozy. She looked at the newspapers and remembered Nel reading them at the table, and she loved him, and she loved her life. She looked up at Mr. Grafton and she loved him, too.

Mr. Grafton filled her glass again.

"Tell me something," she said. "How in the world did an Englishman end up in Fawley, Virginia?"

He chuckled, setting his glass down and crossing his hands in his lap.

"Well, it's quite a long story. My mother was a war bride, you see. A pregnant war bride at that. Her husband, Sgt. Noel Grafton, brought her home to Tidewater, Virginia. Where she lived quite unhappily until the baby was born. Then one day, while Sgt. Grafton was at work in a paper mill or something of that manner, she took the baby back to England and raised him there. That was me, you realize. American born, but raised in the Midlands and my identity scattered somewhere in between. I never felt like an Englishman, you see. Never liked the food, not even the tea, which I drink out of habit. Couldn't bear the Damp and the Quaint. I always gravitated toward American culture. The flicks and the music and pizza and martinis—all of it appealed to me. Even the guns! I have one, you know. A beautiful little thirty-eight in my nightstand drawer. Anyhow, as soon as I was old enough I came to America in search of my lost roots. My father had moved around and settled near here, though I lost his path somewhere next to Martinsville. He's dead by now, I'm certain. But I decided to hang around a bit, just in case he showed up. The rest is history, and this is a most delicious wine."

"But what about your poor mother?" Sally asked. "Didn't you break her heart?"

He smiled a slow smile somewhere beneath his beard. "My dear Mrs. Crane, the English do not expect. Their hearts are not full of hope, and so are far less fragile, far more difficult to break."

"But what do people do if they don't hope?"

"They endure. Surely you're no stranger to that."

Sally peered down at the thin gold rim of wine left in her glass. She wanted it to fill up again, like the story of Tina and the Magic Pot. She wanted to say "Cook, pot, cook!" and find her glass brimming with chardonnay. She did not want to have to reach for the bottle and feel the embarrassment of filling it again.

As usual, Mr. Grafton was perceptive. He reached across the table and filled her glass. She looked at him gratefully and his smile touched her as gently as a kiss.

"Let's go for a walk, shall we?"

Glasses in hand, they walked down the dirt road leading to Rita's house. The weather was warm, humidity hanging in the air like a threat. Sally wished it were breezy and she could feel light and reckless, but instead she felt canned, the air pressing around her and the road leading away from one dead end to another. Behind her was her own strange, stalled existence. And before her, the quiet confinement of Rita and her girls, kept inside their home like some dirty secret. Between the two, of course, was the Perkins home. As they approached it, Sally could not help staring as she always did.

"Do you see that house?" Sally asked, worried that she was beginning to slur her words. "The boy in it died."

"Recently?" Mr. Grafton asked.

"No, years ago. When I was young. Little Ernest Perkins. The flu took him," she said, aware that her language was turning archaic.

"How tragic."

Sally shook her head. "I always heard his mother was relieved because they had so many children."

"That can't be. No mother is relieved at the loss of a child."

Sally looked at him. He was staring at the ground, watching his shoes as they kicked gravel along the red clay. He was wearing brown lace-up oxfords, reheeled, polished to the point that the leather had grown thin. Had he had those shoes when he first came to America? The shoes made her feel sorry for him. Old shoes had always made her feel sad. Any sort of shoes, really. Why was that?

Suddenly she remembered a song her mother used to sing to her as a child. A sad, eerie melody which haunted her and made her weep, but which she begged to hear every night before bed.

"Mother dear, oh mother dear, won't you put my little shoes away?" was how the chorus went. It was all she could remember. But the song was about a little girl who was dying of a fever, and she wanted her mother to put her shoes away and save them for the baby. The song was so scary, even now. Thinking of this poor dying child, who had the clarity to make plans for her own passing. Whose last thoughts were for her shoes, and why not? Wouldn't a dying child's thoughts be for her possessions, the little things that filled her room and gave her definition?

She used to imagine Ernest Perkins lying on his bed, asking for his shoes as his indifferent mother busied herself in the kitchen. Sally felt dizzy. She stopped and fanned herself with her palm. Mr. Grafton touched her back.

"Are you all right, Mrs. Crane?"

"I think we should go home," she said.

"Yes, the heat is too much. Will you take my arm?"

She did. They walked and sipped, as the cicadas made their peculiar, deathlike noise, and something stirred in the distant grass. The magical feeling was wearing off, and the world was starting to look complicated.

"Are you in love with my son?" she asked.

Mr. Grafton stared straight ahead and said, "Oh yes, very much."

"Will you run off with him?"

"No, of course not. He's a homebody. But most of all, he does not share my feelings. In fact, I don't believe he even likes me very much. He thinks I'm pathetic. I make him feel superior. But since he enjoys feeling superior, I think of that as my little gift to him."

"Does Rex love anyone?"

Mr. Grafton made a humming sound and pulled his pipe out of his pocket. He did not light it but chewed on the stem.

"I think his taste runs much younger," he said. "He likes, what we refer to in the vernacular as 'rough trade.' He doesn't realize this about himself, but I see how he looks at those troubled schoolboys who come into the library. The ones with scars and dirt under their fingernails and oil in their hair. If Rex lived in a city, he'd be in a bathhouse or a public john nearly every night. So it's just as well he lives so far away from his desire. He'd probably be sick by now. Better that he stays home and builds models and drinks back his demons."

Sally tried to consider the logic of that statement, but it left her feeling cold.

"I just feel like I've failed as a mother. And if I've failed there, I can't say I've done much of anything."

Mr. Grafton laughed. "Oh, surely you can't believe you've failed after everything I've told you. My parents failed because their concern for me was so minimal. I'd say it would be a fair trade if my mother had made herself happy instead of devoting herself to my concerns. But she did neither. She gave me the most basic care, and gave even less attention to her own concerns. She made the decision not to care about anything at all. My father, three thousand miles away, made a similar decision."

"But you turned out all right," Sally said.

"Oh, I suppose. I'm not a murderer or anything. But Rex has turned out much better. He's quite a remarkable young man. He understands his desires but he's not a slave to them. You should feel proud that you raised a boy who was so confident that he allowed himself to be different. It's an easy task to browbeat a son into conforming, but you didn't do that. Your acquiescence has allowed him to make peace with himself. He's not self-destructive or cruel. He's just different, and content to be so. Give yourself a pat on the back, Mrs. Crane."

Sally didn't think she could do that, but Mr. Grafton's words did comfort her. She thought he should have his own talk show. He was just as compassionate as Oprah, and sounded much more intelligent.

"And then there's Danny," he said, "who is a good soul. Rex says so.

They don't seem to get along, I know, but Rex says it is because Danny is too good. Danny's goodness makes Rex feel inadequate. But it is that example of goodness which has kept Rex from straying too far. If you ask me, you've created the perfect combination. A man who is enslaved by his own goodness, and another who's been humbled by his lack of it. You've given birth to the yin and the yang. Have a drink on Dr. Freud."

By the time they reached the house, Sally was weak-kneed. Mr. Grafton made coffee and they sipped it in front of the evening news. Rex was still sleeping and Nel wasn't home, so she and Mr. Grafton sat together in front of the set like an old couple who were meant for each other, but who had somehow forgotten to spend their lives together.

2

SOMETHING HAD TO be done about the baby. First of all, he cried too much. He cried constantly, in fact. Joyce sometimes had trouble picturing his face when she was away from him. All she could see was that contorted expression, the mouth gaping open like a canyon and beyond it, nothing, no teeth, just gums and a pink, naked throat. He cried about everything. Food. Sleep. Wet diapers. Noise. He cried with relief when he saw her at the end of a day. His feelings overwhelmed him.

Secondly, he was starting to remind her of Rick. Not his face so much. It was his presence. The way it felt when she used to know that Rick was waiting for her, and he would need her, and she'd have to sit still and listen and care and nod. She might have to feed him. At the very least she would have to put her own thoughts aside to make room for his. She would stare at her baby the way she often stared at Rick and think, How did he get here and what does he want?

Of course, Sam's needs were simple. He wanted food, he wanted to be held, he wanted dry clothes. Rick had wanted something bigger, harder to part with. He wanted her sympathy, her concern, her friendship. What did that mean? The truth was, she had never had any idea what Rick was doing in her house, any more than she now understood what he was doing in Whiteville, North Carolina, any more than she understood why his sperm had stayed in her body and created this thing that wanted her every night, no matter how she behaved or what she looked like.

His name was not legally Sam, it was Peter, but she changed her mind after a few months and decided she could not really call him Peter, after her father, since her father had never gone by that name, and since she must have been out of her mind on drugs when she decided to pass that name on in the first place. Why would she have the ghost of her father living in her house in any way, even if it was just a name? Something had come over her in that delivery room, as if she finally saw herself heading toward her own dark fate, each contraction pulling her back to the place she had never escaped.

She did not know anyone named Sam, and when he was about five months old she started calling him that, thinking if she changed his name she could give the two of them a new start. But nothing changed, and she still felt overwhelmed by him, and something had to be done.

It was getting harder to think. She could not remember anything, found herself making one mistake after another at work. Ordering things they did not need, not ordering things they did, losing people's credit accounts, overcharging, undercharging. She could barely face produce day anymore. She just took whatever the farmers brought in. She did not argue. One day she took a whole load of small green tomatoes, believing the farmer when he said they'd ripen better in the store than on the vine. What dope would believe that? Was she born yesterday? It wasn't that she didn't know. It wasn't even that she didn't care. She just couldn't think of what to say. All of her usual arguments deserted her. What did she used to tell them? How did she ever persuade anyone to cooperate with her?

Any strength she had ever possessed had left her. She vaguely recalled feeling something like confidence around the time that she met Rick. She remembered feeling that he couldn't hurt her, and that she in fact had the upper hand. He needed her more. Was that possible? She remembered sending him away, too, and the relief she had experienced afterward, and the lack of concern over whether or not he would return. Now she found herself wondering, at the end of every day, if he would be waiting for her. Somehow he had gotten the news and rushed home to have a look at his son, and to face the possibility of marrying Joyce. That never happened, of course, and she wasn't sure she wanted it to. She wasn't sure of anything at all. When she walked into her apartment, Sam propped on her hip like a bag of groceries, screaming as if he had swallowed a hot coal, she looked around at her featureless place and realized she had finally extracted all meaning from her life, had eradicated her personality so completely that she had no idea what she wanted.

Then, too, there was the matter of Danny and Lydia. Their breakup had left her feeling dazed and disoriented. They were perfect for each other, the shining promise of love and devotion and all those things Joyce wanted to believe in. She had never believed she would have it for herself but she wanted to know it was there, it was possible. And if Danny and Lydia weren't forever, then what was?

She didn't know what had broken them up, why Lydia had suddenly just left like a thief in the night. She didn't know why Danny wouldn't talk about it those days when he dropped by after work to visit her and Sam. He had plenty of opportunity to open up to her if he wanted to. She was not going to ask, but she couldn't help thinking he wanted to tell her. He never did. He just played with Sam and ate his food, and sometimes, when he didn't think Joyce was looking, he'd stare at the wall and cry.

Joyce didn't ask, because there was no point in asking. She knew exactly why it had happened, why every bad thing had ever happened to her family, and would go on happening as long as he was alive.

Lydia had left because of Kyle. And Danny cried at the wall because of Kyle. And Joyce knew that none of them would ever be free as long as he was alive. They all circled around him and cursed and condemned him, but they could not escape his gravity.

"What's your story, Mr. Man?" Danny said, picking up his nephew and bouncing him on his knee. He always talked to Sam as if he were a grown-up. He was the only person who could make Sam stop crying, and he stared at Danny as if he were a giant, his eyes popped wide open so he could see all of him.

"Why are you making life difficult for your mother?" he asked. Then, in a voice meant to be Sam's he said, "Don't ask me. I don't know how I got here."

Joyce opened a can of soup and made some salad and poured Danny a glass of beer. She always kept a six-pack of Bud in the fridge for him. As she served him dinner, she thought how odd it was that her childhood fantasy had come true. Here she was with Danny and a baby, as if they were a family.

"I can't go home," Danny said, sipping the foam from the beer. "I can't face Bonnie and Clyde tonight."

"I can't believe they're still living with you," she said. "You should make them leave."

"Have you ever tried to make Kyle do something?" he asked.

"You could call the police."

"The police can't do anything with him either."

"There has to be some way to get rid of him."

Danny shrugged, bouncing the baby again. Joyce watched the side of his face. He was always so handsome, so good to watch. He had the kind of smile that made you want to walk over broken glass to get him something. But Danny never asked for anything. It was hard to do anything for him, but she wanted to, and one day she would. A thought came to her, a perfect plan, an idea so good it almost seemed complete before it was formed. I could get Lydia back. I could do that for him.

She did not know how, but she knew it had to be done.

"Do you ever hear from her?" she asked him suddenly.

Danny knew just what she meant. He shook his head, still smiling at the baby, but the smile taking on a different color.

"It's Kyle's fault," Joyce reminded him.

"I wish it was, Joyce. That would be easy to fix. She left me, she didn't leave him."

"How do you know?"

"Because I know what made her leave and it was me."

"You never told me what happened."

"It's not worth telling," he said. Then he added, "She found out who I was."

"Danny, don't say that. You're the only thing this family has ever had going for it."

"I never was that guy. You all invented him. You needed him. Sort of like what Lydia did. She needed me to be this strong, uncomplicated guy and then she found out I wasn't. It was bound to happen. I'm glad I got as many years as I did."

"But it's not like you not to fight for something."

At this he laughed. The sound startled Sam, who started to whimper.

"It's *exactly* like me, Joyce. I've never fought for anything in my life. Ask my daddy, he'll tell you what a lousy hunter I am. I couldn't bring down a deer if my family was starving. Kyle was the hunter. And the fighter."

"You don't know what you're saying," Joyce said. Sam was crying full steam now, so she whisked him away, put him in his crib in her room, and closed the door so she wouldn't have to hear it. He'd cry himself out and go to sleep eventually. He always did.

When she came back, Danny had turned on the TV in her kitchen and was staring at it, mesmerized. It was the lawyer talking, the one who was representing the Quality-Mart murderer. He had long, silvery hair and a matching beard. His eyes were a cold blue and he looked smart. He was saying that the charges against his client would never stick. He said the police had violated a dozen different laws and that the arrest was dirty. His client had no prior criminal record and this was nothing short of a witch hunt.

"Something happens when there's violence in an ordinarily peaceful place," the lawyer was saying. "It creates panic and a desperate desire to punish, to set things right. Well, there's nothing wrong with making someone pay, but you have to make sure it's the right person. And in this case, it isn't."

Joyce turned the television off. Danny stared at the blank screen for a second before looking at her.

"I grew up in the same family you did," Joyce said. "I know what went on. Kyle was evil, he was all bad, and he inflicted it on everybody around him except you and Daddy. But Daddy's day was coming, and so was yours. He killed Daddy and he ran your wife away. What I'm wondering is when he'll get his."

"No, he didn't kill Pike. You have to believe that, Joyce."

"You forgive him all you want, but I never will. Never."

Danny stared at her and slowly nodded. "You're right. You should hold on to your anger."

Joyce said, "Sometimes I think it's all I've got."

"No. You've got more. But it's what makes you strong."

Danny stood and went to her. He took her hand and kissed it. He touched her scar lightly with his fingers. Then he held her and she started to cry against him. He smelled like cement and trees and beer—like life, somewhere that she'd never been.

Mr. Oliver wanted to see her. It was the end of the day and she was closing up the cash register. She was ten dollars and eighteen cents short, and this time it was not Jeffrey the bag boy, because he had quit at the beginning of the summer to be a lifeguard at the country club. This time it was her mistake, and she knew she'd have to take the money out of her own purse again, which meant she wouldn't be able to rent a video on the way home. She had started doing that lately, renting animated videos and plopping Sam down in front of them, which actually kept him quiet for twenty minutes or so. While it was quiet she tried to think. How to give Danny something, how to get Lydia back.

But tonight she would not be able to think anyway, because Mr. Oliver wanted to see her and she knew what it was about. She finished counting the money and putting away the receipts anyway, and then she took the long walk back to his tiny office, which was next to the butcher's counter. As a result, Mr. Oliver's office always smelled like raw meat, which she thought was fairly appropriate.

Mr. Oliver was smiling, a bad sign. He was never smiling, and she knew that first he was going to try to be kind to her. She hated that. It was like the kids who'd been told not to point and stare at the scarred lady and so they smiled instead, as if that made a difference. Because everyone forgot that normal people did not smile at other normal people. They smiled at strange people or people they had nothing to say to or people who scared them. They smiled when they didn't understand. Normal people nodded and spoke to other normal people, or ignored them altogether, knowing they were going to be just fine, going to be just normal, so they did not need a boost.

"Joyce, you look tired," Mr. Oliver said. "Are you sleeping?"

"Not right now," she said.

He laughed and leaned forward on his desk, his hands clasped as if in prayer.

"The baby is difficult?"

Joyce shrugged. "He's a baby."

"I suppose I was under the impression that you were"—he paused to cough—"going to find a home for him."

"I found one."

His eyebrows went up, his bald scalp rolling back slightly. "Did you?"

"Yes. He's going to live with me."

His face deflated and everything went back in place. Now the smile was gone, thank God, and he was scowling at her as he always did, as if someone were pinching him under the desk. "I just have to tell you how inappropriate I find that. I'm not the only one, either. Customers ask me about it all the time. Now, I know the whole business wasn't your fault. You were attacked. But that makes it all the more difficult to understand."

"I wasn't attacked."

"What?"

"That's something everybody is saying. I never said it." Joyce had never made an effort to stop that story because she wasn't quite sure how to. The fact was, she was a little bit attacked, at least she was certain Rick saw it that way, but she didn't. She would have said yes if he'd given her the chance.

"Are you telling me that you're acquainted with the father?"

"Yes. I don't know where he is now, but if he walked in the room I'd recognize him."

Mr. Oliver shook his head back and forth slowly, deliberately, his eyes boring into her. Joyce felt foolish. She hated this moment so much and yet she wanted to laugh. And when her eyes fell on the photo of Mrs. Oliver, thin and spiny as a crab, and their dough-faced, retarded boy, and that horrible yellow house in the background, she wanted to laugh even harder. She wanted to ask him who he really thought was worse off.

"Well, you've got to do something about this, Joyce. I don't need to tell you how much your work is suffering. I've had to hire an accountant to clear up the mess you've made of the books. I've got crates full of herbal pasta and scented body scrub that I can't sell. I've got green tomatoes and shriveled corn and cucumbers no bigger than my dick."

She smiled politely. Now that he regarded her as a whore, she supposed he'd talk to her anyway he pleased. She didn't mind. It was amusing to see him unraveling like this.

"Now I know the rest of the world is getting up to whatever they want, and screwing everything that'll sit still, and having babies like rabbits, but it's not how people live around here. So if you don't mind, I expect a little more of my assistant manager than bastard children and bad produce. And the bookkeeping! Have you taken a look, Joyce? My son could do a better job and he's got the mind of a six-year-old. Now, since you've been here so long I'm prepared to listen to why you think you deserve to stay. I'll give you another chance if you can convince me that you want to get back on track."

"I want to," Joyce said.

"And what's your plan?"

"I don't have one, but I was planning to think tonight."

"To think?"

"Yes, sir. To find a plan."

He did not seem convinced and Joyce did not know how to persuade him. Suddenly she pictured herself going home to where she used to live, in that dark house with the curtains always drawn and the heat always on, and the girls around the jigsaw puzzles and her mother saying, "If he comes over here we just won't open the door. No law says we have to open the door, girls. We'll just ignore him like a bad joke."

No, it wasn't true. That was not her home. She had an apartment where she lived and Danny visited and there was a baby, Rick's baby, who cried all the time.

"I'll do better, Mr. Oliver. I will because I can't go back. So I'll figure something out. I have to have this job."

"I want you to have this job, Joyce. God knows I don't want to do without you, but unless you jump on the bandwagon but quick, I won't have much choice."

She stood and smoothed out her skirt and started wringing her hands as her mother always did, standing at the window, watching.

"How long do I have?" she asked.

"End of the week."

"What's today?"

"Tuesday." He looked at her, cocking his head to one side like a bird dog. "You should get some sleep, Joyce. Give that baby to someone who can take care of it and get some sleep. People go all kinds of crazy when they aren't getting their eight hours."

Joyce left, barely remembering to lock the front door, then she headed toward the public parking lot, watching her feet and wringing her hands. She understood what had to be done. She had to see Lydia. It was hard to explain, even to herself, but she knew this was why she could not concentrate. The baby was an excuse, and his crying irritated her mainly because it interrupted her thoughts. She was thinking, planning all the time, devising a way to get Danny's wife back. And no matter how much she thought, nothing came to her. She had no idea how to proceed.

She unlocked her car door and she saw that her hands were trembling. It was then that she knew she was going to do it. She would do it the way she had moved out of her mother's house. She didn't think then, she just acted, and never looked back. But that was just across town. This was getting to Washington, D.C. She knew there must be buses and trains and planes, but the notion of calling them up to ask for a timetable was overwhelming. She could drive. Route 29 went all the way. Surely she could just get on a highway and follow it. But then there was the matter of getting into the city and reading a map and finding a house or an apartment and parking and avoiding one-way streets. . . . Her head began to pound.

She sat behind the steering wheel, rubbing her temples until they felt raw. It was so hard to think. Maybe she should just sleep. Maybe the answer would come to her in a dream, the way dreams came to Joseph in the Bible. Or was it Abraham? It was everybody, of course. Back in the days when all the answers came in dreams.

Her feet hurt. She had been behind the cash register all day. She slipped off her left shoe and rubbed her ankle where it was sore. She stared at her foot and she thought of him. She could feel him touching her there. She closed her eyes and brought it all back. And then her thoughts became clearer, stronger, as if a cloud had lifted.

She went straight home, without stopping by Mrs. Winston's to pick up Sam. Then she went directly to her bedroom and picked up the phone, before she had time to reconsider. She called directory assistance and asked the operator to put her through because she knew if she hung up she'd change her mind. She'd never be able to dial it.

The phone rang six times. She was willing to let it ring ten. That was the deal she made with herself. Just as the seventh was about to begin, the ringing stopped and there was an unnatural space of silence, and then the voice, which sounded ragged and sleepy.

"Hello," he said.

"Hi. Are you busy?"

"Busy?"

"Yeah. It's me. Joyce Crane."

There was another stiff pause, and then an exclamation. "Jesus Christ! Jesus, hold on. Don't hang up."

She heard muffled sounds. She closed her eyes and put her hand over her heart.

"Joyce," Rick said, his voice sounding stronger now, the way she remembered it. "Thank God you called. I tried calling you, but your number's changed and it's unlisted."

"I know," she said. "You could have written."

"I'm terrible at that," he admitted. "But I wanted to call and just see how you were doing."

"I'm fine," she said. "How are you?"

"Oh, you know, living. I'm at an all-boys prep school down here. Keeps me in line. The football team's for shit. Rich kids, scared to get hit. But it's okay."

"Listen," she said. "I have two things to tell you. First, you have a son. And second, I need you to take me somewhere."

"What?"

"I need you to take me somewhere."

"I have a son? What kind of son?"

"Just a normal one," she said. "He's a baby. He looks like you. But that's not why I'm calling."

"Jesus," he said. "Joyce, you should have told me."

"I'm telling you now. But I don't want anything from you like money. I just need a favor. I need a ride to Washington, D.C. Soon, like tomorrow. Can you do that?"

There was a long pause. She could hear voices from his end, high-pitched, arguing tones. She felt sick. And then she heard a laugh track and she knew it was the television. He was alone. Like her. No, not exactly like her. She had Sam.

"Wow," he said. It wasn't much of an answer.

"Will you do it?" she asked him again. "Will you take me?"

"I guess I have to," he said. "I guess I owe you."

3

W HEN LYDIA CAME home from work, she had more energy than she knew what to do with. Her job at the secondhand-book store in Dupont Circle was so much less demanding than teaching, she barely felt she'd done anything at all. Even on the evenings when she tutored high school students, she found herself wide awake and wired after they left. It made her wonder if it had been the teaching that was wearing her out, or the coming home to Danny and his unpredictable behavior. Knowing she had nothing to fear in her two-bedroom detached house in Mount Pleasant gave her extra stamina, and it bothered her that she couldn't think of a better way to use it. She usually just read until her eyelids got heavy, then watched a trashy movie on television, and fell asleep until the shrieking of some evangelist preacher woke her up. Then she went to bed, where she slept hard and didn't dream.

One day in mid-August, when the humidity was particularly bad, she walked home from work, hoping to exhaust herself. But she still didn't feel tired and she was actually relieved to see Hamilton Crider waiting for her. He sat on the front stoop in perfectly creased jeans and a white cotton sweater, watching the neighbors' children chasing Frisbees and hula hoops all over the street. Fireflies were starting to appear, but the children ignored them. They had better things to play with.

Hamilton smiled at her all the way up the walk. Ham was always a smiler. It was one of the things that had driven her crazy about him, one of the things that was so refreshing about Danny. Danny's resting face was a serious one. His smile was a rare treat. But Ham just smiled and smiled, like a simpleton, and if she remembered correctly, he even smiled in his sleep.

"What are you doing here?" she asked.

"I figured it was about time."

She'd been back in town for over a year and she had not contacted Ham at all. It had never occurred to her to do that. It had barely occurred to her to contact anyone from her former life. She had come back to construct a new beginning, not to resurrect her past. And so she rarely saw her old friends, including Camille. Camille had remarried, to a plastic surgeon, and moved to Annandale, an area Lydia had convinced herself it was difficult to get to. She'd worked the same magic on Springfield, where her parents lived. Sometimes she met them in town for Sunday brunch, but the idea of driving into the suburbs was slightly unnerving to her. She had seen all she wanted to of life outside the city.

Ham's smile increased as Lydia got closer to him. He shook his head. "Look at you. You're still beautiful."

"Forget it, pal. You're married."

"My wife doesn't understand me."

"Neither do I."

"Besides, you're married, too."

"Only on paper."

"Now you're splitting hairs. Just fix me a drink and let me sit and look at you."

Finally she smiled back at him; she couldn't help it, staring at his face. It was as contagious as a yawn.

Ham stood and wedged his hands in his pockets. He had changed very little. His blond curls had straightened and retreated a little. There were crow's feet around his eyes, but there always had been. Ham had one of those faces that was permanently forty. He affected that slow, Southern, aristocratic quality. That befuddled, inbred thing, camouflaging a brain as sharp as a straight razor, pretending his wealth was about inheritance and breeding rather than intellectual effort.

Lydia decided to let him in. She was comforted by him because his presence was a constant reminder that whatever great opportunities she might have missed in life, marrying him was not one of them. She would be crazy by now, or fat, or an alcoholic. Or all three.

"I'll let you in," she said, "if you promise not to say I broke your heart."

"Can I say you damaged it?"

"No, you're not damaged, Ham. I've seen damaged people."

He followed her into the house and settled on the couch, waiting for his drink. Lydia smiled as she went into the kitchen to fix it. This is how it would have been. She would have spent her life waiting on Ham. Danny was the opposite. He never expected anything. Sometimes she even found it frustrating how little he relied on her. *No, you can't do this. You cannot have Ham in here if he's going to make you miss Danny.*

She poured an inch of Scotch into a highball glass, splashed some gin over two ice cubes for herself, and joined him in the living room.

"Are you getting divorced?" Ham asked.

"Not at the moment."

Lydia sat down and stared at her windows, thinking no matter what she did, they always looked dirty. It was the pollen and the humidity. D.C. was so horrible in the summer it was almost nice. People came together out of misery, as in a war.

"Are you getting back together?"

"Not at the moment," she repeated.

"Mmm," he said, sipping his Scotch. But she knew he was referring to her and not the drink.

"Ham, you have no idea how much courage it took to come home and admit I was wrong and eat a steady diet of crow for a year. I'm not going back there, if that's what you're asking."

"But if he moved here?"

"He wouldn't," she said. "He doesn't move."

"Not like you," he said. "You and your geographics."

"My what?"

"It's an alcoholic term. When you change locations, thinking it's going to solve your problems. It's called a geographic."

"Where'd you come by this information?"

"I was in AA for a while," he said, sipping his Scotch.

This was somehow not very startling news. Anyone who smiled that much had to have some inner turmoil.

"So why did you stop?" she asked.

"Because I figured AA was going to kill me before the alcohol did. All those people thinking so highly of themselves. They wear themselves out with all that backslapping and crying and confessing. I came home from one of those deals, I felt like I'd run a marathon in August."

"You've changed," she said. "You used to have more compassion."

"That was killing me, too." He ran his thumb along his glass, staring into the liquid as if he was afraid it might evaporate. "You've changed a little yourself."

"How?"

"I don't know. You seem sadder. But calmer, too. And you're more beautiful."

Lydia said nothing to this. She thought it was probably true, except for the latter. That was just an effort to win her back. She didn't mind. It had been a long time since someone had called her beautiful. Danny never did. But somehow it didn't matter, because the way he looked at her made her certain of it. And the way he touched her made her feel it, all the way to her bones.

"Well, old girl," Ham said. "You may have made a big mistake coming back here. It's not that this place won't accept you again. Hell, D.C. accepts anybody. It's that you won't accept it, knowing you can leave. The rest of us don't know that, see, so we get happy with where we are."

"Oh, for God's sake, Ham, you could live in Tahiti if you wanted to."

"But I don't want to. I think I don't want to live anywhere but right here next door to the President. All my roots are here, all my experiences, good and bad. Moving away would feel like looking in a mirror and seeing no reflection."

Lydia couldn't dispute that. It was close to the truth, if not right on target. Living in Fawley had been more like looking in the mirror and seeing someone else's reflection.

"So what was it like?" Ham asked, reading her expression. "Living in East Jesus for all those years."

She shrugged. "It was like living anywhere, only smaller."

"Did you make friends?"

She thought about that, trying to conjure up some of the familiar faces. It was getting harder all the time.

"Not really," she said.

"You must have found somebody to like down there."

She sipped her gin, the ice touching her lips like a cold kiss.

"I liked him," she said. "But he changed."

"People don't really change."

She rolled her eyes. "That's ridiculous. Of course people change. Sometimes they change beyond recognition. He was on the road to it and I didn't want to sit around and watch it."

"And what happens when things around here start to change. Will you run from that too?"

"Don't analyze me, Ham."

"You should have stuck it out, girl."

She shook her head. "I couldn't save him."

He grinned. "I mean you should have stuck it out with me. I know you thought I was boring, but everybody eventually gets boring. In a few years we won't mind being bored. What you want when you're old is a little money, a little quiet, and a past that somebody remembers the same way. We could have had that. I would rather have had it with you. Was it worth it, Lydia? All that mystery and calamity?"

Lydia smiled. "It takes civilization hundreds or thousands of years to determine if a single course of action was successful. So how can we hope to know in one lifetime if the choices we made were correct? Maybe we never know. And maybe not knowing is a kind of blessing."

Ham said, "Bullshit."

"Well, thanks for giving it a chance."

"You've been running from what you want your whole life. You get close and you pack your bags. You pride yourself on being a fighter, but you really just get the battles started. Then you escape to watch it all unfold from the high ground."

"How can you possibly know this about me?" Lydia said. The alcohol dulled her anger, which brewed behind her eyes but refused to make the trip to her tongue.

"I know you better than you think."

"I wish that were true. I'd love for somebody to know me. God knows I haven't been so successful with figuring me out."

Ham laughed. "Lydia, just listen to yourself."

"What kind of advice is that? People don't listen to themselves, Ham. They listen to politicians and preachers and shrinks and talk-show hosts. The last voice they trust is their own. People go around the earth and back to avoid listening to themselves."

"Well, then listen to me. Let's get married. We've always belonged together."

"But you're already married," she said, as if that mattered, as if she'd consider even for a second what he was proposing. She recognized an adolescent need to hear his desire.

"My marriage is a temporary arrangement. I'm circling the airport. Tell me which runway and I'll land."

"You're drunk."

"In vino veritas," he said, grinning.

Lydia tossed back the last of her gin and closed her eyes, listening to the squeals of the children, and to the distant demands of their parents, and to the atonal music and sporadic chatter in the apartment next door at the party that never stopped. Underneath that noise there was the dull roar of an engine idling nearby. Lydia flicked the curtain back with her foot. The car, an old red Mustang, was sitting in front of her house. Two people were in it, staring in the same direction—in her direction. They were vaguely familiar. Her heart began to hammer.

"I need another Scotch," Ham said, shaking his glass.

"Ssh," she said.

"What?" He craned his neck.

She dropped the curtain just as the two people got out. She didn't need to see. She knew, though she didn't want to believe it.

"Ham, you have to go," she said.

"Why?" he asked, observing her as she began to pace around the room as if looking for an escape route.

"Please, I need you to go."

It was too late. The doorbell had rung. She stood, paralyzed, and did not object as Ham moved in his slow gait to the front door. When he opened it, Lydia saw Joyce and Rick standing there, slightly slumped and apologetic, like people soliciting for a political cause.

"I'm sorry," was the first thing Joyce said, "but I'm looking for Lydia Crane."

"She's right here," Ham said. "Though I think she's Lydia Hunt these days."

"Come in," Lydia said from a distance.

"Yes, I'm leaving," he said, taking his cue from Lydia's anxious expression. "Have a nice visit. Thanks for the tea and sympathy, Lydia. We'll continue this discussion at a later date."

As soon as Ham was gone, Lydia felt exposed. She stood a distance from the two visitors, who were strange yet familiar. They had not changed at all. Of course they hadn't. Joyce was still scarred and her eyes were still frightened. Her hair was pulled away from her face, making her look a little less hidden. Next to her Rick looked striking, in his jeans and letter jacket, with that same boyish grin, though his hair was now laced with gray. It was seeing them here in D.C. that was so strange, trying to place them in her new life.

"Surprise," Rick said. "We were in the neighborhood."

"Would you like a drink?" Lydia asked.

"Joyce might. I'm driving."

Joyce shook her head, clutching her purse in both hands and blushing like a newlywed. The image made Lydia wonder if in fact there was a man. If, against all odds, the man was Rick. She had never forgotten the look in his eyes when he saw Joyce's foot.

She motioned and they all sat down. Joyce put a pillow in her lap, as if for protection, and found the courage to speak.

She said, "We've come up here to take you back."

Lydia just nodded, with a pained smile.

Joyce said, "Well, you don't have to go back with us right this minute. But we just—well, I just think you need to be back with Danny. He's miserable without you. He's lost. He still loves you. And what's worse is, I think you still love him."

"Joyce," Lydia said.

"No, I have to keep going. I understand the reason you couldn't stay. It was because of Kyle. Because he moved into your house and you couldn't get away. But Danny will make them leave. He'll do that for you. I know he will."

"Joyce, listen."

"He's learned his lesson, I think. He knows what Kyle is."

"He's always known," Lydia said. "And that isn't even the point. It's not why I left. I mean, not the way you're thinking. It was very . . . complicated."

Joyce waited, ready to hear the complications. Outside a car backfired and she jumped, clutching Rick's arm. Lydia observed the motion and studied Rick's face. He was watching Joyce with respectful concern, as if he understood how delicate she was but didn't mind.

"It's just a car," Lydia said.

"Joyce hasn't ever been in a city like this," Rick explained, as if there were a need. "Tell you the truth, I haven't either. I mean, Atlanta, sure, but they don't have the kind of crime you do. And then there's the President and all. We drove right past the White House, but Joyce was too scared to look at it."

"I looked," she said defensively. "I just didn't want to get out."

"You should," Lydia said. "It's perfectly safe. They do a tour and everything. It's pretty impressive. Bigger than Quality-Mart, even."

Lydia meant to make a joke, but the utterance of those words still created tension. Joyce sat up straight and Rick began to examine a hangnail.

"What?" Lydia said. "Is that still going on?"

Joyce nodded. "They caught the guy. Some kid from North Carolina. But it never went to trial. He had some big lawyer and the charges were dropped. On a technicality. People in town were pretty broken up about it."

"What technicality?" Lydia asked.

"No evidence," Rick said. "And the arrest was dirty. I mean, that's what I hear. I don't live in Fawley anymore."

"You don't? What happened?"

"Well, I was about to go before the Spanish Inquisition, so I decided to spare myself the trouble and resign. Got a much better job down in Whiteville."

Lydia looked at Joyce, who was now surveying the room as if she were a potential buyer. From her expression, Lydia could tell she would not make a serious offer.

"So, if you don't live in Fawley anymore, how did you and Joyce get together?" Lydia went on.

Joyce's head snapped around and her mouth parted. Rick waited, letting her provide the answer.

"I couldn't come up here alone," Joyce said.

"Well, that brings me to my next question," Lydia said. "Which is, if Danny misses me so much, why didn't he come up here to get me?"

"He wouldn't," Joyce said, slightly exasperated, as if Lydia ought to know better. "He'd never do that. He just figures it's your decision and he'd never try to interfere."

Yes, Lydia thought, Danny would never interfere.

The sun was gone now and the room was shadowy and dark. The squeals of the children had gone, too, as though they'd all been called in to late supper or early bedtime. Lydia remembered fondly the days when there were people around to tell her what to do, where to be. Even now she couldn't be sure she was going to bed at the right time or eating the right things. It all seemed so loose and unstructured, being an adult without a family, without even a pet by which to set her clock.

"Right," Lydia said, looking at her lap. She could feel the effects of the gin, loosening her tongue. "Danny wouldn't come after me. Danny doesn't struggle. He retreats."

"That's not true!" Joyce nearly shouted. "And it's not fair. You left him. What did you expect him to do? There is such a thing as pride."

"Yes, and there's such a thing as swallowing it. Look, I don't want to have this argument. I didn't leave Danny just to see if he'd come after me. But I think it does illustrate a certain aspect of his character. The fact that he never called or wrote or even asked why. He just accepted it. From baseball to his job to his marriage, he's an underachiever. Everybody acts like he's a star. But what he really is is a quitter."

"How dare you say that," Joyce snapped, jumping to her feet, still clutching her purse.

"There's only one person on earth that Danny wouldn't quit on. I think we know who that is."

Joyce trembled. She looked miserable, exhausted. "But if you told him, if you'd given him an ultimatum, he'd have chosen you."

"He could still choose me."

Joyce stared at her for a long moment. Lydia felt uncomfortable under her gaze, as if she were being put under a spell. She wondered what was going on in Joyce's mind.

"You just don't understand," Joyce said.

"Yes, people in Fawley kept telling me that. As if it were my fault."

Joyce stared at her for one more long moment, and Lydia felt herself weakening. She was thinking of Danny, sitting at the kitchen table, looking up from the newspaper and smiling at her, as if he couldn't believe his luck. She thought of his serious face, as he leaned forward to kiss her in the darkness of their bedroom, while the wind whistled against the window.

"I have to go now," Joyce said.

She hurried to the door and Rick scrambled to follow her. Lydia sat still, wondering if she wanted to pursue this anymore, or if she just wanted to stay there all evening, watching the shadows grow and remembering Danny.

Finally she stood and went to the door. Joyce was racing across the dark yard, forgetting momentarily her fear of D.C. Rick followed a few steps behind her and Lydia stood on the porch, poised at a moment of truth. If she let them go, she would be as guilty as Danny, just as gutless. Something had to be done.

"Danny knows what Kyle did," Lydia called across the yard, her voice echoing down the quiet street. "I think you know it, too. You're both protecting him. And you know he's not finished doing damage."

"I'm not listening," Joyce said, without looking back.

"He's a murderer."

Rick turned around and took a few steps toward Lydia. But Joyce stayed put, her hand on the car door handle. Lydia waited. And finally Joyce turned, only her head, and their eyes met and locked, even in the darkness.

"You think you bear no responsibility for Kyle," Lydia said. "You think it's enough to distance yourself from him, but it isn't. You have something to answer for."

"I've hated him my whole life," Joyce said, without emotion.

"And Danny has loved him. It's caused equal damage."

Joyce turned back around and jerked at the door handle. It was locked, but she just kept pulling at it, whimpering, her whole body shaking with anger.

Rick watched this, then turned back to Lydia, uncertain of his role.

"I think you need to get her home," Lydia said.

4

ON THE DAYS when Danny did not have to work late, he looked for any excuse to avoid going back to his house. He thought it was odd, now he was single again, that he behaved like a man who was unhappily married. Kyle and Amanda posed as the difficult adolescents he didn't want to face, and Lydia, in her absence, was the wife he could not talk to. Sometimes, when he was absorbed in work, hammering or plastering, he would forget that she was gone. He'd think about some amusing story he'd want to relate to her, and he'd formulate the conversation in his head. He could see her smiling, her green eyes trained on him and absorbing every word. Lydia was a great listener and more than anything else he missed telling her things. Missed it more than he missed making love to her, though he missed that plenty.

He did not miss sex in a generic sense, for he'd stumbled into a couple of clumsy affairs. One was with a stranger, a real estate agent who'd been sent down from Raleigh to try to expand the area around Quality-Mart. Since the murders, the store had actually begun to thrive and the thinking was that a fine community could be established in the vicinity. Gina, the real estate agent, had come into town full of enthusiasm. She had tried to negotiate deals for a condominium, then a housing park with rows of identical homes, fronted by perfectly square lawns and roomy garages and a common park. It all sounded good, but there were no takers. It was as if the region were haunted. People might want to shop there, but they knew better than to live near it.

Gina had met with Danny, hoping to encourage him to involve Howard J. Mecklin in its development. Ben, who was now at the helm of the company after his father's early retirement, sometimes sent Danny on sales pitches. Danny obliged, feeling up to the task as long as he knew that he was still basically a construction worker and no one would try to interfere with that. Ben met with him about once a week to try to talk him back into the office. One of the plans Ben had was to transfer him up to Manassas, where they were opening a second office. He wanted Danny to head it, indeed felt Danny was the only company man capable of the task, but Danny refused. He was happy with his drill and his circular saw, and besides, Manassas was far too close to Lydia. He could not make himself vulnerable to her again.

Danny had disclosed his personal problems to Gina when she first started hitting on him. He gave her the old I'm-still-recovering-from-my-marriage routine, which was actually true, and Gina admitted that she didn't mind, wasn't really looking for a relationship and casual sex would suit her to a T. But that faded fairly quickly, and soon Danny found himself lying in bed next to her at the Howard Johnson's out on Highway 29, his body stiff as a board as she cried about her insecurities, her fears that she couldn't make it in the real estate world, and that in a few years, men wouldn't desire her at all. She wanted children. Was that so extreme? She was pretty and sweet, her eyes just as green as Lydia's, her dark hair cascading across her chest, hiding her tiny breasts.

"No, I think that's fair," Danny said. "You want what you want."

"But you're still in love with your wife," she said, and he realized that she expected him to deny it. When he couldn't, she wept and her tears crawled across his chest and settled in his armpits. Before things could get much worse, she was transferred to Martinsville.

Then there was his affair with Dee, which really didn't constitute an affair, since it only happened a half dozen times, and he always felt horrible when it was over. John was his friend and Danny could scarcely believe he was betraying him, sleeping with his friend's wife (the Reverend's wife, no less) in their own bed, but he'd only consented because Dee swore the marriage was over, it was just a matter of time. John had had a curious revelation and declared himself celibate. Sex was subversive, he'd decided, and it was interfering with his communication with God. Dee was devastated and Danny felt comfortable being with someone who was in the throes of a loss, pining for someone who was still very much there but unavailable.

It felt familiar to make love to Dee, like something he'd always intended but somehow had neglected to do. Sex with Lydia had been different, like some novel experience, something he hadn't believed was possible. He remembered how soft her inner thighs had felt. He loved to kiss her there and when he did, she would gasp and straighten her back. He had made love to Lydia so many times, and it never felt the same twice.

The trouble with Dee was not her inner thighs, which were thin and perfectly appealing. It was that she had wanted to console him, and that took the form of criticizing Lydia.

"I never liked her," she said. "She was always so cold."

"Don't say that," Danny said. "You did like her, and it doesn't make things better to pretend you didn't."

"But, Danny, how could she do that to you?"

"She had her reasons."

"I'll never forgive her."

"You have to. I did."

Dee didn't want to know about it. She wanted to treat their relationship as if they were connected by despair, by equal injustice, and though it was tempting, Danny did not want to buy into it. He did not want to despair. He wanted to go on, to get up tomorrow and hope some more, hope for undefined, amorphous things. He wanted to believe.

He had only recently broken off his relationship with Dee and it was one of the reasons he did not want to go home. She lived only a few doors down and as he walked around the house in the evenings, he could swear he felt her watching him through the windows. Kyle and Amanda watched him, too. Kyle was content to bury himself on the couch and consume massive quantities of beer, but he occasionally sat up and asked Danny bizarre questions about their family. "What was it your father used to do on Christmas? Didn't he always want oyster stew and nobody could open presents until everybody had some?" Or, "What did my Daddy used to say, 'Spit in one hand, wish in the other, and see which one fills up first?' He was a poet, wasn't he? He was a goddamned philosopher."

Danny never answered him, and Kyle never seemed to notice.

Amanda had her own agenda. She moved through the house in a flurry, always cleaning and cooking and attending to Syphilis's needs, but often doing it in a half-dressed state. She wore tank tops, so tight her breasts almost shoved through the cotton. Sometimes she was in her underwear, sometimes in one of Kyle's shirts open to the navel. Danny did his best to ignore her, and Kyle occasionally rose up off the couch and said, "For God's sake, woman, dress yourself. That man hasn't gotten laid in a coon's age."

Kyle had mellowed and was rarely energetic enough to start an argument, let alone cause any physical destruction. Because of this, Danny found it hard to pursue his own private campaign against Kyle. He still harbored the notion that Kyle was responsible for the Quality-Mart murders. But that seemed so long ago, and the town had become convinced that Lenny Whittaker, that scrawny teenager from Durham, had been the real culprit. Now they focused their rage on the system that had let the murderer slip through their grasp. Martha Dawson had never really been convinced about Lenny's guilt, but shortly after he was released she had been diagnosed with terminal liver cancer and didn't have the strength to continue her personal investigation. If Lenny had gone to trial, Danny liked to think that he would have come forward with his suspicions. He never would have let an innocent man be punished for what he still firmly believed was his cousin's crime.

He found himself going out to Kyle's trailer site periodically, after work. He drove out to the blackened patch of land and kicked through the rubble. Time had taken its toll, and grass was starting to grow up around the charred remains. He picked up broken bits of china and sinewy pieces of videotape. Once he found a photograph album, the images distorted by time and fire and weather, the familiar faces all running together until they were barely distinguishable. But he had rescued one shot of him and Kyle during some forgotten summer. They were standing next to the barbecue grill, all of twelve years old, Kyle's leg still intact, Danny's face still full of youthful confidence. Their arms were linked around each other and Kyle clutched a stick, holding it in the air like a scepter. Looking at it, Danny could picture the rest of the family, standing off in the distance, wondering about them, trying to imagine who would win the race. Kyle's face was full of mischief, and Danny's was clouded with doubt. There was no happiness anywhere in the scene, and Danny wondered what might have happened if he could have looked at the picture back then as he did now, knowing what he knew. Would he have recognized the warning—one boy too sure of his own power, the other too frightened of his ability to stop it. Was everything already determined in that picture? Was the story over, even then?

Danny had never found any evidence to support his theory. He'd never gotten a drunken confession out of Kyle. He'd never found a gun lying around the house. He'd never heard another word from the police. It wasn't that his suspicion was any less strong. It just seemed to matter so much less, especially now that he'd lost Lydia. Everything seemed to matter less because of it. So Danny never went to the police and denied Kyle's alibi. He just let things be. Kyle's one true talent was that he could not be caught. Danny was afraid it was a talent he shared with his cousin. In fact, he feared he was better at it than Kyle.

The call came in the middle of the afternoon. This was something Danny had never anticipated. He always pictured the dead of night, the frantic scramble for the phone, the disorienting sensation that ordinary life had been interrupted. His every sleep was tinged with a kind of lightness, an expectation of interruption. But the afternoon felt safe, and whenever he found himself standing on a beam he felt protected from external invasion. Yet there he was, trying to figure dimensions on a site several feet above ground when his cellular phone rang. He answered it angrily, for almost always it was Ben just checking in, asking annoying questions he could not answer at the time.

"What?" he barked into the phone. "This better be good, I'm twenty-five feet from paralysis."

"Danny? You better get down here. It's the police."

"Who's the police?"

"It's me, Les Carlisle. Kyle is hurt. We think he's dead."

"Bullshit," Danny said illogically. He did not believe Kyle could hurt himself in daylight.

"Just come home," Les said.

Danny scrambled down from his post and told his workers he'd be back in a few hours. He refused to accept anything permanent. It wasn't yet four o'clock and he knew Kyle would be passed out on the couch, giving everyone a scare.

He drove home in his pickup, listening to the radio. He could not make himself worry. He just felt annoyed that another one of Kyle's antics was going to cost him a day's work. It was only when he approached his home that he began to feel scared. Three police cars and a fire engine were parked out front. Dee was standing among the crowd, her two rambunctious boys tramping through his geraniums.

"Danny, I'm so sorry," she said, rushing toward him.

Angrily, he pushed her away. "Sorry for what?"

"He's dead in there."

"Who's dead?"

"He's been shot."

She tried to hug him again but he wouldn't have any of it.

"Get out of my flowers," he shouted to the boys. They stopped their game and stared at him, wounded, as if he'd swatted them.

Inside, the scene was no less chaotic. Policemen were everywhere. Danny did not recognize any of them. He did not try to. He moved past them all to the thickest gathering of people, leaning over his couch as if they were searching for spare change. Seeing him, they moved back, allowing him a view of what was causing all the commotion. Kyle lay sprawled on the couch, much as Danny had left him, but for the bloody stain on his white V-necked T-shirt. His arms were splayed, wide open, as if expecting an embrace. His eyes were open, staring at the ceiling, and his lips were in a curious twist—not a smile so much as a grimace, as if he had succumbed to a furious bout of indigestion. But he was dead. This Danny knew without asking anyone. He could feel it, a weightlessness in his cousin's body, a lack of significance to him. Kyle was no longer dangerous.

The police parted and let him have his way. He knelt beside Kyle, holding his hand, his eyes traveling from the wound in his chest to the blankness of his face, over and over, trying to make the connection. Finally Danny looked up, locating Les Carlisle in the crowd.

"Where's Amanda?"

"In the kitchen. They're interrogating her. She wasn't here when it happened."

Danny dropped Kyle's hand, and it fell against the floor. Looking down, Danny saw Kyle's fake leg lying a few feet away, next to the fireplace, where it always stayed when he was watching TV or sleeping.

"How did it happen?" he asked.

"Don't know yet," Les admitted. "But I'm leaning toward suicide."

"Why?"

"Why not? No offense, Danny, but everybody in town knew what Kyle was. He was sure capable of it."

Danny shook his head. He sat on the floor, leaning against the couch, staring at the prosthesis, feeling Kyle's other knee, just as dead, pressing against his back.

"The gun was lying right where you're sitting. And the girl has an air-tight alibi. She was working at the Green Lantern. Got a dozen witnesses."

"It doesn't sound like him," Danny said.

"I know you had some kind of fondness for him, Danny. But let's face it, there was no predicting him."

That was hard to deny. And maybe the guilt had finally gotten to him. Not just the murders, but all those years of destruction, all those lives he had damaged.

"What kind of gun was it?" Danny asked.

"Rifle of some kind. Forensics took it away. Not being a hunting man myself, I couldn't give you the name and number. I just recognize the wound."

Danny recognized the wound too, the same kind he'd put into Kyle's foot two decades ago. He pressed his thumbs to his forehead and repeated silently, "I did not do this. This I did not do."

Les put a hand on his shoulder, trying to coax him to his feet. Danny felt as if he were nailed to the ground.

"Was there a note?" Danny asked.

"We're still looking."

Danny said, "He wasn't wearing his leg."

"Yeah," Les said. "So?"

"I think he'd want to die with his leg on."

"Danny, let us do the detective work, all right?"

Amanda came out of the kitchen then, smoking a cigarette with a vacant expression that remained constant, even when her eyes fell on Danny. She lifted a hand to him, in a strange sort of wave, and followed a policeman out the front door.

"Did she find the body?" Danny asked.

Les stared at him. "Christ, I thought you knew that part. Your cousin found him."

Danny was momentarily confused. Kyle was the only person he

thought of as his cousin. Then he remembered. "Joyce? Joyce found him?"

"Yeah. She's still in the bedroom. Doc Steen's with her, giving her a sedative. She's pretty tore up, I imagine, but we still need a statement."

Of all the things he'd seen and heard so far, this struck the most terror in Danny's heart. Joyce had found him, and Joyce was in the bedroom, and he had no idea what condition she would be in. He had to walk in there now, and face her, and face Jerry Steen, and still resemble something like a rational adult.

He knew that Joyce wouldn't be sorry. If she were devastated, it would only be from the shock of the discovery. All Joyce had for Kyle was cold contempt. Kyle had ruined her life, and why should she forgive him for it? She shouldn't, Danny thought as he began the long walk back to the bedroom. He wouldn't try to make her feel sorry for Kyle, or make her see that her brother was a sad, inept human being, capable of rare bouts of goodness, and that despite everything, he deserved better. There was no sense at all in trying to rescue Joyce from her anger. That train had left the station.

He slowly opened the door. She was pacing, the way Rita did, wringing her hands, and muttering to herself. When she saw Danny she stopped and stared at him. Her face was pale; the scar was even paler, like ice against snow.

Jerry Steen was putting things back in his black bag. Seeing Danny, he smiled, that courteous, detached smile, which basically meant that he didn't give a shit. He'd been through enough with this family.

"She should be fine," Jerry Steen said, as if Danny had asked. "I've given her a mild dose of Valium. She's got two more to get her through the evening. She should get some rest as soon as possible. But she shouldn't drive."

"I'll take her home," Danny said.

"And what about you?"

"What about me?"

"Will you need anything?"

It took Danny a minute to understand he was being offered a sedative. But oddly, he did not feel in need of one. He felt a strange calm descending on him. Not a temporary calm, a result of shock, but a more permanent sensation, as if some puzzle deep inside him had been solved. This was how he was going to feel from now on. Released.

"I'll leave the two of you alone now," Steen said. "My condolences to your family. Particularly your mother," he said to Danny, which was odd. Shouldn't Rita receive special sympathy?

When the door closed behind him, Joyce's countenance changed. She, too, seemed suddenly composed, as if her jitters had been a performance for the doctor.

"Have you told my mother?" was her first question.

Danny shook his head. She stood still as he approached her, and even stiller as he embraced her. She let her chin dig into his shoulder but other than that she did not move.

"I'm sorry," he said.

"I came over. I thought you'd be at home," she said.

"I don't know why you thought that. I'm always at work this time of day. Come here, sit down."

They sat on the bed together. Outside, police cars formed a barricade. Some cops were winding yellow tape around the house, and neighbors were coming out on their porches to have a look. Danny observed all this as he gazed out the window, giving Joyce a moment to calm herself. But she didn't need the moment. Her pulse seemed slow, her breath was even.

"I'm sorry you had to find him like that," Danny said.

Joyce did not respond.

He said, "The police are going to want to talk to you. It's routine. They know it's a suicide."

She looked at him. "They do?"

Danny nodded, searching her face for doubt. Some sort of uncertainty was there, but it was difficult to define.

She went rigid suddenly, and then her body started to quake. He held her close and kissed the top of her head. After a second, he realized that she was laughing. It chilled him. He hoped she would stop and he could make believe it had been a nervous reaction. Instead, it got louder. So loud that he was afraid the police would hear. He held her at arm's length.

"Joyce, don't. Sweetheart, they're gonna think you're crazy. Don't do that."

But she couldn't stop. Finally he had to cover her mouth, and she laughed into his fingers, spit forming like condensation against his palm.

"Please," he said. "Please try to stop."

Finally she managed to get control of herself, but by this time Danny had recognized a panic descending, the old kind that he remembered back when Lydia was around. The pinpricks in his chest, the aching under his armpits, the shallow breath, the burning in his fingertips.

"He always gets the last laugh, doesn't he?" Joyce said. "He beats anybody I've ever seen for always getting the story told his way. He would just love that, Danny. He would love to go out of this world with a story like that."

Danny flexed his fingers. It didn't help. They were turning red and felt as if they might melt. I can't believe it's not over, he thought, staring at his fingers, listening to her.

"So that's how it will be," she said. "But I guess that's how it sort of is. Kyle did do it to himself. Mama always said, 'You made your bed, now lie in it.' Sometimes I think Mama didn't know how to talk to me. She just quoted things at me all the time. A guilty conscience needs no accuser. Your chickens have come home to roost. What doesn't kill you makes you stronger. Danny, what are you doing to your fingers?"

"Nothing. Joyce, look at me."

She did.

"Who killed Kyle?"

"I did," she said simply.

She took his hands and held them against her face, against her scar.

"Your hands are hot," she said. She smiled, and she almost looked pretty, with his hands covering the bad half of her face. Her eyes were so warm, childlike, and she blinked at him, a languid gesture which was almost seductive.

"I wanted to give you something, Danny."

"Oh God," he whispered.

"I went to find Lydia. I found her, too. She's in Washington. I tried to get her to come home, but she wouldn't. And you know why she wouldn't? Because of Kyle. Because she knew the truth and she wanted something to be done. She wanted *you* to do something. I guess she wanted you to prove you loved her more."

"I don't know what you mean," he said weakly. "I loved her more than anything."

"Except Kyle," she said.

"That wasn't love, Joyce. That was . . . something else."

"She wanted you to tell the truth. About Kyle."

Danny swallowed. He said, "It was just a theory."

He pinched the bridge of his nose. He wanted to cry, but he was horrified at the thought of Joyce seeing that. Horrified at the realization that she was stronger than he was. Maybe she always had been.

"Joyce," he said, "you killed him."

"No," she said. "He's been killing himself his whole life. I just finished the job."

"The police won't see it that way."

She stood up and walked across the room. Danny watched her, relieved to feel the tears retreating. Now he was starting to feel angry.

"The police," she said slowly. "You're going to tell them?"

"I have to," he said.

"You wouldn't tell on Kyle? But you'll tell on me?"

Danny looked away. Then he got up and walked over to the window and stood with his back to her for what seemed like an eternity. He was watching the world at work, cleaning up its messes, putting things back together, making sense of it all.

It wasn't fair. Joyce deserved to have her sins absolved, much more than Kyle ever had. If he had known, he would have waited to save her instead. But he hadn't waited, and now he had to turn to her and tell her that he could not possibly keep her secret. Because he already had one.

"So I walked into the house," she said, as if she were mid-story, giving her statement to the police. "And he was lying on the couch, and he just raised up and looked at me and grinned. You know that grin. I hadn't seen him face to face in ten years. And all that hate came right back to me, good as new. I could feel those blinds digging into my face. I could see my life, twisted and bent by his hands. I could see him doing the same to you and I just couldn't let it happen."

Danny shook his head. "You didn't have to kill him."

"Why? Who's going to suffer?"

Danny thought of Amanda and her vacant stare, and the limp wave she gave him on her way to the door.

"I don't know," he said. "Maybe we will."

"You mean, like hell? I've already had mine. At least it will feel familiar. And I don't believe in any kind of God that would punish you."

Danny shook his head. "I'm not good, Joyce."

"Stop it," she said.

"I'm not good," he repeated.

"Danny, come on. You think I don't know who shot Kyle?"

He turned slowly and faced her.

"I was at the window. I saw it all. Why do you think they never found the gun?"

He couldn't speak, couldn't get a breath. It felt as if all the air had been sucked out of the room.

Finally he said, "It was an accident."

"Of course it was," she said. "But a whole person's life shouldn't be ruined because of an accident. You did one wrong thing your whole life. Kyle did a thousand. Who should be punished?"

Danny didn't answer. He didn't want to listen anymore and he didn't want to speak.

Joyce said, "He came at me, Danny. Like Daddy came at Tom Fitzgerald. He had that look in his eyes. He got up without his leg and came at me. He was drunk and still grinning. He saw the gun and said, 'What are you gonna do, shoot me?' I said either that or we'd call the police and have a talk with them. I gave him a choice, Danny. It was more than he ever gave me."

Danny clasped his hands together. Suddenly he was struck by the memory of Kyle pitching a baseball to him, the burn of it landing hard in his mitt. Kyle threw wild pitches, but he caught them. Always.

This was one he couldn't catch.

Joyce put her hand on Danny's arm. "Don't worry. He's in heaven now."

He looked at her and he wanted to laugh. Her face was perfectly still.

"You honestly believe that?"

"Of course," she said. "Why shouldn't God have to live with His mistakes?"

Danny no longer felt like holding back the tears. He let them race down his cheeks and onto his chin and neck. It felt good, better than anything he could remember, except Lydia's touch, her fingers, like a blessing, on his face.

Epilogue

SPRING WAS SUPPOSED to be the best time of year in Washington, D.C., mainly because of the cherry blossoms that bloomed everywhere from the White House lawn to the mall along the reflecting pool. People came from great distances to see the spectacle, as if cherry trees existed nowhere else. But Lydia didn't care for spring in D.C. or anywhere. It had never been her favorite time of year. She only felt hopeful in the fall, when the chill set in, promising more and more cold weather, and the leaves piled up on the ground, and the trees turned black and bare. Fall was nature's version of cleaning house, throwing everything out and starting over.

It was the end of September when Danny called her to say that he was living in Manassas, working in the new branch of the Howard J. Mecklin company as a general manager and vice president. She congratulated him and he thanked her and asked what she was doing. She described her life, relatively unchanged since she had arrived—working in a bookstore, tutoring, and spending time with her friends.

"Seeing someone?" he asked simply, trying to keep the question down to a bare minimum.

"No one special," she said.

"Okay," he said awkwardly. She did not ask the same question of him, for she knew the answer would certainly be no, and she did not want to embarrass him. She couldn't believe that he had moved. She tried to picture him living in Manassas in one of those faux colonial townhouses along Interstate 29, with the planes from Dulles passing overhead at all hours. She pictured him going out the door in the morning, getting into his pickup truck, driving past the Civil War fences and cannons and plaques marking battle sites. It was such an unlikely image, she had trouble believing it.

"I'm sorry about Kyle," she said. She had meant to call him after she heard the news. She even planned what she was going to say. She wrote it down and practiced it. It was some ridiculous speech about how things happened for a reason and good things could come out of tragedy. But it all sounded false and she knew he would hear the insincerity.

"Thanks," Danny responded simply. "We got your flowers. I mean, they were displayed at the funeral. It was nice. White carnations and roses."

"Good," she said.

There was a pause which seemed longer than it probably was. The phone was filled with dead air. She could hear no ambient noise on the other end. She pictured Danny in this place, clean and silent and white, like the flowers. Like heaven.

"How's Joyce?" she asked.

"Oh, fine. The kid's getting big. Starting to crawl."

"What kid?"

"You didn't hear? She had a baby, a boy. With some teacher over in Whiteville. It created a big scandal, but it's starting to die down. The guy comes to visit every other weekend. I think he used to teach at Fawley. Maybe you know him."

"Maybe I do," she said. She was smiling. She felt happy and almost giddy, as if she had suddenly fallen in love. She felt the way she had at Myrtle Beach when she and Danny were sitting in that seafood restaurant. Full of hope and willing to believe in salvation.

She was struck by the image of Joyce's foot, sleek and beautiful, flawlessly formed. She was sure the baby had inherited some of that, the secret evidence of perfection.

They both agreed they should get together, and they went into great detail to spell out their schedules, and finally agreed that a Friday would be the best night, maybe the second Friday in November, if nothing came up. It was one of those plans that would never happen and they both felt it and Lydia hurried to get off the phone.

Lydia did not tell him how close she had come to going to Kyle's funeral. She wanted him to think it had never crossed her mind, but it had. She had even made arrangements to get off work, and had gone so far as to borrow a black dress from Camille. She had started to pay regular visits to Camille and her husband. This recent marriage had brought out the best in Camille. It had calmed her down and lowered her expectations. Her husband, Dr. Todd Roland, was a short man with wispy blond hair and a mild stutter. He adored his wife and lavished attention on her. Beyond pleasing Camille, he only had one other aspiration. He sincerely believed he might make Surgeon General one day, and no one had the heart to tell him otherwise, that a plastic surgeon presented certain negative image problems, even if he did have a number of burn-injury patients.

"Oh, it's his dream, let him have it," Camille said. She was more generous now, not so scathing in her assessments. She was willing to let people live with their follies. She seemed to understand that hope was nothing to sneer at.

"I don't think this is a good idea," Camille had said, as Lydia modeled the dress in front of a floor-length mirror. "You can't rekindle a flame at a funeral. Nobody's thinking about love with some dead body lying nearby in a casket."

"I don't want to rekindle the flame. I just want to pay my respects."

Camille had laughed at Lydia's good intentions. She had not lost her looks, though they had been marked by age. The crow's feet gave her dignity. The lines on her face made her look kinder, less severe.

"Honey, from the minute you saw that man on the beach you loved him. And you still do. You can't run away from something like that."

"For God's sake, Camille, you begged me not to marry Danny. You disowned me."

"I stopped talking to you. That's different. I just didn't understand it then."

"Understand what?"

"That people can be saved by love."

Turning to her, Lydia asked, "Do I look saved to you?"

"No," Camille had admitted. "Not now. But back then you did."

"It's all a myth. If you go around believing in stuff like that, you're asking to get your heart broken. I don't honestly know what love is supposed to do, but I know it can't save you. Love is only as strong as the people in it."

"Exactly," Camille had said, as if this had proven her point.

Lydia had taken the dress home with her, where it still remained in her closet. Every now and then she took it out and looked at it, as if it represented some kind of lost chance.

Maybe she had wanted to see Danny. Maybe she had even wanted to rekindle something. But she could not face his family. And the truth was, more than anything, she could not face going back to Fawley. Driving back there, through that time warp of a town, with its toy store fronts and its epidemic of churches, the pickup trucks and jacked-up cars rumbling through town, all those blandly beguiling faces along the street, and all that quiet concern and distrust settling in the air like dust, she was afraid she would be looking at the manifestation of her breakdown, the hard evidence of her lost years. And sometimes she feared that it wouldn't be like that at all, that it would just be a plain little town, incapable of capturing or deluding anyone, and that she had created the whole nightmare scenario in her mind.

Whatever it was, whether Fawley kept her demons or her delusions, she was going to let them stay there. She could not confront it. Besides, she liked being in her apartment, and she'd gotten some plants and a couple of cats, and going away was more of a problem than it used to be.

The first snow came early that year, the second week in October, and the city ground to a halt. It could never handle snow very well, but this early it constituted a national disaster. The metro stopped running and National Airport closed, and the roads were congested with accidents and stalled cars. Lydia was planning to meet a friend in Adams Morgan at a Vietnamese restaurant and decided to walk there from her place. She was looking forward to the evening. Matt, a fellow clerk in the bookshop and nearly a decade younger than she, was suffering from the illusion that he was in love with her. Lydia didn't mind and was in fact contemplating an affair. She was curious. He was an amazing man to look at, with a thin face and chiseled cheekbones, piercing blue eyes, and dark curls down past his shoulder blades. He often wore his hair in a ponytail, sometimes in a braid. He was an artist. He wrote essays. Not for magazines but for himself. He kept a collection of them and hoped to publish them in a book one day. She found this such an exotic and unlikely ambition that it appealed to her. Why not? Good for him. He probably had an amazing mind, she told herself (though she'd only seen evidence of an average one), and it was time someone revived the form of essay writing. Since Montaigne there had hardly been an essayist worth worrying about.

She knew perfectly well that she just wanted to sleep with him and was trying to find a way to justify it. He was twenty-four. Twenty-four, twenty-four, twenty-four. That was the sound her feet made in the snow. She could not imagine any more what it felt like to be twenty-four. She remembered living in Georgetown then, in a group house, but she couldn't remember much about her housemates. Two guys named Mike and Steve, who argued about everything from Supreme Court rulings to football. And there was a sullen girl named Janine who was always on the phone, talking in low tones and crying. Lydia was just starting to resurrect her relationship with Ham then, and they went out to dinner a lot or cooked on the grill at his place. Sometimes they went to jazz clubs and she remembered feeling lonely and left out, because the erratic, fitful music sounded more like confusion than art. Ham was passionate about jazz, and Lydia, if she remembered correctly, was not passionate about anything except, maybe, passion. She didn't have it and she wanted it and was determined to find it. She vaguely recalled believing in the steadfast, unforgiving laws of intuition. Following that voice meant eventual bliss. Ignoring it ensured disaster. She must have believed, back then, that life was a journey, and like any good journey there was a right way to go. She no longer believed that, but nothing had taken its place. Nothing filled the void. She had always had a credo or at least a theory, and the lack of one made her feel loose and crazy.

"I just can't get a grip on it," she had complained to Camille that day on the phone. "Where's it all leading?"

"Sweetie, it's leading to old age and death. So why worry about that? Just pack everything you can in before it happens." But Lydia had never thought it was about packing in good moments. She thought there was going to be a point, a pinnacle. After circling and circling the lot, she thought there was going to be the equivalent to a good parking space in life.

But what did she care about when she was twenty-four? What did she want? Because the year itself was so lost on her, she had trouble contemplating Matt's motives. Was he sincerely in love with her? He seemed sincere about wanting to sleep with her at least, but men were sincere about that at any age. If Matt really did have strong feelings for her, she'd have to sit down and reckon with that and confront the possibility that she might have to pretend to feel the same way.

Adams Morgan was empty. Many of the restaurants were closed, but the Vietnamese place was open, and Matt sat at a corner table, writing and drinking a glass of wine. His hair was loose, hanging around his shoulders. She wondered if he had stood in front of the mirror and thought, Ponytail tonight? No, I think down.

He smiled when he saw her, grasped her hand and kissed her on the neck. A chill shot through her.

"What are you writing about?" she asked, but he only smiled. Matt never discussed his essays.

"You're cold," he said, keeping hold of her hand even after she sat down.

"It's snowing."

"It's a miracle, isn't it?"

"No, it's not a miracle. It's frozen water."

"But I mean so early. And tonight. It's like it happened just for us."

Lydia struggled to smile. This wasn't going to be easy.

A Vietnamese man of about sixteen took their order. After he had gone away, Matt informed her that he was not Vietnamese but Korean. (He had done extensive traveling in Indochina and had unfortunately brought back a lot of their philosophy with him. He was constantly trying to get her to take herbs.) For some reason it annoyed Lydia that he knew the difference between a Korean and a Vietnamese accent. This did not seem like vital information, an appropriate use of one's time.

"What's wrong with you tonight?" Matt asked. One thing in his favor, he was attuned to her moods and did not possess the typical male oblivion to any emotion other than his own.

"I'm tired. Or the snow depresses me."

"You love winter."

"But this isn't winter, that's why I'm depressed. I know I'm going to invest in it emotionally. And when the fall weather comes back I'll resent it."

"You're so complicated," Matt said, smiling, his sincere blue eyes bearing down on her.

"No, I'm not, Matt. I'm screwed up. Sometimes it looks like the same thing."

He let it go at that. He was content to sip his wine and stare at her, smiling. After the satay arrived, he asked her again, this time with more conviction, about what was bothering her.

"I don't know. Do we have to talk about me? I was hoping we could just finish the food and go home. I mean, go to your place. Or you could come to mine."

He smiled and tossed his hair over his shoulder, keeping one strand between his fingers and twirling it, the way Lydia used to do in high school when she had long hair. It was a strange gesture, seductive and innocent.

He said, "I know you're going to think this sounds crazy. But there's this philosophy, sort of Eastern, sort of Native American—a hybrid, really—that you don't, for lack of a better expression, *lie down* with someone who is holding on to another spirit. Could be another person's spirit, could just be a strong memory. Because if you do, you'll absorb some of that spirit, that negative energy, and you can't rid yourself of it until the other person does. That is to say, I'll be connected to you in a negative way, and so it will end badly."

Lydia stared at him. She could not get her wineglass to her mouth fast enough. Whatever she had felt at twenty-four, this was not it.

"What I'm saying is," he continued, still twirling his hair, "I want to wait until it's right. Until whatever you're burdened with is gone."

She swallowed, put her glass down and said, "Matt, you'll be waiting until your dick falls off. My burdens aren't going anywhere. They're permanent. You know what you call burdens at my age? Personality."

He took her hand again and pressed it to his lips. "I know you're more positive than you pretend. And I want to be with you. God, you're all I ever think about."

The words hit her like a jolt and she felt breathless. It was almost as if Danny's voice had come into the room, as she found herself looking around to see if he had somehow materialized. The room was empty, and the sound of Vietnamese or Korean or some sort of zither music echoed off the tile walls. She began to laugh. Matt's ubiquitous smile faded then and he became quite serious.

"What?" he asked.

"My husband used to say that. Or said it once."

Matt nodded with a solemn expression. "You're not over him."

"Of course I'm not over him. People don't get over each other. It's not like a virus."

"You know what I mean. You're still in love with him."

"I talked to him a while ago. I'm supposed to see him, but I don't know. I guess I am still in love with him. It's just that being with him suddenly got so hard—harder than not being with him. Do you know what

I mean? Every day I was having this conversation in my head. Driving to work, or eating lunch or watching TV, I'd be discussing it with myself. Adding up the pros and cons. Checking myself out to see if I still had some patience left, the energy to argue with myself one more time, to justify what I was doing for one more day. Finally I hit a wall. I was exhausted. So I left."

Matt looked stricken. The food arrived and they ate it in silence. He used his chopsticks expertly, as if he were playing a musical instrument. She could feel his agitation; he was brooding, in the way that her high school students used to do.

"What?" she said.

"Do you really think that kind of connection between human beings is so easy to come by? You just throw it out when it starts to get difficult? When did life ever become about avoiding difficulty?"

"It's not that simple. It only looks that way because you're young."

"Bullshit," he said. "Don't pull the age thing on me. You're not exactly venerable. If you love your husband, you should be with him. If you don't, you should be with me."

"Don't make me lie to you, Matt. Because I'm willing to do that just to find out what it feels like to wake up next to an essayist. Whatever happened to casual sex? Did I miss that stage of my development?"

"Lydia, did it ever occur to you that you're living your life backward? You've already had a taste of permanence, now you want something transient. Comfort is what you're supposed to be working toward, not running away from."

"Let me be the first to tell you. Marriage is anything but comfortable."

"Well, that's your view. But I've had enough casual sex. And now I don't want to sleep with someone who's in it for the experience."

"How can you have had enough of anything? You're twenty-four."

Matt said, "You want to find some solution, Lydia. You want to find that magical formula, but it isn't there. It's like that line from Beckett, 'You're on earth, there's no cure for that.'"

"God, you're a treasure. You're quoting Beckett to me."

"'I can't go on, I'll go on,'" he said, inspired.

"Did I ever tell you why I married my husband?" she asked.

"No."

"Because he told me a funny joke. It was whimsical and it surprised me. I understood it, so I thought I understood him. Honest to God, I believe it was the start of everything. People should not get married for those reasons."

"Why not? Marriage is impractical by nature. We're one of maybe half a dozen species which subscribes to the notion of mating for life. It's like swans and wolves and us. I mean, there are a thousand reasons that we do it, but finding exactly the right reason doesn't seem imperative. Or even possible."

Lydia smiled. She felt so tired. All this conviction was exhausting. Had she ever felt like this? Had she ever thought that life could be boiled down to a handful of aphorisms?

Lydia looked out the window at the snow forming a pale, cold gloss on the street, like some layer of healthy skin growing over a wound. She wanted to be in it. She wanted to touch it, to make a snowball, to listen to the dull whisper that sounded like magic would if it could make a sound. When she was little, Lydia imagined that snow was a kind of glue, cementing everything to the earth.

"I'm lost," Lydia said. "That's how I feel, all the time."

"Everyone is lost," Matt said. "Which means that no one is."

"I'm sure that makes sense to you, but I'm thirty-two and I've had three glasses of wine."

"Let me walk you home."

"I thought you weren't going to lie down with me or whatever."

"I can still take care of you."

Lydia smiled. Wouldn't it be nice if people could really take care of each other? But it wasn't like that. The most they could do was huddle against their own private panic.

"Let's get the check," she said, rubbing her forehead. A dull pain was settling behind her eyes, and she was being attacked by her former life. Memories shot through her brain, uninvited. The phone ringing in the darkness, Danny's truck roaring out into the night to rescue Kyle, and the taste of the thick hot chocolate as she sat and waited for him. She was jealous. Because Danny had fought for something. And it wasn't her.

She and Matt went out into the street, which was empty but for a few students from Georgetown, laughing and hanging on to each other, their heads down, watching their feet. Lydia had trouble standing up. Matt hooked an arm around her waist and their hips bumped together as they walked, creating an uneven rhythm.

"Tell me what your essays are about," Lydia said.

"I don't like to talk about them. It's too personal."

"I want to know."

Matt considered it for a moment, then said, "Teeth."

"What?"

"My most recent essay is about teeth. Taking care of your teeth is an act of faith, an investment in the future. Teeth as a metaphor for hope. Should I go on?"

"No, I don't think so."

She stared up at the sky, at the thick layer of clouds which seemed close enough to touch. Her breath came out of her in streams of smoke, the evidence of her consciousness settling in the air.

"Maybe I'll drive to Manassas tomorrow," Lydia said.

"What's in Manassas?"

"Battlefields."

Their footsteps diminished as the snow accumulated. It was like walking on air, going forward without making a sound. Looking over her shoulder she could see their prints, an erratic, meandering pattern, leading all the way back to where they'd started.